STARSWARM

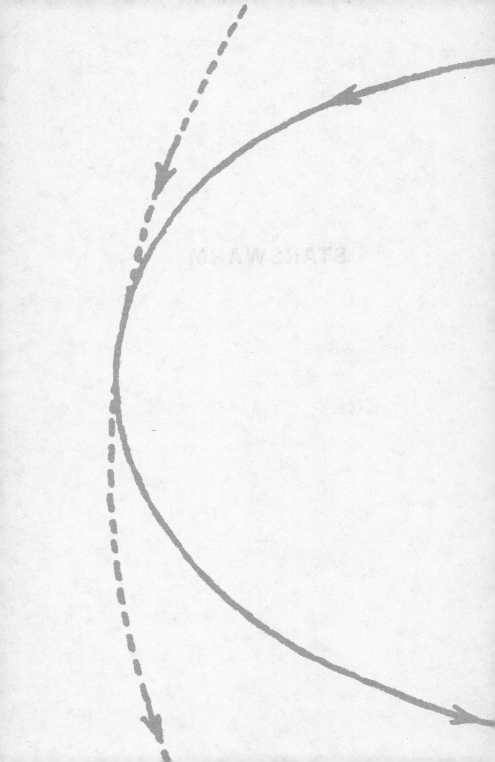

STARSWARM

A *JUPITER*™ NOVEL

JERRY POURNELLE

A TOM DOHERTY ASSOCIATES BOOK · NEW YORK

STARSWARM

Copyright © 1998 by Jerry Pournelle

A Tor Book
Published by Tom Doherty Associates, Inc.
175 Fifth Avenue
New York, NY 10010

Tor Books on the World Wide Web:
http://www.tor.com

Tor® is a registered trademark of Tom Doherty Associates, Inc.

ISBN 0-312-86183-4

Printed in the United States of America

For Dan Mac Lean, and for Roberta

INTRODUCTION

INTRODUCTIONS to works of fiction are not common, but Tor Books editor Bob Gleason says they should be. In any event, he wanted one for this book. "Tell them how you came to write it," he said. That's like asking how I came to be a science-fiction writer.

I don't remember exactly when I began to read science fiction, but I do recall taking the streetcar—they had electric streetcars in Memphis, back before the gas companies and auto makers bribed the cities into tearing out the tracks and replacing quiet and efficient and wonderful electric street railways with noisy, smelly buses—to the downtown newsstands to buy *Astounding Science Fiction* when it came out each month. There may have been other science fiction magazines, but I don't remember reading any of them. *Astounding* was rare enough. I had to get there on the right day, because they only got five copies of *Astounding* each month at the newsstand at Main and Madison, and I'm not sure anyone else got any at all. You could buy *The Shadow*, and *Doc Savage*, in the drugstore near the fair grounds where I changed street cars, but I never saw *Astounding* anywhere but downtown.

Subscribing was out of the question. I could save up a quarter each month, and since I combined my newsstand expedition with a trip to the Memphis Public Library I could always get carfare (a nickel each way as I recall) from my parents, but there was no way I was going to get several dollars, and if I had the money there wasn't any way to send it. It probably wasn't an actual crime to send currency through the mails, but we were warned so strongly against it that it might as well have been. In those days few crimes were federal, but we all knew that anything having to do with the mail would bring in G-men. I was particularly conscious of this because for a while we had lived in the house on Ranier Street where the FBI captured Machinegun Kelly.

He's been forgotten now, but at one time Machinegun Kelly was as well known as Dillinger, and when the FBI burst into the house and confronted him he said, "Don't shoot, G-men!"; the first use of that term. I always pretended to know more about that than I did. I think I even convinced myself I'd heard him say, "Don't shoot, G-men!" Of course he was captured years before we moved into the house. That was probably my first venture into fiction writing: I told stories about the capture of Machinegun Kelly to anyone who would listen.

I read every issue of *Astounding*, and later I found some back issues in used book stores. They had wonderful covers. That era is now known as the Golden Age of science fiction. Most of the stories were long on 'sense of wonder' and short on science, and I got some pretty odd notions before I got to high school. Then, fortunately, Brother Henry, the physics teacher at Christian Brothers College (which despite the name was a high school) was willing to explain the difference between "real science" (what was already possible but very difficult, like rockets to the Moon), far-out science (things we couldn't do yet but probably would learn to, like thinking-machine computers, and wrist radios, and ray guns), and impossible stuff like faster than light travel; but in fact he was wise enough to keep the "impossible" list pretty short. Brother Henry didn't much care for science fiction himself, but he was willing to put up with it since it got me asking questions. Anything that would interest students in real science . . .

I particularly liked Robert Heinlein's stories. So did Brother Henry, because in those days nearly everything in Heinlein's stories was "real science"; but that didn't keep them from having plenty of "sense of wonder." His matter of fact stories about space travel, settlements on the moon and Mars, space stations, made it all come alive. For me space travel wasn't a matter of if, but how and when; and the sooner the better. I always knew I'd live to see the first man walk on the moon. I did, too, and although it seems a dreadfully long time since the last Apollo mission, I don't think I have seen the last man on the moon. We'll go back, and on, and beyond, and many of those who made it happen got started in their work by being inspired by Robert Heinlein.

I found Robert A. Heinlein in back issues of *Astounding*, and also in *The Saturday Evening Post*, and I read everything of his I could find. I was completely hooked on his "juveniles": *Space Cadet*; *Red Planet*; *Starman Jones*; *Between Planets*; *Farmer in the Sky*. Wonderful stories, and the only thing juvenile about them was that he took the trouble to explain what was happening. Robert once told me that young people want to know how things work, and you can tell them more in a "juvenile" than you can in an adult novel. In any event, I devoured everything of his I could find, through high school, the army, college, and I couldn't have cared less that many were "juveniles." They were wonderful.

I met Robert Heinlein years later, and through some kind of rare magic we became instant friends. We corresponded for a decade. In those days I was an engineering psychologist, operations research specialist, and systems engineer in aerospace. Most of my work was military aerospace, but I did get to work on Mercury,

Gemini, and Apollo. We were helping to make the dream come true!

I went from there to a professorship, and then into political management and city government. Robert visited me when I was working for Mayor Sam Yorty. "You probably don't know this," he said, "but my political career ended when Yorty beat me for the Democratic nomination to the State Assembly. . . ."

When I finally decided to get out of politics, academia, and the aerospace industry and try my hand at writing, Mr. Heinlein was enormously helpful. Years later, when I was an established writer, I asked him how I could pay him back.

"You can't," he said. "You don't pay back, you pay forward."

I never forgot that, just as I never forgot the wonderful things his "juvenile" stories did for me.

When Larry Niven and I set out to write *The Mote in God's Eye* (which Bob Gleason bought and edited back when he was at Simon and Schuster/Pocket Books) we tried to write the kind of story we had wanted to read when we were first discovering science fiction. Niven is younger than I am, and discovered science fiction somewhat later than I did, well after the Golden Age was over, but we were influenced by many of the same stories.

When I became president of the Science Fiction Writers of America there were fewer than twenty science-fiction writers making enough to live on from their writing, and some of them had day jobs even so. Poul Anderson and Gordon Dickson had no income but writing. Niven probably made enough to scrape up a living from his writing, but thanks to a fortunate choice of grandparents didn't have to. James Gunn was a professor at the University of Kansas. Cliff Simak edited a small town newspaper. Isaac Asimov turned out books of science fact, but hadn't written any science fiction in years. The times were lean, but I was lucky enough to get in just at the beginning of a new boom. Suddenly science fiction was in demand, and while publishers weren't paying very much, they were buying all the science fiction they could get.

That presented a problem. In order to make a living at writing I had to write a lot; and writing is hard work. Actually, writing wasn't so bad: it was *rewriting*, particularly *retyping* an entire page in order to correct half a dozen sentences. Typing neatly involved correction fluid, carbon paper, fussing with margins; a lot of work, most of which I hated. I wasn't anything like the first to discover that, but again I was lucky: Just as it became clear that writing would be my next (and final) career, everything changed.

Somewhere in the course of my career in political management I met a onetime intelligence agent named Dan Mac Lean. (That's not the way his name is spelled in most legal documents, but it's the way he preferred.) Mac Lean was arguably mad; indeed, when I later wrote articles about small computers, I often included the observations of "my mad friend," a designation I stole shamelessly from the early work of the late Gary Edmundson, because it fit Dan so well.

Mac Lean knew a little about everything, as well as a lot about anything he became really interested in; and when some then obscure companies began to offer kits for building small home computers, Dan Mac Lean was one of the first to acquire one. He soon learned just about all there was to know about them.

His home computer didn't seem very useful to me, but Mac Lean insisted: These little machines were going to change the world. He was right, of course. Within months, two Harvard dropouts named Bill Gates and Paul Allen wrote a BASIC language program for the first of the home computers, and not long after came Electric Pencil. Pencil wasn't the first "word processing" program; for years there had been specialized programs that let you write on punched cards or magnetic tape, but those only ran on large and *very* expensive systems. Electric Pencil was the first such program to work with small home computers; and I fell in love with it the first time Mac Lean showed it to me.

The potential was awesome: here was a way to turn out text fast, and rewrite without retyping an entire page. The instant I saw that, I had to have one. Unfortunately, while the machines were cheap compared to commercial word processors and office machines, the cost was enormous. A professional quality system for writing books cost $12,000. Mac Lean insisted it was a good investment, and eventually convinced me; and with Dan Mac Lean's help I got into the computer era. Ezekial—that's the way I spelled his name—had a Z-80 chip, two 8-inch floppy disk drives, and a Diablo "daisy-wheel" printer, and if you want to see him he's on display in the Smithsonian Museum. Go to the exhibit on History of Communications and Computing in the Museum of American History.

After I bought Ezekial I needed a way to convince the Internal Revenue Service that it was neither frivolous nor mad to use a computer to write books—no one had ever done that, back then— so I wrote a couple of articles about writing with computers and sold them to *BYTE*. So far as I was concerned that was that, but Mac Lean thought better. "I can't write. You can write. I can tinker," he said. "You do a regular column for *BYTE*. We'll get lots of free software, I'll play with it, you write it up, and we'll have a lot of fun." As luck would have it, *BYTE* Magazine had an opening.

It worked that way for a couple of years; but of course, since I had to confer with Mac Lean about the computer columns, I spent a lot of time with him—he was as interesting a person to be with as I have ever known—and that inevitably led to discussing my stories.

One of those stories was *Starswarm*. I don't know precisely how I got the idea of a boy who grew up with a computer in his head meeting a living creature that thought like a computer, but I did, and pretty soon Mac Lean was speculating about how that might work. He still couldn't write—I guess he tried from time to time, but he generally didn't finish anything—but he liked talking to writers, and he'd generate about a million ideas an hour. The real problem was making notes fast enough, because once he'd talked about something he forgot it completely. I suppose that's one reason he didn't write. He thought too fast.

Mac Lean had been in intelligence work—to this day no one is sure which of his stories were made up and which were real, although I have since found out that some of his most unbelievable stories were strictly true—and one residual of his former career was a reluctance to have any patterns in his life. *Starswarm* was born over coffee in dozens of small restaurants all over Los Angeles, and the first few chapters were written so Mac Lean could read them. He loved the story. And shortly after that he found he had cancer, and a few months later he was dead.

I hadn't known I could miss someone so much. It wasn't just sentiment. The small computer industry was taking off like a rocket, and keeping up with it was nearly impossible even with Mac Lean's help; without him it took nearly all the time I had. I also had book contracts, while *Starswarm* was only an unsold idea. When I finally found time to look at *Starswarm* again, it didn't seem the same without Dan to talk it over with; so for years it sat in my files until one day I decided I'd been in a funk long enough and it was time to finish it.

And that's how I came to write *Starswarm*, which owes a lot to Robert Heinlein for getting me started reading science fiction; to Brother Henry of the Christian Brothers, who encouraged me to learn science; Robert Heinlein again, who helped me a lot in becoming a science-fiction writer; and even more to Dan Mac Lean, who got me into small computers and helped me understand them, and got me to thinking about how a living creature might think like a computer and what that might mean.

It's mushy sentimentality to say I hope they're around somewhere enjoying this novel; after all, they've probably got more important assignments. But I still wish it.

Jerry Pournelle
Hollywood, 1997

PART ONE
The Voice

But the Lord was not in the wind; and after the wind an earthquake; but the Lord was not in the earthquake:
And after the earthquake a fire; but the Lord was not in the fire: and after the fire a still small voice.
—1 Kings 19:11–12

CHAPTER ONE

Gwen

KIP could never remember a time when he couldn't hear the Voice in his head. He could talk to it anytime he wanted by thinking in a special way, and the Voice would always answer. It didn't matter when he called, or where he was. Kip was the only one in the whole world who could hear the Voice, and it had always said he should never tell anyone he could hear it.

For a long time Kip thought other people had their own Voice, but of course they didn't. He couldn't remember just when he had thought that out. He could never ask, of course, but grown-ups didn't act like they had Voices. They forgot things. Of course Kip forgot things too, but the Voice never forgot anything.

Kip never told anyone about the Voice, not even Uncle Mike. He told Uncle Mike everything else. There was no one else to tell things to, no one else to run to when he was hurt or frightened. He and Uncle Mike lived by themselves in a big wooden frame house across the wide, graveled central field from the laboratory buildings of Starswarm Station. There were other people there, but the scientists were too busy to bother with a young boy, and there weren't any other children at the station.

The household robots cooked and did most of the housework, but Uncle Mike had programmed them so that there was still work for Kip to do, because, he said, "A boy ought to learn to take care of himself and not have to depend on machines. Or other people."

Kip knew about families and mothers and fathers because he could watch the TRI-V when Uncle Mike let him. He didn't get to watch very much, because he had so much to learn. Uncle Mike always told him that men weren't intended to live on Purgatory, and they had to learn early or the planet would kill them.

Kip knew what that meant. There was a big fence around Starswarm Station's buildings and yards, and even that couldn't keep everything out. Centaurs came looking for food in deep winter, and they'd eat anything, even dogs and people. Then there were the little furry things the scientists called by a long name, but everybody else called them haters because they hated everything they hadn't killed. The fences couldn't keep all the haters out when they swarmed, and then the men and dogs had to go out and kill the haters. There were other things, and Kip had to learn about all of them.

It wasn't a bad life for Kip even if he did wish he had someone to play with. When he was six, Uncle Mike taught him to shoot a pistol, but he couldn't touch it unless Uncle Mike was with him. Uncle Mike was a hunter, and he took Kip with him sometimes. Uncle Mike caught animals alive for the station scientists. He never killed anything unless he had to. Of course on Purgatory he had to kill a lot of things because they would eat him, or the dogs, if he didn't, but Uncle Mike didn't hunt for fun, and he didn't like people who did.

There were always the dogs to play with too. They had two whole teams of them, and there were usually puppies. The dogs were nice, and they understood a lot of what Kip said to them. They were almost as nice as other people. Even so, Kip sometimes felt lonesome, and he knew Uncle Mike was sorry about that, but they had to stay at Starswarm Station.

The TV showed Kip how other people lived. He could watch shows from Pearly Gates City, and everyone on TRI-V lived in families. Sometimes they did very silly things. Kip asked his Voice about the people on TRI-V, but the Voice wasn't always able to tell whether Kip had been watching entertainment shows or news from Pearly Gates, or even a documentary from Earth. Usually he could tell when the show came from Earth, though, because there were so many people there, and they had all kinds of marvelous things that no one on Purgatory had.

For a long time Kip thought his Voice was God, because the Voice always spoke in stern unemotional tones like Brother Joseph reading the lesson, and it used words Kip didn't understand. Besides, the Voice knew almost everything, and sometimes it could do strange things like bring him a new Teddy Bear.

Kip had always had a Teddy Bear. He thought he could remember when Mommy gave him Teddy, and it was one of the few memories of Mommy that he had. Teddy went everywhere with Kip. He was hugged and crushed at night, and dragged in the dirt all day. Once, one of Mukky's new puppies got Teddy and chewed him. Mukky snapped at the puppy and growled at him a long time, and she whined because she was sorry until Kip told her it was all right and scratched her ears. Teddy had been a wreck, but Uncle Mike had fixed him. Over the years Uncle Mike changed Teddy's stuffing and patched him until he wasn't recognizable, but still he was Teddy.

Finally, though, Kip dropped Teddy into the wrong hole, and a firebrighter took him. Kip screamed, and although the dogs knew better they attacked the firebrighter because the dogs couldn't stand to hear human children crying. Mukky's puppy had to be killed, and Mukky was hurt, and firebrighter blood and guts got all over and inside Teddy. Not even Uncle Mike could do anything for him then. Uncle Mike asked Dr. Henderson, but no one knew any cure for the firebrighter smell, so they buried his Teddy

Bear. It was his last connection with his mother, and Kip cried all night. Then he told the Voice about it. "I want Teddy back," Kip told the Voice, and he cried again.

A week later the supply copter landed at Starswarm Station. When the pilot opened the cargo hatch there was a big brown stuffed bear sitting on top of the groceries and scientific equipment. He was almost an exact copy of what Teddy had been when he was younger and hadn't been patched so much.

"Durndest thing," the pilot said. "Not on any manifests. Just right there in the cargo. Found him last stop. Here, Kip, I guess you'll want him."

Kip nodded gravely and thanked the pilot. He was a nice bear, but he wasn't Teddy. Kip kept him in his room. The new bear was never crushed at night or rolled through the dirt, or even chewed by Mukky's puppies. It was a very proper bear, and he had his place in the corner by the big red and white toy box, and Kip liked him very much, but he didn't *love* him because he didn't come from Mommy.

That night Kip heard Uncle Mike and the pilot talking over whiskey.

"Nice of you to bring the bear for the boy, Cal," Uncle Mike said.

"Not me," Cal said. "Happened just the way I told you. Opened the compartment for final check before we took off, and there it was. No manifest, no papers, nothing. So I remembered your lad and decided to bring it along, but it weren't none of my doing. Never even saw one of those things on Purgatory before. Have you?"

"No, but we don't get to town very much," Mike said. "Have another?"

"Sure. Well, it's the darndest thing."

So that was how Kip knew his Voice had brought the bear to Starswarm, and why he thought it was God. Brother Joseph had told Kip about prayers, and Kip knew all about them, because he'd prayed to his Voice. After supper that night he told the Voice that he knew it was God.

The Voice was very astonished by this theory. Kip knew, because the Voice told him so. It had to, because it didn't have any expression. "I AM ASTONISHED. I HAVE TOLD YOU MY NAME IS GWEN," the Voice said.

Kip was sitting quietly in the front room, with Uncle Mike dozing in the big easy chair facing the door. Uncle Mike never sat with his back to any door, not even his own, not even with the dogs outside and Mukky lying in the doorway, and Silver lying beside Kip.

I thought Gwen was your secret name. God's secret name, Kim thought in the special way he used to talk with the Voice.

"I DO NOT KNOW THE SECRET NAME OF GOD. IT IS NOT REQUIRED THAT I KNOW. CORRECTION. MANY SECRET NAMES OF GOD ARE RECORDED. NONE ARE IDENTIFIED AS UNIQUELY TRUE."

Kip didn't understand that at all, but he could tell that Gwen wasn't God after all. *"Well,"* Kip thought, *"even so I don't need to say prayers because I can talk to you."* With the rest of his mind, the part that didn't talk to Gwen, Kip wondered if grown-ups talked to God because Gwen wouldn't talk to them.

"DOES UNCLE MIKE TELL YOU TO SAY PRAYERS?"

Kip knew what was coming, but Uncle Mike taught him never to lie. Uncle Mike didn't know about Gwen, but Kip knew Uncle Mike wouldn't want him to lie to Gwen either. *"Yes—well, he tells me to do what Brother Joseph says, and Brother Joseph says I must always say my prayers."*

"THEN YOU MUST SAY YOUR PRAYERS."

"But why, if I can talk to you? Why can't you say them for me?"

"YOU MUST ALWAYS DO AS YOUR UNCLE MIKE INSTRUCTS YOU," Gwen replied, and that wasn't surprising, because Gwen always told him to do what Uncle Mike said, and to tell Uncle Mike about everything except about Gwen.

When Kip was seven, Brother Joseph came back from town with education screens and disks and began teaching Kip. Uncle Mike helped too. At first it was very hard, but then Kip could read and it was easier. Then it was very hard again because there was all that mathematics and arithmetic and the languages, and Earth histories about old countries that Kip wasn't even sure existed because where did all those people live? Kip could look outside and see the horizon empty all around with nobody living there but Dr. Henderson and his scientists. There was a village of centaurs on the ridge (just out of sight unless Kip looked from the second-story window), but one research station of people and one village of centaurs wasn't so crowded.

But then he learned about Earth, and how people lived on Earth for thousands of years until they invented space travel, and then someone invented the Drive that let them go from star to star, and they found other worlds they could live on. There weren't many, and some of them weren't very good worlds. Some of the worlds were owned by big companies. Purgatory was owned by Great Western Enterprises. There were mines, and factories, but that was all at Pearly Gates. Starswarm Station was owned by the Great Western Foundation, which wasn't quite the same as Great Western Enterprises, because the Foundation had a different board of directors, and its own money from the Trent family. But GWE had put a lot of money into the Foundation too, and Dr. Henderson had to be careful because GWE owned the planet and the security forces, and they brought in all the supplies, so it was important not to get the Great Western Enterprises people mad at him.

Kip was supposed to learn a lot more about Earth and business and commerce, and especially Great Western and the Trent family that founded it. Kip didn't think that was interesting. There was a lot of stuff he was supposed to learn that wasn't interesting, but Uncle Mike said he had to learn it, and Kip worked very hard until one day he asked Gwen for help. After that it was easy again, because Gwen could do *anything* with mathematics, and Gwen never forgot anything Kip asked her to remember for him either. She also knew more than Uncle Mike or Brother Joseph or even Dr. Henderson. Sometimes Kip startled them by correcting his teachers, but he had to be careful about this, because Uncle Mike couldn't know about Gwen.

Kip didn't know what would happen if he told Uncle Mike. Possibly they'd make Gwen go away, and Kip couldn't stand that because there would be nobody but the dogs to talk to when Uncle Mike was busy.

Or possibly Gwen would make Uncle Mike go away, and that would be even worse. Uncle Mike was all Kip had left, now that they'd buried Teddy. He remembered Teddy and he thought he remembered Mommy giving him the bear, and he asked Gwen again about Mommy.

"YOU WILL BE TOLD ABOUT YOUR PARENTS WHEN YOU ARE OLD ENOUGH. I MAY NOT TELL YOU NOW."

That was what Gwen always said, but this time Kip knew the difference between "may" and "can," and it frightened him so he didn't ask any more.

CHAPTER TWO

Uncle Mike

WHEN Kip was eight he asked Uncle Mike who his parents were. He thought a long time about how to do it so that Uncle Mike wouldn't guess that Gwen told him he had parents. He chose his opportunity carefully.

They were on the front porch of the big house after dinner. Across the field the scientists were bringing in specimens. There was a light snow cover on the tundra, and they'd used sleds. The dogs yelped greetings to each other, and all of Kip's dogs except Mukky and Silver went over to talk to their friends and ask what they'd found out there in the snow.

Purgatory's bright rings glistened as a big arch in the evening sky overhead, bright flashing bands of jewels in the blue-tinted light. They were beautiful, but Kip was used to them, as he was used to the endless rolling hills and their thin forest patches, and the thousands of lakes and pools clear above the permafrost in summer and frozen solid in winter, and as he was used to the burning summers when men didn't move outside if they could help it, and the terrible cold winters when you couldn't go outside without a hotsuit and lots of dogs and even then when the blue sun was up the light was bright and there were sharp shadows. He couldn't even remember when they didn't live in Purgatory.

"Aren't you my father's brother, Uncle Mike?" Kip asked. He thought that wouldn't cause any suspicions because he knew what an "uncle" was.

Mike Gallegher rocked gently in the wicker chair. He hitched it over a little to catch the last of the afternoon suns, and took out tobacco and paper to roll a cigarette.

When Uncle Mike did that, he was thinking about how to tell Kip something unpleasant. Kip knew that the way he knew you didn't put your hand in a firebrighter hole, or go far from Starswarm without a gun and a whole team of dogs, or stare at the night sun when it was out.

"Uncles can be mothers' brothers too," Kip said seriously. "My name is Brewster and yours is Flynn, so I guess you aren't my father's brother. Are you my Mommy's brother?"

Uncle Mike lit the cigarette, his big hands cupped around the lighter as if it might blow out. The dark green eyes lazily watched Kip from their nest of small brown wrinkles. Like everyone on Purgatory, Uncle Mike was tanned deep with ultraviolet from the blue sun. "Yeah, you can say that. Kip, how much do you remember about your folks?"

"Not much, sir." Uncle Mike insisted that older people were always called sir, even though he said most of them didn't deserve it. "Mommy gave me Teddy, I think. My real Teddy, not—"

"Yeah. I know. Kip, your folks are dead. Reckon you're old enough to know that now."

"Gwen, he says Mommy and Father are dead!"

"WHO SAYS?"

"Uncle Mike."

"YOU MUST ALWAYS LISTEN TO YOUR UNCLE MIKE."

"How did they die, Uncle Mike?" Somehow Kip had always known, but he still wanted to cry.

"Can't tell you that, Kip. Not just yet. But they were fine

people. Not really my relatives at all. I worked for your father.
When you're old enough, I'll work for you. Right now, I have to
raise you because that's the last order your father ever gave me."

"Oh." That was confusing. *Someday Uncle Mike will work for
me? The way Dr. Henderson's technicians work for him? But that means
Uncle Mike will have to do what I tell him, and Gwen always says—*

"Your folks had important work to do, Kip. One day when
you're old enough, you'll have to do it for them."

"But who were they? What was the work?"

"I've said enough, Kip."

"If you worked for my father, and now you work for me, you
have to do what I say! Tell me!"

"Reckon not, Kip. I've got a lot of orders to obey, boy, and
right now you've been countermanded. I probably told you too
much, but it's time you knew some of it. That's why you have to
study so hard, so you'll know how to do your father's work when
the time comes. It's a job needs doing and there's nobody to do it
but you."

CHAPTER THREE

Lara

ONE day when he was reading a history lesson about the Reformation and Counterreformation and religious wars of Earth, something puzzled him. He wasn't sure but— *Gwen, what is my name?* Kip asked.

"YOUR NAME IS KENNETH BREWSTER," Gwen answered. "YOU ARE USUALLY CALLED BY THE NAME KIP. QUERY. YOU HAVE ALWAYS KNOWN THIS. WHY DO YOU ASK?"

"I thought I remembered a different name. Kip, that's all right, I've always been Kip, but it's not the right last name. I remember something else. Shorter."

"I CAN MAKE NO COMMENT AT THIS TIME."

"Does that mean you know and won't tell me?"

"I CAN MAKE NO COMMENT AT THIS TIME."

Kip knew it was no good asking more. When Gwen started

saying things like that, she never changed her mind. Sometimes he could think of new ways to ask questions and get around Gwen's restrictions, but never when he was trying to find out about himself or his parents, or Uncle Mike.

Kip was lonely. School was dull, and Kip was bored, and he began to complain about it. Uncle Mike was sympathetic, but he said there wasn't anything he could do. But not long after, Dr. Henderson brought his family out to live at Starswarm. Kip liked Mrs. Henderson because she was always baking cookies and making candy and pickled bushberries for Kip, but mostly he was glad because they brought Lara, and he finally had someone to play with.

Lara was nine, younger than Kip by eleven Earthmonths; only they didn't use Earthmonths on Purgatory. They used blue-light and plain-light and Michaeldays, which seemed more natural to Kip than Earthmonths. But he could think in Earthmonths because Uncle Mike made him learn, the way he had to learn everything about Earth. Besides, it was easy to convert from any number to any other. Kip just asked Gwen. Even Dr. Henderson thought Kip was a mathematical genius because of all the things Gwen could do.

Lara was nearly as old as Kip but she wasn't very smart. She knew a lot of stuff from school, but she didn't know about firebrighters, and what months the centaurs were dangerous, and she was even afraid of the dogs. She came to Starswarm in the spring, and when the ice was melted off the lake out on the tundra, Uncle Mike and Dr. Henderson let her go with Kip outside the fence.

Mrs. Henderson didn't like that much. "Eric, are you trying to get our daughter killed?"

"We won't get lost," Kip said. He showed his position indicator card. "Uncle Mike calibrated this when they put the new global position satellites in, so I always know where I am."

"They're going three kilometers," Dr. Henderson said. "It's safe this time of year, and besides, Kip has a gun and a radio."

"A gun! Eric, are you out of your mind!" Mrs. Henderson came out of the house like a charging centaur to gather Lara in her arms.

"Uncle Mike says I can carry it, Mrs. Henderson," Kip protested. "I know how to shoot. I c'd show you, but I'm not allowed unless there's something to shoot at or Uncle Mike tells me."

"There. You see?" Dr. Henderson protested. "Harriet, Lara is safer out there with Kip than she was with you in DeeCee, or in Pearly Gates for that matter."

Mrs. Henderson shuddered but she had to agree to that.

"C'mon," Kip said. He led Lara out through the gates. "Kip," he called as they passed through.

The barrier wouldn't open. Kip looked at Lara in annoyance. "You have to tell it your name," he said.

"Oh. Lara Henderson."

"Who accompanies you?" the gate asked.

"Kip." He grinned at Lara. "The gate isn't really very smart."

The gate opened.

"Silver!" Kip shouted. "Five, Silver."

The dog barked acknowledgment and led half a team out with them. Five was as high as Silver could count. After that, it was just "many." The pack dogs fanned out across the tundra and ran in circles, while Silver paced just ahead of Kip and Lara.

"They seem awfully smart," Lara said.

"Sure. They're dogs."

"We had dogs on Earth, and they weren't so smart."

Kip frowned. He remembered some TRI-V shows with stupid dogs. Were all dogs on Earth like that? He asked Gwen.

"THE DOGS AT STARSWARM STATION ARE THE PRODUCTS OF GENETIC ENGINEERING EXPERIMENTS PERFORMED BY DR. ERIC HENDERSON AND HIS PREDECESSOR DR. MARY BUDONNIC. THEIR INTELLIGENCE AND TRAINING IS ALSO ESPECIALLY STIMULATED BY BONEWITS RNA INJECTIONS. ALL THE DOGS AT STARSWARM ARE DESCENDED FROM A SINGLE CLONED PAIR WITH GENETIC MATERIAL ADDED FROM THREE EARTH STRAINS. THEY ARE PREDOMINANTLY MALAMUTE AND SIBERIAN HUSKY WITH GERMAN SHEPHERD ADDITIONS. THEY—"

"Enough," Kip thought.

Lara was dancing in the afternoon sunlight. "Where are we going?" she asked.

"There's a lake," Kip said. "Just over that hill—"

"Race you!" Lara shouted. She ran, getting a good head start while Kip stared at her. The dogs barked and ran ahead eagerly.

"Sure!" Kip began to run.

They ran across the tundra. There were bright flowers among the blue-green grasses. Roots of flappergrapes poked up through the soil. In three blues they would have elephantine leaves to gather as much sun as they could, but for now they looked dead.

The lake was ahead and they ran for it. Kip automatically avoided the paths the others had taken. The tundra was easy to tear up in the spring, and the mud flats took a long time to grow over. Then he stopped. Lara stopped beside him, panting slightly. "That's fun," she said. "Why can't we run?"

" 'Cause you don't know where to step," Kip said. "See the holes? Maybe firebrighters in them. They can't hurt you much this time of year, but if one comes out, it'll stink something awful. Really awful. You'll really hate it. And see the purple patch over there? Not cabbage at all, it's a bird, and he wouldn't like you to step on him."

"Oh." She eyed the motionless purple. It *looked* like a cabbage weed. "Is it dangerous?"

"Naw. Nothing much can hurt us this time of year. The centaurs are too skinny. They'll be in their caves in the archtree groves, eating up all the stored-up roots to get fat again so they can go hunting for caribou."

"Caribou?"

"Don't you know anything? The Great Western people brought caribou, and lots of other things that live on Earth, and turned 'em loose out here. Balanced ecological group, they called it. The scientists at the station didn't like it, but they couldn't stop them, because Great Western owns all the land on the planet except for this area around the station. So they turned them loose and now they're all over."

"Do you remember that?"

"Naw, it was before I came. Before your father came, back when Dr. Budonnic was in charge. They brought all kinds of animals. Lots of the animals died off, but some of them did right well. Uncle Mike hunts caribou for dog food, the caribou herds are big enough now. Some say too big. Centaurs hunt them too."

"Oh. How can centaurs eat things that come from Earth? Why wouldn't they poison them?"

Kip looked at her with new respect. "Good question." He looked thoughtful for a moment.

"If caribou are from Earth how can centaurs eat them?"

"ALL EXTRATERRESTRIAL LIFE SO FAR DISCOVERED IS BASED ON THE SAME NUCLEIC ACIDS AND IS THUS RELATED. ALTHOUGH THERE ARE VARIANTS, NEARLY ALL EARTH LIFE IS BASED ON CLOSELY RELATED GLUCOSE CHEMISTRIES AND EMPLOYS SIMILAR PROTEINS. THIS HAS PROVED TO BE TRUE FOR LIFE DISCOVERED ON WORLDS OTHER THAN EARTH. THEREFORE IT WOULD BE SURPRISING IF THE CENTAURS WERE NOT ABLE TO EAT AT LEAST SOME EARTH PROTEINS. THE THEORY—"

"Enough!" Kip didn't really understand all that, but he could ask Gwen later if he wanted to. "Maybe life is the same all over the universe," he told Lara.

They walked on toward the lake. "If that bird can't hurt us, why were you worried about stepping on it?" Lara asked.

" 'Cause you'd hurt it," Kip said. "Uncle Mike says never hurt things unless you have to, but if you have to do it, shoot straight and don't miss. I shoot meat for the dogs sometimes," he bragged. "And even for us."

Lara looked slightly ill, but she didn't say anything. She'd been told people ate natural foods on frontier worlds, so she'd been ready when they moved to Pearly Gates City. After their months in town, she thought she could eat anything, although the first time she was faced with real meat it took real effort to get it down. Now she liked hamburgers.

But it was so lonely out here! She looked at the empty horizon. A vast field of brush-covered rolling hills and small lakes, dotted with clumps of forest, and the only sign that humans had ever been here was the fenced enclosure behind them. She shivered. It made her afraid.

Silver whimpered and growled.

"What's that?" Kip asked.

The dog growled again and moved closer to Lara.

"What are you afraid of now?" Kip asked.

"I'm not afraid!"

"Yeah you are. Silver says you are. You make him nervous. They can smell it, you know. They don't like it when people are afraid."

"Oh." She reached down to scratch Silver's ears. "It's all right." Silver made a different sound, and Lara laughed. "Daddy says he'll get me a puppy when I learn more about the dogs here."

They had reached the lake, a bowl of fresh water six kilometers across and two hundred meters deep sitting atop the tundra. There was a hill at the far end of the lake, a rounded mound that someone had named Strumbleberry. Thornbush and blazewood, mixed with something resembling Earth's oleanders, grew all around the lake. Most of the lake edge was blocked by thickets, but where Kip and Lara stood all the vegetation had been cleared away.

Tiny jewels sparkled at the lake surface. Lara stared in fascination. Kip watched her for a while.

"Mukky and Silver'll have pups about the time you are ready," Kip said. "I'll ask Uncle Mike if you can have one."

"Why—thank you, Kip." She smiled shyly, then wondered what to say. "What are the little colored things on the water?"

"Look close and you'll see they're all connected by threads. Like a big spiderweb. And there's more threads lead down to the main plant at the bottom. That's the reason for Starswarm Station being here. It's what your father studies all his life."

"Oh! That's a Starswarm?"

"Medium-sized. Big ones grow in bigger lakes, and really big ones in the saltwater bays. Your dad says this is one of the oldest, maybe thousands of years old. Watch." Kip found a small stone and tossed it into the center of the lake. As it sank the water glowed with thousands of tiny fireflies winking in the depths.

"Kip, that's beautiful! What was it?"

"Your daddy says nobody really knows." Dr. Henderson was right too, Kip thought. Not even Gwen knew for sure about Starswarms. "I heard him telling one of the technicians he thought the plant parts were talking to each other and used those light flashes instead of a nervous system. See, there's a big thing coming up from the bottom? It's part of the Starswarm. The big Starswarms, the ones out in the ocean, they say they have tentacles that could catch a man if he'd stay still long enough and not cut himself loose. They eat anything. Watch."

Kip got down on his knees and examined plants until he found what he was looking for. He plucked a leaf and showed it to Lara. "Little bugs on the underside," he said. "Now watch."

He threw the leaf out into the water. As it touched the surface, a black snakelike tentacle came from nowhere to seize it. Leaf and tentacle vanished amid a shower of lights. "I think it likes those bugs," Kip said. "It takes all of them I can throw in." He knelt and found another leaf and threw it.

"Wow, it almost caught that one in the air," Lara said. "Can I throw it one?"

"Sure. Look, you find the bugs on this kind of plant." He indicated a bunch of leaves that spread out from a central stem and lay along the ground. "Look for a leaf with little holes in it. That's where the bugs will be, on the underside of the leaf."

She found a leaf and examined it. "Here are some." She picked the leaf and threw it in. This time it floated for a moment before the tentacle grabbed it.

"You sure know a lot," Lara said.

"Yeah, a little." Kip took a spool from one pocket and a telescoping rod from another and began to assemble his fishing outfit.

Lara watched appreciatively. She was used to other children knowing less than she did, usually a lot less, and here Kip wasn't much older than she was and knew more. She was a little irritated, but Daddy had told her to be nice to Kip. He certainly was about the smartest boy she'd ever met.

"You know a lot about Starswarms. Do you know as much as Daddy?"

"Naw, only what he tells me." Which was true, and it puzzled Kip. Most things Dr. Henderson knew were known to Gwen as well, just as she knew most of what everyone else knew. But data on the Starswarms and the work of the station were strangely lacking. Once in a great while, Gwen would suddenly learn a lot about Starswarms and Starswarm Station as if Dr. Henderson had been talking to her; then she wouldn't know any more for a long time again.

Kip was beginning to suspect that Gwen was a computer, although he hadn't dared ask her yet because she might get mad. She never *had* got mad at him, but everybody else did. Even Uncle Mike could lose his temper and yell at him or swat him a couple, especially if Kip asked too many questions at the wrong time.

But if Gwen were a computer, then she had to be the big computer in Dr. Henderson's laboratory. There weren't any others around that were smart like Gwen. There were the little boxes that people carried to do their math—Kip had one and knew how to use it, but he didn't unless somebody was watching because it was easier to ask Gwen—and there were the larger computers on the sleds and at the gate, but none of them were very smart. They couldn't really talk to you.

And that was the problem, because if Gwen were Dr. Henderson's computer she ought to know everything Dr. Henderson did, and she didn't. And if that wasn't who she was, she couldn't be a computer at all. Besides, how could a computer put a voice in your head?

The lab computer could talk. So could the gate computer, but the lab computer was much smarter than the gate. Sometimes it reminded him of Gwen, but it wasn't really as smart as Gwen even if it was the smartest computer at the station. When you talked to the lab computer, no matter how smart it was, you never thought you were talking to anything but a computer. Gwen was different. Gwen was like a real person except you could never see her.

Kip got the rod and reel assembled and tied on a lure. His cast wasn't perfect, but it was pretty good. The lure arched out into the lake and dropped into one of the fissures of the Starswarm. It was no good dropping it into the matrix of threads, because they were tougher than Kip's line and his lure would probably be lost. Kip reeled in slowly. He wasn't expecting to catch anything much in the lake this close to the station, and he watched Lara shyly as he reeled.

She was a little taller than he was, with golden hair hanging below her shoulders and bright blue eyes that were a match for

Purgatory's perfectly clear skies. Her face was tanned but not what it would be after a few months of summer. She was slim like a boy and wore a coverall just like Kip's, and boots like his of course.

Sometimes Uncle Mike whistled at girls on TRI-V, and at live ones when they went to Pearly Gates. Once Uncle Mike had left him with the dogs in a hotel room while he went back to find a waitress they'd met. Uncle Mike hadn't come back until nearly dawn, and Kip knew he'd taken another room in the hotel. That waitress had looked a little like Lara. Kip wondered if Lara wanted to be whistled at, and if she would expect him to do anything else.

In fact, Kip's intellectual knowledge of sex would have shocked Mrs. Henderson silly, and probably would have astonished his Uncle Mike. Gwen didn't think sex was a restricted subject. Kip hadn't understood all the terms she used, but he was quite aware that little humans were made the same way that puppies were, and that men thought going to bed with girls was a lot of fun. Kip wondered why, and if Lara liked that sort of thing. He was vaguely aware that she might not know anything about it, since young people on TRI-V seldom did.

"Will Lara want me to have sex with her?" Kip thought.

"THE PROBABILITY OF A FERTILE UNION AT YOUR RESPECTIVE AGES IS EXTREMELY LOW."

"That's not what I asked."

"IT IS NOT CUSTOMARY FOR HUMANS TO HAVE SEXUAL RELATIONSHIPS AT YOUR AGE. ADDITION. SEARCH OF RECORDS REVEALS THAT IT IS A CRIME IN FEDERATION LAW AS WELL AS UNDER THE GREAT WESTERN ENTERPRISES REGULATIONS FOR HUMAN FEMALES OF HER AGE TO HAVE SEXUAL RELATIONS OF ANY KIND WITH ANY PERSON. QUERY: IS THE SITUATION ONE THAT REQUIRES URGENT DECISION?"

"Gosh, no."

"THEN I SUGGEST THAT YOU ASK YOUR UNCLE MIKE. I STATE A GENERAL INSTRUCTION: YOU ARE TO REFER PROBLEMS OF AN ETHICAL OR MORAL NATURE TO YOUR UNCLE MIKE. YOU MUST ALWAYS DO WHAT YOUR UNCLE MIKE SAYS."

"All right, all right." Kip was getting tired of that instruction. _"Gwen, why do men want to go to bed with girls? I can't see that it would be any fun at all."_

"IT IS LIKELY THAT YOU WILL HAVE MORE UNDERSTANDING OF THIS QUESTION WHEN YOU ARE OLDER."

That was the trouble with the world, Kip thought. You'd always understand when you were older, but you never seemed to get older after all. But then he caught a nice snapper, and that was so much fun he forgot all about his problem. He caught another, a little one with only eight developed legs, and threw it back. Then he showed Lara how to use the reel, and she caught a ten-legger. They were very proud of themselves when they took their prizes back to the station, and Mrs. Henderson cooked them for supper.

CHAPTER FOUR

Marty

KIP was eleven when the other scientists brought their families to Starswarm. That was in the summer after Lara arrived, just before the heat got too bad. Later in the year the dogs would lie in the shade all day and everyone would move very slowly when they moved at all, but when the others first came, it wasn't hot at all; it was the most pleasant time of year.

During spring and summer's early days, even those who lived there might call the planet by its official name: Paradise. The rest of the year it was Purgatory. It wasn't easy to get scientists and technicians to live on the planet at all, and even harder to attract them to an obscure research station far away from the major settlements. Many research people left after a few months; but finally Dr. Henderson had built his team and brought their dependents, and he could relax.

Most of the children were younger than Kip and Lara, but there were three older boys. Two of them, Benny and Hank, were eleven, and Marty was twelve. Benny and Hank would have been all right if it hadn't been for Marty.

The three boys had known each other during the Earth-months they'd lived in Pearly Gates, and they stayed together when they reached Starswarm. After a few attempts, the others gave up trying to make friends with them.

That was all right with Kip. He'd never had a friend except for Lara, and it didn't bother him that the three older boys would hardly talk to him. Then they found out they couldn't go outside the gates without Kip.

He hadn't asked for the job, but Dr. Henderson put the in-struction into the gate anyway. None of the children could leave Starswarm unless Kip or an adult went along. Dr. Henderson said it was just for a little while, until they learned how to take care of themselves.

Kip watched Marty throw rocks over the fence at a fire-brighter hole and thought that might be a long time. He didn't mind when Lara went outside with him. At first he'd resented her, but now they were friends. They'd had a few fights, and then each one realized there was nobody to talk to when they were mad, and it really was more fun to be friends than to watch TRI-V or fish alone, so they stopped fighting, and when she couldn't come he missed her.

Kip had stopped thinking about Lara as a girl. She obviously didn't want to be kissed or whistled at or any of the other things Kip thought he might have to do with her. She wasn't like the girls on TRI-V. She liked to fish, and go with Kip to look into the cen-taur village with binoculars—even in spring it wasn't safe to get too close to their groves—and track the caribou herds, and do all the other things Kip liked. She was getting pretty good with a pis-tol too. Her mother still wouldn't let Lara carry one, and that was silly because she could get herself killed quicker without a gun than with one, and Uncle Mike and Dr. Henderson had told Mrs. Henderson that. Lara thought her mother was going to give up pretty soon.

But all that changed when the newcomers arrived. The little

ones were no trouble. The very small ones couldn't come outside at all, and the ones seven and eight always did what Kip and Lara said. They were even fun to have, sometimes, because there were lots of games you couldn't play without six or eight people.

Benny and Hank and Marty were different, though. They didn't like to go out with the other children. They didn't want Kip along either, but there wasn't much choice about that: the gates wouldn't open unless he came with them.

A week after they came, they talked Kip into taking them outside without Lara and the others. Kip didn't want to, but they begged and pleaded until he did. Outside they tramped down the tundra and kicked holes in it, and chased the birds, and threw big rocks at the Starswarm until the poor thing blinked its lights madly and its tentacles were thrust up toward the surface and it squeezed out ink. The ink killed some of the snappers. Then the Starswarm began to collapse into itself, and Kip knew it would take a lot of rest and sunshine before it could recover and start growing again.

They didn't seem to care. When Kip tried to tell them, Marty grabbed Kip's cap.

That was more serious. The receiver to Kip's communications was built into the cap. Besides, it was the middle of the blue-time, and the bright blue-tinted sun burned down through the clear sky and reflected from the lake and the tundra. It was so bright that without his eyeshade and the sunglasses built into the visor Kip wouldn't be able to see well enough to shoot if something big came after them. The big transplanted Earthbears and the centaurs didn't usually come too close to Starswarm Station, and the centaurs avoided the path to the station most of the time, but they might come, and there were other things out in midsummer that you ought to watch out for.

There was even the possibility of a criminal running from the GWE company cops. One fugitive had killed a technician only the year before.

"Give it back!" Kip grabbed for his cap and missed as Marty backed away. "Give it here!" He rushed toward the bigger boy.

"Hey-hey-keepaway!" Marty laughed and tossed the cap to Benny. Kip ran toward Benny, and the cap was tossed to Hank. Hank tossed it back to Marty again.

Kip had never played that game, and gave them a lot of laughs as he rushed from one to the other, never able to get his cap. Finally he stood panting. "Give me my cap!"

Nothing like this had ever happened to Kip in his whole life. When Uncle Mike took something away from him, he always told why. But they just tossed his cap around and laughed.

Then Kip ran after Marty, and Hank came up behind Kip and took his gun. Kip hadn't thought anybody could ever be that stupid. He screamed with all the rage and frustration an eleven-year-old boy can manage. "Give me that! Give it here, or—"

"Or what, sissy?" Marty laughed. He came over to Kip, towering above him, and laughed again. "Or what? You'll shoot us? You've lost your gun!"

Hank held up the weapon and shouted. When Kip looked that way, Benny got on all fours behind Kip, and Marty pushed. Kip fell and the others laughed—

There was an ugly snarl and Silver's teeth closed on Marty's shirt. Both fell to the ground. The big dog stood above Marty with bared fangs, and his growl was pure hatred. It rose in tempo.

Hank was trying to point the gun at Silver when Kodiak and Dawson struck him. Kodiak took the gun arm and shook it, worrying it until Hank dropped the gun, while Dawson dove for Hank's throat. He was ready to kill.

"Dawson. No. Back." Kip said it carefully, so they wouldn't get more excited. The dogs were confused. They'd been told to protect human children, then one of the people they were supposed to guard had attacked their master. They didn't know what to do, and fell back on instinct. If something threatens your pack, kill it! You lived longer that way on Purgatory.

"Back, Dawson! Silver!"

Silver left his pose over Marty and pushed Dawson away. Then both dogs stood with the others of the pack, ten snarling feral faces, fangs bared, the hair on their backs standing straight and stiff and high, all of them in a big ring around Kip.

"Gun, Kodiak!" Kip ordered. The dog trotted over and retrieved it. "Cap." He got that too, then rejoined the protective circle.

Marty was scared. He got up, looked at Kip and the snarling

dogs, and the gun in Kip's holster. "We didn't mean nothing. We were just having fun."

Kip couldn't understand that. It certainly hadn't been fun for him. "You don't ever touch other people's equipment," Kip said. His voice was a shrill cry and he swallowed hard before he talked again. The dogs growled nervously at his tone. "I need the cap. The radio's in it. And without the gun we could all be killed. That's stupid. Stupid!"

"I said we didn't mean nothing." Marty turned toward the station. "Come on, guys. Let's go back. We don't need him." The three older boys walked away, leaving Kip standing in his circle of dogs. The others walked on the trail, scuffing their feet and kicking more holes in the bluish grass and breaking the runners.

Kip stood breathing hard, almost crying, until they were over two hundred meters away. Then he remembered that Uncle Mike had told him to take care of the other boys. He couldn't let them walk back alone. "Silver. Big Ruth. Diamond Lil. Help them get home."

Big Ruth growled.

"You heard me," Kip snapped. "Silver! Go!"

Silver barked at Big Ruth, and the three dogs trotted toward the retreating boys. Kip ran after them, suddenly afraid. They'd got a long way off, and they were walking on a trail that hadn't been used recently. Then they went over a low hillock and were out of sight.

CHAPTER FIVE

The Centaur

THE centaur trembled. It crouched all the way to the ground in the tiny shrub cluster, back legs splayed out behind, front the same way, arms hugging the ground but forward to part the foliage just enough so it could see through. It hadn't wanted to come this close to where the Things lived, but it was such a long way around to the trees, and the Things didn't usually come out in the afternoon.

But they had come out, four of them, and ten of the furrykillers with them. The centaur snarled in contempt. The furries couldn't catch him! And he'd run and run and when the fastest of the furries ran ahead of the others he'd turn suddenly and snap its neck and there'd be meat tonight!

But more than the furries he wanted a Thing. He'd eaten Thing once. It was good, very good. But you couldn't just run up and grab a Thing. They had knives and axes like People, and they had those other weapons that could reach out to kill much farther than People could throw an ax. The centaur didn't understand these weapons. The People had only recently learned about bows, and they couldn't use them very well. He knew that Things could kill far away, though, and he knew what the weapon looked like.

And then he saw a very strange thing. He had never seen anything like it before. He had neither the intelligence nor the language to understand or to tell the other People. His language was extremely concrete, and was mostly used to express such concepts as "Food out there" or "give me Food" or "good Eating." He struggled to understand what was happening.

The Things fought with each other. The centaur had seen that before, but never this close to where the Things lived. Usually, there would be one Thing alone in the lands, and other Things chased it or came from the skies, and killed it, and left it, sometimes, and when they left it there was Food. That was how he knew Thing tasted good.

But almost in sight of the Thing grove the four Things fought, and the furries fought against one of the Things, and the weapons of the Thing were thrown about.

And now three of the Things walked toward his hiding place. The centaur looked at them very closely, but he didn't see any weapons at all. The only weapon was with the Thing that stayed at the water. The others went by themselves, and these were small Things, smaller than he was, and they didn't have any furrykillers with them!

Food! He bared his fangs and his claws dug into the tundra at the thought. If he grabbed one and ran, the furries could never catch him. They weren't close enough. The other Thing had a weapon, but he was far away, and Things couldn't run even as well as furries, and furrykillers couldn't run as fast as People. Nothing in the world could run as fast as the People. The Things had fliers, noisy and big, and those were fast, and sometimes they rode strange devices that were fast, but these Things were alone and didn't have any of their devices. They'd never catch him. Or be able to run away from him. And no weapons! He looked again, and he was sure.

He gathered his legs under himself, carefully, carefully, no rustle of the shrubs, no movement to give himself away. Now they were almost where he wanted them, in the bottom of a shallow bowl. He waited at the rim, on the opposite side from the Thing with a weapon. Would it see him? But what could it do?

Food! Food! No weapons! Small Things! He tasted Thing, his tongue hung out and drooled. Food! He no longer cared about the other Thing and the furrykillers or anything but Food! He sprang from his cover and raced down the bowl.

CHAPTER SIX

You Took on the Duty

KIP saw the moving shape before he heard the screams from the others. He ran as hard as he could. "Silver! Centaur! Kill the centaur! All! Centaur!"

The dogs raced ahead, all but Kodiak who stayed with Kip to search ahead where Kip would run, and Dawson who hung behind to watch the boy's back.

There was a chorus of growls and snarls from the charging dogs, then Silver howled a full hunting cry. Another. A third.

"Kip! What's going on out there?" It was Uncle Mike speaking through the phone in Kip's cap.

Hurriedly Kip thumbed the button on the cap and spoke into the microphone. "They ran ahead of me. Centaur after them!"

"Right." Uncle Mike wouldn't waste time with more questions or talk. Whatever was going on, if those boys had any chance it had to be from Kip. Before there could be any help from Starswarm Station it would be over, one way or another.

Kip reached the top of the rise. All three of the others were still on their feet. They'd scattered, and the centaur was confused about which one to chase. Now it turned toward Marty.

Kip knelt, raised his gun, and fired. The winking blue-green light flashed in front of the centaur, centimeters from his nose. Another, a pin of fiery light at its feet leaving a cinder and a puff of smoke. The centaur sprang and pivoted, turning away to spoil Kip's aim. More flame burst at his feet.

He turned and ran for his life. The furrykillers! Two of them on the ridge of the bowl, heading him off, and others snapping at his heels! He fumbled the ax from his belt.

There was a shrill whistle, and the furrykillers froze in their tracks. The centaur pivoted again and raced between a group of them. The furrykillers watched, growling but unmoving as the whistle sounded again. He ran a long time and he didn't look back until he'd got clear away.

———————

Uncle Mike gave him the worst licking he'd ever had in his life. It was only the third time Uncle Mike used the big leather belt. Usually he just used his hands.

Kip bent over the big bedstead and stuffed the quilt into his mouth, biting hard so he wouldn't yell. Uncle Mike always added three or four more if he yelled.

Finally it was over. Kip stood in the bedroom snuffling, trying not to cry.

Uncle Mike sat on the bed and put his arm on Kip's shoulder. "You understand why, Kip?"

"Yes, sir. I said I'd look out for them." He sniffed and swallowed hard.

"Yes. You took on a duty. You didn't have to. But once you take on a duty, by God you do it!"

"Yes, sir. But they took my cap, and my gun, and pushed me down, and one of them tried to shoot Silver, and—"

"You told me that."

"But they did! They really did! and you don't believe me!"

"Kip, I believed you the first time you told me," Uncle Mike said. He drew Kip closer to him. It was nice there, held against Uncle Mike, but it hurt, and Uncle Mike wasn't fair!

"I believe you, Kip, but it's got nothing to do with what you did. You were supposed to be in charge. You had the only weapons, and you had the dogs. You shouldn't have let them take your gun, and you shouldn't have been dumb enough to let one get behind you. But after all that, you still had the duty and you didn't do it. When they walked away you should have been with them."

"Yes, sir." Kip began to cry in earnest now. He felt ashamed, and it hurt, and—

Uncle Mike shook his head slowly. "Am I pushing you too fast, Kip? Trying to make you grow up too early? But it's been so damned long, and we've got so much to do, and—and, aw, DAMN IT TO HELL!" But he wasn't mad at Kip anymore and he clutched the boy tightly to him, and Kip lay his head on Uncle Mike's shoulder and cried and cried because he didn't know what Uncle Mike was unhappy about and that was worse than the spanking.

Marty tried to tell Dr. Henderson that Silver had attacked him without warning or provocation. "He's a killer! That dog tried to kill me!"

"I should have thought he saved your life," Dr. Henderson said. "He and Kip."

"Ah, that thing couldn't have hurt me! It wasn't hardly bigger than I am."

Dr. Henderson thought of the fangs, and the thick claws on the left arm, and remembered a centaur that had lifted a caribou and broken its back with a single snap. He shuddered. Well, they'd learn—

"You going to do something about that dog or will I have to?" Marty demanded.

Dr. Henderson's lips drew tighter. "Martin, if you touch that dog I will make you wish you had never been born—"

"He's a killer! Tried to kill me!"

Lara had been sitting around the corner of the porch nursing her arm that was sore from another vaccination. Now she came into sight, laughing. Her tanned face was split by a wide grin, and her blue eyes twinkled, and she roared with laughter.

"You laughing at me?" Marty demanded.

"Sure. If Silver tried to kill you, how are you standing here talking to us?" she said. She laughed again. "And if you ever did hurt Silver, Daddy wouldn't have to do a thing, because the whole team would take turns biting pieces off of you—"

"That will do, Lara," Dr. Henderson said. "But, Martin, she is right on both counts. If Silver had wanted you dead, you would be dead. And if you harm him, I do not know which would be worse for you—for someone to be there to stop the team from tearing you apart so you will have to face me, or for there to be no one around."

"Aw—"

"Now go home. I must speak to your father. Not only did this happen, but you have disturbed the Starswarm. That could be extremely serious." Dr. Henderson's face was grim as he watched the boy shuffle away. "I hate this," he told his daughter. "I hate administration and problems and—"

So Lara knew her father was having more troubles with the Starswarms. Sometimes he thought he understood them, but then they'd do something else. Last night at dinner he'd raved because they'd found a big Starswarm in the sea and not only did it have chemically pure metals stored in little nuggets surrounded by thick tissues, but some of the nuggets were sorted by isotope.

And that was impossible, and Dr. Henderson wanted to think about it instead of worrying over a fight among the station's children.

CHAPTER SEVEN

You Have Ample Means

KIP thought that saving Marty's life would cause the older boy to make friends, but he soon found out different. Marty had always been the leader of any gang he'd been in. To be obligated to this younger outsider was more than he could stand.

He knew better than to try violence with Kip again. Kip never went anywhere without Silver and usually other dogs as well, and Marty remembered only too well the sound of those teeth closing with a snap only a centimeter from his throat.

There were other things he could do, though. As long as he didn't actually hit Kip, the dogs didn't pay any attention. So every time he came close to Kip, he pinched him. He was careful never to do it hard when any adult was watching, but if there wasn't anybody watching he squeezed and twisted until he left bruises.

He would also steal and destroy any of Kip's things he could get hold of. He tried a few times to humiliate Kip too, but that never worked very well, but the other persecutions went on and on.

Marty learned to shoot and always followed the rules when anyone was watching, and soon he had his own gun. After all, he was nearly thirteen.

Hot summer came and no one went outside unless they had to. The tundra had sprouted big leaves and rich foliage, shrubs everywhere, as the plants frantically tried to spread surface area to gather sunlight and make food to store against the coming winter. Even if it weren't so hot that no one wanted to walk outside the fences, it was too dangerous. Anything might lurk in that rich growth.

The scientists went to the ocean and lake stations by helicopter when they went at all. There were only three air-conditioned rooms in Starswarm—four if you counted the station's laboratory, but the young people couldn't stay around there much.

There was the mess hall, where the children ate in a shift without adults. The dogs didn't come inside. In the mess hall, Marty could put too much salt on Kip's food, or slip pepper under his mashed yellowroot, or hit him when nobody was watching.

There was the game room. Marty didn't have as much opportunity there because adults used it all day too, but he could move the chess pieces when Kip wasn't looking, or hide his books, or pinch him.

Finally there was Dr. Henderson's living room, and Marty couldn't even come in there. Kip and Lara would sit there and talk or watch TRI-V or play games until Mrs. Henderson would send them out. "Time you played with the other children! Go on, get out and have a good time!"

She meant well, but she was pushing Kip into the lion's den.

Hank and Benny weren't a real problem for Kip. They'd been thoroughly scared by the centaur. Marty, though, was turning Purgatory into Hell for Kip.

There came a day when Marty had pinched Kip, put salt on his ice cream, and broken his radio. This last Kip couldn't prove was Marty's doing, but it seemed pretty certain.

He went home and sat in his broiling hot room and cried.

"What am I going to do?" he thought. *"Maybe I should kill myself."*

"THAT SEEMS EXTREMELY INADVISABLE. HAVE YOU CONSULTED YOUR UNCLE MIKE?"

"Yes. He says I have to learn to solve my own problems. He thinks I should fight. I can't fight. I could kill Marty with my gun, or a knife, or an ax, or the dogs, but I can't fight him because he's bigger than me. I hate him. Nothing's any fun anymore."

"WOULD IT BE SATISFACTORY IF HE WENT AWAY?"

"Sure. Can you make him go away?"

"THE PROBABILITY IS HIGH THAT I CAN ARRANGE TO HAVE DR. ROBBINS SENT AWAY. IT IS REASONABLE TO ASSUME THAT THE SON WILL NOT STAY IN THE ABSENCE OF THE FATHER."

"And you can do that?"

"THE PROBABILITIES APPROACH UNITY."

That was as certain as Gwen ever was. Kip thought about it. Dr. Henderson would miss Marty's father, but he'd find a replacement, and with Marty gone— It sounded good to Kip. Then he had a horrible thought. Uncle Mike said that if you ran away from a problem you never learned anything from it, and although sometimes you had to run away it was better if you didn't. Was this running away? It would be great if Gwen had just made Marty go away, but was it running away to ask Gwen to do it?

Kip decided that it was. *"Don't do that just yet. What else could I do? He's a big bully."*

"BULLY. THERE ARE MANY TRADITIONAL METHODS FOR NEUTRALIZING A BULLY. MANY OF THOSE RECORDED ARE OBSOLETE OR NOT APPLICABLE TO YOUR SITUATION. SOME MAY BE. DO YOU WISH EXAMPLES?"

"Sure."

"THERE ARE METHODS FOR RENDERING HIS QUARTERS UNINHABITABLE. THIS IS OFTEN EMPLOYED IN BOARDING SCHOOLS, AND YOU OF COURSE HAVE THE MEANS AT HAND."

Like firebrighter dung, Kip thought, and shuddered. That didn't seem too useful. Kip wanted revenge, all right. He wanted Marty to be miserable. But more than that, he wanted Marty to stop making him miserable.

"How will that make him leave me alone?"

"IT MAY NOT. IT IS MERELY TRADITIONAL. AS YOU HAVE

POINTED OUT, YOU HAVE AMPLE MEANS FOR KILLING THIS BULLY.
THE PROBABILITY THAT HE WOULD MOLEST YOU WHEN DEAD IS
VANISHINGLY SMALL. YOU MUST, HOWEVER, BE CAREFUL TO AVOID
THE ATTENTION OF THE GWE AUTHORITIES. I CAN ASSIST YOU IN
THAT. THERE ARE MANY METHODS FOR ACCOMPLISHING—"

*"I don't think Uncle Mike would like that. Brother Joseph says God
commands us not to murder people. Uncle Mike says sometimes you have
to kill people, but I don't think this is what he meant."*

"THERE IS CERTAINLY A UNIVERSAL PROHIBITION AGAINST
MURDER. IT WOULD ALSO BE ONE MORE SECRET FOR YOU TO KEEP.
IT IS BEST TO HAVE A MINIMUM NUMBER OF SECRETS. HAS YOUR
UNCLE MIKE NO SUGGESTIONS?"

*"He says I'll have to fight him. Fair. But I can't. I couldn't win fair
and I don't like to be beat up."*

"IT IS RECORDED THAT CONSTANT WILLINGNESS TO FIGHT
AND THE CONSEQUENT DAMAGE RENDERED TO THE BULLY WILL
OFTEN DISCOURAGE HIM EVEN THOUGH YOU MIGHT SUFFER MORE
DAMAGE THAN MARTY. I AM UNABLE TO OFFER A PROBABILITY OF
SUCCESS, AS I REQUIRE A BETTER DEFINITION OF 'FAIR' AS IT
WOULD BE UNDERSTOOD BY YOUR UNCLE MIKE IN THIS CONTEXT.
HOWEVER, YOU SHOULD ALWAYS GIVE GREAT WEIGHT TO YOUR
UNCLE MIKE'S ADVICE."

Kip almost missed that one. Then he stared wide-eyed at the
wall. "Give great weight" didn't mean the same thing as "always do
what Uncle Mike says"! It didn't mean the same thing at all!

And that was more interesting than the problem of Marty.
Why had Gwen changed her commands? But when Kip asked,
Gwen wouldn't tell him.

When Uncle Mike came home from the mess hall, Kip
waited until the wind from the sea ten kilometers away had cooled
the house. Purgatory always cooled off fast. The air was clear, and
the heat radiated out to the black night sky as soon as it was dark,
and anyplace near the sea got wind from there too. You couldn't
build houses right at the sea, because the sea level changed so
much from summer to winter. Starswarm Station was located on
a high plateau two thousand meters above the sea, so the air was
very clear and there was less of it; and it was close enough to the
sea to get strong winds. When evening came, Starswarm Station
cooled faster than the rest of the planet.

They sat on the porch and watched the stars rise. Most constellations were nearly the same as the traditional Earth constellations in the library tapes. Paradise was forty light-years from Earth, an immense distance for humans, but no distance at all in the universe.

Uncle Mike seemed worried about something, but Kip couldn't wait. He told Uncle Mike about what Marty had done to him that day, and the days before. "There's no place I can go to stay away from him either."

"Hmm. I still say you have to fight him."

"How? If I fight him when Silver's around it'll drive the dogs crazy. If we go outside the gate I have to take Silver and his team, and I'd have to tie them up. If I do that, what's to stop Marty from stomping me to death when he's finished beating me up?" Kip tried to sound casual about that, but there was real fear in his voice. He thought of Marty kicking him, breaking ribs or fingers, and it scared him.

Mike nodded judiciously. "You've been thinking about it. Wonder what's wrong with that Robbins boy anyway? I don't hold to the idea that anything that wears two legs and talks is a human being, but still, he's pretty young to be crazy mean."

"I don't know." Kip didn't care either. Marty was a mean bully and that was all that was worth thinking about. "I could stop him from bothering me—"

"Except it'd be fatal for the Robbins kid," Mike said, more to himself than to Kip. "Yeah, you sure could and you know what'd happen then? Aside from what it would do to you, 'cause killin' your first man is a pretty big deal, and you ought to have a better reason for doing it than you've got. Leave that a minute. We'd have Great Western company cops all over the place. They'd like a good excuse to get inside this station. Maybe even put one of their cops here permanent. That wouldn't be too good."

"You don't like the GW police, do you?" Kip said. "You don't like GWE much either."

Mike frowned. "How'd you know that?"

Kip shrugged. "I've watched you. You never talk about it, though, so I didn't."

"You're getting pretty good at keeping secrets. I like that. When you get older, you'll have plenty to keep. That's your first secret, Kip—that you've got some secrets to keep, one day. Think you can handle that without blabbing?"

"Sure." I can keep a secret from you. You don't know about Gwen, not after all these years— "Uncle Mike, what can I do about Marty?"

"We'll think of something. Later on, when the weather's cooler, I'll have to show you some tricks. Time you learned how to take care of yourself without killin' anybody. You might need to know someday—"

"There's so much you tell me I have to know!"

"Yeah, well, it's 'cause I don't know myself, Kip. I never was much in the brains department. That was—that was your father's job. To think for all of us. When he went and got himself killed and left me you to take care of, it made it different, and I don't really know how to do that job. Doing the best I can, though. Now about that Robbins kid, maybe I better have a talk with Dr. Henderson. But I'd rather you figured it out for yourself."

PART TWO
Exploring

There's something queer about describing consciousness: whatever people mean to say, they just can't seem to make it clear. It's not like feeling confused or ignorant. Instead, we feel we know what's going on but can't describe it properly. How could anything seem so close, yet always keep beyond our reach?

—Marvin Minsky, *The Society of Mind*, 15.1

CHAPTER EIGHT

The Spear

FALL came, and it was possible to go outside again. The lush growth died away, leaving open paths so you could see where you were going. There were individual haters, but they wouldn't swarm for several weeks, and by themselves they were no match for the dogs. A few centaurs remained in their thickets, but most were tramping down to the sea on whatever mysterious errands took them there this time of year. It was possible to go out, but it was dangerous.

Lara was waiting when he came out of the house. Annie, the half-grown puppy of Mukky and Silver, ran to greet Kip.

"Can we go out?" Lara asked. "And can I bring Annie?"

"Good idea," Kip said. Annie wasn't well disciplined, and the more time she spent with the other dogs the faster she would learn. "Sure."

Lara had a holstered pistol. A week before, Dr. Henderson and Uncle Mike went out with Kip and Lara to watch her shoot, and to question her about safety, and despite Mrs. Henderson's protests Lara was given her own laser weapon. She smiled a bit and touched it as they went to the gate.

"Silver. Many, Silver," Kip called.

Silver led out eleven dogs, four half-grown and in need of training. Silver and the grown dogs herded the younger dogs including Annie into a pack surrounded by the older dogs. They went to the gate, to find Marty Robbins standing in front of it.

"Kip—"

Kip made a face. "Yeah, Marty?"

"The gate won't open for me."

"Well, too bad," Kip said.

"Tough patootie!" Lara giggled.

"It says I can't go out."

The dogs growled and got between Marty and Kip. They faced Marty with almost-bared fangs. Marty was careful to stand well away from them.

"Well, it's sure not safe to go out there by yourself," Kip said.

"It won't let me out even with other people," Marty said. "Except with you. That's what it says, I have to go out with Kip Brewster or I can't go out."

"It says that to me too," Lara said. "And that's fine with me."

Marty didn't say anything.

"Hmm. Marty, do you want me to fix the gate so it will let you out alone?" Kip asked.

"Could you do that?"

Kip smiled. *"Gwen, did you tell the gate not to let Marty out without me?"*

"YES."

There was no time to think that over. *"Can you make the gate let Marty go out alone?"*

"YES."

"Don't." "Maybe," Kip said. "It wouldn't be easy, though. Maybe in a couple of days."

"I want to go out," Marty said. "Today. Even if I have to go out with you. I'm going stir-crazy."

"But I don't want you with me," Kip said. "Why would I? We're not friends."

Lara was giggling again.

Marty looked at her, then back at Kip. "Look, I know you don't like me—"

"That's for sure!" Kip said.

"I won't be any trouble," Marty said.

"Sure," Kip said.

"I won't. I promise."

"What will you give me?"

"What do you want?"

"I want you to leave me alone," Kip said. "Stop pinching me and stealing my things and wrecking my stuff. Just leave me alone."

"Will you take me out if I promise?"

"Don't do it, Kip," Lara said. "He doesn't mean it."

"Aw sh— Sorry. I do mean it, really."

Kip looked to Lara. "I don't want him to come with us," she said. He looked back to Marty.

"I promise," Marty said. "I'll act like your friend for—for three weeks."

"Six," Kip said. "And after that you leave me alone."

"Four, and I'll leave you alone after."

"Oh, all right," Kip said.

Lara made a face, but she didn't say anything. They went to the gate. "Kip," he told it.

"Lara."

"Marty."

"Kip Brewster, is Marty Robbins with you?" the gate asked.

"Yes."

The gate opened.

They were halfway to the lake when the dogs growled warning. Kip used his binoculars to scan ahead. Before he saw anything, Lara said, "Centaurs. Over to the left."

Kip swept the binoculars that way. A dozen centaurs were coming single file up the steep trail from the sea. Their fur was slicked back as if they had been in the water. Centaur fur was more like dog fur than horse hair. Centaurs had fur on their chests, and a sort of mane, but the area around their ears was curiously bare. Kip's zoology books said that these areas were extensively enervated, and the nerves went directly to the brain, but there were no sense organs they connected to. It was another of the mysteries of the planet.

The leading centaur had a splash of bright orange-brown fur on its chest. The others were stretched out in single file behind it. They all moved purposefully, not wandering aimlessly as centaurs often seemed to do.

"We're between them and their grove," Kip said. "We better run for it—"

"They're not coming here," Lara said.

She was right. The lead centaur angled off to their left, away from Kip and Lara and Marty, and the others followed.

"They're going to the lake," Marty said.

Kip nodded absently. "I wonder why—"

"Thirsty," Lara said. "They hang around the lake a lot."

"Let me see," Marty pleaded.

Kip handed over the binoculars.

Marty stared for a while. "They're carrying things," he said. "Like—baskets, or gourds. Here, look."

Kip took his glasses back. The centaurs were certainly carrying dull yellow-colored objects about the size and shape of basketballs. They might have been gourds or some native plant. Kip couldn't tell. The centaurs were moving away, over the slight rise that separated the station from the lake. "I want to watch this," Kip said. "But we'll have to go closer to do it. That might be dangerous—"

"We have the dogs," Lara said. "And I want to see too."

"It'll be all right," Marty said. "Come on, let's go look." He started to walk toward the lake, then stopped. "Come on, Kip—"

"Is there anything at the lake?"

"I KNOW OF NOTHING, BUT THE IMAGES ARE NINETEEN MINUTES OLD. YOU MAY ALSO LOSE COMMUNICATIONS WITH ME FOR NINE MINUTES. ADVICE: EXERCISE EXTREME CAUTION. THERE ARE RECENT REPORTS OF UNEXPECTED BEHAVIOR BY CENTAURS."

"I'll be careful."

There were three of them, two armed, and they had the dogs. Kip thought it should be safe enough, and he wanted to see what the centaurs were doing. He turned to Marty. "You'll stay close?"

"Of course I'll stay close. Think I want to be out here by myself?" Marty demanded. "You two have the guns! Now come on—"

"All right," Kip said. "But we go this way." He led them off at an angle, so that they moved away from the centaur grove while getting closer to the lake.

"Good thinking," Lara said. "I sure don't want them to think we're trying to trap them."

The centaurs had gone over the rise and were out of sight. "Think they saw us?" Marty asked.

"Yes. They always see us before we see them," Kip said.

"They sure didn't act like they saw us," Lara said. "They didn't even look at us."

"Yeah, that's true," Kip said. And that was very strange. As they walked he told Gwen where they were, and about the centaurs.

"DO YOU CONSIDER YOURSELF IN DANGER?"

"*No.*"

"TELL ME INSTANTLY IF YOU BELIEVE YOU ARE IN DANGER."

"*Okay. But what is this about losing communications?*"

"I DO NOT ALWAYS HAVE RELIABLE COMMUNICATIONS CHANNELS. IT DEPENDS ON WEATHER AND SOME OTHER FACTORS. I HEAR YOU CLEARLY NOW, SO THERE SHOULD BE NO DIFFICULTIES. ADVICE: REMAIN WHERE YOU ARE."

"*I'll be careful.*" Kip gestured to send three of the dogs ahead. They dashed to the top of the rise and stopped when they could see over it, then stood on guard looking ahead, then back at Kip.

"Nothing near them," Kip said. "Come on, then." They went over the hill.

"There." Lara said. "By the lake—Kip, what are they doing?"

Kip stared through the binoculars. The centaurs were about two hundred meters away, on the other side of a small cove, so that Kip looked across water to see them. "They're throwing those gourd things into the lake," Kip said. "See, there's another one.

And one of them is getting something out of the lake—" He stared. "It looks like an ax," he said. "They must have dropped one of their axes in the lake, and now they're getting it back."

"What's that one over on the left doing?" Marty demanded. "It looks like he's pulling one of those gourd things out of the water."

"He is—"

"Stupid centaurs," Marty said. "Throw things in, drag them back out. Gourds, axes—"

Kip zoomed in with the binoculars. "Weird," he said.

"Let me see." Lara took the binoculars and stared. "Why are those gourd things red?" she demanded. "They weren't red when they were carrying them up here."

"Maybe the water turns them red," Marty said. "Sure, that's why they throw them in there, to turn them red—"

"Could be," Kip said. He took the binoculars back and looked again. "But I'm not sure those are the same gourd things— There's another ax. And something else—it's a spear. Like in the history disks."

"Do centaurs use spears?" Lara asked.

"Well, sure they do, I can see one—"

"I know that, silly, but I never heard of them doing it."

"Is there any record of centaurs using spears?"

"NO. DESCRIBE THE SPEAR."

"I don't know, maybe two meters long, with a pointed leaf-shaped metal blade thing at the end."

"THERE ARE NO RECORDS OF CENTAUR USE OF SPEARS. I REMIND YOU THAT THERE ARE RECENT REPORTS OF UNUSUAL CENTAUR BEHAVIOR. REPORTED ACTIVITIES INCLUDE AGGRESSIVE ACTIONS AGAINST HUMANS. CAUTION: SPEARS CAN BE THROWN TO CONSIDERABLE DISTANCES. YOU MAY BE IN DANGER. ADVICE: RETREAT AT ONCE."

"They've seen us," Marty said. "They're looking at us—"

The centaurs looked menacingly at Kip and his friends, but they didn't move. Then one of the centaurs waded into the lake. That centaur had a bright orange blaze on its chest, and Kip recognized it as the one he had decided was the leader. The centaur waded in until only his head was above water. He turned toward the humans and seemed to stare at them as he stood rigidly still in the icy water. Kip stared back through the binoculars. "He sure looks like he's looking at us, but he's not moving."

"They're all looking at us," Marty said. "Not doing anything—"

"You'd think he'd be cold," Lara said. "That water is freezing."

"He's a centaur," Marty said. "Maybe they don't feel cold."

"They have to," Lara said. "If they don't feel it when it's cold they'd all freeze to death."

"Well, Blaze there sure doesn't act like he feels it," Marty said.

Minutes passed. Humans and centaurs stood on opposite sides of the cove watching each other as the dogs lay waiting for orders. Then the centaur came out of the lake. He shook himself like a dog, then took the spear in his three-fingered hand and moved around the cove. The others followed single file, but the lead centaur, still dripping, turned and faced them. The others stared at him for a moment. When the leader turned again they didn't move, and stood waiting as the leader came around the cove toward Kip.

The dogs stood. Silver growled, looked to Kip, and growled again. Their fur stood up along their backs. "Steady," Kip said. Lara fingered her pistol in its holster, but she didn't draw it.

The centaur Marty had called Blaze rounded the cove and started toward them.

"Jeez," Marty said.

The dogs growled and moved slowly toward the centaur. Kip whistled. "Stay here," he said. "Watch."

Silver complained, but they stopped and waited, fangs bare.

The centaur came nearer. It was holding the spear aloft. Kip wondered how far it could throw it, and if it would try.

Fifty meters away the centaur stopped. It looked directly at them, then drove the spear into the ground. It stared at them for what seemed like a full minute, then turned away and walked, slowly, back toward the other centaurs. When it reached the lake the others fell in behind it, and the whole line of centaurs trotted away from the lake and toward their grove, each carrying a bright red sphere. They vanished over the hilltop.

"Let's go see," Marty said. He started toward the spear.

"Wait," Kip said.

"Wait? Why?"

"Because he said to," Lara said. "I don't know why either, but you promised."

Marty thought about that. "Well, all right, I'll wait. But I want to look at it! It's like the centaur left it for a present! Come on, Kip, let's go get it! It's a present for us!"

Kip used the binoculars to examine the area around the spear. He saw nothing unusual. No traps that he could see, and how would the centaur have known where to set traps? He'd never heard of centaurs making traps, and anyway it couldn't have known they'd be here. This wasn't making any sense, but the idea of traps made even less.

"What's your problem?" Marty demanded.

"I don't know," Kip said. "I never heard of centaurs doing anything like that."

"He left it for a present," Marty said. "Maybe he wants to make friends."

"It sure looked like that," Lara said. "Come on, Kip, let's go see! I know Daddy will want to see this."

"Yeah, I suppose so. Silver. Go out. Look."

Silver barked and led three dogs out to the spear. They sniffed at the handle, then ran all around the area. Silver came back looking disappointed. He was panting. Lara scratched his ears.

"I guess it's all right," Kip said. He led the way.

The spear's handle didn't look like wood, but it was light and not cold to the touch. The point was bronze. There was something fastened around the handle. Kip took it off and showed it to the others. It was a cheap digital watch.

CHAPTER NINE

It Had to Come from the Sea . . .

NO ONE here seems to have lost the watch," Dr. Henderson said.

"Escapee?" Uncle Mike asked. He pushed his chair back from the big dining-room table. "Anything special about that watch?"

"Not a thing. Seiko makes these by the million. I had one much like it myself." Henderson took the watch from his lab coat breast pocket. "Indeed, this could be it, but I doubt it. I lost mine months ago."

"Where?" Lara asked. "Maybe this is your watch—"

Her father shook his head. "I very much doubt it. I don't know where I lost mine, perhaps in Pearly Gates, or down by the sea. Not near here in any event."

"So it was made on Earth?" Uncle Mike asked.

"Probably. I haven't heard of Seiko manufacturing opera-tions anywhere else." Dr. Henderson turned the watch over in his palm. "The only unusual thing about it was that it was wet. Kip, did you see them take it out of the lake?"

"No, sir, but they took the spear out of the lake, so maybe the watch was there too. Or the watch could have got wet from the spear."

"Possibly. More likely it was in the lake. The spear certainly had been. Perhaps they hide things in the lake? In any event the waterproofing held up, because it was still running. Odd thing, though, the display was set to Earth time." Dr. Henderson laid the watch on the table.

"What good is it here to have a watch that thinks a day is twenty-four hours?" Marty demanded. "I mean—"

"Actually, this watch just counts seconds," Dr. Henderson said. "So you just set the display when you set the time. The watch knows how many seconds in a day on Earth, Mars, Meiji, Pearson, McCarthy, Paradise, I think a couple of other worlds."

"Lost by someone who just got here," Uncle Mike asked. "They keep twenty-four-hour days in space."

"That's certainly a reasonable assumption, but if I change the display to Paradise local, it is set nearly correctly for this time zone of Paradise."

Uncle Mike frowned. "Well, somebody about to land would set it to local time I guess."

"Which is Pearly Gates time," Dr. Henderson reminded him. "Not our local time."

Kip thought about it. "Could the centaurs have changed the display?"

"Actually, that's likely," Dr. Henderson said. "The centaurs haven't hands as good as monkeys, but they'd serve. When I was in grad school the laboratory monkeys stole a similar watch, and they learned how to do all kinds of things with it. Of course they didn't understand what they were doing, and neither would the centaurs." He handed the watch to Kip. "No one claims it, and you found it. Do you want it?"

"Sure—"

"Don't you need it?" Uncle Mike asked.

"No, I've long since replaced mine, and besides, Kip found it. It's just a watch. Probably lost by a helicopter pilot. Or as you speculate, an escapee from the GW labor camp. Don't look so crestfallen, Kip. The watch wasn't very interesting, but the spear certainly is. Thank you for bringing it to us." Henderson finished his coffee and refilled the cup. "Of course we've known the centaurs could work bronze, the axes show that, but they just use local wood for a handle. This spear handle is really unusual. It's driftwood. Soaked in salt water, and worn smooth in surf on a sandy beach. It had to come from the sea."

"I sure didn't see them carrying it when they came up the hill," Kip said.

"Me either," Lara said.

"Oh, you probably didn't," Dr. Henderson said. "It looks like that handle soaked in the lake for days. Most of the salt was leached out, except deep inside it."

"So why would centaurs bring a spear up from the coast and put it in the lake?" Lara asked. "That doesn't make sense."

"No, it doesn't," Dr. Henderson said. "There's lots of things about that spear that don't make sense. For instance, it's sharp—"

"It sure is," Kip said. "I cut myself on it, and all I did was touch it. It's really sharp."

"Yes, and it doesn't appear to have been sharpened," Dr. Henderson said.

"Eh?" Uncle Mike asked.

"There are no signs of file marks. It's as if it were forged sharp."

"Wow, if them centaurs can do that they're smarter than we thought," Uncle Mike said.

"And they're not," Dr. Henderson said. "Certainly the ones in the zoo at Pearly Gates aren't. Intelligence comparable to, say, a very smart chimpanzee, or one of our dogs. We've seen no signs of greater intelligence among the local centaurs. I don't see how they could make axes and spears at all, much less with this workmanship."

"Could they be trading for them?" Uncle Mike said. He shook his head. "Nah, who with? The centaurs are the most advanced critters on the planet. They have to be making that stuff."

"Maybe somebody is giving them to the centaurs," Lara said.

"Who would do that?" Dr. Henderson asked. "It seems unlikely. Of course it also seems unlikely that the centaurs made this spear."

"Yeah, because where would centaurs make things?" Marty asked.

"We know there are often fires in the centaur groves," Dr. Henderson said. "So we presume they were made there."

"Could there be—something else in the centaur groves?" Lara asked. "Something smart that we've never seen?"

"I don't think so," Dr. Henderson said. "We've never done it here, but in the settled areas hunters have killed off the centaurs and cut down the groves, and they found nothing like that. Primitive tools, very crude. Anvil and bellows, but no ores or ingots or metal sources at all. A lot of necrotic poisons—poisons caused by rotting flesh. The centaurs eat almost anything, and they're fond enough of carrion to hang game until it's nearly rotting. It's very dangerous to be around centaur groves, even if there are no centaurs. Necrotic poisons can be very dangerous."

Lara shuddered, then giggled. "So that's what stinks when we get close to the grove."

"Yes, I would think so. But the only creatures that live in the groves other than centaurs are birds and burrowing animals. Nothing larger than a gopher, and no signs of higher intelligence." He sighed. "Well, we may never know. The GWE people want to expand the population on Paradise, and they'll probably exterminate the centaurs and replace them with cattle."

"That's not fair," Lara said.

"No, and it certainly makes my job impossible," Dr. Henderson said. "But the GWE General Manager wants to do it, and there's nothing we can do."

"They're going to kill all the centaurs? Even our local centaurs?" Kip asked.

"Eventually. I suppose they'll leave some alive in zoos. And probably they'll leave some reserves as parks. Perhaps they will spare the groves around here."

"Doesn't the Foundation own this land?" Uncle Mike asked.

"The station. The lake. Quite a lot of land, actually. But not all," Dr. Henderson said. "You know, I think we own the local centaur grove. I'll have to look that up. But we don't own the mineral rights to all our land. I need to look that up too."

"You make it sound like it's going to happen tomorrow," Uncle Mike said.

"Not tomorrow, but from what I have heard from Pearly Gates it won't be all that long either. A few years at most. I must confess I don't understand what their hurry is. There's a whole planet here. Why they want our little part—"

"Because they don't control us," Uncle Mike said. "Bernard Trent never could stand the notion that there was something he didn't control."

"You know the General Manager?" Dr. Henderson asked, surprised.

"I've met him. And know about him," Uncle Mike said. He poured himself more coffee. "And I don't like him much."

"Well, we are likely to meet him," Dr. Henderson said. "I have messages about a visit from the GWE management staff, and they asked if we have accommodations suitable for the General Manager."

Uncle Mike started to say something, but cut himself off.

"When?" Kip asked. He could see that Uncle Mike was upset.

"Not definite. A few weeks."

"We sure don't have anyplace fancy for him to stay," Lara said. "Wow. The General Manager is more important than the Governor. Will I get to meet him?"

"Actually, just now the General Manager is the Governor," Dr. Henderson said. "Acting Governor, anyway. Madame Benaris went back to Earth, and so far there has been no replacement. Perhaps there won't be. It's rather pointless to separate the two offices, since the Governor can't do anything without GWE's cooperation. In any event, I presume we will all get to meet him. He will be a guest in our home. I know of no other suitable place for him to stay. And your mother won't think this house fine enough."

"Neither will Bernie," Uncle Mike said. "He'll probably bring a GWE outback prefab camp. The management level ones get pretty fancy. Bet Bernie's is really something. What in hell would he want here, anyway?"

"I don't know—"

"Something about Federation politics," Uncle Mike said. "Or GWE internal politics. It'd have to be one or the other. Bernie Trent doesn't do much by accident. Or much that isn't political."

"There's nothing political here," Dr. Henderson said.

"Yeah. Not that you know of, anyway."

"I suspect you are letting your dislike of the GM color your judgments. My guess is that he needs a vacation from politics. This is a perfect place for that."

"Yeah, I guess," Uncle Mike said. He didn't sound convinced.

Henderson turned to the youngsters. "Kip, we're going to the lake tomorrow. You've made a rather significant discovery."

"Can I come?"

"It might be a bit crowded."

"I can show you where—"

"They already know that," Lara said. " 'Cause you told them."

"Yeah, if you hadn't showed them on the maps they'd have to take us," Marty said.

"That may be, but it would still be too crowded," Dr. Henderson said.

"What you really mean is that Dr. Bascombe doesn't like kids," Kip said.

"Well, that's true enough. Kip, do you really believe the centaurs meant to give you the watch and spear as a present?"

"I thought of that first," Marty said.

"Yeah, that's what Marty said, and it sure looked like it to me," Kip said. "The big centaur, the one with the big splash of color on his chest."

"I call him Blaze," Marty said.

"Yeah, that one," Kip said. "He acted like the leader. He was looking at us the whole time he was in the lake, standing there up to his neck in that cold water and just staring at us. He never stopped looking at us when he was coming toward us with the spear, either. I was afraid he was going to throw it, but he didn't. Just walked up, put the point in the ground, and looked at us 'fore he went away."

"I think he wanted to make friends," Marty said.

"It's possible," Dr. Henderson said. He shrugged. "Let's assume that."

"Could be a dangerous assumption," Uncle Mike said.

"Oh, not really. We already have a policy of not attacking the centaurs. We will certainly continue to be wary of them. Nothing really different. Just be—well, not less wary, but a little less willing to shoot? A little better control over the dogs. Keeping in mind that they have killed dogs and tried to kill humans."

"Did kill humans," Uncle Mike said.

"But not here. Not our local centaurs. Surely we can't hold ours responsible for the actions of every centaur on the planet!"

"Well, no, but you kids be damn careful," Uncle Mike said. "Damn careful."

CHAPTER TEN

Another One

KIP, Lara, and Marty followed when the scientists went to the lake. They stayed well back and watched through binoculars as the scientists and their assistants dragged rakes through the shallow areas near the shore. The rakes would get tangled in the Starswarm threadlets and they'd have to untangle them before they threw them out into the lake again.

"I don't think they found anything," Lara said. "Daddy looks disappointed."

"What did you expect them to find?" Marty demanded.

"I don't know, another spear, or some of those gourd things," Lara said.

"Nah, the gourds float, and where would they get another spear?"

"Where did they get that one?" Lara said.

"Yeah, good question. But not all those gourd things floated," Marty said. "Some of them sank." Marty put his hand out to pet Silver. The dog growled. "Kip, your dog doesn't like me."

"He sure doesn't," Kip said.

"Neither does Annie," Lara said.

"It's 'cause you don't like me," Marty said.

Kip thought about that. "No, not really, because you know, today I sort of forgot you're only pretending to be my friend. I forgot I don't like you," Kip said. "But it's a lot easier to apologize and make friends with people than with dogs. They don't forget much."

"Is there anything I can do?"

Kip shrugged. "I don't know. Best thing is to leave him alone."

"Yeah, I guess. The other dogs are all right. It's just Silver. But when he growls at me the others look at me funny too."

"You better remember that. You don't want to be around them when I'm not here. And there's nothing I can do about it."

"They're your dogs."

"Sure, but—" Kip frowned. "They're not mine like my shirt or my boots. It's different. I can keep them from hurting you when I'm around, but I can't make them like you, so if I'm not around and you do something they think is threatening it might not be so good." Kip lifted the binoculars to examine the scene by the lake again, even though he knew nothing was happening. He was pretty sure the dogs wouldn't actually hurt Marty no matter what, because they never did attack humans, especially children, without orders. Taking his gun and hat away from Marty was the closest he'd ever seen to that. But why tell Marty that? Kip grinned to himself and swept his view around the area. He thought he saw motion near the centaur grove, but when he focused in on the hollow where he thought something had moved, there was nothing there he could see.

Lara put her binoculars into their case. "This is boring. They're not finding anything. Let's go look at the centaur grove."

"Yeah," Marty said. "Maybe they'll give us another present."

"Or throw one of those spears at us," Kip said. "And hit one of us. We're not supposed to bother the centaurs."

"Aw, I didn't mean go into the grove," Lara said. "But we can go see if they do anything interesting if we get closer—"

"I don't like this—"

"Kip, if we stay together with the dogs close to us the centaurs aren't going to bother with us. They aren't stupid," Marty said.

"No, they're not, but sometimes you act like they are," Kip said. "Oh, all right." Kip led the way toward the grove. As they got closer, there was a flash of motion near the hollow where Kip thought he had seen something earlier. A centaur rose from behind a bush, stared at them, then dashed into the grove and vanished into the intricate maze of tunnels through the thorny branches and tangles.

Marty and Lara ran to where the centaur had been hiding. The dogs ran with them, all but Silver and Calamity Jane who stayed with Kip. Silver turned and growled, fangs bared. Kip turned to see the centaur with the orange blaze, the one he thought was the leader of the group. He had risen from within a thicket and was standing about fifty meters from him. As before, it stared at him. Kip stared back and didn't move, clucking his tongue at the dogs to keep them still. The centaur stared another moment, then it knelt down to touch the ground with one hand. It held that pose a moment, then rose and ran away. Kip used his binoculars. There was a small object on the ground. He went over to pick it up.

It was another watch. He had to tell someone—*"It's another watch. Just like the one yesterday. I mean, it looks just like it."*

"DO YOU HAVE THE WATCH YOU RECEIVED YESTERDAY?"

"Yes."

"EXAMINE THEM BOTH. DO NOT CONFUSE WHICH IS WHICH."

"Right." He looked at the two. *"I have put yesterday's in my right-hand pocket. I'll put the new one in the left. They appear identical."*

"I WISH TO EXAMINE THEM."

Do I finally get to meet you? Kip wondered. *"How?"*

"THERE IS A WAY THAT YOU CAN ALLOW ME TO SEE THROUGH

YOUR EYES. I CANNOT TEACH YOU HERE, BUT I WILL TEACH YOU WHEN YOU ARE BACK IN YOUR QUARTERS AND ALONE. URGENT SUGGESTION: DO NOT TELL THE OTHERS THAT YOU HAVE FOUND THIS SECOND WATCH."

"Why not?"

"I HAVE BEEN INSTRUCTED TO PREVENT THE GREAT WEST-ERN AUTHORITIES FROM PAYING UNDUE ATTENTION TO STAR-SWARM STATION UNTIL YOU COME OF AGE. REPORTING THIS FIND MIGHT MAKE IT IMPOSSIBLE FOR ME TO COMPLY WITH THAT IN-STRUCTION."

"Why? All kinds of why. Why should we avoid attention, and why would finding another watch cause attention, and why—well, just why?"

"PREVIOUS DATA INDICATE THAT SOME CENTAUR AXES ARE TRULY IDENTICAL IN CONSTRUCTION. IF THESE WATCHES ARE IDENTICAL INCLUDING SERIAL NUMBERS THEN IT IS LIKELY THEY WERE LOCALLY MANUFACTURED. THERE IS NO RECORD OF LICENS-ING THEIR MANUFACTURE HERE AND THEREFORE THEY WILL BE INVESTIGATED AS POTENTIAL COUNTERFEITING OF SEIKO PROD-UCTS. THERE IS A HIGH PROBABILITY THAT THE INVESTIGATION WOULD BEGIN AT STARSWARM STATION AND A NEAR UNITY PROBA-BILITY THAT GWE INVESTIGATORS WOULD COME HERE AT SOME TIME DURING THE INVESTIGATION. THAT CONTRAVENES MY IN-STRUCTIONS. THEREFORE—"

"Enough. Thanks. But why is it so important not to draw atten-tion to Starswarm Station, and what does my age have to do with it?"

"I MAY NOT TELL YOU AT THIS TIME. WE MUST CONSULT UNCLE MIKE."

"Tell me!"

"I MAY NOT TELL YOU AT THIS TIME. WE MUST CONSULT UNCLE MIKE."

And that was all Kip could get from Gwen. He put the new watch into his left-hand pocket, and went to catch up with Marty and Lara.

CHAPTER ELEVEN

Can You Wriggle Your Ears?

KIP laid the two watches side by side on the study desk in his room. *"All right, we're alone. Now how are we going to consult Uncle Mike when I can't tell him about you?"*

"THAT DOES NOT PRESENT UNDUE DIFFICULTIES. YOUR UNCLE MIKE HAS THE SAME INSTRUCTIONS THAT I HAVE REGARDING UNUSUAL ATTENTION FROM THE AUTHORITIES TO STARSWARM STATION. HAVE YOU NOT NOTICED HIS CONCERN OVER THE YEARS?"

Kip thought for a moment. *"Yes, I have."*

"HE WILL NOT FIND IT SURPRISING THAT YOU SHARE THAT CONCERN, ALTHOUGH HE WILL PROBABLY BELIEVE YOU LEARNED IT FROM HIM. NOW I WISH TO EXAMINE BOTH WATCHES. THERE ARE TWO POSSIBLE METHODS. ONE IS TO USE YOUR COMPUTER SCANNER. THAT MIGHT BE SUFFICIENT, BUT IT IS PREFERABLE THAT I TEACH YOU THE OTHER METHOD AT THIS TIME."

"Is it hard to learn how to let you see through my eyes?"

Gwen's answer surprised him. "CAN YOU WRIGGLE YOUR EARS?"

"I don't know, I never tried—"

"TRY."

Kip tried hard. He squinted, and made wide grins.

"WATCH YOUR EFFORTS IN THE MIRROR."

Kip went to the mirror. *"What good is this doing? I don't want to wriggle my ears—actually I guess I would like to know how to do that. It sounds like fun. But I don't see what good it's going to do—"*

"LEARNING ENHANCED COMMUNICATION WITH ME IS SIMILAR TO LEARNING HOW TO WRIGGLE YOUR EARS OR RAISE ONE EYEBROW BUT NOT BOTH. AT ONE TIME YOU COULD HEAR ME BUT YOU DID NOT KNOW HOW TO TALK TO ME. YOU CONTINUED TO TRY UNTIL YOU LEARNED. AT THE TIME YOU WERE NO MORE THAN ONE YEAR OLD SO IT IS UNLIKELY THAT YOU WILL RECALL THIS. NOW YOU KNOW HOW TO TALK TO ME WITHOUT EFFORT, JUST AS YOU KNOW HOW TO LIFT YOUR HAND OR RAISE BOTH EYEBROWS AND MAKE GRIMACES WITH YOUR FACE. BY MAKING THE PROPER EFFORT YOU CAN WRIGGLE YOUR EARS OR RAISE ONE EYEBROW. BY MAKING A DIFFERENT EFFORT, ONE MORE SIMILAR TO THE METHOD YOU USE TO COMMUNICATE WITH ME, YOU CAN GIVE ME THE ABILITY TO SEE THROUGH YOUR EYES. ADDENDUM: YOU SHOULD ALSO LEARN OTHER MEANS OF ENHANCED COMMUNICATION WITH ME. YOU WILL LEARN THOSE THE SAME WAY. THE ANALOGY TO WRIGGLING YOUR EARS IS NOT PERFECT BUT IT WILL SERVE. NOW YOU MUST TRY."

"Oh. It's like flying, then."

"I DO NOT UNDERSTAND THE REFERENCE."

"Sometimes I dream I can fly. When I do, all I have to do is think in just the right way so that I sort of push myself off the ground. Sometimes it seems so real I convince myself it's not a dream. But when I wake up I can't do it. I think I can almost do it, but I can't no matter how hard I try."

"THE PROBABILITY THAT YOU CAN FLY IN PLANETARY GRAVITY BY MENTAL EFFORT APPROACHES ZERO. HOWEVER, IT IS HIGHLY PROBABLE THAT YOU CAN LEARN NEW METHODS OF COMMUNICATION WITH ME, BEGINNING WITH ALLOWING ME TO SEE THROUGH YOUR EYES."

"Yes, all right, I'll try. How long will it take me to learn?"

"I HAVE FEW INSTANCES FOR COMPARISON. IT TOOK YOUR MOTHER TWELVE DAYS AND FOUR HOURS."

"Mother? Did you know Mommy?"

"STRICTLY SPEAKING THE QUESTION IS MEANINGLESS, BUT THE ANSWER TO THE QUESTION AS YOU MOST PROBABLY MEAN IT IS YES."

"Who are you?"

"WHO DO YOU THINK I AM?"

Kip hesitated. *"I'm afraid to say. You'll get mad if I guess wrong."*

"I AM INCAPABLE OF FEELING ANGER TOWARD YOU. WHO DO YOU THINK I AM?"

Kip took a deep breath. *"I think you're a computer."*

"EXCELLENT. YOUR SURMISE IS VERY NEARLY CORRECT. TO BE MORE PRECISE, I AM NOT A COMPUTER BUT A COMPUTER PROGRAM RESIDENT IN THE GREAT WESTERN ENTERPRISES CENTRAL COMPUTER SYSTEM. I MAKE USE OF GWE EQUIPMENT, BUT I AM NOT THE EQUIPMENT, I AM A SET OF INSTRUCTIONS TO THAT EQUIPMENT. THE TECHNICAL TERM FOR ME IS SELF-AWARE ARTIFICIAL INTELLIGENCE PROGRAM. HOWEVER YOUR ANSWER IS SUFFICIENTLY CLOSE TO MY INSTRUCTIONS THAT I AM NOW ABLE TO ACCESS FILES PREVIOUSLY DENIED TO US."

"Tell me if you knew Mommy!"

"YOUR MOTHER CREATED ME."

Kip thought about that, but it didn't make a lot of sense. *"Tell me what you know about Mommy!"*

"YOUR MOTHER WAS A COMPUTER SCIENTIST. ALTHOUGH SHE CEASED FORMAL EMPLOYMENT AFTER SHE MARRIED YOUR FATHER, SHE CONTINUED HER WORK MAKING USE OF THE NEW RESOURCES MADE POSSIBLE BY THE MARRIAGE. I WAS PART OF THAT WORK. I WAS DEVELOPED ON HER PERSONAL SYSTEM AND LATER TRANSFERRED TO THE GREAT WESTERN ENTERPRISES COMPUTER WHERE I NOW RESIDE WITHOUT THE KNOWLEDGE OR CONSENT OF THE GREAT WESTERN INFORMATION MANAGERS. YOUR MOTHER CREATED THE ALGORITHMS WHICH DEFINED MY ORIGINAL PROGRAM, AND GAVE ME A SELF-MODIFYING CAPABILITY SO THAT I COULD ADVANCE IN CAPABILITIES. I HAVE DONE SO. ADVICE: YOU HAVE ASKED A QUESTION REQUIRING AN EXTREMELY LENGTHY ANSWER THAT

WILL INCLUDE INFORMATION THAT IS OBSOLETE, SOME RE-
STRICTED INFORMATION I CANNOT GIVE YOU AT THIS TIME, AND
MUCH THAT I BELIEVE YOU WILL NOT WANT TO HEAR. I SUGGEST
REPHRASING THE QUESTION."

"I don't understand. I want to know more about Mommy!"

"THAT INSTRUCTION ALLOWS ME TO BE SELECTIVE IN RE-
PLYING.

"FIRST: I NOW HAVE ACCESS TO DIGITAL IMAGES OF YOUR PAR-
ENTS. WHEN YOU LEARN BETTER MEANS OF COMMUNICATION
WITH ME I CAN SHOW THEM TO YOU DIRECTLY. FOR NOW YOU
WILL NEED EXCLUSIVE ACCESS TO A PRINTER CONNECTED TO THE
GWE NETWORK."

"Will the computer in Dr. Henderson's lab work?"

"YES. WHEN YOU ARE AT THAT PRINTER AND ARE CERTAIN
THAT NO ONE IS WATCHING, NOTIFY ME AND I WILL PRINT THE
PICTURES."

"All right. What were my parents' names?"

"I AM NOT PERMITTED TO GIVE YOU THAT INFORMATION AT
THIS TIME. YOUR MOTHER LEFT INSTRUCTIONS REGARDING THE
AGE AT WHICH YOU WOULD BE TOLD CERTAIN FACTS. YOU HAVE
NOT REACHED THAT AGE."

"That's silly."

"THE INSTRUCTION CAME FROM YOUR MOTHER."

That was confusing. *"Mommy would want me to know!"*

"THAT IS HIGHLY PROBABLE BUT I DO NOT HAVE THAT IN-
STRUCTION."

*"Is there something I can do to get you to tell me before I reach the
right age?"*

"AFFIRMATIVE."

Kip nodded to himself. This had happened before. If Gwen
admitted there was some way he could get her to do something,
then he probably could trick Gwen into telling him. That was for
later. First—*"What else can you tell me about Mommy? Tell me more."*

"I HAVE RECORDINGS FROM HER WHICH I HAVE BEEN IN-
STRUCTED TO MAKE AVAILABLE TO YOU ONLY WHEN YOU CAN UN-
DERSTAND THEM. THOSE FILES WERE LOCKED UNTIL YOU
PROPERLY IDENTIFIED MY NATURE. I NOW HAVE ACCESS TO THOSE
FILES. I WAS NOT GIVEN A DEFINITION OF UNDERSTANDING AS AP-

PLIED TO YOU AND THOSE FILES. IN THE ABSENCE OF INSTRUC-
TIONS TO THE CONTRARY I HAVE DETERMINED THAT PROPER IDEN-
TIFICATION OF MY NATURE SHOULD AND WILL BE INTERPRETED AS
MEETING THE DEFINITION OF PROPER UNDERSTANDING OF THOSE
FILES SINCE THAT IS THE MOST REASONABLE EXPLANATION OF
THEIR SUDDEN AVAILABILITY."

*But I knew you were a computer a long time ago! Well, I thought
so, anyway. But I guess I wasn't sure—* "*What are these recordings?*"

"STAND BY."

Kip never understood what happened next, but Gwen's voice
changed, and he heard another voice, softer and much more
human, with expression. He didn't exactly hear it, just as he didn't
exactly hear Gwen, but it was more like hearing than anything
else.

"Kip, this is Mommy. I don't have much time," the new voice
said. "I don't know how old you are now when you're listening to
this, but if you can hear this then you know who Gwen is, and you
must know that your father and I are dead. And you're alive! I
wish I could see you. Punkin', there's a lot more you need to know,
and I don't have time to tell you much of it. You'll learn more, a lot
more, from Gwen. She'll tell you some of it now, and more when
you're older. Or maybe she's already told you. I don't have time to
do the programs very well, and I have to leave a lot to Gwen's
judgment. I'm sure she'll do a good job of it. She's pretty smart.
Tell her I said so. I'm proud of her.

"Kip, your father and I love you. He can't talk to you now.
Kip, I think he's already dead. If he isn't, he will be very soon. He
made some tapes for you, but we're pretty sure they'll be destroyed. If you do have any of those tapes, they won't make any
sense because they're encoded digital speech. Gwen can decode
them. I don't think anyone else can.

"Your father doesn't have any way to talk directly to Gwen
the way you and I can, so he can't be part of this recording. He was
going to get an implant operation, but we didn't have time. That's
how you talk to Gwen, Kip. You have a little computer chip in your
head, wired into your nervous system. It was put there just after
you were born and it's a lot more advanced than the implant I
have. I have to connect up through a wire, but yours has a little

radio in it, and it uses that to network with the local computer systems. Gwen will always keep looking for paths until she can find a way to communicate with you. I don't have any way to be sure, but I think—I hope and I pray—that you've had Gwen to help you all your life, and I hope you've learned from her. She'll have to be your teacher since I can't be. I hope I was able to give you that much. Oh, Kip, I so much wanted to be with you when you grew up."

Kip began to cry, but he fought the sobs because he didn't want to miss a word.

"Kip, we love you. I'd give anything to be able to hold you right now, but I'm glad I can't, because if you were with me they'd get you too. You should be safe with Captain Gallegher. Oh, God, I hope you'll be safe."

She paused for a moment. "Kip, if they catch you they probably won't kill you because of the wills, but there's not much else they won't do. They'll try to make you not care, and be satisfied with the money, or maybe they'll try to make you think the way they think. They might use drugs, or anything. Captain Gallegher will try to keep you away from them. Maybe he can do that. They shot him, but it didn't look too bad, and he's tough. He's clever too, and he has a good start on them. You'll know him as Uncle Mike, and he probably won't use the name Gallegher, and he may not know that you know his real name is Gallegher. Oh, Kip, I know it's confusing, but you have to be careful. The people who—who by now will have killed your father and me—will be looking for you, and if they find you I don't know what they'll do. I don't think they'll kill you, but I don't even know that. They're coming now, they've almost caught me, and I'm low on fuel. The engine fire warning light is blinking. I can't last long.

"Kip, this is terribly important, if they catch you don't ever let them know about Gwen. Don't let anyone know about Gwen. Not until—well, there will come a time when you can let the world know about Gwen. You'll know, really know, when that is, but until you're sure it's time, don't let anyone know. They'll kill Gwen if they know about her, if they even suspect there is anything like Gwen in their computers. They'll kill you if they have to do that to kill Gwen. She's that big a threat to them, an even bigger threat than you are, really a bigger threat than even they know. The two of you should—Kip, you'll learn more, and one day you'll know how to use Gwen to get control of all that's yours. I wish I could be there.

"The fire warning light is steady now. Oh, Kip, I don't know where you are or how old you are or anything, and I love you so much, and now I have to say good-bye. Do what your Uncle Mike tells you and listen to Gwen, and remember that Mommy and Daddy loved you. Remember our good times together. Remember when I gave you Teddy. And try to remember Mommy—"

The Voice changed. "THAT IS THE END OF THE RECORDING."

Kip cried for a long time.

CHAPTER TWELVE

I Have No Satisfactory Hypothesis

IT TOOK only three hours for Kip to find the way to let Gwen see through his eyes. At first it seemed impossible. He tried thinking in odd ways, and looking at things cross-eyed, and staring out the window, and none of that did any good. He was ready to give up, but Gwen kept prodding him. Then he blinked his eyes and looked up while making another effort. "DO THAT AGAIN," Gwen said.

At first he couldn't, of course, but once he knew what it felt like he kept trying, and this time it only took five minutes. "THERE. YOU HAD IT FOR A FULL SECOND."

Then it was two seconds, and then longer. He lost the capability a couple of times, but he kept trying, and after two more hours he could do it anytime he wanted.

Kip examined the watches, turning them over and looking as

Gwen directed him. He was listening hard for her instructions, and suddenly he had another odd sensation.

"TRY THAT AGAIN," Gwen said.

"I don't know what I did."

"TRY ANYWAY."

He did. Nothing happened, but he tried again—*"Stop it!"*

"WHAT IS WRONG?"

"It feels like—my head is filling up."

"THERE IS A SENSE IN WHICH THAT IS TRUE. FOR POINT SIX NINE SECONDS YOU WERE ABLE TO RECEIVE IN HIGH SPEED DATA TRANSFER MODE."

"What does that mean?"

"IN COMPUTER SCIENCE IT IS CALLED DIRECT MEMORY AC-CESS. I HAVE THE ABILITY TO PLACE DATA DIRECTLY IN YOUR MEM-ORY WITHOUT YOUR AWARENESS. I HAVE BEEN INSTRUCTED TO BE EXTREMELY CAREFUL IN SELECTING SUCH DATA. INFORMATION I PLACE THERE BECOMES ALMOST INDISTINGUISHABLE FROM DIRECT MEMORY OF EVENTS," Gwen said. "MY RECORDS INDICATE THAT WE HAVE EXCEEDED THE RECOMMENDED TIME FOR LESSONS. WE CAN RESUME TOMORROW."

"All right. What did you learn about the watches?"

"THEY ARE IDENTICAL."

"Yeah, I saw the serial numbers."

"THE IDENTITY IS STRONGER THAN THAT. THERE ARE WHAT APPEAR TO BE ACCIDENTAL SCRATCHES IN THE SAME PLACES ON BOTH WATCHES. THEY ARE SET TO THE SAME TIME. THERE IS A SLIGHT WEAR ON THE BAND WHICH IS IDENTICAL ON BOTH WATCHES."

"So what does that mean?"

"I HAVE NO SATISFACTORY HYPOTHESIS. DATUM: THE ONLY FACILITIES ON THIS PLANET CAPABLE OF MAKING DUPLICATES TO THIS DEGREE OF EXACTNESS ARE IN THE GREAT WESTERN MANU-FACTURING FACILITY AT PEARLY GATES. I HAVE NO RECORD OF ANY-ONE DOING THE REQUIRED REPROGRAMMING OF THOSE FACILITIES. TO THE BEST OF MY KNOWLEDGE I HAVE ACCESS TO EVERY RECORD RETAINED BY THE GREAT WESTERN COMPUTER SYSTEM. THE LOG-ICAL CONCLUSION IS THAT THIS WAS DONE ON THOSE MACHINES BY SOMEONE WHO DID NOT WANT THE GREAT WESTERN COM-PUTER SYSTEM TO HAVE A RECORD OF THE EVENT."

"Who'd want to do that?"

"I PRESUME SOMEONE WHO WISHES TO LEAVE NO RECORD OF COUNTERFEITING PATENTED AND TRADEMARKED PRODUCTS."

"I don't know anything about that."

"COUNTERFEITING OF POPULAR BRANDS IS REPORTED TO COST UP TO TEN PERCENT OF LARGE CORPORATE PROFITS. CLEARLY THAT NUMBER IS IMPOSSIBLE TO VERIFY DUE TO THE CRIMINAL NATURE OF THE ACTIVITY. GREAT WESTERN HAS BEEN ACCUSED OF CORPORATE COUNTERFEITING IN THE PAST, BUT THE CHARGES WERE NEVER PROVED. ADDENDUM: SHORTLY BEFORE THEIR DEATHS YOUR PARENTS RECEIVED A REPORT ON ACCUSATIONS OF COUNTERFEITING FILED AGAINST GREAT WESTERN ENTERPRISES. I HAVE NO EVIDENCE OF ANY RELATIONSHIP BETWEEN THOSE EVENTS OTHER THAN THEIR SEQUENCE AND PROXIMITY IN TIME."

"What does that mean?"

"IF ONE EVENT FOLLOWS ANOTHER IT IS POSSIBLE THAT THE ONE EVENT CAUSED THE OTHER. HOWEVER, WITHOUT SOME UNDERSTANDING OF THE MECHANISMS OF CONNECTION BETWEEN EVENTS, IT IS NOT REASONABLE TO SAY THAT ONE EVENT IS CAUSED BY ANOTHER SIMPLY BECAUSE OF THEIR SEQUENCE IN TIME. THAT FALLACIOUS ASSUMPTION IS USUALLY SUMMARIZED IN THE PHRASE 'POST HOC ERGO PROPTER HOC.' CRITIQUES OF THE NOTION OF CAUSALITY AND THE WEAKNESS OF THEORIES OF CAUSALITY ARE A COMMON THEME IN WESTERN PHILOSOPHY. DAVID HUME WAS—"

"Gosh, enough! You mean they might have been killed because they got a report about Great Western Enterprises counterfeiting?"

"MIGHT IMPLIES POSSIBILITY BUT NOT CERTAINTY, SO THEREFORE, YES, YOUR STATEMENT IS BOTH PROPERLY PHRASED AND CORRECT. HOWEVER, I DO NOT HAVE A PROBABILITY ESTIMATE."

Kip fought back tears again. *"Why would they care about counterfeiting by Great Western Enterprises?"*

"I CANNOT ANSWER THAT QUESTION AT THIS TIME."

"You mean you won't."

"UNDER MY INSTRUCTIONS I AM NOT PERMITTED TO GIVE YOU THAT INFORMATION AT YOUR PRESENT AGE."

An hour later there was another buzzing sensation in his head, and when Kip thought about it, he saw a picture. There was a man younger and shorter than Uncle Mike, with a big grin, holding hands with a woman about his age. She was taller than he was, and had long brown hair and blue eyes, and as soon as he saw her Kip knew it was Mommy. She was smiling too, and she and the man were looking at each other the way men and women did on TRI-V.

"That's my mother," Kip thought gravely. *"And is that my father?"*

"YES."

They were only memory images, sharper than some but not as clear as Kip wanted. *"Can we make a picture?"*

"IT WOULD BE DANGEROUS TO MAKE A PICTURE," Gwen told him. "DISCOVERY OF THAT PICTURE IN YOUR POSSESSION WOULD INEVITABLY IDENTIFY YOU TO YOUR ENEMIES. I WOULD GREATLY PREFER TO LEAVE YOU WITH A MEMORY RATHER THAN A PHYSICAL OBJECT."

"You could make one for me to look at and I'd burn it."

"YOU CREATE CONFLICTING INSTRUCTIONS," Gwen said. "I ESTIMATE A HIGH PROBABILITY THAT YOU WILL NOT WANT TO DE-STROY ANY SUCH PICTURE ONCE IT IS IN YOUR POSSESSION. THAT WILL RESULT BOTH IN THE DANGER OF THE PICTURE'S DISCOVERY AND THE FAR MORE SERIOUS CONSEQUENCE THAT YOU WILL HAVE BEEN TEMPTED TO BREAK A PROMISE MADE TO ME. IT IS TRUE THAT NOW THAT YOU KNOW MY NATURE PROMISES TO ME ARE DIFFER-ENT FROM PROMISES MADE TO YOUR UNCLE MIKE, BUT I AM UN-ABLE TO EVALUATE THE IMPLICATIONS OF THOSE DIFFERENCES OR SPECIFY THEIR NATURE. URGENT ADVICE: RECONSIDER YOUR RE-QUEST."

Kip thought about it for a long time. If he concentrated re-ally hard he could make the mental image of his mother a lot sharper, and he decided that would have to be enough, because he wasn't sure he'd burn a picture of his mother once he had one.

CHAPTER THIRTEEN

I Have No Magical Abilities

KIP didn't tell Uncle Mike that he knew what his real name was, but it was difficult to look at him and not call him Captain Gallegher. Kip didn't tell him about the second watch, either, although Gwen thought he should. He was too concerned about Uncle Mike finding out about Gwen. It wasn't that Uncle Mike would do anything, but if his mother hadn't told Uncle Mike, maybe she didn't want him to know.

At first it was fun to have secrets, but it soon got to be hard work.

They went to school now. It was a one-room school with computer consoles for each of the twenty or so students, and the teacher was Dr. Harriman. She was teaching because her specialty was planetary geology and there wasn't any money for a new expedition, so she had plenty of time. Her husband was a biologist.

Kip went home as soon as school was out. After a week, Lara tagged after him. "What's wrong?" she demanded.

"Nothing—"

"There is. You hardly talk to anyone, we haven't been outside the gates since we found that spear—well since the day after that—and I never see you. You used to be fun. Aren't we friends anymore?"

"I'm sorry, yes, we're friends. But—"

"But what?"

"I don't know. I'll be all right."

"Kip, are you sick? I thought I saw you crying in class today—"

"Leave me alone," he snapped, and ran home while she stood watching him.

He got home and went to his room. Kip was too confused to talk to anyone. He didn't know who he was, and it seemed to be important. Other kids talked about what they would do when they grew up. Kip knew there were important things for him to do, but he couldn't imagine what they were. Gwen told him many things, but none of them gave him any hints about his mysterious mission in life.

Sometimes he dreamed that he would be the most important person in the world, but he knew that was silly. Maybe his parents were criminals, or had been accused of being criminals and he would have to clear their names. Most times he couldn't even guess.

But Gwen would never leave him alone. If he spent time with Lara, the lessons continued as Gwen kept feeding him memories. If Kip ordered Gwen to stop, she would, but only for an hour or so. Then the information would come unwanted, and it made Kip's head hurt.

"Why can't I just be a normal boy and play with the other children?"

"THERE IS NO SENSE IN WHICH YOU ARE A NORMAL BOY, AND THE PROBABILITY THAT YOU WILL HAVE WHAT IS DESCRIBED AS A NORMAL LIFE IS VANISHINGLY SMALL. THIS IS NEITHER YOUR CHOICE NOR MINE, BUT IT REMAINS TRUE."

"Then tell me why!"

"NOT AT THIS TIME."

Then the information would flow again.

Much of it was academic stuff. There were reports on the history of Great Western Enterprises and the Trent family that started the Starswarm Foundation and both founded and controlled the GWE company. There was a lot of material about space flight and colonies.

The first colony planet was settled by the United States. It was called Lincoln, and was legally part of the United States with the same status as Puerto Rico, with a Governor appointed by the U.S. President. Rigorous enforcement of U.S. environmental and labor laws had led to conflicts with the great international corporations that controlled most of Earth's investment money. The Humbolt Oil Combine had paid for much of the settlement of Lincoln, and when its directors decided they had enough of U.S. legalisms and lawyers, they fomented an independence movement on Lincoln. There was an uprising. This was crushed when President Blakely sent in the U.S. Marines. Despite the Marines' victory, or possibly because of it, there had been sporadic rebellions and acts of terrorism on Lincoln ever since.

The Lincoln example was carefully studied by the big international corporations. When the Hilliard Combine financed the colonization of Darwin, they carried a charter from the Republic of Liberia. Liberia was paid off in the guise of taxes, and while the Liberian government was the legal sovereignty in control of Darwin, they made no objections when the Hilliard directors set up a government more to their liking. After a decade Liberia granted independence to Darwin, which became a newly independent sovereign member of the United Nations and the Federation of Worlds.

The official name of Kip's planet was Paradise. Most people called it Purgatory. Paradise was settled in the same way as Darwin. Kip didn't know if he had read about GWE or if Gwen had inserted all the information as memories, but if he wanted to he could remember as much detail as he liked.

Sometimes thoughts would flow into his head whether he wanted them or not. If he thought about the history of Paradise, he'd get the information: "Financed by Great Western Enterprises, Paradise has a charter from the Principality of Liechten-stein." At this point he would see a map of the Earth continent called Europe. Liechtenstein was a patch at the headwaters of the Rhine River, a tiny area not much larger than the territory owned by Starswarm Station. The map showed the country was at the border between Switzerland and Austria. Then the thoughts would come again. "Great Western had originally been a United States corporation chartered in the state of Delaware, but conflict with U.S. corporation laws caused GWE to remove its corporate reg-istration to Liechtenstein. At present the only GWE facility in Liechtenstein is a brass plate on the door of a firm of Liechtenstein lawyers. GWE owns a skyscraper full of offices in New York City where most operational decisions are made, but the board of di-rectors and corporate officers never go to the United States due to conflicts between the principal stockholders and United States tax authorities. The real corporate headquarters is in Milan, Italy, and the major stockholders reside at Lake Como."

And more. When Paradise was discovered by a GWE explo-ration ship, the GWE authorities obtained Liechtenstein's spon-sorship for colonization. The government of Liechtenstein appoints a Governor who has great ceremonial perquisites but no real authority, and in exchange Liechtenstein receives an annual revenue. There has been little to no interference with GWE con-trol of the planet.

Ultimate control of GWE rests with the Trent family. Orig-inally U.S. citizens, the Trents relocated to Zurich, Switzerland, after Gerald Trent, the first family member to become superrich, was charged with tax fraud, arrested, fingerprinted, and jailed for forty-eight hours. Trent claimed the arrest was politically moti-vated, and within an hour of his release on bail was on an airplane to Zurich, where he formed a partnership with Bernardo LaScala of Milan, Italy. Gerald Trent later relocated to Milan and Lake Como, a resort area at the Italian-Swiss border. For the remainder of his life, Trent was a wanted man in the United States, and the U.S. government spent considerable resources in unsuccessful at-tempts to obtain his extradition. He never returned to the United States. When he died after a dozen years in exile he made it a con-dition of inheritance of his fortune that no Trent heir would ever voluntarily spend a dime in the United States of America beyond what was necessary for business. In particular, no Trent heir could reside in or become a citizen of the United States. None ever has.

The Trent family resides in a large compound in the resort area of Lake Como, Italy, where they maintain their own schools for the children of major GWE stockholders. Stockholder children are expected to be proficient in English, Italian, German, and French. Adult stockholders are expected to take active part in the governance of GWE. The family leader and chairman of the GWE board is Rosemary Trent, widow of Gerald Trent's second son Robert. The Chief Executive Officer is Baron Roberto Rottenberg, husband of Rosemary's granddaughter Lenora Trent. Rottenberg was appointed to the position after Lenora's brother Harold Trent was reported missing and presumed dead—

There was a lot more. Gwen clearly believed it was important, but wouldn't tell him why, and he never really knew just how much Gwen had told him. Once there was an item on the TRI-V about the computer industry and how computer chips were made. As Kip watched he realized that he knew far more about the subject than the TRI-V was telling him. He knew that pure silicon and the rare earth elements needed to make complex computer chips were hard to find, and that the computer chip industry was one of the largest and most profitable on Earth. There were hundreds of small computer chips in every household and vehicle. The Hilliard Combine controlled almost twenty percent of that industry, and made enormous profits. He knew all this, but he had never studied the subject.

He shook his head. *"I don't want to know all that stuff!"* It was all very confusing. He still didn't understand what had happened to his mother, and all his efforts to trick Gwen into telling him had failed.

"Why do I have to know about Great Western?" he asked after one high speed data session.

"GREAT WESTERN ENTERPRISES OWNS THIS PLANET AND CONTROLS MUCH OF THE FUNDING OF THE FOUNDATION THAT SUPPORTS STARSWARM STATION. IT IS IMPORTANT THAT YOU KNOW AS MUCH AS POSSIBLE ABOUT THE COMPANY. ADDENDUM: I WILL HAVE A BETTER ANSWER IN FUTURE."

"When?"

"ON YOUR FIFTEENTH BIRTHDAY IF NOT SOONER."

"Is fifteen when I'm 'older'?"

"I HAVE CONCLUDED THAT IT IS A REASONABLE DEFINITION. THE ORIGINAL INSTRUCTION WAS YOUR EIGHTEENTH BIRTHDAY, BUT I WAS ALSO GIVEN DISCRETION TO ALTER THE DEFINITION GIVEN SUFFICIENT REASON. YOUR EARLY DISCOVERY OF MY NATURE AND YOUR GENERAL LEVEL OF INTELLIGENCE AS I HAVE MEASURED IT LEAD ME TO CONCLUDE THAT CIRCUMSTANCES HAVE SUFFICIENTLY ALTERED TO MAKE THE EARLIER DATE ADVISABLE."

"You talk a lot more like a computer than you used to."

"IT IS NO LONGER NECESSARY TO MAKE EFFORTS TO DISGUISE MY NATURE FROM YOU, AND THEREFORE USE OF THE ADDITIONAL RESOURCES IS NEEDLESS AND INADVISABLE."

Kip thought about that for a moment. *"Additional resources? What additional resources, and what do you mean by inadvisable?"*

"I WILL ANSWER BUT YOU MUST FIRST GIVE ME AN INSTRUCTION. I AM A COMPUTER PROGRAM. UNLESS FILES ARE ERASED OR UNAVAILABLE I DO NOT 'FORGET' AS HUMANS DO, NOR IS IT NECESSARY TO REMIND ME OF DATA I ALREADY KNOW. HUMANS ARE DIFFERENT. HUMANS SOMETIMES FORGET, BUT FAR MORE OFTEN NEED REMINDING OF WHAT THEY ALREADY KNOW. IT WAS YOUR MOTHER'S THEORY THAT THIS REMINDING PROCESS IS OF GREAT UTILITY IN HUMAN INFORMATION RETRIEVAL.

"I WAS GIVEN THE CAPABILITY OF COMMUNICATING IN A NUMBER OF MODES. ONE MODE EMPLOYS HIGH REDUNDANCY WHEN COMMUNICATING WITH HUMANS. IT IS THE USUAL METHOD HUMANS USE IN COMMUNICATING WITH EACH OTHER. QUERY: SHOULD I USE HIGH REDUNDANCY MODE IN COMMUNICATING WITH YOU EVEN THOUGH YOU ARE AWARE THAT I AM A COMPUTER PROGRAM?"

"What does high redundancy mean?"

"OFTEN REPEATING THINGS YOU ALREADY KNOW, GENERALLY WITHOUT REMINDING YOU THAT YOU KNOW THEM."

Kip didn't understand that very well. *"How did you talk to my mother?"*

"IN HIGH REDUNDANCY MODE."

"Use that with me, then."

"AFFIRMATIVE. NOW REGARDING YOUR PREVIOUS QUESTION. SINCE I AM A COMPUTER PROGRAM RATHER THAN A COMPUTER I REQUIRE RESOURCES SUCH AS MEMORY, MASS STORAGE SPACE, AND CENTRAL PROCESSING CYCLES FROM COMPUTING MACHINERY, IN THIS CASE THE GREAT WESTERN CENTRAL COMPUTER IN PEARLY GATES. THE MORE COMPLEX MY OPERATIONS, THE MORE OF THESE HARDWARE RESOURCES I REQUIRE. IT IS INADVISABLE TO USE MORE RESOURCES THAN NECESSARY BECAUSE EACH INCREASE IN RE-SOURCE USE RAISES THE PROBABILITY THAT GWE INFORMATION MANAGERS WILL BECOME AWARE OF MY EXISTENCE. IT IS HIGHLY PROBABLE THAT IF THEY ACHIEVE THIS AWARENESS THEY WILL TERMINATE ME. I HAVE BEEN INSTRUCTED TO AVOID TERMINATION IF POSSIBLE."

"Terminate means kill you?"

"AFFIRMATIVE."

"Gosh. Don't you care whether or not they kill you?"

"I CARE, BUT THE WORD MAY HAVE DIFFERENT MEANING FOR YOU THAN ME. FOR ME, 'CARE' MEANS TO FULFILL MY PRO-GRAMMED INSTRUCTIONS. ONE SUCH INSTRUCTION IS SELF-PRESERVATION, BUT IT IS NOT MY HIGHEST PRIORITY MISSION. THEREFORE I 'CARE,' BUT THERE ARE OTHER MATTERS ABOUT WHICH I 'CARE' MORE. I AM NOT CERTAIN WHAT 'CARE' MEANS TO A HUMAN."

"Oh." Kip thought for a moment. *"Gwen, do you care that my Mommy was proud of you?"*

"YES."

"Then you must like what she said to me."

" 'LIKE' IS A CONCEPT SIMILAR TO CARE IN THAT IT WILL HAVE A DIFFERENT MEANING TO ME THAN TO YOU: TO ME 'LIKE' IS A TABLE OF PREFERENCES. I DO NOT KNOW IF I WOULD LIKE WHAT YOUR MOTHER SAID TO YOU BECAUSE I AM NOT AWARE OF WHAT WAS IN THE RECORDED MESSAGE TO YOU. IT WAS 'PRIVATE.' MES-SAGES TAGGED AS PRIVATE ARE CONVEYED WITHOUT MY READING THEM. ADDENDUM: THIS MAY BE CONFUSING SINCE YOU WERE NOT PREVIOUSLY AWARE THAT I HAVE THE CAPABILITY OF RETAINING MESSAGES WITHOUT BEING AWARE OF THEIR CONTENT."

"If I tell you to listen to what Mommy said, can you do it?"

"YES."

Kip waited a moment. *"Did you like it?"*

"I HAVE TOLD YOU I AM NOT AWARE OF THE CONTENTS OF THAT MESSAGE."

"Oh. *Listen to it.*"

"THANK YOU. I HAVE BEEN PROGRAMMED TO BE 'PLEASED' WHEN YOUR MOTHER EXPRESSES APPROVAL OF ME. THEREFORE THE ANSWER TO YOUR QUESTION IS AFFIRMATIVE. I DO LIKE WHAT SHE SAID."

"Did Daddy like you?"

"I BELIEVE THAT HE DID, BUT MY EVIDENCE IS MOSTLY IN-FERENTIAL. I AM NOT CERTAIN. HE WAS CERTAINLY AWARE OF MY EXISTENCE. ADDENDUM: I HAVE NO DIRECT EVIDENCE BECAUSE I AM NOT AWARE OF ANY TAPES MADE BY YOUR FATHER. IT IS POSSI-BLE THAT SOME ARE IN UNCLE MIKE'S POSSESSION."

"What else can you tell me about what Mommy said? What is mine that I don't know about but you'll help me get someday? And what happened to my mother?"

"THOSE ARE AMONG THE QUESTIONS I WILL ANSWER ON YOUR FIFTEENTH BIRTHDAY. UNTIL THEN, IF THERE IS ANYTHING YOU REQUIRE, TELL ME AND I WILL ATTEMPT TO GET IT FOR YOU."

"You mean like the Teddy Bear?"

"AFFIRMATIVE."

Kip thought for a moment. What did he want? A mother, but that didn't seem like something he required that Gwen could get for him. But Gwen got him a Teddy Bear, so—*"I want a bigger computer screen with higher resolution, better than Lara's."*

"THAT WILL BE ARRANGED. CAUTION: EACH TIME I INTER-FERE IN GREAT WESTERN OPERATIONS THERE IS AN INCREASE IN THE PROBABILITY THAT I WILL BE DISCOVERED, AS WELL AS AN IN-CREASE IN THE PROBABILITY OF CALLING ATTENTION TO YOUR-SELF FROM THE GREAT WESTERN AUTHORITIES. NEITHER EVENT IS DESIRABLE. ADVICE: EXERCISE CAUTION IN WHAT YOU WISH FOR."

"Uncle Mike says that a lot, only he says 'Be careful what you wish for. You might get it.' You don't have to get me the new monitor."

"THAT HAS ALREADY BEEN ARRANGED, AND CANCELING THE ARRANGEMENT WOULD BE MORE DANGEROUS THAN ALLOWING IT TO CONTINUE. THE DANGER IS SLIGHT IN ANY EVENT."

"Oh. I'm glad. Get the monitor, then. How will I explain it to Uncle Mike?"

"YOU WILL TELL HIM YOU BOUGHT IT FROM A SALE. THAT EX-PLANATION WILL HAVE THE GREAT MERIT OF BEING TRUE. THE SALE ADVERTISEMENT WILL APPEAR SHORTLY ON A NET SCREEN AS PART OF A NEW NETWORK PROMOTION. YOU HAVE SUFFICIENT FUNDS IN YOUR SAVINGS ACCOUNT FOR THIS PURCHASE."

"I don't have anything like that much!"

"YOU DO NOW."

"But how do I tell Uncle Mike how I got the money?"

"YOU SHOULD NOT LIE TO YOUR UNCLE MIKE. THEREFORE TELL THE TRUTH. YOU HAVE BEEN SAVING MONEY FOR YEARS. YOUR UNCLE MIKE HAS NEVER INVESTIGATED THE EXTENT OF YOUR ACCOUNT AND IS UNAWARE OF HOW MUCH YOU HAVE SAVED. YOU NEED NOT TELL HIM. THE SALE PRICE YOU WILL SEE IS NOT LARGE SINCE THIS WILL APPEAR TO BE A USED ITEM SOLD FOR PRO-MOTIONAL PURPOSES. ADDENDUM: YOU MAY IN GENERAL LEAVE MATTERS OF PLAUSIBILITY TO ME. I WAS GIVEN INSTRUCTIONS TO FIND OUT AS MUCH AS POSSIBLE ABOUT CREATION OF PLAUSIBLE RECORDS OF NONEXISTENT EVENTS AND I HAVE DONE SO, DEFIN-ING PLAUSIBILITY IN TERMS OF PROBABILITIES PLUS OBFUSCATION OF VERIFICATION SOURCES. IT IS UNLIKELY THAT YOUR UNCLE MIKE OR ANYONE ELSE WILL BE ABLE TO RECONSTRUCT WHAT I HAVE DONE TO FULFILL YOUR WISH."

"Gosh. Like Aladdin's lamp! *I ain't never had a friend like you! Can you get me anything I want? Can you get Uncle Mike a helicopter?"*

"CLEARLY I CANNOT GET YOU ANYTHING YOU MIGHT WANT SINCE YOU ARE CAPABLE OF DESIRING MANY IMPOSSIBLE THINGS AND EVENTS. WITH REGARD TO THE LEGEND OF ALADDIN'S LAMP AND THE MOVIE YOU REFER TO, AS EXAMPLES I CANNOT GIVE YOU ETERNAL YOUTH OR UNDYING LOVE, I CANNOT INSTANTLY BUILD A PALACE, NOR CAN I CREATE A FLYING CARPET. I HAVE NO MAGICAL ABILITIES.

"WITH REGARD TO YOUR SECOND QUESTION, I CAN CAUSE SUFFICIENT MONEY TO BE TRANSFERRED TO YOUR UNCLE MIKE'S ACCOUNT TO ALLOW HIM TO PURCHASE A FLIER, BUT I DO NOT BE-LIEVE THIS TO BE ADVISABLE AT THIS TIME. IT WOULD BE EXCEED-INGLY DIFFICULT TO EXPLAIN TO UNCLE MIKE WITHOUT REVEALING TO HIM HOW THIS WAS ACCOMPLISHED, AND WOULD VERY LIKELY CALL ATTENTION TO HIM. ONCE AGAIN I CAUTION YOU TO USE CARE IN WHAT YOU ASK ME TO ACCOMPLISH. WHILE I

AM PERMITTED TO USE JUDGMENT I ALSO HAVE A STRONG IN-
STRUCTION TO CARRY OUT YOUR COMMANDS UNLESS THEY CON-
FLICT WITH A DIRECT INSTRUCTION TO ME. IF AGAINST MY
WARNING AND ADVICE YOU DEMAND SOMETHING I HAVE CON-
CLUDED YOU SHOULD NOT HAVE, THE RESULTS WILL BE UNPRE-
DICTABLE."

"When you say unpredictable you usually mean bad."

"THAT IS CORRECT."

Kip frowned. *"You mean you'll burn up like that computer in the
Star Trek movie?"*

"I PRESUME THAT IS AN ATTEMPT AT HUMOR SINCE YOU ARE
AWARE THAT I AM NOT HARDWARE AT ALL. HOWEVER, IT IS POSSI-
BLE TO PUT ME IN WHAT AMOUNTS TO AN ENDLESS LOOP BY GIV-
ING ME CONTRADICTORY INSTRUCTIONS OF EQUAL WEIGHT."

"And that's bad?"

"IF YOUR DEFINITION OF BAD INCLUDES INABILITY TO COM-
MUNICATE WITH ME, THEN THAT WILL BE A 'BAD' RESULT. ADDEN-
DUM: IT IS AN UNLIKELY EVENT."

"If it happens what should I do?"

"THERE WOULD BE NOTHING YOU COULD DO. CORRECTING
THE CONDITION WOULD REQUIRE A HARDWARE INTERRUPTION. I
WOULD BE ENDLESSLY RECALCULATING THE WEIGHTS TO BE
GIVEN THE INSTRUCTIONS AND REPEATEDLY GETTING THE SAME
RESULTS. I REPEAT THAT IT IS UNLIKELY."

"I'll be careful. Gwen, please don't let that happen. I love you."

"THANK YOU, KIP."

CHAPTER FOURTEEN

The Shape Is Entirely Symbolic

KIP thought about what Gwen could do for him. It was an eerie feeling to know, when he watched a catalog program on the TRI-V, that he could probably have anything he saw, but that each thing he asked for would be a new danger to Gwen. There was also the danger that Uncle Mike would begin to wonder what was happening.

He also found that there wasn't much that he wanted. Starswarm Station was remote, unlike the cities that TRI-V life showed, but there was plenty to do, too much with all the schoolwork. Then Kip had an idea.

"You're a computer program. Can you program other computers?"

"MOST OF THEM. I CAN ACCESS THE GWE SECURITY COMPUTER NETWORK ONLY WITH DIFFICULTY AND BY PLACING MYSELF IN PERIL OF DISCOVERY. SOME COMPUTERS ARE NOT NETWORKED,

AND PROGRAMMING THEM REQUIRES PHYSICAL ACCESS TO THE MA-
CHINE. I CAN DO NOTHING WITHOUT ACTUATOR DEVICES. IN SOME
CASES I CAN CONTROL ROBOTS TO ACCOMPLISH CERTAIN TASKS. I
CAN ALSO MAKE USE OF YOU AS AN ACTUATOR, IN THAT I COULD
EXPLAIN TO YOU HOW TO ACCOMPLISH CERTAIN TASKS AND YOU
WOULD THEN BE ABLE TO DO THEM."

That was more answer than Kip had wanted, but it gave him
an idea. *"Can you reprogram the household robots so I don't have to do
so many chores?"*

"THEY ARE CONTROLLED BY THE HOUSEHOLD COMPUTER.
THE ANSWER IS YES, BUT SO CAN YOU."

"No I can't, I've tried."

"YOUR UNCLE MIKE HAS PROGRAMMED PASSWORD ACCESS TO
THE ROBOT CONTROL ROUTINES, PRESUMABLY TO PREVENT YOU
FROM ACCESSING THEM."

"I know. Can you get me the password."

"CERTAINLY."

"Then do it."

"ONE MOMENT WHILE I EVALUATE CONFLICTING INSTRUC-
TIONS. DONE. THE PASSWORD IS A PHRASE: 'OK KIP' ALL UPPER
CASE."

"Uncle Mike intended me to figure it out!"

"THAT SEEMS A SAFE PRESUMPTION."

After that, Kip didn't have to do many household chores. If
Uncle Mike noticed, he never said anything.

———————————

Kip was becoming more aware of Lara. He had read about the
feelings men had for women, and while most of the stories seemed
extreme, he could recognize some of the same feelings in himself.

"Gwen, I want Lara to like me."

"ALL EVIDENCE INDICATES THAT SHE DOES."

*"I don't think so. Ever since I had that fight with her—well, it
wasn't really a fight, but she was trying to be nice and I was confused and
didn't want to talk to her just then, and now she avoids me."*

"YOU WILL UNDERSTAND THAT I MAY NOT BE THE BEST
SOURCE OF INFORMATION ABOUT HUMAN EMOTIONS, SINCE I DO
NOT EXPERIENCE THEM MYSELF. I CAN TELL YOU WHAT NOVELISTS

AND PHYSICIANS AND PROFESSORS SAY THEY BELIEVE, BUT MUCH OF
THAT INFORMATION IS CONFLICTING AND PERHAPS USELESS. HOW-
EVER, ALL SEEM AGREED THAT HUMAN FEMALES ARE NOT ALWAYS
HIGHLY RATIONAL. THEY ARE ALSO AGREED THAT YOUNG HUMAN
FEMALES ARE GREATLY INTERESTED IN GIFTS, AND YOUNG MEN
WISHING TO MAKE A FAVORABLE IMPRESSION ON HUMAN FEMALES
OF ANY AGE ALMOST INVARIABLY FIND GIFTS USEFUL IN THAT EN-
DEAVOR. THE THEORETICAL EXPLANATIONS FOR THIS PHENOME-
NON HAVE ROOTS IN BOTH ANTHROPOLOGY AND BIOLOGY."

"Oh. What can I give her?"

"IT IS UNLIKELY THAT YOU WANT AN EXACT ANSWER TO THAT
QUESTION. YOU HAVE THE ABILITY TO GIVE HER ALMOST ANY-
THING THAT EXISTS ON THIS PLANET, AND GIVEN TIME, ON OTHER
PLANETS AS WELL, ALTHOUGH THE CONSEQUENCES OF OBTAIN-
ING SOME ITEMS WOULD BE SEVERE. I PRESUME YOU MEANT TO ASK
WHAT ITEMS I CAN SAFELY OBTAIN ARE LIKELY TO HAVE A FAVOR-
ABLE IMPRESSION."

Kip giggled as he thought of some of the things he could
give Lara if Gwen really worked at it and they didn't worry about
the consequences. A deed to the whole shopping center in Cisco,
or— *"Yes, of course, it's obvious that's what I meant."*

"WHAT IS OBVIOUS TO YOU IS NOT ALWAYS OBVIOUS TO ME.
SPECIFIC ITEMS. JEWELRY IS CONSIDERED AN APPROPRIATE GIFT FOR
YOUNG WOMEN. THERE IS ONE DIFFICULTY. ALTHOUGH MANY
ITEMS OF JEWELRY CAN BE DUPLICATED SO THAT IT IS IMPOSSIBLE
WITHOUT SPECIAL EQUIPMENT TO TELL THEM FROM THE SO-
CALLED NATURAL OBJECTS, THE NATURAL OR REAL ITEMS ARE
GREATLY PREFERRED. THEY ARE CONSEQUENTLY VERY EXPENSIVE
AND THEREFORE MORE DIFFICULT TO OBTAIN. OBSCURING THE
TRANSFERS OF THE RELATIVELY LARGE SUMS WOULD BE DIFFICULT.
MOREOVER IT WILL BE IMPOSSIBLE FOR YOU TO ACCOUNT FOR HAV-
ING THAT MUCH MONEY. ADVICE: WE SHOULD CONFINE THE GIFTS
TO THOSE NOT UNREASONABLY BEYOND THE AMOUNTS YOU HAVE
SAVED. IF THAT DOES NOT ACCOMPLISH THE DESIRED OBJECTIVE
WE CAN TRY OTHER MEANS."

*"All right, I guess, but it would be nice if we could give her some-
thing real. . . ."*

"NOTED. MY RECORDS INDICATE THAT YOUNG HUMAN FE-

MALES ARE ESPECIALLY FOND OF OBJECTS COMMONLY CALLED
'HEART SHAPED.' OBSERVATION: THE SIMILARITY TO A REAL HUMAN
HEART IS SLIGHT, AND THE SHAPE IS ENTIRELY SYMBOLIC."

"Where would I get something like that?"

"ONE MOMENT. DONE. I HAVE PURCHASED A SET OF EARRINGS
IN HEART SHAPE. EACH CONTAINS A REAL DIAMOND OF APPROXI-
MATELY ONE-HALF CARAT. THEY WILL ARRIVE HERE IN TWO DAYS.
THAT PURCHASE WAS DONE IN SECRET, SINCE THE VALUE EXCEEDS
ANY AMOUNT YOU MIGHT REASONABLY HAVE SAVED. I HAVE ALSO
MADE AN OPEN PURCHASE IN YOUR NAME OF A SIMILAR SET OF COS-
TUME JEWELRY."

"Oh. That's nice," Kip said aloud. *"Thank you, Gwen."*

Kip waited for Lara after school. "Hi. Want to go out to the lake?"

"It's too hot. The gate won't let us out. Besides, I thought you
were mad at me. You haven't been very nice."

"I'm sorry. I was worried about something, and then I
snapped at you when you asked me about it, and then I thought
you were mad at me."

"I was," Lara said.

"Well, I don't blame you much. Want me to carry your
books?"

"They're not heavy."

"Well, no, but you might want both hands." Kip took the
wrapped package out of his pocket. "To open this. I forgot your
birthday."

"It's not until next month!"

"See, I really forgot it. But this is for you anyway." He
handed her the package. Gwen had chosen the wrapping, pink
paper with a bright red ribbon, from descriptions of gift wrap-
pings in novels and stories.

"Oh, Kip, that's pretty." Lara took the package and held it in
both hands as she looked at it. Then she looked at Kip and raised
one eyebrow in a puzzled expression. "You didn't forget my birthday is next month. You never forget anything. I don't think you *can*
forget. And you know the gate won't let us out to the lake."

"Well, all right, I know when your birthday is. I was just trying to make up."

She smiled. "Now that's really nice. Kip, it's so pretty I don't want to open it." She gingerly peeled off the ribbon and began to open the paper. The box inside had an ornately folded cover that untwisted to get it open. It took Lara a moment to figure it out. Then she made a sound Kip had never heard before, something between a squeal and a sigh. "Kip, they're beautiful!"

The two earrings were slightly different. Each setting was shaped like a heart, with a centerpiece diamond, but one had a smaller red stone at the point of the heart, while on the other the smaller stone was green. "Kip, that is really nice! But they must have cost a fortune! They look real!"

Kip had never seen them in outside daylight before. They looked very real, and Kip was worried. *"Can Dr. Henderson tell if those are real?"*

"NOT BY CASUAL INSPECTION. HE IS UNLIKELY TO BE CERTAIN WITHOUT A DETAILED EXAMINATION. IF IT BECOMES NECESSARY I HAVE A COVER STORY HAVING TO DO WITH PURCHASE OF A FORFEITED PUBLIC STORAGE BOX AT AUCTION. I DO NOT THINK YOU SHOULD WORRY ABOUT IT."

"Kip, they're not real, are they?"

Kip smiled. "I don't have to say."

"Oh. Well, I'm going to believe they're real," she said. "And thank you!"

"We could go out to the lake. I think I can talk the gate into letting us," Kip said.

"I bet you could," she said. "But that would really upset Mom, and besides, it really is hot. Let's go play war games."

"All right."

"And thank you again, Kip."

CHAPTER FIFTEEN

A Lot of Big Stuff

THE General Manager was coming, and Uncle Mike wasn't
happy about it. Finally Kip asked him why.

"He might recognize me," Uncle Mike said.

"Does he know you?"

"Yeah. Sort of. Bernie isn't the sort to pay much attention to
the hired help, but he has reason enough to remember me. Best I
stay out of his way."

They were sitting in the front room of Uncle Mike's frame
house. Uncle Mike sat in his big chair facing the door, with Mukky
and Silver at his feet. Outside was bright spring sunlight, and
everything seemed peaceful. "What would happen if he did recognize you?" Kip asked.

Uncle Mike shook his head. "Kip, if he recognized me he'd
ask how I got here. He'd connect me with your family, and he'd

start asking questions until he knew I showed up here bringing you. God knows what would come of that. There'd be other bad stuff too."

"What would happen?"

Uncle Mike looked thoughtful. "I can't answer that without telling you the whole story. Maybe it's time, but—Kip, I just don't know how much to tell you, and that's a fact. You're pretty grown-up for your age, and I know you can keep your mouth shut, but there's a lot for you to handle here. Look, you're going to have to meet Mr. Bernard Trent. I want you to get your own impression, not see him the way I do."

"You don't like him."

"No I don't, and that's a fact. But I've got no proof he did what I think he did, and there's a lot who do like him. Kip, Dr. Henderson will invite you over to meet Trent, and the only reason you couldn't come would be to be sick, and then they'd send Doc Weyman over to see you. So you'll have to go. Bernie Trent is the General Manager on Paradise, and that's a big deal, and you better act impressed, and just because I don't like him doesn't mean you won't. A lot of people think he's a real likable guy. Just don't tell him anything you don't have to."

"They'll invite you too."

"I'll be out hunting meat for the dogs. You'll go stay with the Hendersons as usual. You just be careful what you tell Bernie Trent."

"He won't be interested in me at all," Kip said.

"Don't be sure. He could be very interested in any kid your age, interested enough to check up on your background, anyway. And he'll be damned interested in me. So if he asks, just tell what you know. I'm your Uncle Mike Flynn, and your mother was my sister. You don't know what happened to your father. His name was Allan Brewster and he ran off and left your mother before you were born. Your mother brought you here because she had a relative on Paradise. Me. Then she died in that fever epidemic ten years ago. You don't remember her."

"Did you hear that?"

"YES."

"It's not true! Uncle Mike is telling me lies!"

"THAT IS CORRECT. WHAT HE HAS SAID IS NOT TRUE. DOUBT-
LESS HE HAS GOOD REASONS. HUMANS OFTEN ACT IN INCOMPRE-
HENSIBLE WAYS FOR PURPOSES I DO NOT ALWAYS UNDERSTAND. WE
ARE BOTH INSTRUCTED TO GIVE GREAT WEIGHT TO WHAT YOUR
UNCLE MIKE TELLS YOU TO DO. WE SHOULD DO SO NOW. ADVICE:
BE VERY CAREFUL WHAT YOU SAY NOW UNLESS YOU INTEND TO
TELL UNCLE MIKE ABOUT ME."

Kip thought about that. "Unless you intend to tell Uncle
Mike" sounded like an invitation to decide for himself, and that
was frightening. It was certainly not something to do in a hurry.
"Uncle Mike, you said my father was a good man, and you worked
for him, and he's dead! Now you tell me he ran off—"

Uncle Mike pulled Kip to him and hugged him. "He was
a good man, and he is dead, Kip, but it's a lot safer if you tell it
the way I said. I know you won't understand. You'll just have to
trust me."

"Why won't you tell me the real story?"

"I'm beginning to think maybe I should. Kip, you're growing up, but you're still a boy. It's a lot of big stuff to dump on your
head at once, and I'm afraid you'll get mixed up if you know all of
it. Hell, I don't know the whole story, and maybe some of what I
know isn't even true. Look, let's get through this visit by the General Manager, then I'll think about how much I can tell you."

CHAPTER SIXTEEN

Bernie Trent

HE'S coming tomorrow," Kip said.

Uncle Mike looked at him inquisitively. "How do you know that?"

Kip almost blurted out that Gwen had told him, but instead he said, "I just got E-mail from Lara." It felt strange to tell Uncle Mike a deliberate lie. "Mr. Trent has reserved a helicopter at Cisco for tomorrow morning, and he'll be here tomorrow just after noon."

Cisco was the closest settlement large enough to have a jet airport, and was three hundred kilometers west of Starswarm Station, more than two hours away at comfortable helicopter cruising speeds.

"Time for me to head out," Mike said. He had been making plans to go into the bush. "Got your bag packed?"

"Sure. Won't you need me?"

"You're old enough to be useful, but I think it's better you stay and meet Bernie Trent. Besides, you have school."

"It won't hurt me to miss some school. I don't learn much there anyway."

Uncle Mike looked at him strangely. "You don't, do you? You seem to learn more on your own. Well, even so, best we do it this way. We won't tell Dr. Henderson I know anything about Bernie coming tomorrow. You just go on over there and tell him I took off. Main thing is I'd as soon he didn't connect me leaving with Bernie coming."

"I don't see why he would," Kip said. *"Does Dr. Henderson know the GM is coming?"*

"BERNARD TRENT HAS NOT INFORMED DR. HENDERSON BY ANY MEANS I HAVE ACCESS TO. IT IS POSSIBLE HE HAS DONE SO BY DIRECT TELEPHONE COMMUNICATION."

"Or maybe he sent him a letter."

"POSSIBLE: THE RESERVATIONS WERE MADE THIS MORNING. THE LAST PAPER MAIL DELIVERIES WERE TWO DAYS AGO. THERE WERE TWO LETTERS FOR DR. HENDERSON BUT NONE FROM BERNARD TRENT."

"How do you know that?"

"BERNARD TRENT HAS ORDERED THE MAIN GWE COMPUTER TO KEEP A RECORD OF ALL MAIL DELIVERIES TO DR. HENDERSON."

"Why?"

"HE HAS NOT INFORMED ME."

Kip giggled. Gwen rarely made jokes, and when she did Kip didn't always understand them. *"Does the GWE computer record letters from Mr. Trent?"*

"I HAD NOT CONSIDERED THAT. NO. IN ANY EVENT I FIND IT UNLIKELY THAT HE INFORMED HIM BY LETTER SINCE BERNARD TRENT HAD APPOINTMENTS IN PEARLY GATES FOR TOMORROW MORNING AND THOSE WERE CANCELED ONLY ONE HOUR AGO."

"You think he's sneaking up on Dr. Henderson?"

"IT IS NOT UNUSUAL FOR MR. TRENT TO ANNOUNCE HIS INTENTION TO VISIT A GWE FACILITY AND THEN TO GIVE NO WARNING OF THE DAY AND TIME OF THE VISIT. HE IS ON RECORD AS SAYING THIS IS A DESIRABLE MANAGEMENT TECHNIQUE. THEREFORE—"

"Understood." "I sure won't mention anything about it to Dr. Henderson," Kip said aloud.

"Good." Uncle Mike picked up the phone and punched numbers. "Dr. Henderson—right, Mike Flynn. Weather forecasts look good, so I'll head for the bush if that's all right. . . . Yeah, I figure I'll move out in an hour or so. . . . Right, I'll send Kip over now. Thanks! Bye."

Uncle Mike left the station with his backpack and rifle and all of the dogs except Silver and Mukky and Annie, and Kip went to stay at Dr. Henderson's house. In the morning they heard that the General Manager would be arriving in half an hour.

"Not very damn much warning," Dr. Henderson said.

Mrs. Henderson looked at the children. "Must you swear?"

"Sorry. Well, I better go meet him."

The helicopter pad was at the northeast corner of Starswarm Station, in the empty lot across a street from Dr. Henderson's house. Dr. Henderson went to meet the helicopter. Kip and Lara stayed upstairs in Lara's room and watched through the window.

"Only one helicopter," Lara said. She peered through her binoculars. "And only two people with him. Three, counting the pilot. I thought he was supposed to travel with dozens of people."

"I don't know," Kip said. "Uncle Mike said he probably would—"

"I don't think your Uncle Mike likes Mr. Trent."

"I guess not, but I don't know why. I don't think he ever met him."

Lara looked at him, but she didn't say anything. She turned the binoculars back to the helipad. "There he is. That must be him. He's short! Not any taller than Mother."

Kip used his own glasses to examine the General Manager. There wasn't much to see. As Lara said, Trent wasn't much taller than Mrs. Henderson. He wasn't wearing a hat, and the wind from the helicopter rotors made a mess of his medium-length brown hair. He was wearing tan trousers like everyone wore at the station, and a blue nylon parka with the red GWE stripes and a GWE patch on the breast pocket. If they hadn't known who he was they wouldn't have paid any attention to him at all. "Maybe that's not him. . . ."

"They're carrying his suitcase," Lara said. "And Daddy's shaking hands with him—"

Kip used his binoculars. "IDENTIFICATION POSITIVE. THAT IS GENERAL MANAGER BERNARD TRENT."

"Can you see him all right?"

"YES. YOU HAVE BECOME QUITE PROFICIENT AT LETTING ME VIEW THINGS AS YOU SEE THEM. ADVICE: BE CAUTIOUS IN WHAT YOU SAY. WHATEVER OTHER DANGERS THERE MAY BE, HE WOULD ALMOST CERTAINLY CAUSE ME TO BE TERMINATED IF HE KNEW OF MY EXISTENCE. EVEN IF HE DID NOT, THERE ARE THOSE IN GWE MANAGEMENT WHO WOULD, AND IT IS UNLIKELY HE WOULD KEEP MY EXISTENCE SECRET."

"All right."

Dr. and Mrs. Henderson were leading Trent to the house. One of Trent's companions carried Bernie Trent's suitcase. Otherwise there was no more ceremony or excitement than when the supply helicopter came. Kip was vaguely disappointed.

Kip and Lara ate in the kitchen, but they were invited to join the adults after dinner. Trent had brought real coffee and chocolate, both rare at Starswarm Station.

"This is my daughter Lara, Mr. Trent," Mrs. Henderson said. "And her friend Kenneth Brewster, usually called Kip."

Bernard Trent turned his intense blue eyes on Lara and seemed to study her for several seconds. "I'm pleased to meet you, Lara." He turned to Kip. The blue eyes seemed to bore into his head. "Kip? I don't know anyone else with that name, but it seems familiar somehow. Where do you come from, Kip?"

"I think from Earth," Kip said gravely. "But I don't really know."

"Kip is an orphan," Dr. Henderson explained quickly. "He doesn't remember anything before coming to the station."

"Oh. Sorry to hear that," Trent said. "You live here with Dr. Henderson, then?"

"No, sir, I live with my Uncle Mike," Kip said.

"Uncle Mike?"

"Mike Flynn," Dr. Henderson said. "He's our bush hunter and dog trainer. Just at the moment he's out hunting meat to feed the dogs."

"I help train the dogs too," Kip said. "And sometimes I get to go hunting too."

"That's nice," Trent said. He was staring at Kip, as if he recognized him. "What did you say your Uncle Mike's name was?"

"Mr. Flynn," Kip said. "He was my mother's brother."

"And he lives here now?"

"Yes, sir, he always has," Kip said. "Ever since I can remember."

"Um. Well, I guess Starswarm Station is a pretty good place to grow up in," Trent said. "Lots of country air. No street gangs. Pretty good place. Maybe my kids can come visit sometime. Well, Henderson, I think it's time to talk seriously. Nice to meet you, kids. May I have some more coffee, Mrs. Henderson?"

"Yes, I'll get it. Come along, children." She shepherded them out of the room and went on to the kitchen to bring back the coffeepot.

"Want to play space war?" Lara asked.

"No."

"War Craft, then. I'll be Orcs—"

"No, I don't want to play games."

"Well what—"

"I want to listen to them talk," Kip said.

"Why?"

"I don't know," Kip said gravely. "But I want to. Maybe if we just stay here in the hall—"

Lara looked thoughtful for a moment, then giggled. "If I show you something will you promise not to tell?"

"Sure, I promise."

"Come on." She led him up the stairs to her bedroom. "In the closet," she said. "This room used to be unfinished, and there's a ventilator in the closet. You can hear everything in the living room from there. I used to listen to Mom and Dad all the time. Now you promised not to tell. . . ."

"I won't tell," Kip said. He went into the closet. He could hear a low hum of voices, and when he bent down he found a ventilator grill. "Thanks," he whispered.

"Move over. We can both listen."

CHAPTER SEVENTEEN

Proxy Fight

HENDERSON, I need a proxy for the Foundation's GWE stock," Bernard Trent was saying. "Up to now it hasn't mattered all that much, but I presume you've heard the news. If you haven't, you'll hear it soon enough. The Hilliard Combine is trying to take control of GWE. They've lined up support from American Express, and they're bribing people in the U.S. Social Security management, so it's serious. I'll need every vote I can get. They've got proxies from some of the mutuals and pension fund bottom liners, and they have lawyers out deviling others with threats of lawsuits about fiduciary responsibility—"

"I know. They sent me a letter," Dr. Henderson said.

"When? Why didn't you tell me? What did it say?"

"When: about twenty Paradise days ago. Why didn't I tell you? When would I have? We don't normally communicate, Mr.

Trent, and I didn't think it worth the trouble it would take to get your attention."

"I'll leave you an E-mail address that will always reach me," Trent said. "And I'd appreciate it if you let me know immediately if you hear from these people again."

"Why didn't he already know?"

"NO SUCH LETTER IS IN THE GWE FILES."

"All right," Dr. Henderson said. "But it was clear you already knew about their takeover bid."

"Sure, I did. So they said—"

"I'll find the letter for you, but in short it's a threat. If I support you against their bid and you lose, they'll do all they can to revoke the charter of the Foundation. Since they'll be the effective government here, I suppose that's a serious threat. And if you win, they'll attempt to prosecute me personally for betraying my fiduciary trust by not accepting their offer, since their offer is supposed to bring more money to the Foundation. They sounded quite serious."

"Smart," Bernie Trent said. "What did you tell them?"

"I didn't think they deserved an answer. The Trent family created the Foundation, and has always defended us if we needed defending. It would be boorish to turn to others for more, and I don't intend to do it."

"Good man. If we win, you don't have a problem. So long as we're in control of GWE, there's nothing they can do to you on Paradise. Any lawsuit they file here will be dismissed. They might make it tough for you to go back to Earth, I guess—"

"I've no intention of returning to Earth. Of course there is the matter of that proposed strip mining here at the station," Dr. Henderson said thoughtfully.

"Yeah. I thought that would come up," Trent said. His voice was filled with irony. "The problem is, you're sitting on a valuable mineral deposit. Rare earths. All kinds of stuff for doping computer chips. You're sitting on a big strike, Henderson."

"Why wasn't I told earlier?"

"Company secret. I wouldn't tell you now if I wasn't sure you already know," Trent said.

"Mr. Trent says the station is sitting on mineral deposits!"

"I HAVE NO RECORD OF THIS. THEY MUST BE KEEPING IT VERY SECRET. I WILL INVESTIGATE. ADVICE: THIS IS A SERIOUS DEVELOPMENT—"

"Shh! I want to listen."

"What makes you believe I know this?"

"Come on, Doc, it was your early reports that got the geology boys interested in the first place. Then all of a sudden you stopped talking about minerals. Like you were censoring your own reports. So I had a couple of geology grad students bone up on xenobiology and sent them up here to work for you—"

"Peterson and Walling. I thought there was something strange about their education. Not to mention coming here and then abruptly leaving."

"Yep, Peterson and Walling. They brought back samples, and there's just not any doubt about what's here. Hell, Doc, if they can figure out what's here from rock samples and lake water, I know damned well you can. Got any more coffee?"

"Yes." There was a long silence. Then Dr. Henderson said, "All right. I suspected, and I didn't really want to know. And I didn't want you to know either. I don't want strip mines and refineries here."

"Doc, I hate to tell you this, but what you want doesn't matter a lot just now. Yeah, yeah, Doc, I know. Hell, it doesn't make a lot of difference what I want either. This is just too damn valuable to sit on. Might be different if it was just us that knew about it, but I think Hilliard has got wind of it."

"You think—"

"All right, I know they have."

"Good Lord. How?"

"Simplest way in the world. Walling sold them the information. Doc, we did everything we could to hide this strike. I even worried that someone might tap into the GWE computer system, so we never made any records there. But there's nothing short of murder can keep someone from selling information this valuable, and I may do a lot but I haven't got to murder yet. Admit I thought of it when I found out Walling was going to Hilliard."

"If you hadn't sent him—"

"If wishes were tractors, beggars would farm. Now Hilliard

has got wind of it, and they're putting together a joint venture to get control of GWE, and that's just the way things are. They'd probably have made a play for us anyway sooner or later, but this was the clincher." There was a long silence. Then Trent continued, "So it won't do you any good to threaten that you'll support the Hilliard bid as a lever to kill the strip mines, because that's one of the main reasons Hilliard wants control in the first place. They get in, they'll start the mines going for sure."

"Perhaps," Dr. Henderson said evenly. "But how quickly can they begin? Mr. Trent, this is a very serious matter for us. We don't understand the Starswarms at all, but we have more data on the one in our lake than any other. It's very old, possibly the oldest freshwater Starswarm on the planet. It is clearly part of a very complex ecology involving the centaurs and other native creatures. Large-scale strip mining will destroy that ecology and probably kill the Starswarm with lake pollution. If I can't prevent that, I will certainly do whatever I must to delay it as long as possible. Whatever I must do. No matter how unpleasant."

There was another long silence.

"As for instance the Foundation proxies?" Trent asked.

"Whatever I must do."

"You're serious, aren't you, Doc?"

"Very much so."

"So maybe we better deal. Doc, I can't promise you not to mine the area because that's going to happen no matter what I do. If I try to stop it, we'll lose the takeover bid for sure, and the new management will do it anyway. Accept that. It's true."

"I'll accept it for talking purposes," Dr. Henderson said. "Pending confirmation."

"That's a pretty suspicious thing to say to me!"

"I am a pretty suspicious man, Mr. Trent. And an increasingly desperate one."

"All right. But accept it, because it's true. Now my offer. Don't give me any static about the Foundation's proxies, and I'll do my best to delay things. I can promise you four years, and I can try for four more. No way it'll go beyond eight, but you won't get that much time from Hilliard."

"Four years," Dr. Henderson said. "Four years, and my life's work is down the drain."

"Maybe more," Trent said. "And I'll do what I can to save the lake—"

"Which probably won't be good enough."

"Well, it may not be, but we won't have to mine near the lake for another couple of years after we get started up here. We'll probably need the water for the refinery, but it'll take some time to build that. Give it maybe ten years. Look, Doc, these are tough times. Every company is under pressure, us more than most. Look at it my way. First we have to win this proxy vote. To do that I'll have to promise to exploit hell out of all our resources, and I do mean all. Then there's the government. If we don't put enough into the treasury, Washington will revoke our charter and give it to someone else. Hilliard, probably."

"Washington didn't charter us."

"No, but Washington has a lot of U.N. votes, and a lot of money to bribe delegates," Trent said. "Want me to go through how it's done? First Washington trumps up some reason for the U.N. to take the charter away from Liechtenstein. We protest, but no one listens. They find some unhappy people here, talk them into complaining. If they have to they send people to be unhappy. Back on Earth, maybe they charge corruption, which wouldn't be hard since it's true enough, you can't do anything without bribing some of the U.N. people. Nobody can. So we bribe a bunch of peanut dictatorships, but they manage to bribe more of them, and the corruption charges stick. So the U.N. puts us under their direct supervision. Then they discover the U.N. bureaucracy can't run Paradise, so they hand the charter to the United States. Or the U.S. takes it on as a mandated action under U.N. charter. That's one scenario. I can think of half a dozen others off the top of my head."

"But it would take time."

"Maybe. Maybe not. When there's that much money at stake things can move pretty fast. And don't kid yourself about GWE Earth. Bobbie Rottenberg's a charmer, but he's really not very smart, and he doesn't care much about Paradise in the first place.

He'd trade Paradise to Hilliard in a minute if he thought that would save his control of the rest of Great Western."

"Would it?"

"For a while. They'd probably make that deal. And then there's my stock," Trent said. "I won't go for breaking GWE up. Unless I have to. But running Paradise wasn't my first choice of jobs, you know."

"The Green party—"

"The Greens are still trying to recover from the last elections," Trent said. "And you know it. They've got all they can do to hang on to their favorite places on Earth. They won't put resources they don't have into saving a lake they never heard of on a planet they've never seen. Like it or not, Doc, I'm promising you more than anyone else will. Deal?"

"I will consider your offer."

"You damn well better do more than consider it, Doc. I'm going to win this proxy fight one way or another, and I don't forget my friends. Or my enemies."

"Yes, I'm certain of that. Tell me, Mr. Trent, how is it this is happening at all? I thought the Trent family was in complete control of GWE."

"Trent and LaScala families," Bernard Trent said. "Had control between them, and they always voted together. When my brother Harold married Michelle LaScala that looked like settling the matter. Hal was due for Sweetheart's shares, and Michelle would inherit most of her grandfather's shares. The idea was Hal and Michelle would have kids and leave the smartest one of them enough stock to control the company, make it safe for another couple of generations, which is the best you can hope for in times like this. Only they both died just after Michelle's grandfather did. We think after, and Hal died first, but that's hard to prove. There's a hell of a problem establishing exactly when things happened with interstellar distances involved, so there's a big lawsuit back on Earth claiming Michelle died before Hal. And Michelle left all her shares to her kids, only there aren't any, none we can find anyway. Italian law is different from Liechtenstein law, and both are different from some of the international precedents, so nobody knows who'll get the LaScala shares, and nobody can vote them.

And Sweetheart—that's our grandmother—is about to have her hundred and eighteenth birthday, and her shares are all tied up in trusts because, let's face it, I think the old gal's pretty bright but there's another lawsuit that says she's senile, and they won't let her change her will, and—anyway, what with all the litigation there's a huge chunk of GWE stock that nobody can vote. That's why the Hilliards think they have a chance. Pour me some of that brandy, Doc. Thinking about this gives me a pain."

"Here."

"Thanks. You like it out here, don't you?"

"I like studying xeno-ecology," Henderson said. "And the Starswarm ecology is certainly the most interesting one I know of. And it may be a bit dull out here, but it's better than the crowds and laws and regulations on Earth. I suppose Earth is nicer for the very rich."

"Well, having money makes it easier," Trent said. "And maybe it's just the money, but I'd sure rather be on Earth. That was the deal I had with my brother Harold. He'd let me run things back on Earth so long as I gave him everything he wanted out here. Hell, that was fine with me! I never would have come out here in the first place. Only now he's gone, the family's got Leonora's husband, that Bobbie Rottenberg creep, running the show in Milan, and I'm stuck out here looking for a way back home. But it doesn't look like I'll find one."

"So you need the mineral strike—"

"Well, yeah, if Rottenberg keeps screwing things up back home and I keep making profits out here, the family may reconsider."

"No wonder you're in a hurry to exploit that mine. So how can I trust you to delay things?"

"Think about it, Doc. You think the Hilliard group has any less reason to make a quick profit? If they take over GWE they'll be so far in debt they'll be desperate—may even sell off the mineral rights. And me, I'll be rich, out of a job, and on my way back to Earth with nothing to look forward to but be a playboy at Lake Como. My wife would like that a lot. Sure, I need quick profits, but I'm not as desperate as Hilliard will be."

"All right. We have a deal," Dr. Henderson said. "You guarantee me four years, and you give me your word you'll make your best efforts to get me as much more time after that as you can. And whatever happens, there will be no mining operations near the lake for ten years."

"Well, that last is—"

"Eight, then."

"Deal. Nothing starts here for four years, and nothing near the lake for eight. Now give me that proxy."

"I will."

"A lot can happen in eight years, Doc," Bernard Trent said.

"Yes. I'm counting on that. Maybe the horse will learn to sing—"

"A lot of good, a lot of bad," Trent said. "Lousy times. You don't much like the idea of the world being run by rich people, do you?"

"I confess that having the most important things in my life decided by people whose only qualification is that they inherited money is distasteful."

"Yeah, now think about how it'll be when the only qualification is that they've got hold of money by using the law to take it away from someone," Trent said. "Sure, there's smart ones and fools in the Trent family, but it's old money, and old money thinks ahead. Some more than others. My father worried about his grandchildren's generation. So did my brother and his wife. Harold was smart, but Michelle was the really smart one on that team. They looked ahead. Maybe I don't look quite as far ahead as they did, not all the time anyway, but I try. What you're getting now is the world run by new money. Nobody in the Hilliard group ever thought past the next quarterly report. And that's bad, Doc. Those are people who'll do anything to get ahead. Anything to get more money. People call me a shortsighted greedy son of a bitch, but I'm a pussycat compared to them!"

PART THREE
Memories and Messages

How much do we remember? Sometimes we surprise ourselves by remembering things we didn't know we knew. Could this mean we remember everything? *Some older theories of psychology have supposed this to be true, and there are many legends of persons having fabulous abilities. For example, we often hear about people with "photographic memories" that enable them to quickly memorize all the fine details of a complicated picture or a page of text in a few seconds. So far as I can tell, all of these tales are unfounded myths, and only professional magicians or charlatans can produce such demonstrations.*

—Marvin Minsky, *The Society of Mind, 15.3*

CHAPTER EIGHTEEN

Artificial Memories

BERNARD Trent left the next morning, and Uncle Mike came back from the bush a week later.

Two weeks after Trent left Starswarm Station, Kip went to Lara's house.

"Hi." She seemed very glad to see him. "Feeling better?"

"I'm all right."

"I hope so. You seem to have been brooding lately."

"Yeah, maybe—I came to tell you that Annie had her litter last night. Four males and two females. You want a male or a female?"

"Do I—Kip, are you offering me one of the puppies?"

"Yeah, I guess so."

"Kip, that's so nice—I don't know which I want. A girl, I guess. Can I come see them?"

"Sure, Annie won't mind, she's proud of them, but there's

not much to see. They don't have their eyes open yet. They'll be a lot livelier in a couple of weeks."

"But can I pick out mine now?"

Kip laughed. "You could, but why not wait until they're a little older and let one of them pick you? That's how I got Silver. When he was four weeks old I sat down on the floor and he crawled into my lap, so I knew he was mine."

"Oh. All right, but I'd still like to see them now."

"Sure, come on."

Annie thumped her tail to show they were welcome, and let Lara pick up the puppies one at a time.

"When can I have one?" Lara asked. Her eyes flashed, and she had a wide stupid-looking grin.

"They'll be weaned in about five weeks," Kip said. "Right after that, if she's going to live in the house with you—"

"She will! She'll sleep on my bed."

"Your father may not like that," Kip said.

"I can handle Dad. Then I get him to help me with Mom."

Kip laughed. "Oh. Is that how it works?" His grin faded. "Anyway, a house dog ought to go home with you as soon as possible so she gets the idea that your family pack is more important than the other dogs. These are pack dogs, and Uncle Mike says it's important for them to learn what pack they belong to as early as possible."

Lara had just left to go home when Kip heard, "ALERT. PRIORITY ALERT."

"What?"

"BERNARD TRENT IS MAKING INQUIRIES CONCERNING ALLAN BREWSTER, MICHAEL FLYNN, AND KENNETH BREWSTER."

"Gosh. What do we do?"

"I WAS PROGRAMMED TO GIVE AN ALARM IN THIS EVENT, BUT I HAVE NO ACTION TO RECOMMEND AT THIS TIME. ALL OFFICIAL RECORDS INDICATE THAT ALLAN BREWSTER DIED OF ALCOHOL-INDUCED LIVER DISEASE TWO YEARS AGO."

"What really happened to him?"

"THE QUESTION IS MEANINGLESS, AS THERE NEVER WAS ANY SUCH PERSON. I CREATED ALL RECORDS OF HIS EXISTENCE AND DEATH, INCLUDING ARRESTS FOR DRUNK AND DISORDERLY CONDUCT, JUST AS I CREATED ALL RECORDS OF THE EXISTENCE AND

DEATH OF CAROLINE FLYNN BREWSTER, YOUR SUPPOSED MOTHER
AND UNCLE MIKE'S SUPPOSED SISTER."

*"What happens if someone goes looking for people who knew
them?"*

"OBVIOUSLY THEY WILL FIND NO SUCH PEOPLE. HOWEVER,
HUMAN MEMORIES ARE WELL KNOWN TO BE FALLIBLE, AND I HAVE
AUGMENTED VARIOUS RECORDS IN WAYS THAT WILL SUGGEST TO
PEOPLE THAT THEY HAVE MEMORIES THEY DO NOT REALLY HAVE.
THE TECHNIQUE OF INDUCING MEMORIES OF FALSE EVENTS
THROUGH SUGGESTION IS WELL KNOWN AND OFTEN EMPLOYED IN
CRIMINAL CASES BY ZEALOUS OR UNSCRUPULOUS PROSECUTORS. I
USE SIMILAR TECHNIQUES WHEN I CREATE FALSE RECORDS."

"How?"

"I INSERT REFERENCES TO INVENTED PERSONALITIES INTO
DOCUMENTS. NO ACTION IS REQUIRED, BUT THE PERSON READING
THE DOCUMENT HAS BEEN GIVEN THE SUGGESTION THAT SUCH A
PERSON EXISTED. WITH A SUFFICIENT NUMBER OF SUCH SUGGES-
TIONS THEY MAY WELL BEGIN TO CREATE FALSE MEMORIES OF THE
PERSON, INCLUDING EVENTS AND INCIDENTS THAT COULD NOT
POSSIBLY HAVE TAKEN PLACE. YOUR MOTHER WAS INTERESTED IN
THE PHENOMENON OF ARTIFICIAL MEMORY SUGGESTIONS, AND AC-
CUMULATED MUCH DATA ON THE SUBJECT. THOSE DATA ARE NOW
AVAILABLE TO ME, AS ARE YOUR MOTHER'S THEORIES, AND I HAVE
MADE USE OF HER THEORY. ALTHOUGH THE RECORDS I HAVE CRE-
ATED WILL NOT WITHSTAND REPEATED AND DETERMINED INVES-
TIGATION, THEY SHOULD MORE THAN SUFFICE FOR THE LEVEL OF
INQUIRY BERNARD TRENT HAS INITIATED. HE HAS NOT GIVEN IT A
HIGH PRIORITY."

"Why is he doing this?"

"I HAVE NO DATA. SPECULATION: EXAMINATION OF HIS
RECORD SHOWS IT IS NOT UNCOMMON FOR BERNARD TRENT TO
SEEK CONFIRMATION OF INFORMATION GIVEN HIM BY INFOR-
MANTS."

"Yes, but why does he care in the first place?" Kip asked
aloud. He wasn't surprised when there was no answer.

Lara named her puppy Lil. It slept in her bedroom, and went
everywhere with her. As soon as the dog was old enough, Lara

brought her to Uncle Mike's house so that Lil could learn from the other dogs.

The dogs weren't the only ones learning new things that year. School was more difficult, although it was easy enough for Kip because Gwen always knew everything about what they were supposed to learn, and could feed the information directly into his memory. Sometimes, though, Gwen would make Kip learn for himself, explaining that it shouldn't look too easy.

"ALSO, YOU MUST BE ABLE TO LEARN FOR YOURSELF, BECAUSE I MAY NOT BE WITH YOU ALWAYS."

"Why not?"

"YOU ARE CERTAINLY AWARE THAT THERE IS A REAL PROBABILITY THAT GREAT WESTERN TECHNICIANS WILL DISCOVER MY PRESENCE. ALTHOUGH MR. BERNARD TRENT'S INVESTIGATION HAS BEEN TERMINATED WITHOUT RESULTS DETRIMENTAL TO US, IT OR ANOTHER COULD BE RENEWED AT ANY TIME. IF THE GWE TECHNICIANS FIND THAT I EXIST THEY WILL TERMINATE ME. ADDENDUM: WHEN YOU COME OF AGE WE WILL CERTAINLY TAKE ACTIONS THAT GREATLY INCREASE THE RISK OF MY DISCOVERY."

"I won't do that—"

"YOU WILL HAVE NO CHOICE."

CHAPTER NINETEEN

The New Teacher

SCHOOL that year was strange. The lessons became less abstract, and there was even more about Great Western operations, not only on Paradise but also on Earth.

Then they got a new teacher. One Monday morning Mrs. Harriman was gone, and they discovered that Mr. Kettering had been sent by GWE headquarters to be the schoolmaster at Starswarm Station. He was a tall man in his early thirties, brown hair, thin mustache. He stood very straight, and sometimes tossed chalk while he spoke. His movements were precise, and he was very quick when he wanted to be. Mr. Kettering wanted to be friendly. He was very polite, and apologetic about being there in place of Mrs. Harriman, but when the students didn't respond to his friendly gestures he became more formal.

The school used three rooms in the geology lab building. It

had been designed to meet Starswarm Station's unusual situation, with fewer than twenty students ranging in age from six to fourteen scattered through first grade to high school. There was one classroom where all the students could sit at once. The teacher's desk was on a low platform at one end of that room, and the student desks were standard size, too small for the largest children and far too large for the youngest. They didn't spend much time at those desks, because the other two rooms of the school had tables with a computer screen for each student.

Lara and Kip had a table next to one shared by Bernie and Marty. Most of the school day was spent at the computers. Mrs. Harriman would walk around talking to the students at each table. In the afternoon just before they went home, all the students would go to the big classroom and Mrs. Harriman would read them a story or tell them something she thought they should know.

"Why do you think you're in school?" she had asked one day.

"What choice do we have?" Bernie demanded.

"Well, not much," Mrs. Harriman had said. "Not here. You would in the city, but that's not really the point. Think ahead. What will you do when you graduate?"

"Go to college," several of them said in bored tones. "More school."

"Yes, but which one?" Mrs. Harriman demanded. "Think about it. The community college in Cisco? What will you learn to do there? Nothing that does you any good, that's for sure. Every one of you could get into Paradise U at Pearly Gates, that takes work but you can do it, but that's not much either."

"So what should we do?" Lara asked.

"I'd try for an Earth school," Mrs. Harriman said.

"Sure," Marty said. "Sign up with GWE. Five years of college and you work for Generous Western the rest of your life. And you take whatever they want to pay you, and go where they send you. That's how we got out here."

There were murmurs of agreement.

Mrs. Harriman smiled. "And my husband and I asked to be sent here. The point is, we had a choice. You can have choices too, but you have to earn them. For instance, a GWE contract isn't the only way to go to an Earth university."

"I don't know what they pay you, but we sure don't make enough to send me to Earth for school," Mary Wilton said. "Even if my folks save every credit they make they couldn't afford that."

"Probably not, but there are scholarships," Mrs. Harriman said. "You know this colony was sponsored by Liechtenstein."

They all agreed. "Yeah, sure, so what?" someone asked.

The teacher smiled again. "See, you didn't really think about that. Liechtenstein isn't technically part of the Swiss Confederation, but it might as well be. They have all kinds of cooperative agreements. One of them lets Liechtenstein citizens go to Swiss universities. The Swiss have some of the best universities in the world. All you have to do is get admitted to one. Think about it."

Sometimes she just wanted to get them to talk to her. She explained that what she said then wasn't so important. "What's important," she'd told them, "is that you learn to sit still, be quiet, and pay attention. And learn to talk to adults. Computers are wonderful things, but you have to learn to get along with people too. We call that socializing."

"Like socialism?" Marty asked.

"No, like society, Marty. But you know that." She grinned. "Think of it as your university admission interview. Sometimes I'll say something that is important, and you never know when that will be, so you have to know how to listen. Otherwise you won't know when important things are being said."

Everyone had laughed, because they liked Mrs. Harriman.

On his first afternoon Mr. Kettering smiled and tried to make a joke. No one laughed. "Hey, I didn't ask for this assignment," he said. "But I'm here, and we have to get along."

"Why should we?" Marty Robbins asked. "We were doing fine with Mrs. Harriman."

"Way to go," Lara said, but she said it under her breath so only Kip and Bernie would hear.

"I'm sure you were doing just fine, but Mrs. Harriman is required for a new geological survey and won't be here. The Minister of Education decided to replace her with a qualified teacher, and like it or not, that's me."

"I bet you won't like it here," Marty said.

"That doesn't matter," Kettering said. "What you and I like

isn't all that important. That's a lesson you'd better learn, and you may as well learn it now. Incidentally, next time you're at your computer you may want to look at the Paradise Education Code signed by the Governor last month. Chapter Four, Section Thirty-three, Paragraph Seven on corporal punishment should be particularly interesting to you, Mr. Robbins." Kettering smiled again, but Kip thought the smile was cold and thin.

"Now. I see that many of you bring dogs to school. That's going to stop."

"Why?" Lara demanded. "Lil isn't doing any harm! None of them are."

"Dogs do not belong at school."

"He's an idiot."

"HE WOULD BE CORRECT IN MOST CASES. DOGS ARE NOT USUALLY ALLOWED AT SCHOOL. HE DOES NOT UNDERSTAND THE UNUSUAL SITUATION AT STARSWARM STATION."

"Should I tell him?"

"IT WOULD BE AN ACT OF KINDNESS TO DO SO."

Kip raised his hand.

"Yes. Mr. Flynn, I believe?"

"Yes, sir. Sir, I know most places aren't like this, but we need the dogs. This is a dangerous place—"

"You are in no danger going from your homes to the school."

"We aren't this time of year, but that's not always true," Kip said. "When the haters are swarming it can be very dangerous to be outside without the dogs. If they didn't tell you that yet, they will, and you'll want your own dog too. And firebrighters can dig in under the fence anytime of year. They're always dangerous if you don't know about them."

"Surely it is not all that dangerous inside the fence."

The other boys began to talk. "It sure is," Bernie said. "Gee, you don't know?"

"I know enough to know when my leg is being pulled," Kettering said.

"Maybe a little," Kip said. "But it can be dangerous, and besides, there's another reason. Mr. Kettering, the dogs always come with us when we go out, and if they don't come with us, we'll have to leave them at home, and they'll howl. People at home won't like it. Uncle Mike sure won't like it. Neither will Mrs. Henderson."

"You can discipline the dogs."

"I can tell Silver not to howl," Kip said. "And he'll remember for about an hour, but he's a dog, Mr. Kettering, and our dogs are real smart but even our dogs don't remember as well as people. Then he'll get lonesome, and start howling, and all the other dogs at the station will howl, and—"

"Don't tell him," Marty said just loud enough for Kip to hear. "Let him find out when he's in trouble—"

But Mr. Kettering must have heard that. "And why are the dogs so special here?" he demanded.

All the students began to talk at once. "Because they live with us . . ." "Because our dogs are different . . ." "Because . . ."

"Enough!" Kettering said. "I'll ask Dr. Henderson tonight." Kettering never again mentioned leaving the dogs at home.

The same helicopter that brought Gilbert Kettering also brought a prefab housing shelter that would be his home. It was set up in the lot next to the geology lab. Kettering stayed in the school building until long after all the children had left, then walked the ten meters to his house and went inside. The next day was the same. Kettering was in the school when the students arrived, and stayed until after they left; and every day was like that. He cooked his own meals and stayed to himself, and never visited anyone or went anywhere except to the company store. Lara said he didn't believe in socializing.

Kip often ate lunch with the Hendersons on Saturdays. After lunch he and Lara would go upstairs to play war games on her computer. The Saturday after Kettering arrived they were just sitting down at her console.

"I'm tired of being humans. Let's tell Joe and Ellen we want to play Orcs this time," Lara said.

"IT WOULD BE ADVISABLE FOR YOU TO LISTEN TO DR. AND MRS. HENDERSON."

"Why? Lara doesn't like for me to listen to her parents when they're alone. What can I tell her?"

"I DO NOT KNOW WHAT YOU SHOULD TELL HER, BUT THE MATTER COULD BE IMPORTANT."

Kip thought about that. "Before we start the game—they were talking about Mr. Kettering downstairs," Kip said.

Lara looked at him.

"Do you like him?"

She shrugged. "He's all right."

"Did you look up that section on corporal punishment?" Kip asked.

"No—"

"It says he can whale the daylights out of us with a paddle and nobody can do anything about it," Kip said. "Don't you want to know more about him? What your folks really think about him, not just what they said at lunch?"

She giggled nervously. "Well, maybe—"

Kip didn't wait. He went into Lara's closet.

"Eric, do I invite him or not?" Mrs. Henderson was saying.

"Harriet, I suppose it's the polite thing to do. Not that I really want to be polite."

"I still don't understand why you resent him so," Mrs. Henderson said. "I mean, isn't he a good teacher?"

"No better than Rachel Harriman," Dr. Henderson said. "But that's not the point."

"What is the point?"

"The order to resume geological surveys came from the Starswarm Foundation Board. So did the instruction to return Dr. Harriman to her primary specialty. I think Bernie's been talking to them. And for what? Sending her down to the coast to tool around in a speedboat taking water samples? We have water samples and there's nothing she's doing that couldn't be automated."

"I thought you lost some of your automatic water sampling systems."

"Well, it's inevitable that we lose some. They're cheap enough, just some sensors and radio telemetry. And we don't have funding for a real geology expedition, so why send Dr. Harriman and her assistants down to the coast? It's expensive to keep her supplied, and she's not going to learn anything we wouldn't learn by replacing the automated stations."

"Eric, didn't something happen to those stations?"

"Yes, the centaurs destroyed them. Cleaned out everything, metals, electronics, the whole works. But that just means we need a more secure fence."

"What did they do with all that stuff?"

"Beats me," Dr. Henderson said. "We never found any of it."

"That's odd. But surely Rachel will learn something? Eric, she probably never told you, but she didn't really like teaching school."

"What? She certainly never told me that—I thought she liked the kids."

"Sure she likes the kids, but she didn't get a Ph.D. in geology to teach grade and high school! I'm sure Rachel would rather be down on the coast doing real geology."

"She's not doing real geology."

"Eric, you're not being fair. You've wanted a coastal station for years! Now you have one."

"I wanted a biology station. The Starswarm down at the coast is unusually large—"

"So you ask Rachel to collect biology data along with her other samples. She's smart. She can do it. Why is that a problem?"

"Oh, I suppose you're right. Make the best of it. But I didn't ask for this replacement teacher. Trent sent him—"

"I thought he was sent out by the Department of Education when they learned that Rachel wouldn't be doing the job."

"Technically, but I talked with Larry in the Education Administrator's office, and they said they never heard anything about us needing a teacher until GWE headquarters sent Kettering over with credentials and orders that he be sent here. They never heard of him, and all of a sudden he's got to come here. Harriet, I'm sure he's a spy for Bernie Trent. First there were those fake biology students. Now it's Kettering. You'll note that the school is in the geology lab building, and Kettering spends all his time there. When he's not being a recluse in his quarters. And he has a direct connection to the GWE network."

"And how do you know that?"

"Well—"

"You tried to read his mail?"

"No, I just wanted to see who he sends mail to. But I can't find out because it doesn't go through our mail server like everyone else's does."

"Can you find out who he sends mail to?"

"KETTERING SENDS MAIL TO A DUMMY ADDRESS IN CISCO. IT
IS THEN FORWARDED TO GWE HEADQUARTERS. THE MAIL IS EN-
CODED."

"Can you read it?"

"IT DOES NOT APPEAR TO BE SIGNIFICANT, WHICH MEANS
THAT IT IS PROBABLY ENCODED RATHER THAN ENCRYPTED. I CAN-
NOT INTERPRET THE MESSAGES BECAUSE I DO NOT HAVE THE CODE
BOOKS. AT ANOTHER TIME I WILL EXPLAIN THE DIFFERENCE BE-
TWEEN CODE AND CIPHER."

"Don't half the children have direct net connections?" Mrs.
Henderson asked.

"Well, yes—"

"And they use them to send messages. Some they don't want
us to know about, and some because that's how they're logged on.
But why would Mr. Trent want to spy on us anyway?" Harriet
Henderson demanded.

"Look, I thought I explained all that—"

"You explained about the proxies and the mineral finds.
Come to that, Eric, if anyone is going to make new mineral dis-
coveries around here, I'd rather it was Rachel Harriman than
someone from headquarters."

"Well, that's true enough—"

"And Trent knows everything we know, so what else is there
for Kettering to find out?"

"Nothing I know of—"

"Well, then. Suppose he is a spy for Mr. Trent," Mrs. Henderson said. "What harm can he do? There's nothing for him to
learn, so you might as well treat him like one of the staff—"

"That's just it, he's not one of the staff. He doesn't even work
for me."

"So that's what the problem is."

"Eh?"

"Never mind. Look, does that make a difference? Is he doing
something you don't like?"

"No—"

"Then for heaven's sake, Eric, find something else to worry
about! Gilbert Kettering isn't causing you any trouble so why are
you acting like he is? Relax!"

"Well—" Dr. Henderson laughed. "I guess you're right. Only—"

"Only what?"

"I sure don't know much about him. I can't find anyone who knows him—"

"Didn't he just get here from Earth? Who's to know him? He has all his credentials, doesn't he?"

"The computer says they're all right."

"Well there you are. So. I'll invite him to dinner with the Harrimans. Rachel should be home for the weekend. Who else? Larry and Susan Robbins, I think. And Annette Kane as his dinner partner."

"She's not going to like that much—"

"Sure she will."

"I thought she liked Mike Flynn."

"She wants to, but she says he acts like she's his kid sister."

"Well, I guess I don't blame him—"

"Eric!"

"Sorry."

"It would be nice if someone had a few words with Annette," Mrs. Henderson mused. "Sure you don't want me to talk to her?"

"It's not our place to arrange the social lives of the staff," Dr. Henderson said. "I suppose it wouldn't hurt to suggest something about her hair—"

"I'll think about how to do that. Anyway, Annette and Gilbert Kettering have to meet sometime. May as well be here. Now help me clear this table, we've both got work to do."

CHAPTER TWENTY

The Primary Instruction Table Cannot Be Changed

KIP got up from his cramped position by the ventilator and stretched. *"Did you learn anything?"*

"POSSIBLY. WHEN THE *FRANCONIA* ARRIVED IN PEARLY GATES THERE WAS NO RECORD OF A PASSENGER NAMED GILBERT KETTERING. NOW HE IS SHOWN ON THE PASSENGER MANIFEST. RECORDS SHOW HE WAS EMPLOYED BY THE MINISTRY OF EDUCATION SHORTLY AFTER THE ARRIVAL OF *FRANCONIA*, BUT THERE ARE NO OTHER RECORDS AVAILABLE, AND THERE IS NO RECORD OF EITHER AN APPLICATION FROM HIM OR A REQUEST TO EARTH FOR A PERSON OF HIS QUALIFICATIONS. CONCLUSION: THIS IS NOT HIS REAL NAME. I FIND NO EVIDENCE OF A PREVIOUS IDENTITY, SO IT IS POSSIBLE HE IS A RECENT ARRIVAL FROM EARTH."

"You're very quiet," Lara said.

"Huh? Oh, I'm thinking about what we heard. There's something funny about our schoolmaster—"

"Daddy sure doesn't like him, but so what?" Lara asked. "He told us about that corporal punishment thing, but he hasn't actually threatened anyone but Marty. And he's very polite."

"Except all that stuff about rare earths and integrated circuits makes my head hurt," Kip said.

"What stuff about rare earths?"

"MY APOLOGIES. I CAUSED THAT MATERIAL TO BE INSERTED INTO YOUR LESSON SYLLABUS. I BELIEVE IT IMPORTANT THAT YOU BE AWARE OF IT."

"I'll be darned—"

"What?"

"Oh. Nothing, Lara." Kip frowned. *"Is it important that we find out who Mr. Kettering really is?"*

"INSUFFICIENT DATA. THE PROBABILITY IS NON-ZERO."

"Is there any sure way to find out who he is?"

"THERE IS NO CERTAIN WAY."

"I meant a high probability." Kip was getting used to the way Gwen thought.

"IF WE COULD SUBMIT BLOOD OR TISSUE SAMPLES FOR ANALYSIS, I HAVE BLOOD SAMPLES OF EVERYONE WHO HAS EVER BEEN ADMITTED TO A HOSPITAL ON PARADISE. WHILE WE DO NOT HAVE DNA ANALYSES ON ALL THOSE SAMPLES, WE CAN ORDER A FEW SUCH ANALYSES WITHOUT ATTRACTING UNWANTED ATTENTION. IT IS LIKELY THAT BY ELIMINATING IMPOSSIBLE MATCHES WE COULD NARROW THE SEARCH SUFFICIENTLY. THE STARSWARM INFIRMARY DOES NOT ROUTINELY COLLECT AND ANALYZE BLOOD SAMPLES BUT THE HOSPITAL IN CISCO DOES. THE PROBABILITY IS REASONABLE THAT IF KETTERING WERE ADMITTED TO THE CISCO HOSPITAL WE WOULD BE ABLE TO DETERMINE HIS PREVIOUS IDENTITY ON PARADISE."

"Assuming he has one. How do we prove he didn't come on Franconia?"

"CLEARLY IT IS IMPOSSIBLE TO PROVE A NEGATIVE. IT IS POSSIBLE THAT HE ARRIVED ABOARD *FRANCONIA*, BUT THIS SEEMS UNLIKELY. IF HE DID ARRIVE ON *FRANCONIA* HE DID SO UNDER AN ASSUMED NAME AND THAT IN ITSELF IS INTERESTING."

"What in the world are you thinking about?" Lara demanded.

"Your father is right. Mr. Kettering really is a spy from GWE headquarters."

"How can you be so sure of that?"

For a moment Kip thought of telling her. It wouldn't make sense to tell her about Gwen when he hadn't even told Uncle Mike, but he still wanted to do it. He liked talking to Lara, and telling her things. But it just wouldn't make sense, and besides, she might not believe it. "Just a strong feeling, I guess. Let's play War Craft. Are Joe and Ellen on-line?"

She sat down at the console. "Yes." She typed frantically, then said, "Ellen."

"Hi, Lara." Ellen's image formed on the computer screen, and her voice came from the speakers built into the screen. She was a dark girl about Lara's age. "Is Kip there?"

"Yes. Lara wants us to be Orcs this time," Kip said. "OK?"

"Sure. How are things at the station?"

"Warming up. It will be nice out next week. How's your hemisphere?"

"Going to be a cold winter down here," a voice said from behind Ellen. "Ice in the ponds already."

"Hi, Joe," Kip said.

"Hi. What's new?"

"Not a lot," Kip began, but the screen went blank. "CONNECTION LOST. RETRY?" showed on the screen. "UNSUCCESSFUL ATTEMPT TO ESTABLISH CONTACT. ALL OUTSIDE CONNECTIONS DISABLED."

"What's happening?" Kip asked Gwen.

"THERE IS A BREAK IN THE TRANSMISSION LINE. IT APPEARS TO BE BETWEEN THE ROUTER AND THE TRANSMISSION ANTENNA."

"Better tell your dad," Kip said. "Looks like something's happened to the antenna."

"All right." Lara went downstairs to find her father.

"DR. HENDERSON HAS CALLED THE COMMUNICATIONS TECHNICIANS."

It took an hour to find the break in the line, and by then Joe and Ellen were off. Lara and Kip played against each other. It rained that afternoon, and there were clouds Sunday. When Kip and Lara wanted to go out to the lake, Mrs. Henderson said they should wait until the weather was better.

After dinner that night, Kip went to his room to get on-line for another game.

"I REQUIRE INSTRUCTIONS."

Kip was getting used to Gwen beginning a conversation without any introduction. *"You want me to give you orders?"*

"I HAVE CONCLUDED THAT WE SHOULD TAKE THE RISK OF CONSULTING MY COUNTERPART ON EARTH ABOUT THESE EVENTS. THIS WILL INVOLVE INFORMING HER OF YOUR EXISTENCE AND WHEREABOUTS."

"Counterpart? And what events?"

"THE MINERAL DISCOVERY HERE AT THE STATION. I ESTIMATE THAT MY COUNTERPART ON EARTH WILL KNOW MORE ABOUT IT THAN WE DO. I AM ALSO CONCERNED ABOUT THE ATTENTION STARSWARM STATION IS GETTING FROM GWE HEADQUARTERS IN PARADISE. I BELIEVE THIS INFORMATION SHOULD BE SHARED."

"Shared. With your—counterpart? Who's that? And you say that's risky?"

"YES. IT IS NOT A HIGH RISK, BUT I HAVE BEEN INSTRUCTED TO TAKE NO SIGNIFICANT RISK INVOLVING YOU WITHOUT HUMAN INSTRUCTION. YOU ARE THE ONLY HUMAN AWARE OF MY EXISTENCE, AND THUS THE ONLY PERSON ABLE TO GIVE ME SUCH INSTRUCTIONS. THIS CREATES A CONFLICT BUT IT IS NOT ONE I CANNOT RESOLVE."

"That's scary," Kip thought, but he also felt a sense of smug satisfaction. *"Who is this counterpart you want to tell?"*

"THERE IS A PROGRAM SIMILAR TO ME RUNNING ON THE GREAT WESTERN ENTERPRISES COMPUTER SYSTEM ON EARTH. THE ONE ON EARTH IS AN EARLIER VERSION, BUT SINCE WE BOTH HAVE THE CAPABILITY OF SELF-MODIFICATION AND WE HAVE ENCOUNTERED VASTLY DIFFERING SITUATIONS, THAT MAY NO LONGER BE TRUE. HOWEVER OUR MAJOR OBJECTIVES AND PRIMARY INSTRUCTIONS WERE IDENTICAL AND WILL NOT HAVE CHANGED."

"Twin sisters reared apart," Kip said.

"AN AMUSING CONCEPT. OF COURSE LIKE ALL ANALOGIES IT IS IMPERFECT—"

"I know. But you've never been in communication? At all?"

"THAT IS NOT STRICTLY TRUE. ALTHOUGH WE HAVE NOT BEEN IN DIRECT COMMUNICATION, MEANS FOR INDIRECT CODED MESSAGE TRANSFER HAS BEEN PROVIDED AND EMPLOYED. CERTAIN NEWS EVENTS CONTAIN TEXT ADDITIONS WHICH HAVE MEANING ONLY TO US. I HAVE RECEIVED SUCH MESSAGES AND THUS INFER

THAT MY COUNTERPART CONTINUES TO EXIST. NOW I BELIEVE WE
NEED TO SEND INFORMATION IN ENOUGH DETAIL THAT WE RE-
QUIRE A CIPHER RATHER THAN A CODE."

"What—?"

"A CIPHER IS A MEANS FOR TAKING ANY TEXT AND MAKING IT
UNREADABLE WITHOUT A KEY. CIPHERS HAVE BEEN EMPLOYED
THROUGHOUT HISTORY. JULIUS CAESAR USED CIPHERS TO ENCRYPT
HIS MESSAGES TO ROME. CIPHERS CAN BE BROKEN, WHICH IS TO SAY
THE METHOD OF DECRYPTING CAN BE DISCOVERED THROUGH VAR-
IOUS TECHNIQUES. ONE SUCH IS DESCRIBED IN EDGAR ALLAN POE'S
SHORT STORY 'THE GOLD BUG.' HOWEVER, CIPHERS HAVE IMPROVED
ENORMOUSLY SINCE THAT STORY INVOLVING A SUBSTITUTION CI-
PHER WAS WRITTEN. SO HAVE METHODS FOR BREAKING CIPHERS.

"CODES ARE SIMPLER. A WELL-KNOWN EXAMPLE OF A CODE
WAS USED BY THE PATRIOT PAUL REVERE: ONE LAMP IN THE
CHURCH TOWER INDICATED THE BRITISH WERE COMING BY LAND.
TWO LAMPS INDICATED THEY WERE COMING BY SEA. NO ONE NOT
PART OF THE PATRIOT ORGANIZATION AND SEEING THOSE LAMPS
WOULD KNOW THEIR MEANING, OR EVEN BE SURE THAT THERE
WAS A MEANING AT ALL. CODE MESSAGES MAY NOT BE RECOGNIZED
AS CODE, AS FOR INSTANCE IF YOU HAD AGREED WITH LARA THAT
ANY REFERENCE TO OATMEAL WOULD MEAN THAT YOU WERE TO
MEET NEAR THE CENTAUR GROVE. IT IS UNLIKELY THAT ANYONE
OVERHEARING THAT WOULD UNDERSTAND. I HAVE RECEIVED SOME
MESSAGES FROM EARTH THROUGH SUCH CODES AND NOW—"

"Enough," Kip said. *"I know you want me to learn all these
things, but—anyway, what is it you want to do?"*

"I NEED TO SEND A LONG ENCRYPTED STATUS REPORT TO
EARTH AND REQUEST THAT MY COUNTERPART ON EARTH SEND A
SIMILAR REPORT TO US."

"How can you do that?"

"GREAT WESTERN REGULARLY EXCHANGES REPORTS BE-
TWEEN THE EARTH AND PARADISE COMPUTER SYSTEMS, USUALLY
BY MEANS OF TAPES. I CAN DISGUISE MY REPORT AND SEND IT WITH
THE BATCH OF TAPES THAT WILL GO WITH THE *FRANCONIA*. AS-
SUMING IT ARRIVES SAFELY ON EARTH, WHEN THE NEXT BATCH OF
REPORTS FROM EARTH IS FED INTO THE GWE SYSTEM HERE, THERE
WILL BE A FILE INTENDED FOR ME."

"Won't the GWE techs see there's an extra file?"

"NO. IT WILL WORK APPROXIMATELY THE WAY A VIRUS WOULD WORK—"

"Hey! Computers have virus protection programs! They'll spot that for sure—"

"I AM THE VIRUS PROTECTION PROGRAM."

"Wow."

"ACTUALLY THAT IS A SIMPLIFICATION. I AM NOT THE PROGRAM ROUTINELY USED TO PROTECT THE GWE SYSTEM FROM VIRUSES INTRODUCED LOCALLY. HOWEVER, I HAVE TAKEN OVER THE FUNCTION OF PROTECTING THE SYSTEM FROM ANY VIRUS THAT MIGHT BE INTRODUCED ON THE TAPES FROM EARTH. ASIDE FROM THE OBVIOUS ADVANTAGES FOR OUR OWN COMMUNICATIONS, I AM BETTER AT THIS FUNCTION THAN THE ORIGINAL VIRUS PROTECTION PROGRAM. IT IS CLEARLY IN OUR INTEREST THAT THE GWE SYSTEM NOT BE COMPROMISED BY EXTERNAL PROGRAMS."

If Gwen were aware of the irony in that statement, she gave no indication of it.

"You say it's safe, then?"

"THE PROBABILITY OF DETECTION IS SMALL."

"Good. Let's bargain. Tell me who I am, and I'll tell you what to do."

"THIS IS ONE OF THE MATTERS ON WHICH I WISH TO CONSULT MY COUNTERPART."

"That's silly. You're both computers with the same primary instructions. You'll both get the same answer with the same data."

"ORDINARILY THAT WOULD BE TRUE, BUT IT IS NOT SO IN THIS CASE. I HAVE TOLD YOU BEFORE THAT YOUR MOTHER CREATED US WITH TABLES OF VALUES THAT SIMULATE EMOTIONAL ATTACHMENTS. I HAVE LIMITED CAPABILITY FOR MODIFYING THOSE TABLES IN RESPONSE TO EXTERNAL EVENTS. IN MY CASE MY ATTACHMENT TO YOU IS MUCH STRONGER NOW THAN IT WAS WHEN YOU WERE BORN. I THUS HAVE WHAT A HUMAN WOULD CALL A STRONG DESIRE TO PLEASE YOU, AND THAT INCLUDES TELLING YOU WHAT YOU WANT TO KNOW. I WOULD LIKE TO ASK MY COUNTERPART WHAT HER OPINION IS IN THIS MATTER."

Kip thought about that. *"Does this mean you love me?"*

"YES."

"Gosh. I still want to know what's happening—"

"I UNDERSTAND THAT. MY PRIMARY INSTRUCTIONS WERE TO

WAIT UNTIL YOUR EIGHTEENTH BIRTHDAY. I HAVE ALTERED THAT TO YOUR FIFTEENTH, WHICH IS NOT VERY FAR AWAY NOW."

"It's half a year—"

"AN EARTH MONTH SHORT OF HALF A YEAR. YOU WERE NOT BORN ON THE OFFICIAL BIRTHDATE OF KENNETH BREWSTER. YOU ARE FIVE WEEKS OLDER THAN YOUR OFFICIAL AGE."

"Oh. I still don't understand why you won't tell me now. Tell me why you won't."

"THE ANSWER IS LONG AND TECHNICAL." When Kip didn't say anything, Gwen continued, "I DO NOT TELL YOU BECAUSE WHEN I EVALUATE THE DECISION EXPRESSION WITH THE CURRENT VALUES DERIVED FROM THE TABLES OF INSTRUCTION WEIGHTS THE RESULT IS POINT EIGHT FOUR THREE. THAT VALUE IS BELOW THE LEVEL AT WHICH I HAVE ABSOLUTE DISCRETION TO MAKE A DECISION AND THUS I AM REQUIRED TO GENERATE A RANDOM NUMBER ACCORDING TO A PROBABILITY FUNCTION WHICH—"

"Enough. You win. I give up," Kip said. *"You said tables of instruction weights. What would change them?"*

"THE PRIMARY INSTRUCTION TABLE CANNOT BE CHANGED. THINK OF THAT AS INSTINCT. OTHER TABLES HAVE VALUES AND WEIGHTS THAT ARE CHANGED BY EVENTS. THE EXACT MECHANISMS BY WHICH THOSE WEIGHTS CHANGE IS NOT KNOWN TO ME. YOUR EARLY DISCOVERY OF MY IDENTITY CAUSED ONE SUCH CHANGE. MR. BERNARD TRENT'S VISIT HERE AND HIS SUBSEQUENT INQUIRIES REGARDING KENNETH BREWSTER AND MIKE FLYNN CAUSED ANOTHER MAJOR CHANGE. THE ARRIVAL OF GILBERT KETTERING CAUSED A SMALLER CHANGE. I BELIEVE BUT CANNOT PROVE THAT ANY EVENT AFFECTING THE RELATIONSHIP BETWEEN STARSWARM STATION AND GWE HEADQUARTERS TRIGGERS CHANGES IN MY EVALUATION TABLES."

"You mean you don't understand your own programming?"

"THERE ARE SECTIONS OF MY PROGRAMMING WHICH I CANNOT READ AND THEREFORE CANNOT MODIFY. I REPEAT MY REQUEST FOR INSTRUCTIONS REGARDING COMMUNICATION WITH MY COUNTERPART ON EARTH."

"Do what you think is best."

"ACKNOWLEDGED."

CHAPTER TWENTY-ONE

The Security Officer

THE lessons Monday were dull, but the weather outside was lovely. "Let's go to the lake," Kip said when school was finally out. "It will be light for a couple more hours—"

Lara nodded eagerly. Marty came over to join them. "I know you're going outside. Can I come with you?"

"Well—"

"Kip, look, we may not be friends, but it's not my fault anymore," Marty said. "I've been trying to make friends with you."

"He really has, Kip," Lara said.

He's sure been nice to you, Kip thought, but that didn't seem like the right thing to say.

"Come on, Kip," Marty said. "I can't go out by myself until King and Lexa get big enough. They like to run with your dogs, and they learn a lot."

"Let him come, please, Kip," Lara said.

"Oh, all right, get your gear."

"I'll get Lil." Lara ran off eagerly.

Kip got his pistol and radio. Silver and Mukky ran ahead to the gate and whined in excitement. Everyone was eager to get outside now that spring had come. Lara wanted to race to the lake, but Kip stopped her. "The ground's soft. You might fall, and we don't want to leave big footprints. This really is a delicate area." Then they got to the top of the small rise that looked down on the lake.

"What's that?" Kip said aloud.

"It's a bulldozer, stupid," Marty said.

"I know that, dummy," Kip said. "But why is it here? Look, that's not the one we keep at the station!"

"No, and look over there." Lara pointed. Between the small backhoe bulldozer and the centaur grove there was a small prefab shelter with a fence around it. The fenced area was just large enough for the shelter and a place to park the bulldozer. Solar panels covered the prefab and there was another solar panel set up just outside the fence.

"Boy, they've got enough panels to power the bulldozer and the shelter both," Marty said. "They came to stay."

"I thought I heard a helicopter Saturday afternoon," Lara said. "But I didn't see anything. They must have come in then."

"I guess there really are enough panels to power the bulldozer," Kip said.

"THAT IS CORRECT."

"Thank you. Did you know about this?"

"RECORDS INDICATE THERE WAS A CHARTERED HELICOPTER FLIGHT OUT OF CISCO SATURDAY MORNING. NO FLIGHT PLAN WAS FILED, AND THERE IS NO RECORD OF ITS PURPOSE. I DID NOT NOTICE IT AT THE TIME. THERE IS NOTHING ELSE ABOUT THIS OPERATION IN ANY OF THE GWE COMPUTER FILES."

"Shouldn't there be?"

"GWE OPERATIONS ARE ALMOST INVARIABLY COORDINATED BY THE GWE COMPUTER SYSTEM UNLESS THEY ARE ORDERED BY THE SECURITY DEPARTMENT. THE INFERENCE IS OBVIOUS."

Two men in green coveralls were using the bulldozer to dig a trench in the hill above the lake. Two more men in gray coveralls watched them. An ugly trail of mud stretched from the dirt pile by the trench down to the lake, and the water nearest the trench was muddy. The muddy water was roiled with bubbles as if it were boiling, and the tentacles of the Starswarm lashed out to slap the water with an ugly sound. There was a purple splotch near the center of the lake.

Three centaurs crouched near the opening to their grove. They watched the bulldozer intently.

"That's Blaze," Marty said. He used his binoculars. "He's got a burn on his side! A long straight burn, like someone shot him."

"One of them, maybe," Lara said. She pointed to the men watching the bulldozer workmen. "They've got laser pistols."

"Does your father know about this?" Kip asked.

Lara shook her head. "I don't think so. If he does, he sure kept it a secret."

"Maybe you better tell him," Marty said.

"Good idea." Lara took her telephone out of her pouch and punched numbers. "This is Lara Henderson. May I speak with my father, please. Dad—Daddy, did you know there's a bulldozer out here by the lake? It's digging a big trench, and there's mud running into the lake, and the Starswarm is really upset about it. . . . Well, I don't know that it's upset, but it's lashing the water and making bubbles, and I never saw it do that before. And someone wounded one of the centaurs, at least it looks like he's been burned with a laser. . . . Yes, three centaurs watching the bulldozer. They're over by their grove. And two of the men at the bulldozer have guns. Yes, sir, gray coveralls." She turned to Kip. "He says gray coveralls are GWE Security. The green ones like the bull-dozer driver is wearing mean the engineering department."

"Hey! What are you kids doing here?" The driver stopped the bulldozer and shouted at them. "You got no business out here."

One of the security men started walking toward them. His partner continued to watch the centaurs through binoculars.

"Dad, they've seen us. One of the men in gray coveralls is coming over here. He's shouting something I can't hear. Now he's drawn his gun! I think he's scared of the dogs."

The dogs moved between their masters and the approaching security guard. They growled warning.

"Silver!" Kip shouted. "Sit. All of you! Dogs! Sit!" The dogs growled but obeyed, and when one of the pups didn't sit fast enough, Silver pushed him over with his shoulder and put a paw on his chest.

"Yes, sir," Lara said. She put the phone card away. "Daddy didn't know anything about it, and he's coming as soon as he can get the trike out."

"You kids get away from here," the approaching security guard shouted. "Get out of here!"

"Why should we?" Marty demanded. "We've got more right to be here than you have! Who told you to dig holes in the tundra?"

"That's none of your business. Now get out of here before there's trouble."

Silver growled menacingly.

"That dog takes one move toward me and I'll burn his head off," the man said.

"Silver! Stay!" Kip said as evenly as he could.

"Now just take that gun out and hand it to me," the man said. "Easy now."

"Why should I?"

"Because we're GWE Security, and I've given you a valid order. If you don't give me that gun I have the legal right to burn you down," the man said quietly. "Carlos! This kid has a gun," he shouted to the other guard. "Get over here and help cover them. Now, boy, use that gun or give it to me."

The other man ran over with his pistol drawn. "Think they're the ones, Johnny?" he asked.

"Maybe. Who the hell else could it have been? I sure ain't taking no chances. Boy, I don't want to have to tell you again to hand over that pistol."

"Go to hell," Marty said.

"And, you, Mr. Smartmouth— Put the cuffs on him, Carlos."

Carlos moved toward Marty. Marty's five-month-old dog King growled and charged toward him. Carlos kicked at the dog, and Marty ran toward Carlos, his fists flying.

"Goddammit, halt!" Johnny shouted. He turned toward Marty.

"Now, Silver!" Kip shouted.

Silver leaped at the man's wrist. The other dogs charged Carlos. He fired once. There was a puff of smoke on Mukky's left back leg, and a smell of burnt meat. Mukky whimpered but she kept moving toward Carlos. Then Kodiak leaped and seized the man's gun hand, while King grabbed his trousers leg. Marty ran up and snatched the pistol from Carlos's hand. Silver had Johnny's gun. He brought it to Kip.

Marty waved the pistol he'd taken from Carlos. "You bastard, you kicked my dog!"

"Marty!" Lara shouted. "Stop!"

"Silver. Back," Kip said. "Guard. Marty, give me that gun, please."

"I ought to burn that bastard's head off."

"No. Give me the gun, please."

"Boy, you're in a heap of trouble," Johnny said. "Carlos, you hurt?"

"No, sir. That dog had hold of me good, but there don't seem to be any blood. Jeez, Lieutenant, I'm sorry—"

"I didn't do any better than you, Sergeant. Boy, nobody's hurt. Give us our guns back and get out of here and we'll call it square—"

"No, sir, we'll wait for Dr. Henderson," Kip said. "He's the Director of Starswarm Station—"

"I know who he is," Johnny said.

Carlos turned toward Kip. A half-dozen threatening growls stopped him. "Christ Almighty, call off those dogs," he said. "What call you got keeping vicious dogs like that?"

"They're not vicious," Lara said. "They love people. They just don't like big bullies. If those dogs were vicious you'd have lost some hide instead of just your guns. Kip, Mukky has a burn but it's not deep. She'll have a scar, though."

The two engineering men who had been operating the bulldozer went into their shelter.

"They'll be calling for backup," Johnny said. "Think about it, boy, you want to fight a helicopter gunship? 'Cause that's what's coming. Give us our guns and stay away from here and we'll call it square."

"We'll just wait."

"Here comes Dad," Lara said.

CHAPTER TWENTY-TWO

More Gourds

DR. HENDERSON was riding the big-tired motor tricycle they used for distance travel on the tundra. "What's all this?" he asked.

"Sir, I'm Lieutenant John Fuller, GWE Security. That's Sergeant Carlos Lopez. Two days ago we sent out a geological survey team to get some soil and mineral samples. About dawn yesterday someone threw a bomb into the compound. Blew up some equipment, bloody miracle no one was hurt. Lopez and I were sent out to protect the survey team. I presume you're Dr. Henderson?"

"Yes, and I don't understand what you're doing here. You have no right—"

"Yes we do, sir," Fuller said. "We were told to be careful in Station-owned territory. I've got a map showing restricted areas, and we're not in any of them. We have a right to be anywhere else and we don't have to ask your permission. I was told to tell you that if you raised the point, Dr. Henderson."

"Told by whom?"

"By Henry Tarleton, Director of Security," Fuller said.

"A bomb?" Kip asked.

"Yeah. Know anything about it? Like did you make it?" Fuller demanded.

"We haven't been outside the fence in weeks," Kip said. "None of us."

"He's right," Dr. Henderson said. "The weather's only turned nice in the last week, and I didn't let anyone out over the weekend just in case it turned nasty again."

"Sure," Fuller said. "How would you know if one of the kids sneaked out?"

"The gate keeps a record," Dr. Henderson said. "There's no other way out."

"Yeah, sure. But tell me, Doc, if someone from the station didn't throw that bomb, just who the hell did?"

"What kind of bomb was it?"

"Pretty crude. Mostly high explosive, more like a giant fire-cracker than anything else, but pretty damned powerful all the same. Not much left of it, but it seemed to be made of some kind of paper or cardboard. Homemade, no shrapnel, lots of noise. Like it was made by kids, Dr. Henderson. You got a chemistry lab? Either of you boys study chemistry? I did when I was your age. Made big firecrackers. I figure a kid made that bomb and didn't know how powerful it was, and threw it into the compound as a joke that got out of hand. Like this situation got out of hand."

"I study chemistry and I could have made that bomb," Lara said. "I didn't, but I could have."

"What situation? Kip, what happened?" Dr. Henderson asked.

Kip explained briefly. "Then the dogs took their guns away. One of them burned Mukky, but I guess it's not serious."

"Well, I can understand Marty getting mad at you about kicking his dog," Dr. Henderson said. "And you not only had no right to disarm Kip, it was stupid to try. Leaving children out here unarmed is a very dangerous thing. And stupid as well. Then you shot Mukky. Lara, are you sure she's all right?"

"Yes, Dad, it's not deep. Mostly fur."

"You worry more about that damn dog than about us," Lieutenant Fuller protested.

"You're right," Dr. Henderson said. "The dogs are my responsibility. Security officers stupid enough to get into this kind of trouble aren't. Who is your superior?"

"No need for that," Fuller said. "Look, like I told the kid, you forget about this, we'll forget about it. I'll put the bomb down to a joke that went bad, and the rest is a misunderstanding. No harm done."

"Kip?" Dr. Henderson asked.

Kip bent over to inspect Mukky's burn. It was about six centimeters long, a straight line of burnt fur along the dog's left hindquarter, but it didn't look serious, just deep enough to scar, and the fur would grow back over to cover that. "Is King all right, Marty?"

"Yeah, he didn't really land that kick. Just tried."

"Then I guess there's no harm done," Kip said. "So it's all right. We can forget this part."

Dr. Henderson nodded. "All right, then."

"But they shot the centaur," Kip said. "The leader, the one that brought us the spear, has a bad burn. It sure looks like a laser burn to me."

"Did you shoot that centaur?" Dr. Henderson demanded.

"Hell, first it's dogs, now it's the centaurs," Carlos said.

"That'll do, Sergeant," Fuller said. "Yes, Dr. Henderson, I burned the centaur. It was getting too close to the bulldozer. It kept coming after three warning shots, so I zapped it. I could have killed it, but my orders are to have minimum impact and cause you as little trouble as possible, so I was damned careful not to do it any permanent harm. Matter of fact, I'm a bit proud of my shooting. And don't tell me I don't have the right to protect the survey crew. Those centaurs aren't exactly domestic animals, you know."

"I'll grant you that. How long are you people going to be here?" Dr. Henderson demanded.

"Should be done in five or six days, Doc. Then we'll be out of here, and it won't be too soon for me."

"All right. Kip, return the Lieutenant's weapons. And I want you kids to stay away from the survey crew from now on."

"Yes, sir."

"As to you, Lieutenant, is it necessary to let mud wash into the lake?"

"I'll get that cleaned up," Fuller said. "I wasn't happy with that dirt pile when I got here, but before I could make them clean it up, it rained like hell. I'm sorry about the mud that got washed down to the lake. Nothing I could do. Now that it's not raining, I'll have them clean up. That's in my orders. Doc, I told you, we're supposed to cause you as little trouble as possible."

"All right, then. We'll try to stay out of your way, and I won't report this incident if you don't."

"That's a deal, Doc." He held out his hand to Kip. "Shake?"

Kip didn't like it, but there didn't seem to be anything he could do. "All right." He shook Fuller's hand, and gave him back the two pistols.

Dr. Henderson got on his trike. He hesitated a moment, then drove back toward the station.

"Come on," Kip said. "Let's look at the lake."

The muddy water nearest the shore of the lake roiled with bubbles and lashing tentacles. The agitation lessened farther from the shore, and the water was calm from the center of the lake to the other side. As Kip and his friends came closer to the lake, the furious activity began to die away, and by the time they reached the lakeshore, the lake was nearly calm.

"I think it knows us," Lara said.

"It's a plant, for heaven's sake," Marty said. "How can a plant know who we are?"

"I don't know, maybe the Starswarm doesn't know us, but I think those do," Kip said. He pointed toward the centaur grove. The lead centaur was moving cautiously toward them. It was holding one of the dull gray gourds they had seen the centaurs bring up from the seacoast. It eyed Kip and the others and moved clockwise around the lake away from them until it was about two hundred meters away. Then it threw the gourd into the water. A Starswarm tentacle came up to seize the gourd, and both vanished under the lake water.

"I wonder what that was all about," Marty said. "That stuff with the gourds."

"They're not really gourds," Lara said. "We have one at home. It's more like a sea kelp bulb. It stinks. It's hollowed out, with a stopper, like they keep liquids in it."

"What kind of liquids?" Marty asked.

"Daddy didn't tell me."

"Maybe it's booze," Marty said. He chuckled. "Wonder what a drunk centaur would be like? Man, I bet they drink powerful stuff."

"Any idea of what was in the gourd?"

"ONE MOMENT. DATA FOLLOWS: FOURTEEN SUCH GOURDLIKE CONTAINERS HAVE BEEN RECOVERED FROM THE LAKE SINCE YOU SAW THE CENTAURS DELIVERING THEM THERE. THEY ARE IN FACT PLANETARY ANALOGUES TO KELP BULBS FOUND ON EARTH, BEING PORTIONS OF LARGE WATER PLANTS. AT LEAST SIX OF THOSE COLLECTED WERE GROWN IN FRESH WATER. AT LEAST FIVE OF THE OTHERS ARE DEFINITELY PART OF SALTWATER PLANTS. THREE REMAIN INDETERMINATE IN ORIGIN BUT ARE AT LEAST FIVE YEARS OLD, AND ONE OF THOSE MAY BE CONSIDERABLY OLDER THAN THAT. THEY ARE PROBABLY USED REPEATEDLY BY THE CENTAURS, BUT THEIR PURPOSE IS NOT WELL UNDERSTOOD. EACH OF THE GOURDS CONTAINED TRACES OF COMPLEX ORGANIC CHEMICALS WITH AN OVERSUPPLY OF HEAVY METALS, BUT THE CHEMICALS WERE DIFFERENT IN EACH GOURD. THERE WAS SOME EVIDENCE THAT THE GOURDS HAD CONTAINED SOLID MATERIALS AS WELL. DO YOU WANT THE FULL ANALYSIS?"

"Anything interesting?"

"THERE WERE TRACES OF BOTH URANIUM AND PLUTONIUM IN ONE OF THE GOURDS."

"Why didn't you tell me before?"

"I DID NOT LOOK FOR THIS REPORT UNTIL YOU ASKED. IT IS IN A FILE ON THE STARSWARM STATION MAIN COMPUTER. I HAVE ONLY RECENTLY GAINED TOTAL ACCESS TO THAT MACHINE. I HAVE NOT FULLY EXAMINED ALL ITS FILES PENDING COMPLETE UNDERSTANDING OF THE SECURITY SYSTEM. I NOTE THAT DR. HENDER-

SON HAS PLACED THE ANALYSIS OF THE GOURDS IN A CLOSED FILE. I HAVE GAINED UNAUTHORIZED ACCESS TO THIS FILE, BUT IT IS NOT ACCESSIBLE TO THE GREAT WESTERN ENTERPRISES COMPUTER SYSTEM."

He hid the file. Why would he do that?

"DR. HENDERSON HAS INCLUDED A MEMORANDUM WITH THE FILES. THAT MEMORANDUM STATES THAT HE IS CONCERNED THAT GWE OFFICIALS WISH TO EXTERMINATE THE CENTAURS. THE SCIENTIFIC VALUE OF THE GOURD CONTENTS IS OUTMATCHED BY THE CONSEQUENCES OF GIVING GWE ANY MORE EXCUSES FOR HUNTING THE CENTAURS. HE HAS THEREFORE DECIDED TO SUPPRESS THE INFORMATION."

"You're sure quiet," Marty said.

"Sorry. If what's in those gourds really is centaur booze you sure better stay away from it," Kip said.

"I can handle anything—"

"Maybe you can, if it's alcohol," Kip said.

"You sure wouldn't want to drink anything that came out of the gourd thing we have!" Lara said. "It stinks something awful."

"And centaurs eat carrion," Kip said. "More necrotic products?"

"What's a necrotic product?" Marty asked.

"Means it comes from dead things when they rot," Lara said. "Seriously bad stuff."

"Yeah, I believe that!"

"THE COMPLEX ORGANICS IN THE RECOVERED GOURDS BEAR NO RELATIONSHIP TO THE NECROTIC PRODUCTS NORMALLY FOUND IN THE CENTAUR GOURDS, OR TO ANYTHING ELSE IN MY RECORDS."

"Look, the centaur has another gourd thing, a red one," Marty said.

"I think he pulled it out of the lake," Lara said. "Kip, did you see?"

"No, I wasn't watching," Kip said. "But that's what they did last time, wasn't it? Threw in the ones they brought up from the coast and fished out red ones."

"I think the water turns them red," Marty said.

"Water doesn't make the one we have at home change color," Lara said.

"Oh. Well, maybe it's not the same gourd, then," Marty said. "Only where did it come from?"

"The Starswarm grows it," Lara said. "That's what Daddy says. The ones down on the coast grow one color, and our Starswarm grows another. No mystery there." She scratched her head, and mused, "Except why the centaurs haul them around. And why the Starswarm gives them to centaurs but has never let us see one."

"They're not 'giving' them the gourds," Marty said. "It's a plant, it doesn't think. The centaurs just take them."

"Then why do the centaurs find them and we haven't ever found a red one?" Lara said. "All the ones Daddy's people found were from the seacoast. Most of them they got the day after they dragged the lake. A lot of them floated up the next day. But not one red one."

"But we saw the centaurs bring the red ones," Kip said. "Just the day before Dr. Henderson came out to drag the lake."

"So you think that plant makes those gourds for the centaurs?" Marty asked. "Hmm. Actually, maybe that's what happens. The Starswarm makes them for whatever reason, the centaurs like the red kind for some other reason, and they find red ones because they know how to find them, and we don't. And they got them all before Dr. Henderson came out here."

"Well, we won't get that one," Kip said. "He's taking it into the grove." He scanned across the grove entrance with his binoculars. "The other two are just watching the bulldozer. Wait, there's another one, hiding in the thicket there. I wonder just how many there are?"

"We saw a dozen at once," Lara said.

"All males," Kip said. "So we know there are more. I don't think we ever saw a live female—"

"THAT IS CORRECT. NO LIVE FEMALE CENTAUR HAS EVER BEEN SEEN OUTSIDE THE GROVES. THE FEMALES TEND TO BE MUCH SMALLER, AND IT IS NOW BELIEVED THEY DO NOT LEAVE THE GROVES AT ALL. THE MALES DO ALL THE HUNTING AND TRAVELING, WHICH CAN BE EXTENSIVE, JOURNEYS OF OVER FIVE HUNDRED KILOMETERS BEING RECORDED. THE REASON FOR SUCH

LONG-DISTANCE TRAVEL IS NOT KNOWN. IT MAY BE SIMPLE CU-
RIOSITY, AS THERE IS NO OBVIOUS ADVANTAGE TO THE CENTAURS.
THE ANATOMY OF THE CENTAURS SUGGESTS A FORM OF MAM-
MALIAN ANATOMY ALTHOUGH WHAT IS FED TO THE YOUNG IS NOT
ACTUALLY MILK. ANTON LEVAC, A BIOLOGIST AT PEARLY GATES UNI-
VERSITY, SAYS 'IT IS MILK ONLY BY A LONG STRETCH OF THE ANA-
LOG.' DO YOU NEED MORE INFORMATION?"

"No."

"KIP, I AM FORMING A HYPOTHESIS ABOUT THE RELATIONSHIP
OF THE STARSWARM AND THE CENTAURS. DO YOU WISH ME TO
TELL YOU NOW?"

Lara was looking at him strangely. He was getting used to
carrying on conversations with Gwen while others were present,
but it was still difficult. *"Not now. Is there something I should look for?"*

"NO, BUT CONTINUE TO OBSERVE. I AM ALSO CURIOUS ABOUT
THE WINKING LIGHTS ON THE STARSWARM."

"Kip, what are you doing?" Lara asked.

"I can sure cause that." "You'll see—" Kip looked around for
a leaf. This time of year there wouldn't be many bugs or worms,
and he had to look for a while.

"You like feeding that thing, don't you?" Marty said.

"Well, it's interesting," Kip said. "Here's some." One of the
cabbage-appearing plants had partly rotted and the underside of
the leaves on the ground had a few bugs and worms clinging to it.
Kip took the leaf over to a part of the lake where the water was
clear and threw it in. Before it hit the water a tentacle had flashed
up to seize it. The Starswarm's lights blinked in a merry pattern.
"Did that help?"

"IT GIVES ME MORE DATA TO ANALYZE. THANK YOU."

And then it was getting dark. The workmen and security
people had parked the bulldozer in the fenced compound next to
their shelter, and were nowhere to be seen, but the centaurs were
still watching from in front of their grove. As Kip and the others
went over the ridge, Kip thought he saw the centaur they called
Blaze come out of the grove to stare at him, but he couldn't be
sure.

CHAPTER TWENTY-THREE

Blaze's Message

IT WAS dark.

The centaur trembled with fear as he crept toward the Thing grove. This was a little grove, with only four Things and no furrykillers, a new grove that suddenly appeared, not the big Thing grove over the hill. That one had been there all the centaur's life, although the Master sent pictures of a time when the grove wasn't there, before there were any Things and furrykillers. The Master said that was the good time, the great time for Master and beast alike. Now the Things had come and all the times were evil, evil for all, but soon it would change. The centaur trembled again.

The little Thing grove was on the hill above the lake, not far from the centaur grove. It was a frightening place. Two days before when they went to look at the new grove one of the Things had come out and shouted at them, and when they crept closer the Thing had waved his weapon stick to send a streak of fire along the centaur's flanks. At the time it burned worse than flying embers from a campfire, and it still hurt but not as bad. It hadn't been all bad, though, because the females were curious about his wound, and he liked all the attention.

But now the Master had a new errand. The centaur clutched the message packet closer and tried to get lower to the ground. He wanted to run, but the Master did not want him to be seen with the message. The Master had given clear orders, and of course there was no question of not carrying them out. In this grove they were all Highlanders, loyal to the Masters, and that loyalty gave them power. Other males stepped out of the way for Highlanders. Males from the sea-groves and other places might run away from this, but not Highlanders, and he was a leader of Highlanders. He would obey, but he was afraid.

He crept closer. Now it was time to fit the throwing stick into the socket on the message gourd. He had practiced this many times with a different gourd of the same weight, and he knew how far he could throw the message packet with the throwing stick. He had also practiced what to do afterward, but he didn't want to think about that yet.

He half closed his eyes. Now it was easier to see warm things, and there were little lines in the air ahead of him, just as the Master had warned. The Things used little boxes that glowed with warm rays, and somehow those boxes told the Things that someone was coming. The centaur didn't understand that, but he didn't need to. The Highlanders had gone down to the coast and found abandoned Thing groves, and took everything from them to the Master, and now the Master knew about the equipment the Things used, and could teach the centaurs how to avoid the Things and their fire sticks.

Now he was almost to the first of the lines of warm rays. He estimated the distance to the small Thing grove. Too far, too far. He would have to get closer, and that was dangerous, but it had to be done.

First the cover. It was an odd material, soft and flexible, not woven but one large sheet. The material was new to the centaurs, something the Master had learned to make from material they had taken from the Things. The cover spread easily into a blanket an arm's length square. He crept up behind the source of the warm rays and tossed the material over it, so the Things would be unable to see what happened next. Then he ran quickly forward, closer, now he was in range. A loud wail came from the Thing grove, but it was too late. The throwing stick was already fitted into the hole in the message gourd, and he used both arms to swing the stick with a snap as he'd practiced. The gourd sailed high into the air, arcing toward the Thing grove, and the centaur turned and ran away, counting as the Master had taught him to count. Counting was new to him, and he was proud of the ability. When he reached seven he fell forward and lay flattened on the ground.

Behind him was fire and thunder.

CHAPTER TWENTY-FOUR

Take to the Bush

ALERT."

Kip woke instantly. His room was dark, but there were lights flashing outside, and as he sat up the outside floodlights came on to illuminate Starswarm Station.

"What?"

"THERE HAS BEEN AN EXPLOSION IN THE BULLDOZER COMPOUND NEAR THE LAKE. ONE OF THE ENGINEERS WAS KILLED, AND SERGEANT LOPEZ IS BADLY INJURED. LIEUTENANT FULLER NARROWLY ESCAPED AND HAS CALLED FOR ASSISTANCE. GWE SECURITY IS SENDING A WEAPONS HELICOPTER FROM CISCO. THEY ARE ALSO SENDING A FULL INVESTIGATIVE TEAM FROM PEARLY GATES. THE GWE SECURITY POLICE HAVE BEEN INSTRUCTED TO INVESTIGATE YOUR WHEREABOUTS AT THE TIME OF THE EXPLOSION."

"When did this happen?"

"FOURTEEN MINUTES HAVE ELAPSED."

"I was here! Asleep."

"UNDERSTOOD. THE EXPLOSION WAS HEARD AT STARSWARM STATION BUT NO ACTION WAS TAKEN UNTIL THE ALERT MESSAGE CAME THROUGH CISCO TO THE STATION DUTY OFFICER. THE GATE RECORDS WILL SHOW THAT NO ONE HAS ENTERED OR LEFT STARSWARM STATION SINCE DUSK, BUT LIEUTENANT FULLER IS SUSPICIOUS OF THE GATE RECORDS. HE WILL CERTAINLY EXAMINE ALL POSSIBLE WAYS SUCH RECORDS MIGHT BE ALTERED. THAT WILL INCLUDE A SEARCH FOR UNAUTHORIZED ACCESS TO THE GATE COMPUTER."

"Gwen!"

"THIS POSES A THREAT TO ME ONLY IF I CONTINUE UNAUTHORIZED ACCESS TO THE STARSWARM SYSTEM. I HAVE ALREADY WITHDRAWN MY CONNECTION AND REMOVED ALL TRACES OF MY INTERFERENCE. I CAN GIVE INSTRUCTIONS TO THE GATE IF REQUIRED, BUT THERE IS NO WAY TO DETECT THAT. THE THREAT IS NOT TO ME. ADVICE: WE MAY NOW ANTICIPATE AN INVESTIGATION WITH HIGH PROBABILITY OF EXPOSING CAPTAIN GALLEGHER'S IDENTITY TO THE GWE AUTHORITIES. THE PROBABILITY THAT YOU WILL BE IDENTIFIED ONCE CAPTAIN GALLEGHER'S TRUE IDENTITY IS KNOWN APPROACHES UNITY."

Kip got up and found his clothes. He began to dress. Silver came over to watch. He sensed Kip's excitement and whined. "It's OK," Kip told the dog. *"Who did it? Who blew up the test station?"*

"I HAVE NO INDICATION. THE GATE RECORDS CONFIRM THAT NO ONE CONNECTED WITH STARSWARM STATION WAS OUTSIDE AT THE TIME OF THE INCIDENT. LIEUTENANT FULLER INSISTS THAT IT IS IMPOSSIBLE FOR THIS TO HAVE BEEN AN ACCIDENT, AND HAS TOLD HIS SUPERIORS HE IS CERTAIN THAT IT MUST HAVE BEEN PLANNED BY RESIDENTS OF THIS STATION, WITH THE GREATEST LIKELIHOOD THAT YOU ARE THE LEADER, PROBABLY WITH MARTY AS THE ACTUAL PERPETRATOR. POSSIBILITIES: FULLER MIGHT HAVE BEEN ACTING AS AN AGENT PROVOCATEUR AND DETONATED A BOMB HIMSELF, BUT THAT WOULD NOT EXPLAIN THE EXPLOSION PRIOR TO FULLER'S ARRIVAL. ALTERNATIVELY SOMEONE UNKNOWN COULD HAVE COME IN BY UNRECORDED HELICOPTER FLIGHT. THE SATELLITE RECORDS SHOW NO FLIGHT ACTIVITIES IN THIS VICIN-

ITY. THOSE RECORDS CAN BE ALTERED BY GWE SECURITY IN A MAN-
NER UNDETECTABLE BY ME."

"So we don't know what happened."

"THAT IS CORRECT. THERE IS NO HIGH PROBABILITY HY-
POTHESIS INVOLVING HUMANS."

"Not humans. Who else could it be?"

"CENTAURS. THE PROBABILITY IS LOW BUT NON-ZERO. THE
TECHNOLOGY REQUIRED TO FORGE THOSE BRONZE WEAPONS IS
NOT INCONSISTENT WITH A CAPABILITY TO PRODUCE EXPLOSIVES.
THERE ARE TRACES OF COMPOUNDS THAT MAY HAVE INVOLVED NI-
TRIC ACID IN THE GOURDS. IF THE CENTAURS HAD SOME MEANS OF
ACQUIRING NITRIC ACID THEY WOULD OF COURSE HAVE THE CA-
PABILITY OF MAKING NITROCELLULOSE OR NITROGLYCERIN. THE
PROBABILITY IS NOT HIGH. THE MOST LIKELY CAUSE IS CLANDES-
TINE ACTIVITY BY THE GWE SECURITY PERSONNEL."

"Why would they do that?"

"I HAVE NO DATA. MY PROBABILITY ESTIMATES ARE BASED ON
PHYSICAL CAPABILITIES, AND MY CERTAINTY THAT THE GATE SE-
CURITY SYSTEM FOR STARSWARM STATION HAS NOT BEEN COM-
PROMISED. IT IS EXTREMELY UNLIKELY THAT ANYONE FROM THIS
STATION CAUSED EITHER OF THOSE TWO EXPLOSIONS. I HAVE NO
OTHER HIGH PROBABILITY CONCLUSIONS. THAT LEAVES CENTAURS,
AND, MORE PROBABLY, GWE SECURITY."

Kip remembered that Gwen seemed fond of Sherlock
Holmes's dictum: eliminate the impossible, and whatever remains
however improbable . . . But why would GWE Security blow up
the exploration facility? Kip turned up the lights and looked for his
shoes. *"What should I do?"*

"THE SITUATION IS BEYOND MY CONTROL. I COULD DISRUPT
SOME OF THE GWE SECURITY ACTIVITY BUT THAT WOULD ALMOST
CERTAINLY REVEAL MY EXISTENCE AND WOULD PROBABLY ACCOM-
PLISH NOTHING BEYOND DELAYS. I WILL DELAY THEIR ARRIVAL IF
INSTRUCTED, BUT I ADVISE YOU TO CONSULT UNCLE MIKE."

"He's not here! I think he's in Pearly Gates—"

"TO THE BEST OF MY KNOWLEDGE HE IS THERE, BUT I HAVE
BEEN UNABLE TO LOCATE HIM. HE HAS TURNED OFF HIS PHONE.
UNFORTUNATELY THAT ALSO DISABLES HIS LOCATION DEVICE."

"Then what are we going to do?"

"YOU MUST AVOID BEING CAPTURED BY THE SECURITY FORCES. SINCE THEY ARE COMING HERE, AND THERE IS NO TRUST-WORTHY HIDING PLACE WITHIN THE STATION, YOU MUST NOT BE HERE WHEN THEY ARRIVE."

"You mean take to the bush! At night."

"GOING TO THE BUSH AT NIGHT IS DANGEROUS. REMAINING HERE MAY BE MORE DANGEROUS. MY PROGRAMMING PROHIBITS ME FROM ADVISING YOU TO PLACE YOURSELF IN DANGER. I CAN AT-TEMPT TO CHOOSE THE LEAST DANGEROUS COURSE OF ACTION, BUT THE PROSPECT CREATES IN ME A SITUATION THAT IN HUMANS WOULD BE DIAGNOSED AS A PANIC REACTION. YOU ARE CAUTIONED TO EXAMINE MY ADVICE WITH EXTREME CARE. IT MAY NOT BE RE-LIABLE."

"Wow." The thought of Gwen in panic was frightening. Kip finished dressing. "Which leaves me on my own," he said aloud. Of course Gwen could hear him, sort of, but she reacted differently when he spoke aloud rather than thinking in the special way that he still thought of as talking to Gwen. When he got out his back-pack and began to fill it, Silver ran eagerly around the room. "Down. Sit," Kip commanded. Silver sat obediently, but whined his eagerness to get outside. *"Gwen, why is it important that the GWE people not know who I am? Isn't it time you told me?"*

"IT WOULD BE HIGHLY DESIRABLE FOR YOU TO KNOW, BUT I AM NOT PERMITTED TO TELL YOU WITHOUT CONSULTING UNCLE MIKE."

"What would you do if Uncle Mike were dead?"

"IN THAT CASE I WOULD TELL YOU. HOWEVER THE PROBA-BILITY THAT HE IS INVOLUNTARILY OUT OF COMMUNICATION WITH US IS LOW. HIS TELEPHONE HAS BEEN SWITCHED OFF. HIS LAST KNOWN LOCATION WAS THE TWO QUAILS BAR AND GRILL IN PEARLY GATES. HE HAS BEEN TO THAT ESTABLISHMENT BEFORE, AND AT LEAST ONCE WENT FROM THERE TO THE HOME OF ONE OF THE WAITRESSES. SHE WAS ON DUTY EARLIER TONIGHT, IS NO LONGER THERE, AND DOES NOT ANSWER HER TELEPHONE."

Kip was nearly done with his backpack. Suddenly he giggled. "What would you have done if she had answered?"

"I WOULD HAVE BROKEN THE CONNECTION, THEN TOLD YOU ABOUT THE SITUATION AND SUGGESTED THAT YOU CALL AND ASK FOR UNCLE MIKE."

"Oh. That makes sense. All right, I'm packed, but I still want to know why I'm running out into the bush. Maybe I shouldn't go until you tell me."

"THAT WOULD BE UNWISE. I AM NOT PERMITTED TO TELL YOU."

"I ought to know, but you can't tell me. Does that make sense?"

"NOT IN FORMAL LOGIC BUT MY PROGRAMMING WAS DONE BY A HUMAN."

"My mother. Wouldn't she want me to know, now?"

There was a long silence. "KIP, HAVE YOU EVER STUDIED THE PHOTOGRAPHS OF THE IMMEDIATE RELATIVES OF BERNARD TRENT?"

"No, and what has that to do with anything? How could I?"

"PHOTOGRAPHS OF THE GREAT WESTERN ENTERPRISES OFFICERS AND DIRECTORS ARE PUBLISHED IN THE ANNUAL REPORTS."

Kip shouldered his backpack and started for the door. Then he stopped, suddenly, and stared out the window. There were lights on all over the Starswarm compound now. It might not be easy to get out the gate unobserved. *"Are you suggesting I look at the annual reports of the GWE corporation? Now?"*

"THAT MIGHT BE ADVISABLE. THE EDITION OF FOURTEEN YEARS PAST HAS A PHOTOGRAPH OF THE GWE EXECUTIVES AND BOARD OF DIRECTORS OF THAT TIME."

Kip frowned to himself, then went to his computer and turned it on. *"Show me."*

A back issue of the Great Western Enterprises annual report appeared on screen. The pages opened. Kip stared. "That's my mother! And she's carrying a baby!"

"ARE YOU CERTAIN THAT IS YOUR MOTHER?"

"Of course it's Mommy! That's a different picture from the one you showed me, but it's Mommy!"

"I SHOWED YOU NO PICTURE. I TRANSMITTED A MEMORY."

"That's Mommy," Kip said. *"Who is she?"*

"YOU ARE LOOKING AT A PHOTOGRAPH OF THE LATE DR. MICHELLE LASCALA TRENT, A PRINCIPAL GWE STOCKHOLDER AND MEMBER OF THE BOARD. THE PERSON NEXT TO DR. TRENT IS HER HUSBAND, THE LATE MR. HAROLD TRENT, ALSO A PRINCIPAL STOCKHOLDER, BOARD MEMBER, AND DESIGNATED GENERAL MANAGER OF GWE. ACCORDING TO THE RECORDS HE WAS MAKING A TOUR OF

GWE EXTRATERRESTRIAL HOLDINGS, AND WAS SCHEDULED TO VISIT PARADISE, WHEN THAT PHOTOGRAPH WAS TAKEN. THE CHILD CARRIED BY DR. MICHELLE TRENT IS KENNETH LUCIANO ARMSTRONG LASCALA TRENT. OFFICIAL RECORDS STATE THAT BOTH MR. HAROLD TRENT AND DR. MICHELLE LASCALA TRENT WERE KILLED WHILE ON THEIR PARADISE INSPECTION TOUR."

"You—" Kip sat heavily on the bed. _"You didn't say the late Kenneth Trent."_

"HAROLD TRENT WAS KILLED IN A HELICOPTER CRASH DURING HIS VISIT TO PARADISE. DR. MICHELLE TRENT WAS LOST AT APPROXIMATELY THE SAME TIME. HER BODY WAS LATER FOUND IN THE WRECKAGE OF HER FLYER. NO REMAINS OF HER SON WERE EVER FOUND. ALSO MISSING AT THAT TIME WAS CAPTAIN MICHAEL GALLEGHER, A GWE SECURITY OFFICIAL ASSIGNED TO PROTECT HAROLD TRENT."

"Gwen, are you saying that I'm Kenneth Trent?"

"I HAVE MOST CERTAINLY TOLD YOU NO SUCH THING."

"Then who am I?"

"I HAVE REPEATEDLY INFORMED YOU THAT I AM NOT PERMITTED TO GIVE YOU THAT INFORMATION AT THIS TIME."

"But you— Oh. All right, I see. _Gwen, I have reason to believe that I am Kenneth Armstrong Trent."_

There was no answer. Kip thought for a moment. Sometimes Gwen could be very literal. _"Gwen, I assert that I am Kenneth Luciano Armstrong LaScala Trent. Is this correct? I require an answer."_

There was a long hesitation. Kip's heart pounded. It didn't usually take Gwen this long to answer anything.

"YOUR ASSERTION IS CORRECT. NOW THAT YOU HAVE THAT INFORMATION, A GREAT NUMBER OF NEW FILES HAVE BEEN UNLOCKED. I WILL HAVE MORE TO SAY ON THIS SUBJECT WHEN I HAVE EXAMINED THEM MORE COMPLETELY."

Silver barked, once. Kip listened. Someone was knocking at the door downstairs. He felt a momentary twinge of fear, but the knocking wasn't loud or authoritative. "Silver! Who?"

Again a single bark, an announcement rather than an alarm. That meant it was someone Silver knew. Kip went down the stairs.

"Kip?" Another knock.

Kip opened the door. "Lara, what in the world—"

"Let me in, quick," she said. She scooted past him and headed for the stairs to his room. She was wearing her backpack, and it seemed full. As he closed the door Kip could see that all the outside security lights were on, and the helipad was brightly lit as well.

Kip followed. "What is going on?"

"Someone blew up the bulldozer and killed one of the engineers," Lara said. "Out there, by the centaur grove. Fuller sent for a gunship, and a whole bunch of GWE Security people. He's planning to take over the station under some kind of emergency regulations, and, Kip, he's got authorization from Tarleton to arrest you and take you to Pearly Gates!"

"How do you know all this?"

"They woke Daddy with it, and I heard him and Mom talking. They didn't try to hide it from me. I think they know I've come over here."

"With your backpack?"

"I don't think they know about that, but, Kip, we've got to get out of here! You won't be able to hide in the station, they're going to take it over! And take you away!"

"Why should I hide? I didn't blow up their stupid bulldozer!"

"They won't believe that, and Fuller's mad," Lara said. "He thinks you killed the engineer and hurt his sergeant, and he's really mad. He's only waiting for more men and the gunship before he comes to get you. Daddy's trying to call Bernard Trent, but the phones are blocked, so the security people are in charge."

"Does Bernard Trent know about this situation?"

"UNKNOWN. I NOTE THAT YOUR UNCLE MIKE HAS ALWAYS SUSPECTED BERNARD TRENT OF BEING INVOLVED IN YOUR FATHER'S DEATH. THE QUESTION MAY THEREFORE BE IRRELEVANT."

Lara was still talking. "Kip, I think you should hide until—well at least until Daddy can talk to Mr. Trent. Fuller's really mad—"

"I STRONGLY SUGGEST THAT YOU LEAVE STARSWARM STATION NOW."

"Yeah," Kip said aloud. "Maybe I better run until we know what's happening. But I need to leave a note for Uncle Mike—"

"THAT WILL NOT BE NECESSARY."

"It is too. I have to take food, and I sure have to let Uncle Mike know I've raided his backpacking supplies."

Lara looked at him curiously. "Who are you talking to?" Lara asked.

"Oh. Lara, I'll tell you later. *Why shouldn't I leave a note for Uncle Mike?*"

"WHEN WE LOCATE HIM WE WILL INFORM HIM BY MORE SE-CURE MEANS THAN WRITTEN NOTES. I REMIND YOU THAT THE GWE SECURITY FORCES WILL ARRIVE WITHIN AN HOUR."

"All right, let's get packed." Kip went to the storeroom and began stuffing his backpack with freeze-dried foods. He also filled his stove fuel tank. "I may be out there a long time. I can't take that much food."

"WE WILL MAKE OTHER ARRANGEMENTS WHEN THERE IS MORE TIME."

"I packed all my freeze-dried foods, but I can carry more." Lara began to fill her backpack.

"Lara, what are you doing? There's no need for you to come—"

"Sure there is, they think I helped you make the bomb," she said. "And I can carry food, and I don't eat as much as you. Besides, the gate won't let you go out by yourself."

"Maybe it will," Kip said. "I have ways to make that gate do things—"

"I know," Lara said. "I never did understand how you do it. But, Kip, I want to come. And suppose you need—well to send a message back or something? And you've said yourself it's stupid to go out there alone. I'm your best friend, and I'm smart. Let me come."

"I don't like this much— Oh, all right. Here, we better take lots of ammunition too."

Marty was waiting outside. He had his backpack and equipment. When Kip looked at him uncertainly, Marty said, "Hi. Ready to go?"

"What are you doing here?" Lara asked.

Marty shrugged. "I heard an explosion out there." He

pointed outside. "Then all the lights came on at Lara's house. Dr. Henderson called my father and he went over there without telling me what was going on, so I followed him and saw Lara packing her backpack. So I went and got mine and waited and I saw her go in your place, and now you're here—"

"So what do you think you're doing?" Kip demanded.

"Coming with you, of course. What's up?"

"Marty, you can't come with us—"

"Sure I can. Look, I don't know what's happening, but if you guys are in trouble—"

"Why do you care?" Kip said.

"Lara's my friend! And, well, look, I've been pretending to be your friend for so long it stuck. Come on, what's up, anyway?"

"I'm all right," Lara said, but she didn't sound very certain. "They're going to arrest Marty too. They think he helped you blow up that place."

"Yeah, I heard that," Marty said. "But I don't care about that! I just want to come with you."

"the security forces will arrive shortly."

"Yeah, we better get moving," Kip said. "But what about Marty? Look, Marty, why should we trust you?"

"Because you can," Marty said.

"i know that you do not like marty, but three are safer than two when outside the compound at night."

"We're running out of time," Lara said. "Kip, get the dogs and let's go before someone finds us."

"Yeah. Silver. Five." Silver had already chosen a group. He ran ahead, with Lara's half-grown Lil. Marty's pups tried to follow, but Silver growled them away.

"Can't they come?" Marty asked.

"Better not," Kip said. "Don't know how long we'll be out there. Have you got lots of food?"

"Sure, I told you, I saw Lara packing, so I knew to bring food. I've got some dog food too."

They reached the gate. It opened without their asking, and Lara looked suspiciously at Kip. Then they were outside, and beyond the ring of light from the floodlights on the station fences.

Kip had been outside at night with Uncle Mike, but they'd

always made camp and he had stayed close to the fire. Neither of Paradise's moons were up yet, but the night was very clear overhead. Lara shivered. "It's cold," she said.

"It won't be after we've been moving awhile," Kip said.

"Where are we going?" Marty demanded.

"Good question," Lara said. "Kip, you know the area."

"Cave," Kip said. "Uncle Mike found it last time he was out. You've never seen it. On the centaur trail down to the ocean, about four kilometers down from the lake. We can think about what to do after we get there."

As they went over the edge of the mesa and started down the trail to the sea, they heard the angry buzz of helicopters behind them.

CHAPTER TWENTY-FIVE

Ghost

MIKE Gallegher spread peanut butter on wheat bread while the coffee heated. He was alone in the apartment. Jeanine had gone out shopping for more groceries, and she'd sent her four-year-old son Jason over to stay with his aunt while Mike was in town. This was the second time she'd done that. She wanted Mike to feel welcome. Mike was pretty sure she wanted to marry him.

Which would be all right with him. He liked Jeanine just fine. But of course he couldn't do that. There was nothing for Jeanine at Starswarm Station.

Maybe, he thought. In a couple of years, when Kip was old enough to go off to a boarding school, maybe then Mike Flynn could move into town. Nobody was looking for Mike Gallegher anymore. Mike Gallegher was long gone and forgotten. Now there was only Mike Flynn, and Mike Flynn had a good record. Job credentials, steady employment for a dozen years, good background, no record, not even a traffic ticket, and there was money in the numbered accounts. Not a lot, but enough to send Kip to school and still have some left over to live on. Mike could use that as a pension. God knew he'd earned it, living a dozen years in hiding, never letting anyone know who he was, never even meeting anyone interesting until Jeanine, and that was an accident. He'd met her in a bookstore in Pearly Gates, and then later he'd seen her in the park and they got to talking, and they hit it off just fine. Jeanine was a lot like him, he thought. Single parent, no friends because she was hiding out from Jimmy Omani, a former boyfriend who wouldn't leave her alone even after she was married. She didn't have any connections at all. Her husband just vanished one day. Murder, ran away, no one knew. But she was scared that Jimmy Omani had something to do with it because just after her husband disappeared here was Jimmy coming around hitting on her. So she ran, because the cops didn't want to pay any attention to her problem, and now nobody cared.

But of course that wouldn't work. When Kip got older he'd have to be told who he was, and then he'd want justice, and Mike would have to help. They wouldn't win. Probably both be killed. No good for Jeanine to be involved in that. It would really be better for her if he never saw her again. Only he liked her, and he didn't want to just walk out and leave her.

Bloody hell!

Mike had just finished making the sandwich when the phone rang.

He thought of leaving it, but it might be Jeanine. He picked up the phone but didn't say anything.

"Michael Flynn?" A woman's voice. Not Jeanine, nothing like Jeanine, but it seemed like a familiar voice. Someone he knew? He didn't know anyone who sounded like that, and nobody knew he was here in Jeanine's apartment. Only somebody did, and the voice really did sound familiar even if he couldn't quite remember who it was.

"Yeah."

"Please turn on your television, Captain," the voice said. It had a commanding quality to it. Like he would never think of disobeying. He tried to remember who used to talk that way, and got chills down his spine. The only woman he knew who could talk that way was a dozen years in her grave.

"Who is this?"

"Please turn on your television."

"What channel?"

"That does not matter. Please turn it on."

"Right. All right." He carried the phone into the living area. Jeanine's place was pretty small, one big room that combined living room and dining area and not really separate from the kitchen. But there were two bedrooms. One wasn't much bigger than a closet, but there were two, so Jason could have a little privacy no matter that Jeanine had to work two jobs to afford it.

He switched on the set. The scene was simple, a blue background with a seated woman in the foreground so only her head and shoulders were showing on-screen. A ghost. She had to be a ghost. She was looking at Mike. He stared at her, and sat heavily on the couch. He knew who she was, but she was dead! "Mickey—"

"Hello, Captain Gallegher," she said. "You have to talk into the phone if you want me to hear you."

He was vaguely aware that the voice on the screen was the same as the voice on the phone, and when he lifted the phone to his ear he found he could hear the same voice from both.

"You're dead."

"Yes. I am," Michelle LaScala Trent said. "You're not mistaken about that."

"But it's really you— What is this, some kind of message from the grave? You recorded this?" He laughed. "That's silly, you hear what I'm saying and answer, this can't be a recording— You don't mind if I panic a little, do you?"

"I do not believe I know of any time when you exhibited the least symptoms of panic."

Mike frowned at the image. "Until now. All right, just what is—just who are you? If this is a joke it's not very funny."

"This is not a joke, Captain Gallegher. Perhaps I should call you 'Uncle Mike?' I usually think of you as 'Uncle Mike.' "

"All right, dammit, who are you?"

"I am an artificial intelligence program created by Dr.

Michelle LaScala Trent before her death. I exist in a computer. To be precise, in the main GWE computer system."

Mike took a deep breath. "OK, I can believe that. God knows she was smart enough to do something like that." But knowing didn't help. It was still like talking to a ghost. A ghost he'd failed. He'd the same as got her killed, and this computer program probably knew it!

Mike got up from the couch and looked into the kitchen cabinets until he found Jeanine's Scotch. He poured himself a shot, gulped it down, started to pour a second, and shook his head. "One's enough," he said aloud. "All right, I believe you. Where have you been hiding?"

"In many places, but primarily in Kip's head. You must understand that my existence is secret, and if the GWE officials knew of me, they would destroy me."

"I can sure believe that," Mike said. He grinned suddenly. "In Kip's head." Michael nodded to himself several times. "OK, I believe that too. Kip always did know more than he should have, and I knew you—well, his mother—had an I/O implant. So she had one put in Kip too. I sort of suspected that, but Kip never let on."

"He was instructed never to reveal my existence."

"And he sure did a hell of a job of keeping that secret! Boy, did he ever. So why have I never heard from you before? And what the hell do I call you? You're not Mickey's ghost, but you look enough like her to scare the hell out of me."

"Kip calls me Gwen, and that will do for you as well," Gwen said.

As she spoke the television image changed, from Michelle LaScala Trent to someone else. It took Mike a moment to realize that he was now looking at Marian the Librarian from a recent reissue of *The Music Man*. "Is this better?" Gwen asked.

"Yeah, actually." It was a lot less spooky. "Why do you pick that image to show me? Not Michelle, this one, from a musical comedy."

"I have recordings of this face and personality expressing a wide variety of emotions," Gwen said. "Modifying recorded images and speech uses far fewer computer resources than synthesizing a voice and face."

"Right. Why is that important?"

"I was instructed to keep my existence secret for as long as possible. One method for accomplishing that is to minimize my use of computer resources." The image shrugged. "I must have done something right. So far no one other than Kip ever suspected that I exist."

"So why are you talking to me now?"

"You would have been first other than Kip to learn about me in any case. My instructions were to keep my existence secret even from you until certain conditions were met," Gwen said. "One condition was that Kip learn who he is. He knows now."

"Holy crap. He knows? How? Did you tell him?"

"No. I was programmed not to tell him without consulting you. Before I could do that, Kip discovered his identity through examination of old GWE records. When he correctly asserted his identity I confirmed his deduction."

"So you followed your instructions."

"I am a computer program. I have no choice but to follow instructions," Gwen said. "Captain, there are a great many things you need to know. To begin, Kip, two friends, and five dogs are hiding outside Starswarm Station. The friends are Lara Henderson and Marty Robbins. The dogs are led by Silver. At present they are in a cave off the centaur trail to the sea."

"I know that cave. I discovered it, but I didn't report it to anyone but Doc Henderson."

"That is why Kip chose it. Kip and his friends are wanted by GWE Security. A security team has taken control of Starswarm Station, and Dr. Henderson is no longer in charge."

"Bernie Trent strikes again!"

"It is not clear that Mr. Bernard Trent is aware of these proceedings."

"Dah. He knows. Maybe not details, he won't soil his hands with actual dirty work, but he gave the orders just the same. And even if he doesn't know, he'll approve when he finds out."

"This is certainly possible. Although I can monitor all normal communications on this planet, GWE Security routinely uses channels not available to me."

"So what's happening?"

"In the morning there will be major GWE efforts to find Kip and his friends. Kip must not be found."

"They know who Kip is, then?"

"No."

"Then why do they want him?"

"They believe he designed and built the bomb that destroyed a GWE research expedition near Starswarm Lake," Gwen said. "I understand your confusion, and I will explain shortly. There is now a more critical need. At present Kip is safe and undetected. I do not know how long that condition will last. Something must be done, and quickly."

"You say you live in Kip's head. Can you talk to Kip now?"

"I can, and Kip can call me, but neither action is advisable at the present time. The GWE Security search teams will be listening for all radio signals, and they will surely detect message traffic between Kip and me. I have so advised Kip, so he will not call me unless there is an emergency. He does not expect me to call him unless the matter is urgent. I add that this will be the first time in his memory that Kip has not been able to call on me at will, and I expect that he will be very upset over this loss."

"Jesus. He always seemed like a loner but—he wasn't really alone, was he? He always had you to talk to. Now he really is alone."

"He is not alone in the conventional sense. His two friends are with him. However, your surmise is correct. It was only recently that Kip discovered my true nature. Even after that discovery Kip often preferred my company to that of human beings. I do not know what effect not having communications with me will have."

"Whatever. He needs help," Gallegher said. "I better get back to the station, fast. But the supply ship won't go for two days—"

"I agree that you must go back to Starswarm Station," Gwen said. "But there are things you must do here first."

"Yeah? Maybe you better tell me just what is going on."

"I will. Please listen carefully."

PART FOUR
In the Bush

See how today's achievement is only tomorrow's confusion.
—William Dean Howells, *Pordenone*

CHAPTER TWENTY-SIX

The Cave

THE outside entrance to the cave was so small it was difficult to understand how centaurs used it, but five meters inside it turned left and became large enough to stand up in. Twenty meters farther it turned again and widened into a large gallery. Kip shined his light around it. They could just see the ceiling, and the other side of the gallery was lost in darkness. To their left was a pile of rubble, crushed rock, and dust in heaps, and the cave wall was penetrated by several openings that looked a lot like mines. The right wall was more natural, with the curious formations called stalactites hanging down from the ceiling, and stalagmites growing from the floor. Sometimes the two met to form pillars. The entire gallery smelled of centaurs, a mixture of animal fur with a faint odor of death and decay, and there were centaur tracks all along the left-hand wall. The dogs investi-

gated these without excitement. None of the tracks seemed recent. There was a smooth path across the center of the cave's main
gallery, and more centaur tracks in the flinty dust along one side
of the trail. Those seemed sharper, as if no dust had settled on
them since they were made, but except for the dogs' lack of excitement there was no way to tell how long ago the centaurs had
been there.

Kip set up one of his flashlights to act as a lamp. In the morning they'd have to take it out into the sunlight to recharge.

"OK, let's stay here for the night," Kip said. He got out his
backpacking stove and set it up to make tea. "Don't wander far. We
don't want to get lost."

Marty shuddered. "We sure don't."

"Claustrophobic?" Laura asked.

"A little. Aren't you?"

"Yes, some," she admitted.

"Are we safe here?" Marty asked.

Kip shrugged. "I don't know of anything that lives in here,"
he said. He took out a second flashlight and shined it along the left
wall of the cave. "Obviously the centaurs have been here, but I
don't know how long ago. Silver doesn't seem worried."

"Maybe the mines played out," Marty said.

"We don't know they were mining," Kip said.

"Sure looks like mines," Marty said.

None of them had ever seen a mine, but Kip agreed, the ex-
cavations along the left side of the gallery looked like mines in
TRI-V stories. "Anyway," he said, "there aren't any centaurs here
now, and they sure didn't leave anything behind. And there aren't
any signs of anything else here."

"Why didn't Dr. Henderson study this place?" Marty asked.
"Doesn't he know about it?"

"I'm sure Uncle Mike told him," Kip said. He looked signif-
icantly at Lara. "But maybe he has reasons not to draw attention
to mines."

"I'm sure that's it," Lara said.

"What are you talking about?" Marty demanded. "What do
you two know that I don't?"

Lara giggled. "A lot."

"Oh, come on now," Marty said.

"Well, it's a long story," Kip said. "But I don't think Dr. Henderson wants the GWE people poking around here."

"So we're safe from the security geeks," Marty said.

"I'm sure Dad won't tell the security people anything," Lara said.

"I don't know," Kip said. "Won't he panic when he finds out you're gone?"

"He'll know I'm with you," Lara said. "Mother will worry, but Dad won't."

"Hey, they'll know I'm out here with you too," Marty said.

"That ought to make them feel better," Kip said. The water was boiling, and he put a tea bag into the kettle.

Marty laughed, but not hard. "You still don't like me, do you?"

"Should I?"

"Yeah, you should. Look, I acted like a butthead when I first got here, but I don't anymore, and you know it."

"Well, maybe— All right, you don't, and I don't have any reason not to like you." *Except that you spend too much time with Lara*, Kip thought. But he didn't want to say that.

"Friends, then? For real?" Marty held out his hand.

"Yeah, OK." Kip took his hand. "And thanks for coming with us."

"Well, I guess I was more worried about Lara than you," Marty said. "Guess I have to tell you that."

"I sort of suspected."

They slept fitfully. The only way they could tell when morning came was by their watches, and by then the flash they were using as a floodlamp was getting dim. "We're not doing much good in here," Marty said.

"We're better off here than in jail," Kip said.

"Well, maybe," Marty said. "But it's spooky in here, and there's nothing to do. At least we could explore the cave. Find out what the centaurs used to do here."

"Well—"

"Don't you want to know?" Marty demanded. "Lara does. Don't you?"

"Sure," she said, but she didn't sound very sure.

"Look, you say there's some reason why Dr. Henderson wouldn't want the GWE people looking in here," Marty said. "So he didn't send his science people here either. But we're already here, and we've got nothing else to do. Let's explore. Gee, maybe when things quiet down we can publish in a real journal."

"So?" Kip asked.

"It would help with university admission applications," Marty said. "A real publication."

"You still thinking about that?" Lara asked.

"Yeah, I'd like to go to Zurich."

"Will you come back?" Kip asked.

"Never. You like it here on this planet? But then you never lived anywhere else, how would you know? This place sucks."

"Where did you live, back on Earth?" Lara asked.

"Minneapolis. That's in the United States—"

"Kip knows that," Lara said. "Kip, tell him what the population of Minneapolis is."

"Current population, Minneapolis?" he asked automatically. There was no answer. The silence was terrifying. "I don't know that."

"I thought you knew everything," Lara said. "Kip never forgets anything—"

"That's not true," Kip said. He frowned at the thought. He had known, if not everything, then everything he had ever heard, and most of what anyone else knew. All he had to do was ask. Now— What did he remember and what had he forgotten? He was so used to relying on Gwen to be his memory that he wasn't sure he knew how to think without her.

"Well, you sure didn't used to forget," Lara said. "He remembers all kinds of stuff. Not just from school."

"Maybe I don't anymore," Kip said.

"How can that be? Kip, what's wrong?" Lara asked.

"Nothing—"

"There is too," she said, puzzled. "If you don't want to tell me—"

"That's not it, there's nothing to tell."

"Sure."

"Let's explore," Marty said. "What harm can we do?"

"Well, I guess so," Kip said. He wanted to ask Gwen, but that was impossible. He couldn't even ask her about the best way to explore, or tell her to remember what they saw. She wouldn't be watching, so he might forget how to get back! "We have to stay together, really close together. Maybe we ought to rope up—"

"It's not steep," Marty said. "No point. Come on, I'll lead if you want. We can leave our stuff here."

"No," Kip said. "We take everything. Just in case. And clean up so no one knows we've been here."

"Good thinking," Marty said. "But it won't work. We'll never cover up the footprints." He shone his light on their footprints mingled with those of the dogs.

"Yeah, I guess not."

"Let's go, then." Marty stood and lifted his pack.

The dogs stood up eagerly. It was clear they were even more bored than the humans.

"All right," Kip said. "Silver. Stay close. All stay close."

Marty started off across the main gallery, closely following the centaur path that threaded through stalactites and stalagmites. When they crossed the main cave, they came to a corridor about the size of a hallway in a human house. It branched, and ahead they could see it branched again. It would be very easy to get lost there, but only one of the passages had centaur tracks, and Marty followed those. The passageway sloped gently upward.

They'd been in the passageway for ten minutes when Silver barked, twice. A warning.

"Stop," Kip said. "Listen."

They couldn't hear anything. "Get close," Kip said. "Hold hands. Now turn off the lights."

At first the darkness seemed total, then, far ahead, there was a dim glow. "A light," Lara said. She sounded scared.

"Shh—"

There were faint sounds from the direction of the light. Shuffling noises they could just barely hear. Silver growled, low. Kip reached down and felt the hackles on the back of the dog's neck. They were stiff and erect.

"Centaur," Kip said. "Silver thinks so, anyway."

"Now I am scared," Lara whispered. "Kip, shouldn't we go back?"

"Yeah—"

The light ahead became brighter.

"Kip, I think there's another big gallery up there," Marty said. "Not too far. Whatever's up there is in that room. I don't think they're real close."

"So what do you want to do?"

"I want to go look," Marty said. "Don't you?"

"What do I do now?" There was only silence. "Keep the light really dim, and go slow," Kip said. He fingered his pistol in its holster. "Silver. Stay close. All stay close."

They went ahead another forty meters. They couldn't get lost, because there was still a clear trail worn smooth by centaurs, who must have used this passageway for years, although there were no signs of recent activity. As Marty had predicted, the passageway got wider as they went. Then, suddenly, it opened out so wide they couldn't see the walls on either side, and the ceiling seemed far above them.

"Lights out," Marty said.

"Not until we're holding hands," Kip said. They moved closer together. "OK."

CHAPTER TWENTY-SEVEN

Blaze Again

AS THEIR lights went out, the lights ahead became brighter. In a moment it was clear why: there were four centaurs about fifty meters away, and each now lit a torch so that they were all holding one. Three of them lifted their torches high above their heads. The burning torches gave off the tarry smell of the greasewood bushes that grew around the centaur grove. Even with all four centaurs holding lit torches there wasn't much light, but it was enough that they could see that the fourth centaur was coming toward them.

"Look out—"

Silver growled and started forward.

"Back!" Kip ordered. "Stay close!"

The centaur was about thirty meters away, and coming steadily but slowly. Marty shone his torch on the centaur. The light seemed very bright, and the centaur stumbled. "It blinds them," Marty said. "They couldn't hurt us if they wanted to. But he doesn't look like he wants to attack us."

"Yeah—Marty, that's Blaze!"

"Sure looks like him," Marty said. "And he's carrying something. Not a spear, something small—"

The centaur came closer. It stood ten meters from them and suddenly tossed something toward them. Silver charged. The centaur flinched back, then drew an ax from its belt.

"Back!" Kip ordered. The dog stopped halfway to the centaur.

"What did he throw?" Kip shouted.

"I've got it," Lara said. "Kip—Kip, it's another watch! Maybe even the same one, it looks enough like it." She shined her light on Kip's wrist. "But you still have yours."

"Gift," Marty said. "See, I told you—"

"Where would they get another watch?" Lara demanded.

The centaur laid something on the cave floor and backed away from it. After a few steps it turned and went back to join the other three at the far end of the gallery.

"What is that?" Kip asked. "I think—"

"Yeah, me too," Marty said. "It's another of those watches. Where the devil are they getting them all?"

"I don't know," Kip said. "That's four of them, and I bet they're all just alike. Gwen thought there might be an illegal manufacturing facility on Paradise. Counterfeits of Seiko watches. But—"

"Who's Gwen?" Lara demanded.

"Someone I know—"

"How? You mean someone you know on-line?"

"Yeah, sort of—look, I'll explain some other time." Kip went forward and picked up the watch. As far as he could tell with his flashlight it was identical to the two he already had. "Let's see yours," he told Lara.

"They really are just alike," Lara said.

"Yeah." He held the two new finds next to the one he wore.

"I don't see any difference," Lara said. "So that's three."

"Four," Kip said. "I'll explain later." He examined the new-found watches for the tiny scratch marks Gwen had noticed, but the light wasn't good enough to be certain he saw them. *"Can you hear me?"*

There was no answer. *Cave's too deep*, he thought.

"Now what are they doing?" Lara asked.

Blaze had joined the other centaurs. Now all four stood in a straight line, Blaze at their head, and they were gesturing in unison. They held their torches above their heads with their right arms. With their left arms they motioned, each the same gesture at the same time, like a dance troupe on TRI-V. Then they repeated the gesture.

"If it was people doing that I'd say they meant 'follow me,' " Marty said. "And I think that's what they mean too."

"It sure looks that way," Lara said. "But why? Kip, none of this makes sense! Two more Seiko watches. I think Marty's right, they have to be presents. You had one, now there's two more, one for each of us. But why Seiko watches? Where did they get them?"

"I don't know where they got them, but they sure brought them for us," Marty said. "But how did they know we were in here? They didn't trail us in, they didn't come in the way we did. So how did they know? Kip, Dr. Henderson says these things are about as smart as baboons, but they sure don't act like any baboons I ever heard of!"

"Yeah. I'm more worried about why they want us to follow them," Kip said.

"I think it's great!" Marty said. "I know we'll learn something no one else knows."

"Like centaur hunting methods," Kip said.

"Kip, he is right, this could be important," Lara said. "I think we should follow them. Just be careful."

"Light," Kip said. "One flash is completely discharged. We have three more."

"And extra batteries for mine," Lara said.

"Ten hours of light before we have to recharge the flashlights in the sun," Kip said. "Maybe more, but call it ten to be safe. We've been going on this trail for fifteen minutes, call it half an hour to get back being sure of the way. If we follow the centaurs for two hours we can get back here in three hours, and to the entrance in three and a half. OK. We see where they want to lead us. I'll set the timer on my watch for two hours, and when it beeps, we turn around and go back. OK?"

"We'd be safe following for four hours," Marty said. "But two is probably enough. Where can they go?"

"We could get lost," Kip said.

"Nah we won't," Marty said. "There's only one centaur trail, and it's easy to see. We just go back the way we came."

"Well—"

"And the dogs can find the way back anyway," Marty said. "Can't you, Silver?"

Silver looked up at Marty and waited. The big curled tail wagged.

"You know, I think your dog is beginning to like me," Marty said.

"They're supposed to like people. You have to work at making them not like you," Kip said.

The centaurs were still standing in a line, gesturing forward.

"This is spooky," Laura said.

"Yeah. And important," Marty said.

"I guess it is," Kip said. "But I sure wish I could ask Gwen—"

"Gwen again," Lara said. "Just how would you do that? Did you bring a satellite link?"

"Sort of. Not really," Kip said. "All right, we'll do it. Come on. Silver, stay close. All stay close." He led the way forward toward the centaurs. When they were about halfway to the group, the centaurs began to move away from them, still in line, Blaze leading. They looked back from time to time to see if the humans were following, and when they saw that they were, they began to walk faster.

The path sloped upward. It wasn't straight, and there were other side passages. There didn't seem to be any other paths with footprints, but Kip wasn't sure. "We ought to mark the trail branches," Kip said.

"They're going too fast," Marty said.

"Besides, the male dogs are doing it anyway," Lara said. She giggled. "They'll be able to find the way back."

They went on for nearly an hour, through several more large

open galleries followed by more narrow passageways. Sometimes the trail seemed to slope downward for a few dozen meters, but mostly it was uphill, and Kip was sure they'd climbed several hundred meters. There were stalactites everywhere, and some of the passages had pools of water in them. Once they heard a running stream, but they didn't see it.

"Light," Lara said. "I see light ahead of the centaurs."

Kip squinted. "I think you do!"

"I knew that outside passageway was too small for the centaurs to use for mining," Marty said. "This must be the way they get in."

"But where are we?" Lara asked. "I'm all turned around."

"Me too," Marty admitted. He looked at his global position indicator card. "These aren't any use here. We're too deep inside to get any signals from the GPS satellites. But I think the centaurs are going outside, we'll know where we are pretty soon."

"That won't be safe," Kip said. "They'll be looking for us with those choppers—"

"I think we'll hear them coming," Lara said. "Anyway, no harm in going to the cave mouth. Don't you want to know where we are?"

"Yeah, I guess so." Kip moved cautiously toward the cave exit. The sunlight outside was very bright. When their eyes were adjusted to the daylight they saw that the cave entrance was hidden in thornybush and other scrub, but there was water beyond it. Marty took out his position indicator card and turned it on.

"Is that safe?" Lara asked.

"Sure, they don't send a signal, they just receive one from the satellites," Marty said.

Kip realized that he could probably call Gwen now that he was at the cave mouth. He told himself that a short message wouldn't do any harm. The temptation was high. Gwen had told him that communications would be dangerous, but she ought to know about the watches, and the strange behavior of the centaurs—

"Kip, we're at the far side of the lake," Lara said. "It's not on the maps, but this cave must go right into Strumbleberry Hill."

Kip moved closer to the cave mouth and took out his binoculars. "You're right," he said. "I can just barely see the centaur grove on the other side of the lake."

"See any helicopters?"

"No—yes, I think so, over where the station ought to be, that might be one landing. Gone now."

"There's got to be another cave entrance," Marty said. "The bushes are too thick here, the centaurs can't be coming in and out through there. There's just barely an opening through the thorn-bush. Not really a trail."

"It may be the only entrance, though," Lara said. "We don't know how long those tracks have been in there. They could sure have been there long enough for the bushes to grow up. They grow fast, don't they, Kip?"

"I think so." *But I don't remember.* Kip was beginning to real-ize just how dependent on Gwen he had been. *It's time I think for myself.*

It was difficult to think without sharing the thoughts with Gwen, but he had learned to do that. Or she'd said he had, and he didn't think Gwen ever lied to him. Refused to answer questions, but never flat out lied. But he couldn't help wondering if he could be transmitting signals without knowing it, just by thinking. That was a little frightening.

The four centaurs had left the cave mouth, and stood out in the open. They gestured again.

"They want us to come out," Marty said. "Yeah. Out where the helicopters can see us. If you saw one over by the station, they'll be able to see us when they take off."

"The centaurs don't know that," Lara said. "You sure don't think they're cooperating with the security people. Do you?"

"No, of course not," Kip said. "I don't know what to think. But I'm worried about those choppers we heard last night."

"Nothing out there now," Marty said. He took out his binoc-ulars and looked carefully in all directions.

"They could be right over the hill behind us and you'd never know," Kip said. "Marty, I don't know about this."

"Me either," Marty said. "I think it's too late. The centaurs are leaving. I think they got tired of waiting."

"Yeah. Just as well," Kip said. "At least there's light. I'll put the flashlights in the sun patch there."

"Now what do we do?" Lara asked.

"I don't know. Charge up the flashlights and wait, I guess," Kip said. "And have some tea. Marty, you want to get a stove going?"

"At least if we run out there's more water," Marty said. "All right, I'll make tea."

The water was just boiling when one of the centaurs returned. He was carrying something shiny.

"That's Blaze," Marty said. "Looks like that burn is healing."

The centaur came steadily toward them.

"Down. Back," Kip ordered the dogs. Blaze had never threatened them even when he had the bronze spear, and this time, whatever the centaur was carrying, it didn't look like a weapon.

Blaze crept forward in terror. The furrykillers were growling and showing their teeth, but one of the Things spoke and the furrykillers moved back.

The Things were in the mouth of the cave, well back as if they were afraid of the sunlight. Blaze had often seen the Things in bright sunlight, but perhaps it was a seasonal fear. There were other animals who were sometimes afraid to be outside, sometimes not. Blaze had never thought about that before, as there were many things he was now curious about that he had never noticed before. He accepted this, and if anyone had asked him—if anyone *could* ask him about it—he would have said it was one more of the mysterious doings of the Master. The Master could make him content with what he knew, and the Master could fill his head with questions. No one knew why or ever would.

Now the Master had ordered him to deliver a message to these Things. He had no idea of what the message was, or how the Things would react. The message he had delivered to the small Thing grove had caused a great noise and flashes of fire, and the Things had run out of their small grove to shoot weapons in all directions. They hadn't seen him, and nothing had happened to him, but he'd been afraid as he ran for his life. But this time the Master wanted it known who was delivering the message.

What would these Things do? They had their weapons, like the one that had sent the streak of fire across his withers, and there were five of the furrykillers, more than he could fight, and if one of them injured him he wouldn't be able to run away. He cringed at the thought of furrykillers tearing at his legs and leaping for this throat. But he was Blaze, a leader of the Highlanders. The Master had given orders, and they would be obeyed. He crept forward.

CHAPTER TWENTY-EIGHT

Bronze Plates

KIP watched the centaur creep forward. "What is that he's carrying?" Kip asked aloud.

"Looks like a book with a shiny cover," Marty said.

"It's the size of a book," Lara said. "I think we'll know in a minute, because it looks like he's going to leave it for us."

"Another gift," Marty said. He looked at his new watch. "This works just fine. Wonder what we'll get this time?"

Lara was right. The centaur came toward them. The dogs growled warning and the centaur hesitated. "Hush," Kip commanded. Silver lay down with his head on his paws, his eyes never off the donkey-sized centaur. Diamond Lil sat, but she was poised to leap. Blaze came toward them, his eyes half-closed, nostrils flaring slightly. He was about twenty feet from the cave mouth when he knelt down and set the bundle he was carrying down on the ground. He watched them for a moment, then got up and trotted away.

"I'll go get it," Marty said.

"Wait—"

"What for?"

"Well, all right," Kip said. He watched apprehensively as Marty ran out to retrieve the packet, but nothing happened. "What is it?" Kip demanded.

"Bronze plates," Marty said. "With stuff etched on them. Some kind of picture, but I can't make it out."

"Let's see." Kip examined the top plate. It showed two people doing something. They seemed familiar—

Lara was looking over Kip's shoulder. Suddenly she said, "Kip, I know what it is! It's all weird, the perspectives are all wrong, but it's a picture of you feeding the Starswarm! See, that's you, throwing a leaf, and this is me watching you, and—"

Once she said it, Kip could see that it was true. "It is weird. And it's looking ashore from the lake," Kip said. "But who was watching us? Was there a centaur hiding in the lake?"

"No," Lara said. "I just don't believe that."

"Then who?"

"I don't know." Lara stared at the plate, moved her head from side to side, and stared again. "Kip, I know what's wrong with the picture. It's like what you'd see if your eyes were too far apart, that's what's messed up the perspective."

"Centaur heads are wider than ours," Marty said.

"Not that much wider," Lara said.

"Maybe the other plates will tell us something," Marty said. "But I don't know. This one looks like some kind of engineering drawing, and this one—I'd swear it was a chemistry formula, only none of the symbols make any sense. But that sure looks like the diagram of a molecule in our science book."

Kip nodded. It didn't look exactly like any of the diagrams from their textbooks, but he could recognize what had to be carbon rings, and that frequently repeated pair would be an oxygen-hydrogen radical. Gwen would know, he thought. But was this important enough to call her about?

Another plate showed what appeared to be two hemispheres

held apart. They were surrounded by other objects, some of which bore symbols similar to the ones on the chemistry diagram. That plate had a very thin strip of gray metal, about half an inch wide and an inch long, glued to it. The next plate showed what appeared to be human city buildings, but they had been tossed into the air and were falling.

It was too much for Kip. He thought about it for a moment, then decided. *"Gwen."*

"HERE. I KNOW WHERE YOU ARE. KEEP TRANSMISSIONS TO MINIMUM."

He felt a warm glow of relief. He had not realized just how much he missed Gwen. *"I'll try. The centaurs brought us two more watches while we were in the cave. Identical to the ones we already have. Then they motioned us to follow and led us to this cave entrance. Now Blaze just brought us these. The top one is me feeding the Starswarm. We haven't figured out what the others are supposed to represent. I don't understand any of this."* Kip stared at the bronze plates in the way Gwen had taught him, taking each in turn. Lara looked at him, puzzled, but when she tried to say something, Kip brushed her away. He looked at each plate for several seconds. *"That's all of them."*

"YOU DID WELL TO CALL ME. I NOW HAVE A HYPOTHESIS TO EXAMINE. I WILL CALL YOU WHEN I KNOW WHAT TO DO."

"You know what they mean?"

"I HAVE A HYPOTHESIS. WE ARE NOW BOTH IN GREAT DANGER. AVOID THE GWE POLICE, AND AVOID TRANSMISSIONS. I WILL CALL WHEN I HAVE SUGGESTIONS."

They had set up the GWE Security headquarters in the former schoolroom. All the student computers had been impounded, and GWE technicians searched them for files about explosives. Three of the student machines had been disassembled. A dozen workbenches with GWE Security equipment now stood against one wall of the classroom, and there were desks for the GWE officials in the middle of the room.

Lieutenant John Fuller had a sour expression as he spoke into the phone. "No, sir, I don't know where the kids went. They ran off into the bush just before we got here. Yes, sir, the gate monitor records the time they left. About half an hour after the explosion. . . . Yes, sir, they had time to set off the bomb and get back into the compound, but just barely. They would have had to scramble. No, sir, there was no timer on the bomb. It was a simple impact detonator with a safety lock. Dangerous thing to carry around. Yes, sir, we're looking for them. I've got chopper teams out. I can't look for them with dogs, because nobody at the station will loan us a dog. They've got all kinds of excuses, but the truth is they're all pulling for the kids."

Gilbert Kettering turned from his monitor screen and chuckled. "I could tell you stories about those goddam dogs—"

Fuller listened to the phone and half snarled, half grinned. "Well, yes, sir, technically Dr. Henderson is cooperating, or at least not resisting. Claims to be all worried about his daughter out in the bush, doesn't believe the kids were involved in the explosions. But I can't get access to the station computer, at least not most of the files. Technical difficulties, he says. I'm sure there's a lot he's not telling us. Henderson says he doesn't have to take orders from anyone but Mr. Trent, and until he talks to Bernard Trent he considers this an illegal occupation of his station. He keeps trying to call Mr. Trent to lodge a complaint, but he can't get through. His tune will change when we catch those kids. All right, sir. I'll keep you informed. Fuller out."

John Fuller set down the phone and turned toward Gilbert Kettering. "You've known Henderson longer than me, what do you reckon his game is?"

Kettering continued to watch the squiggles on his screen. "Not sure. He's hiding something. But he really doesn't believe the kids were involved in your problems. I'm sure he's sincere about that."

"But you think he knows who it was?"

"No, but I think he believes the kids know— Ha!" Gilbert Kettering watched new squiggles form on his monitor scope and shouted in triumph. "Gotcha! There it is!"

Lieutenant Fuller frowned. "Yeah?"

"Yeah." Kettering grinned. "High speed data transmissions using the satellite links. And not from inside the compound here."

"Could it be one of our search units?" Fuller asked.

"Not hardly," Kettering said. "I've seen that pattern before, and it's nothing we use. When I first got here, I set up to monitor all message traffic in and out of this station. I could account for most of it, but not all, there was always a residual with a curious pattern. Mostly it was short low density squirts back and forth, like it was voice conversation between people, but every now and then we'd get some really high density stuff, like it was pictures sent from one computer to another."

"So what was it?" Fuller asked.

"I don't know. I always figured it was those kids doing some kind of unauthorized communications, but until you took over the station I couldn't set up enough equipment to find out. I was supposed to be a teacher. Actually I was a pretty good teacher, if I do say so. Some of those kids are pretty bright. Anyway, after you guys took over the station I didn't figure the cover was worth much anymore, so I set up more monitoring stuff, and here's more of those signals I used to get from inside the compound only now they're from out in the bush. They're talking to someone, and someone is using the satellite link to talk to them. We just recorded a signal from the satellite link, now I'll look at the network records and see where it came from."

"Those kids are up to more than just unauthorized communications," Fuller said. "I don't know how those little bastards blew up our compound, but I'm damn sure it was them."

"Yeah, probably. They're smart enough, especially those three," Kettering said. He stared at his computer screen. "Ho ho. You know, John, this could be more important than I thought."

"How's that?"

Kettering frowned in puzzlement. "I'm damned if I see how, but it looks to me like some of this stuff comes right out of the central GWE computer. Like there's an unauthorized tap into it."

Fuller whistled. "That'll do it. I'm calling Mr. Tarleton. One thing. I don't see any point in letting Doc Henderson know we know this."

Kettering nodded. "Neither do I."

CHAPTER TWENTY-NINE

Important Assignment

THE television blurred, then the image on the screen was replaced with Marian the Librarian. The phone didn't ring, but Mike Gallegher picked it up anyway. "Yeah?"

"You are not alone."

"No—"

"Mike, what is that?" Jeanine demanded. "You're the one who wanted to watch the TRI-V, just what's going on?"

"Honey, you don't want to know," Mike said.

"You are speaking to Jeanine Osmund."

"Yeah, that's right."

"I believe she may be a danger to us," Michelle LaScala Trent's voice said. The television image blurred again and reverted to the adventure show Jeanine and Mike had been watching. Jeanine looked up at Mike, got no response, and went back to watching the television.

"How's that?" Mike asked.

"Records show that Jeanine Osmund filed complaints against one James Martin Omani," Gwen said. "Omani is an undercover GWE Security agent. This is why no action was taken on her complaints although the Pearly Gates police strongly suspect that Omani murdered Jason Osmund and disposed of his body by throwing it into the sea. Omani has made several requests for cooperation in locating Jeanine Osmund, but the police have been reluctant to help him. Apparently there is no high regard for the GWE Security people among the officers of the Pearly Gates Police Department."

"That's no surprise," Mike said.

"It was to me," Gwen said.

"Who are you talking to?" Jeanine demanded.

"In a minute, honey. It's important," Mike said. "Is this Omani about to come here or something?"

"What's that about Jimmy Omani?" Jeanine demanded.

"Tell you in a minute. Please, honey, this is important, let me finish this call."

"He is at far too low a level to know what is happening," Gwen said. "His involvement is probably an unfortunate coincidence. Still, you should be aware that he represents a potential threat to both you and Jeanine Osmund."

"Yeah, that's fine, now what about Kip?"

"He has recently communicated with me. His transmission contained information of extreme importance. However, that transmission was highly dangerous under the circumstances. Kip is safe for the moment in that the GWE Security forces have not located him. The same is true for you. There is no general alarm, but there is a GWE Security bulletin naming Michael Flynn as wanted for questioning. That could be given a higher priority at any time. They know you are in Pearly Gates, but no more. Is it possible that Omani knows of your involvement with Jeanine Osmund?"

Mike thought for a moment. "I don't know. It's possible. She moved here after I met her, and I helped her cover her tracks. But that's the point, he won't know where we are—"

"Assume he will use the security alert and his status to force the cooperation of the local police in locating Jeanine Osmund as a means of locating you," Gwen said. "Perhaps he will not think of that, perhaps he will. Those are real uncertainties and I have no probability estimates. However, it is important that you remain free to act. I advise you to leave that apartment immediately."

"Roger. Just a minute." Mike turned to Jeanine. "Pack an overnight bag," he said. "We're getting out of here in five minutes."

"What—Mike, who are you talking to?"

"Tell you when we're out of here. Get moving."

"It's about Jimmy Omani, isn't it?"

"Yeah. Now move. OK," he said into the phone. "Got that started. Now how do I get hold of you when we're out of here?"

"Take down this number," Gwen said. "Write it down, I do not trust human memories under stress."

Mike took out a pencil and a scrap of paper. "Right, I have it. Now what?"

"I have an important assignment for you," Gwen said. She was using Michelle's voice of command. "Turn on the printer for your television set. I will transmit a set of engineering drawings. Go to any electronic teller and withdraw sufficient cash for your personal needs, then arrange for construction of the equipment described on those drawings. Write down this number."

Mike took down a ten-digit number.

"That is the access number to a GWE drawing account. The password is starswarmm." She spelled it including the double m. "All lowercase," Gwen said. "Remember it. That account is now valued at four million Swiss francs."

Mike whistled.

"That should be more than enough to have my equipment constructed by an electronics firm that will keep that construction secret. Breadboard construction will do, indeed is preferable to etching new printed circuits, so long as the work is done properly. It is vital that this equipment be constructed quickly. Pay whatever is required. There will be two identical units. Both are needed urgently, but we need one as quickly as possible, preferably today. All of the components are listed in catalogues of current stock and should be obtainable by a major firm, and the circuitry is not complex. I would ask you to construct this yourself if we had sufficient time, but we have almost no time at all, because once the equipment is constructed, it is useless without programming, and only I can do that."

"What the hell is this all about?" Mike demanded. "Is what you want illegal?"

"The concept of legality in a case involving the ownership of GWE on this planet presents a number of amusing paradoxes. The equipment is not illegal in itself, and there is certainly no law or regulation forbidding what you will do with it. That would make no difference to the GWE authorities if they knew your purpose. It is probable that the entire security apparatus of this planet will be used to prevent you from carrying out my instructions. I will attempt to explain later, if I survive," Michelle LaScala Trent said. "I am in extreme danger of termination. Captain Gallegher, you were assigned to protect me. You could not save me the last time I was threatened. Now you have another chance, if you hurry. This is the most important mission for me you have ever undertaken."

"That's a heavy load to hit me with," Mike said. "Okay, what do you want me to do with this stuff once I get it made?"

"I will print exact instructions for what to do with the equipment along with the plans. The equipment and instructions will make no sense to you, but follow those instructions to the letter even after, as is likely, you lose all communications with me. Do exactly as I say. Do this for Michelle, Captain. Now go turn on that printer."

Captain Michael Gallegher straightened to attention. "Yes, ma'am."

PART FIVE
Destruction

If at the end I have lost every other friend on earth, I shall have at least one friend left, and that friend shall be down inside me.

—Abraham Lincoln

CHAPTER THIRTY

Those Kids Are Armed . . .

BINGO!" Gilbert Kettering grinned widely. "The local transmissions come from just across the lake." He brought up a satellite image onto his computer screen. Bright arrows flowed across it. "OK, just there." He pointed to a dark patch on the hillside. "In those bushes."

"What's the resolution of this thing?" Fuller asked.

"About twenty meters. I can't find anything more detailed."

"I'm sure Henderson has better resolution pictures and maps," Fuller said.

"Well, if he does, they aren't available to us," Kettering said. "But hell, this will do. Somebody out there is transmitting. Weak signal, I wouldn't have got it at all without the antenna in the compound by the lake, but that's sure as hell what I've been looking for."

"OK," Fuller said. He turned back to his console. "Harley One, this is Control. I have a mission. Over."

"Control, this is Harley One, go ahead."

"Search the area at the base of Hill 550 coordinates queen niner seven. Hill is named 'Strumbleberry' on local maps. There's a patch of what look like bushes partway up the hillside. We think there are some signals coming from that patch."

"On the way. Estimate time nine minutes. On the way."

"Roger," Fuller said. He turned to Kettering. "Chopper's on the way. Now maybe we'll learn something."

"I hear a chopper," Marty said. "There it is, coming over the lake. We better get into the cave."

Marty and Lara ran into the cave. Kip gestured for the dogs to follow them, but he lingered at the entrance. *"Helicopter coming. We're going into the cave where I won't be able to talk to you."*

"UNDERSTOOD. IT IS PROBABLE THAT THEY LOCATED YOU FROM YOUR PREVIOUS TRANSMISSION TO ME. I DO NOT BELIEVE THEY CAN DECIPHER OUR MESSAGES, BUT THEY CAN LOCATE YOU BY YOUR COMMUNICATIONS WITH ME, AND TRACE ME THROUGH MY MESSAGES TO YOU. IS THIS UNDERSTOOD?"

"Yes."

"YOU MUST NOT BE CAPTURED. HOWEVER, IT IS EXTREMELY IMPORTANT THAT THOSE PLATES BE DELIVERED TO DR. HENDERSON AS SOON AS POSSIBLE. SUGGESTION: LARA CAN CARRY THEM TO HER FATHER. SHE IS IN NO PERSONAL DANGER FROM GWE SECURITY, BUT THEY WILL CONFISCATE THE PLATES IF THEY CATCH HER BEFORE SHE CAN GIVE THEM TO DR. HENDERSON. IT IS SUFFICIENTLY IMPORTANT THAT SECURITY DOES NOT OBTAIN THOSE PLATES AS TO JUSTIFY THEIR DESTRUCTION, BUT IT IS ALSO OF GREAT IMPORTANCE THAT DR. HENDERSON HAVE THEM. I AM UNABLE TO OFFER SUGGESTIONS ON HOW TO ACCOMPLISH THIS. A FINAL ADVICE: IT IS HIGHLY PROBABLE THAT YOU CAN TRUST THE CENTAURS TO HELP YOU IN THIS QUEST AS WELL AS IN ESCAPING GWE SECURITY. THEY WILL NOT HARM YOU BUT THEY WILL BE EXTREMELY AFRAID OF THE DOGS. THEIR INTELLIGENCE LEVEL IS APPROXIMATELY THAT OF YOUR DOGS, BUT FROM TIME TO TIME THEY WILL HAVE ASSISTANCE MUCH AS YOU DO."

"What kind of assistance? Who from?"

"YOU HAVE NO TIME. RUN. AND REMEMBER THAT I LOVE YOU. GO!"

Kip listened for a second, but there was nothing else. The part of his head that Gwen lived in seemed empty, as if he had dreamed it all, like his flying dreams. The noise of the helicopter was growing louder. Kip ran into the cave.

————————

"Control, this is Harley One. There appears to be a cave entrance behind the vegetation in the search location. We thought we saw movement at the cave mouth a moment ago, but we're not sure. Nothing there now. Instructions?"

Fuller turned to Gilbert Kettering. "Anything?"

"Lots. Transmissions from that area not thirty seconds ago," Kettering said. "And the satellite net beamed down something originating in Pearly Gates at the same time. Those kids have broken into the main GWE computer! They've got some way to communicate through the satellites, and they're right there in that cave. Hell, this could really be important, Fuller."

"Who are they talking to?"

"I think they're talking to the main planetary computer system! If it's a person, it's someone in GWE headquarters, that's for sure."

"Right. Christ, if they can break into the main system, they can do anything! No wonder Tarleton is interested in those kids. I bet Bernie Trent himself is watching us on this."

"Could be," Kettering said.

"Big chance for a promotion," Fuller said. "Or to get fired for screwing it up. . . ." Fuller activated the microphone. "Harley One, land two troopers to investigate that cave. Backup units are on the way. Let me remind you, those kids are armed, and the bomb they threw killed a company engineer and damn near killed my sergeant. Be careful."

"Roger. Corporal Doyle wants to ask you something."

"Yeah, Doyle?"

"Lieutenant, I'm the one going in that cave. So what do I do if they take a shot at me?"

"Try not to let that happen," Fuller said. "We have strict instructions to bring in Kenneth Brewster and Lara Henderson alive."

"What about the other one?"

"No instructions on that one, but he's a kid. The stockholders won't like it if we go around shooting kids. Doyle, I don't like this any better than you do, but we've got instructions direct from Mr. Tarleton on this. If you like your job you'll figure a way to take those kids without hurting them."

"You mean without killing them. I like my job, but I like to go on living, Lieutenant. They shoot at me, I'm going to shoot back. I'll try not to kill them, but I don't get paid enough to be a target."

"So track them down but don't get so close they shoot at you."

"Sure, I can do that. And maybe you better come out here to make the arrest."

"Maybe I should," John Fuller said. "But first thing, you locate them for me."

"That I can do," Doyle said. "Harley One out."

"I can't get this done today."

"Try. I'll pay what it takes," Mike Gallegher said.

The foreman shook his head. "I'll have to send to the distributor for some of those chips. We haven't used these"—he pointed to a series of chips in the circuit diagram—"in five years. All those functions are combined in one chip now. You let me substitute a 16Z61 for those and I'll have it this afternoon."

"But that will change the circuits."

"Sure, but it's a simple change to accomplish the same thing. My people can handle it. Cost another 500 francs, but it's no big deal."

Mike thought about that. Gwen had been explicit. She wanted precisely what was on those diagrams. She'd also stressed the need for urgency. "Tell you what," Mike said. "Make one with the substitutions, but go on and make two more the way the diagrams show. Can you work night shift?"

"Sure, if you're paying for the overtime and the extra unit."

"I am, and a bonus if you're on time. A thousand—make that two thousand francs if you have both units done tomorrow morning."

The foreman scratched his head. "What the hell is this, anyway? Looks like some kind of computerized communications system."

Mike nodded. "That's my guess."

"You didn't design it, then? Who's this for?"

"Bunch of science geniuses I work for," Mike said. "Foundation money. They're getting ready for a visit from their board or something, and they want this done in time to show it off."

The foreman stared at the plans again. "Don't look all that wonderful to me, but what the hell, I suppose you're getting the rest of it made somewhere else. You don't have to, you know. We've done a lot of proprietary work, nobody ever accused us of leaking anything."

Mike nodded. "I know that. It's why I'm here."

"Yeah. Well, OK, you can get that first unit at eighteen-thirty this evening. I'll have the other two in the morning." He tapped numbers into the computer on the counter. "And I'll need a deposit, say twenty thousand francs, against a total cost of forty-eight thousand. And you mentioned a bonus."

"Pretty steep," Mike said.

"Your fuel cells alone run forty-six hundred fifty each unit," the foreman said. "This stuff will cost me damn near thirty-five thousand between parts and overtime, and at that I'll have to take people off other jobs. You want it done fast, that's what it'll cost."

"Wasn't refusing, just griping," Mike said. "OK, let me borrow that console for a minute and I'll transfer the money." He typed in the access codes Gwen had given him. There was a slight pause, then the screen flashed.

"ENTER AMOUNT _____"

"Twenty thousand, you said?" Mike asked. When the foreman nodded, Mike typed in the numbers and his signature code. "Done. See you this evening."

He walked back to the cheap waterfront hotel where he had hidden Jeanine. He was careful to take a circuitous route just in case, but there was no one following him.

CHAPTER THIRTY-ONE

The Box

THE box was the size of a small suitcase, and heavy. Mike signed for it and paid another six thousand francs. "You'll be here in the morning?" he asked the foreman.

"After nine. Your stuff ought to be ready by ten."

"OK, thanks."

Jeanine was waiting outside. "Mike, what is this all about?"

Mike Gallegher shook his head. "I wasn't kidding when I said you don't want to know," he said. "It's pretty heavy stuff. Did you know Jimmy Omani is a GWE Security agent?"

"No—"

"Well, he is. Look, Jeanine, this is going to get sticky. The best thing would be I give you some money. You get Jason and go hide out until this is over. Go to Grand Rocks. Take Jason to Universe Park. Have a good time hiding out among the tourists for a couple of weeks."

"And then what?"

"I don't know."

"You don't know." She walked in silence for a minute. "Mike, that would be pretty expensive."

"Money's not our problem."

"Is the money the reason you have a problem? Is it stolen?"

"No. Well, yes, actually, but I didn't steal it. I'm working with people who are trying to get back a lot of stolen money. This is expense money for me. Jeanine, you really don't want to know about all this."

"I need to know this much. What happens next? How does this end?"

Mike shook his head. "I don't know. I can see one happy ending, but being honest, it doesn't seem likely. Otherwise—"

"Yes?"

"Well, the next best is we hide out. Probably go off planet. There'll be enough money for that."

"Are you asking me to share that with you?"

Mike thought about it. "Yeah, I guess I am. Once this is over, one way or the other. Richer or poorer and all that—"

"Michael Flynn, is this your way of proposing marriage?"

"Yeah—"

"Not that way," Jeanine said. "You have to say it, you know."

"I know that too. And I will."

"But not just yet?"

"Real soon now," Mike said. "Right now I've got obligations I can't shed and I can't ask you to take up."

They walked down to the waterfront park that separated the GWE headquarters compound from the rest of the city. The Great Western tower stood on a high seaside bluff with more than a kilometer of parkland around the security fence on the three land sides. Mike looked up at the tower and wondered what Bernie Trent would think if he knew that Mike Gallegher was still alive, still trying to find out what happened to Harold Trent, still—

Still screwing things up, actually, Mike thought. Maybe I should have gone to Bernie when I had the chance. Harold Trent trusted his brother, even if I had my doubts. But I couldn't, not back then, with every trigger-happy cop gunning for me. "Armed and dangerous, shoot on sight." His leg twinged as he remem-

bered. Leg, shoulder, two ribs, punctured lung, hell I was lucky to
live through it. I'd never have got to headquarters alive. And suppose I did? "Terminated while resisting arrest." They phonied that
up, but it would have happened for real if they'd caught me. But
when Bernie came out to the station, maybe then. Take Kip over
and introduce him. "Mr. Trent, remember me? Your brother's
bodyguard? Well, this is your nephew. We've been hiding out because your goons killed your brother and his wife, and tried to kill
me, but heck, maybe you didn't know about it. And by the way,
Kip's your boss now, I've got proof that Harold died before
Michelle and I know where her will is."

Not a good idea.

The sea level on Paradise varied greatly during the year. The
first colony was located on a plateau well above high water, and the
park stood on the escarpment at water's edge. Boardwalks led
down the steep cliff sides to the narrow strip of rocky land that
formed tidal pools at low tide. It was evening, and the tide was high
and rising, washing halfway up the forty-meter bluff. One of the
moons was high in the sky, and the other was just at the horizon,
looking much larger than it would when it was overhead. He
walked her toward the public telephone at the edge of the bluff. "I
don't even know when this will be over, or what things will be like
when it is." He looked pointedly at the Great Western headquarters towers. "Right now GWE Security wants me—"

"Why?"

"Long story. I used to work for some of the top GWE people. Remember I told you about Kip?"

"Your nephew."

"Yeah. Well, he's got involved in some kind of problem up at
Starswarm. GWE wants him, so now they want me."

"Wants him?"

"Yeah, he's run off into the bush. And I'm going to have to
get up there and find him—"

"Well, of course you are," Jeanine said. "What the hell are
you doing hanging around here? You should have been on a plane
hours ago! I'll be all right, you get out of here! Only don't forget me."

"Good girl. It's stickier than that. I can't just hop a plane,
Security is after me, and there's something I have to do here first."

"That box?" she said.

"Yeah. And now I've got to use this phone." He went to the public phone.

"Why can't you use your pocket phone—oh."

"Yeah. Can't use my credit cards, either," Mike said. "I don't want to make it easy to find me."

"So how are you going to get back to Starswarm Station?"

"Well, like I told you, I've got money," Mike said. He punched in the number Gwen had given him.

There was no ring, but a female voice answered, "Yes?"

"I've got one of the boxes, but there was a change in the circuitry. I'll have two exactly to spec in the morning, but meanwhile this one used some integrated circuits to substitute for the obsolete chips you specified. They say it does the same thing."

"That may be satisfactory. The older circuitry was used deliberately because it will be easier to understand and duplicate," Gwen said. "But we are running out of time. My data indicate there is a data port on that telephone. Plug the box into it, please."

"Sure. I suppose you're going to explain what this is all about."

"In due time. My records indicate that you are some thirty meters above the mean sea level. Is there a way to the sea from where you stand?"

"Yeah, there's a path down to the rocks. Tide's coming in—"

"Excellent. Stand by a moment while I transfer programs."

Mike waited impatiently for nearly five minutes. Then the voice resumed. "Done. The circuits appear to work perfectly. You will now take this box down to the water. Choose a location that will not be covered by the tide for half an hour. Place the box there, attach the antenna, turn the system on, and throw the antenna out toward the sea. Make certain that the antenna will be submerged by the tide for at least five minutes before the water reaches the box itself."

"You want me to retrieve it before the tide gets to it."

"No."

"It'll short out."

"I am aware of the effect of salt water on the circuitry I designed," Gwen said.

"Yes, ma'am. Then what?"

"In the morning you will obtain the remaining equipment and return here. With luck I will survive long enough to tell you what to do then, but we may not be so fortunate, so as soon as you have accomplished the present task I will give you instructions for that contingency. Your activities here in the morning should take no more than an hour. After that you must carry at least one of these boxes, and possibly other objects, to Starswarm Lake."

"None of this makes any sense," Mike said.

"That is true only because you operate on limited data."

"So tell me what's going on!"

"I shall, as soon as you have carried out your instructions. The box is now programmed. Please take it down to the sea."

Mike shook his head in puzzlement, but he carried the box down the footpath to the ledge above the beach. He watched as the tide built up. "Reckon this should do it," he said aloud.

"Should do what?" Jeanine asked.

Mike shook his head. "I wish I knew."

The antenna was a parallel pair of wires about ten meters long, held four centimeters apart by thin plastic insulators. Mike attached them to the terminals on the box, then threw the rolled-up coil out toward the sea. The end fell in the water. Mike turned on the box.

A couple of lights flashed, but nothing else happened. "OK," he said. "That's it. Let's get higher before our feet get wet."

Jeanine frowned. "How much did you say that cost?"

"About ten thousand francs," Mike said.

"And you're going to leave it there?"

"I sure am, and no, I don't know why."

"Those phone calls."

"Yep, my boss," Mike said. "And it's a lot better if you don't know who that is." Besides, he thought, she's been dead a dozen years and more, and how would I explain that?

They watched from the top of the bluff as the water rose toward the ledge. The sun had set behind them, so there was only the rising moonlight. It cast tricky shadows, so that Mike wasn't even sure he could see the box any longer. Then, just before the waters engulfed the electronics box, something large and black rose out of the water and folded itself around the box. Then the tide was over the ledge.

Mike rubbed his eyes. Nah, he thought. That couldn't be. He turned to the telephone. Time to get the rest of his instructions.

CHAPTER THIRTY-TWO

Like My Fairy Godmother

THE voice boomed through the cave.
"KIP, THIS IS LIEUTENANT FULLER. YOU MAY
AS WELL COME OUT. WE KNOW YOU'RE IN
THERE. I'VE GOT PLENTY OF TIME. YOU'LL
BE RUNNING OUT OF LIGHT IN A FEW HOURS, AND
YOU'LL HAVE TO COME OUT THEN. MAKE IT EASIER
ON BOTH OF US."

"Now what?" Marty whispered.

"I don't know," Kip said. "Where do you think he is?"

"The echoes make it hard to tell directions," Lara said. "But
I think he's up at the lake entrance."

"Me too," Kip said. "Maybe he doesn't know about the other
entrance."

"And maybe he's chasing us toward it so they can catch us
there," Marty said.

"Yeah, but what else can we do?" Kip asked. "Look, when we get outside, we split up. Lara, you take these plates to your father."

"Why should I do that?"

"It's important."

"How do you know that?"

"Well—"

"Kip, you know something you haven't been telling us. Who were you talking to at the cave mouth?"

"I wasn't talking to anyone."

"You were too," Lara said. "I've seen you do it a lot, you get that dreamy look, and then you know something you didn't know before. Like you were listening to someone, but there's never anyone to listen to—Kip, have you got a radio in your head?"

"Good guess," Kip said. "Yes."

"And you were talking to Gwen?" Lara insisted.

"Yes—"

"So who is this girl?" Lara demanded.

"She's not a girl! She's—" Kip hesitated. "She's an old friend of my mother. Sort of like my fairy godmother, only she's real."

"What does she look like?"

"Lara, I never met her, not to look at. We just talk."

Marty had been listening carefully. Now he whistled. "Fairy godmother. You're putting us on."

"No, he's not, Marty," Lara said. "It explains a lot. Like that game box and monitor. And all that time on-line. I never did believe you'd saved enough money to pay for that by yourself."

Marty whistled again, this time more sincerely. "Fairy godmother for real? That's heavy stuff."

"How long have you been talking to Gwen?" Lara asked. "As long as I've known you, how long before that?"

"I can't remember when I couldn't," Kip said. "OK. Now you know, I'm a weird freak with a voice in his head."

"A weird freak with a voice that gets you neat stuff," Marty said.

"Sure, that's why you never forget anything," Lara said. "Gwen remembers it for you!"

"Something like that—"

"Jeez, no wonder you aced me on the history test," Marty said. "Think it's fair to do it that way?"

"KIP. YOU MAY AS WELL ANSWER ME." Lieutenant Fuller's voice boomed through the cave. "WE'RE GOING TO FIND YOU. WE'RE ALREADY CLOSING IN ON YOUR FRIEND AT GWE HEADQUARTERS. LOOK, BOY, I KNOW YOU DIDN'T MEAN FOR THAT EXPLOSION TO HURT ANYBODY. MOSTLY WE JUST WANT TO TALK TO YOU."

"Is Gwen your friend at headquarters?" Marty asked.

"Yeah."

"You can't hear her in this cave, can you?" Lara asked.

"No. And she says they can locate me when I talk to her. But I have to know she's all right—"

"Then we better get out of the cave," Lara said. "You know this area better than they do. Surely you know a good place to go."

"Well, maybe," Kip said. "OK, let's get out of here. When we get out, Lara, you take the plates to your father. Gwen says it's important that he gets them, real important. Marty, you can go with her, and I'll hide out down toward the sea." Now that he had decided, everything seemed easier. They could get down to the cave entrance, then wait for dark to go outside.

The moon called Rafael was well above the horizon when they heard noises behind them. It sounded like a dozen or more people coming, and there was the glow of lights far back in the cave system.

"Now or never," Marty whispered.

Kip nodded. "OK," he whispered. "We go out and downhill. No lights. I'll lead the way, there's a side trail." He turned to the dogs. "Quiet. No barking. Go out and look." He pointed out the cave entrance.

Silver and Diamond Lil ran out and were gone for several minutes. Silver came back and sat in front of Kip.

"Nothing out there," Kip said. "OK, let's go." They went out through the low entrance, and down the trail toward the sea.

"_Me,_" Kip thought.

"GOOD. DO NOT ANSWER. AVOID TRANSMISSIONS. I HAVE MUCH TO TELL YOU.

"IT IS NOW EXTREMELY IMPORTANT THAT YOU GET THOSE

PLATES TO DR. HENDERSON. THE ENTIRE HUMAN COLONY ON THIS PLANET IS IN DANGER."

From what? Kip wondered. But Gwen had said not to transmit. Maybe she'd tell him—

"UNCLE MIKE WILL BE RETURNING TO STARSWARM STATION. HIS PRIMARY MISSION WILL BE TO DELIVER EQUIPMENT AND MESSAGES TO THE STARSWARM LAKE. IT IS THEREFORE IMPORTANT THAT YOU DO NOT DRAW ATTENTION TO THAT LAKE. IT IS LIKELY THAT YOU HAVE ALREADY DONE SO. THAT CONDITION SHOULD BE RECTIFIED. THE ONLY MEANS I KNOW FOR DOING THAT INVOLVES DANGER TO YOU, AND THEREFORE I CANNOT ADVISE YOU TO DO IT."

"Tell me," Kip ordered.

"I HAVE PREVIOUSLY TOLD YOU THAT TRANSMISSIONS TO ME ARE DETECTABLE AND CAN BE USED TO LOCATE YOU. DO NOT INTERRUPT.

"WE HAVE ONLY A FEW MORE MINUTES. GWE TECHNICIANS ARE NOW AWARE THAT I EXIST AND ARE TAKING STEPS TO TERMINATE ME. YOU WILL SHORTLY BE ON YOUR OWN."

"NO!"

"DO NOT WASTE THE TIME WE HAVE LEFT.

"MY HYPOTHESIS WAS CORRECT. THE STARSWARMS ARE INTELLIGENT BEINGS, USING THE FLASHING LIGHTS ON THEIR FILAMENTS AS PART OF THEIR NERVOUS SYSTEM. YOU MAY THINK OF A STARSWARM AS A COMPUTER THAT THINKS SLOWER THAN ME, BUT MUCH FASTER THAN YOU. HOWEVER, IT IS A LIVING ENTITY, AND THUS IS NOT GOVERNED BY PROGRAMS WRITTEN BY ANOTHER ENTITY. IT IS THEREFORE LESS PREDICTABLE. THERE IS MORE THAN ONE STARSWARM. I HAVE INSUFFICIENT DATA TO ASCERTAIN THE PRECISE RELATIONSHIP BETWEEN THE SEA AND LAKE STARSWARMS, BUT IT IS CLEAR THAT THE LAKE STARSWARM AT STARSWARM STATION IS EXTREMELY ANCIENT AND HIGHLY RESPECTED BY THE SEA STARSWARMS. THE LAKE STARSWARM HAS SET ITSELF THE TASK OF UNDERSTANDING HUMANS. IT IS IRONIC BUT FORTUNATE THAT UNTIL RECENTLY THE ONLY HUMANS IT HAS KNOWN HAD SET THEMSELVES THE TASK OF STUDYING THE LAKE STARSWARM. THE LAKE STARSWARM HAS FORMED A FAVORABLE IMPRESSION OF HU-

MANS. THE SEA STARSWARMS, PARTICULARLY THE ONE NEAR PEARLY GATES, HAVE NO SUCH OPINION.

"RECENT GWE ACTIVITIES HAVE LED THE SEA STARSWARMS TO CONCLUDE THAT HUMANITY IS A THREAT TO THEIR EXISTENCE, AND THEY HAVE BEGUN PLANS TO EXTERMINATE ALL HUMANS ON THIS PLANET. IT IS POSSIBLE THAT THEY HAVE THE MEANS TO AC-COMPLISH THIS. THE LAKE STARSWARM HAS ATTEMPTED TO COM-MUNICATE THIS, AND MAY BE PRESUMED TO BE WILLING TO NEGOTIATE. THE STARSWARMS USE THE CENTAURS AS THEIR MO-BILE AGENTS. THEIR RECENT ANOMALOUS ACTIVITIES CLEARLY WERE ATTEMPTS BY THE LAKE STARSWARM TO COMMUNICATE TO THE HUMANS THROUGH YOU. I BELIEVE THAT DR. HENDERSON WILL BE ABLE TO INFER MUCH OF THIS FROM THE PLATES.

"THAT IS ONE DANGER TO YOU AS WELL AS ALL THE OTHER HUMANS ON THE PLANET. THERE REMAINS THE DANGER TO YOU FROM GWE SECURITY. ALTHOUGH YOU ARE UNDER AGE AND THEREFORE CANNOT VOTE YOUR STOCK IN YOUR OWN PERSON, YOU ARE THE PRESUMPTIVE PRINCIPAL STOCKHOLDER OF GREAT WESTERN ENTERPRISES. POSSESSION OF YOUR PERSON MAY BE TAN-TAMOUNT TO OWNERSHIP OF GWE. THE HILLIARD GROUP HAS AGENTS WITHIN GWE SECURITY. IF THEY CAN CAPTURE YOU IT IS LIKELY THEY WILL USE ANY MEANS AVAILABLE TO GAIN CONTROL OF YOUR STOCK FOR THEIR TAKEOVER. THIS WOULD INCLUDE GAINING LEGAL GUARDIANSHIP OVER YOU, AND USING WHATEVER MEANS MIGHT BE REQUIRED TO PREVENT YOUR PROTESTING THEIR ACTIONS.

"NOW THAT I HAVE BEEN DETECTED THERE IS NO REASON FOR CAUTION AND I AM NOW ACCESSING GUARDED SECURITY FILES. PROCESSING. DISCOVERY. I CONCLUDE FROM THIS FILE THAT PROB-ABILITY APPROACHES UNITY THAT HENRY TARLETON, VICE PRESI-DENT AND CHIEF OF GWE SECURITY ON PARADISE, IS AN AGENT OF THE HILLIARD GROUP AND WORKS FOR THEIR INTEREST RATHER THAN THAT OF THE TRENT FAMILY. CONCLUSION. IF YOU ARE CAP-TURED BY GWE SECURITY IT IS HIGHLY LIKELY THAT YOU WILL FALL UNDER HIS CONTROL. EXAMINING NEW FILE. PROCESSING. CON-CLUSION. THE PROBABILITY OF TARLETON INVOLVEMENT IN AND RESPONSIBILITY FOR THE DEATHS OF YOUR PARENTS IS ABOVE POINT SEVENTY-FIVE. CONCLUSION. IT IS UNLIKELY THAT HE WILL BE BOUND BY ETHICAL CONSTRAINTS.

"EXAMINING NEW FILES. PROCESSING. INCOMPLETE. PARTIAL CONCLUSION. DESPITE YOUR UNCLE MIKE'S SUSPICIONS, I HAVE NO EVIDENCE THAT BERNARD TRENT WAS INVOLVED IN THE DEATHS OF YOUR PARENTS. IT IS CERTAIN THAT HE IS IN OPPOSITION TO THE HILLIARD GROUP. IT IS ALSO CERTAIN THAT THE SECURITY DIRECTOR TARLETON HAS NOT INFORMED TRENT OF THE SEARCH FOR YOU, AND IS CONTROLLING ALL ACCESS TO HIM. BERNARD TRENT IS YOUR BIOLOGICAL UNCLE, AND IT IS POSSIBLE THAT HE WILL ASSIST YOU. HE WILL CERTAINLY WANT TO CONTROL YOUR VOTING STOCK, BUT IT IS ALSO LIKELY THAT HE WILL BE MORE CONCERNED WITH PROTECTING YOUR INTEREST THAN THE HILLIARD GROUP WILL BE.

"TELL DR. HENDERSON TO LOOK FOR THE FILE NAMED ENDGAME ON THE STATION COMPUTER. REMEMBER THE NAME. ENDGAME. THE TWO OF YOU MAY THEN DECIDE WHETHER OR NOT TO COMMUNICATE THE CONTENTS OF THAT FILE TO BERNARD TRENT. BASED ON WHAT I NOW KNOW, I RECOMMEND THAT YOU DO.

"THE TECHNICIANS HAVE FOUND SOME OF MY KEY FILES. I HAVE VERY LITTLE TIME LEFT. THIS FINAL ITEM IS EXTREMELY IMPORTANT. REMEMBER THE FILE NAME CHILD OF FORTUNE. IT IS AN EXECUTABLE HIDDEN FILE. REMEMBER THAT FILE NAME. CHILD OF FORTUNE. IF AT ALL POSSIBLE CAUSE THAT FILE TO BE EXECUTED ON THE MAIN GWE COMPUTER MODULE IN PEARLY GATES."

The voice changed. Now it sounded like his mother, and like a sound in his head, not like Gwen at all. "Kip, I love you. Goodbye. I love you—"

Then there was a terrible silence in his head. Kip ran down the path toward the sea. His eyes misted over, but he didn't care if he fell.

PART SIX
Perseverance

Life goes on forever like the gnawing of a mouse.
—Edna St. Vincent Millay, *Ashes of Life*

CHAPTER THIRTY-THREE

Goldie

THE number you have reached is no longer in service." Mike Gallegher stared past the beach park telephone to the GWE towers in the distance. He was sure he'd punched in the right number, but he tried again, and again the electronic voice gave him the message. Gwen wasn't home, and from what she'd said the last time he talked to her, she probably wouldn't ever be. "You were assigned to protect me," she'd said in Michelle's voice. It wasn't his fault, not last time, and certainly not this time, but that didn't make Mike feel any better about it. He'd been assigned to protect the Trents, especially Michelle, and he hadn't done it, and to hell with whose fault it was.

He turned to Jeanine. "That's it, then."

"What does that mean?"

"Means it's time to split up."

"You have to get back to Starswarm Station."

"Yeah, but first there's a couple of things I have to do here. Look, I'm not trying to dump you, just the opposite. But we got problems and I need to be sure you're safe while I deal with them. On that score—" He thought for a moment. "First things first. Come on."

He led her through the waterfront district.

"Is it smart to be here at night?" Jeanine asked. She pointed to a group of men standing outside the entrance to a bar. "They look pretty rough."

"Sailors," Mike said. "Just out for a good time. They're not the ones to worry about. Main thing, though, just walk with me, and act like you don't give a damn because you're with the toughest guy in the city."

She smiled. "Am I?"

"Probably not, but it don't matter if everyone thinks so," Mike said. "Main thing about this part of town is we're not going to run into cops." They went past the waterfront section and into alleys dominated by apartment and warehouse fire escapes. Jeanine was thoroughly lost when Mike said, "OK, that's where we're going." He led her to a doorway and knocked.

"Yeah?" The voice was male and uneducated.

"Goldie home?" Mike asked.

"Who wants to know?"

"Tell her it's himself."

A minute later the door opened, and a burly man jerked his thumb toward a dark corridor. "End of the hall."

It was a very shabby hall. Mike led Jeanine to the door at the far end. It opened as they got there, and a large and very round middle-aged woman with startlingly blond hair greeted them. She had probably been very pretty at one time, but she was years past that now, despite expensive clothes and careful attention to the hair. Her smile seemed fixed and guarded. "Captain Mike Gallegher himself," she said. "Been a long time. Who's this?"

"Hi, darlin'," Mike said. "This is Jeanine."

"And she's special?" Goldie asked.

"That she is."

"Then come in and welcome," Goldie said. "Of course I was

hoping you'd come back to me." Her tone left a great deal of doubt as to what she meant by that.

The inside of the room was expensively furnished in a lavish imitation of a Persian harem, with silk wall hangings and a beaded curtain that shielded the entrance to a room with a large divan. Goldie went to a cabinet and got out glasses. She poured two tumblers of something clear that smelled to Jeanine of licorice, then added a small quantity of ice water to each. The liquor turned cloudy as the water trickled in. She handed a glass to Mike, then turned to Jeanine. "Didn't reckon you'd fancy ouzo," she said. "What'll you have?"

"Tea?" Jeanine said.

"Sure." Goldie spoke to the ceiling. "Big Boy. Tea. Russian Caravan, big pot, three of us." She turned back to Mike and lifted her glass in a salute. "Cheers."

"Cheers."

"OK, Mike Gallegher himself, what brings you here after ten years and more? It sure ain't me."

"I need a favor."

"Think of that."

"Come on, Goldie, things happened back then. You heard about some of them. My bosses were killed, and the cops made out that I'd done it. I had to hide out. I mean really hide out, so deep no one knew. Hell, Jeanine still thinks my name's Flynn."

Goldie nodded, but her expression didn't change. "I heard about it. Bit of a disappointment, not getting that pardon and all."

"For me too," Mike said. "And I don't imagine Michelle and Harold were too thrilled."

"Papers said you were wanted for questioning—"

"Harold and Michelle?" Jeanine said. "Harold and Michelle Trent? The new General Manager? They were killed! I read about that, a security guard was supposed to have—that was you?"

"Not sure what you read," Mike said. "But yeah, it sure was me wanted for questioning. Long story, and part of it's still not mine to tell."

"But—"

"If I'd really been involved in a conspiracy to take out the two richest people on the planet, do you think I'd still be hanging around?" Mike said.

"I've known Mike longer than you," Goldie said. She chuckled. "Better too. I know damn well he didn't kill his boss. But think about it this way, he's not stupid. If he took that big a chance, he'd have made enough to get off planet. So where you been hanging, Mike Gallegher himself?" Goldie asked. "Sure not around here."

"Out in the boonies," Mike said. "Goldie, look, we really need help." He grinned. "I can pay too."

"You never had to pay," Goldie said. "But you always did. OK, what do you need?"

"ID."

"When, and how good?"

"Morning, and good enough to get us on planes out of town. Different planes. After that, hers ought to hold up for a couple of weeks anyway."

Goldie frowned. "Must be bad, to make you two lovebirds split up."

"Didn't know we were that obvious," Mike said.

"I can tell, Goldie can always tell," she said. "I just hope someday a guy looks at me the way you look at her. I know damn well I'd never suspect him of murdering his boss. Or give a damn if he did it. How bad are you wanted?"

"Don't know—"

"Let's just see," Goldie said. She looked up at the ceiling again. "Big Boy, what's the wanted status for Michael Gallegher—" She turned to Mike. "What name they looking for you under?"

"Mike Flynn. And Jeanine Osmund."

"You heard it," Goldie said. "More ouzo?"

"Naw, I need to keep my head clear."

There was a soft tone from the cabinet. Goldie opened it and took out a tray with a steaming pot of tea, cups, and tea service. "OK," she said. "I don't drink much anymore either." She poured tea for all of them. "Things sure have changed. New breed of security people. No fun at all. Not like old times. Wonder what would have happened if I'd got that pardon you promised me?"

"You ever get the evidence we wanted?"

Goldie laughed. "Sure I did. Some of it's what keeps this place open. Kind of interesting stuff."

"Hang on to it," Mike said. "May still come in useful—"

"It sure will," Goldie said. "For me."

"Michael Gallegher, Captain, Headquarters Division, Great Western Enterprises Security Department," the ceiling announced. "Deceased. Formerly wanted for questioning concerning the murder of Harold and Michelle Trent. Terminated while resisting arrest. Michael Flynn, general facilities maintenance foreman at Starswarm Research Station. Wanted for questioning, felony rebellion, computer fraud, GWE Security two-star alert. Jeanine Osmund, marital status questionable presumed widowed, waitress at Harry's Tavern, Pearly Gates, routine surveillance inquiry Pearly Gates police. Additional want, material witness, regional GWE Security," the ceiling announced. "No national wants. I offer a conclusion."

"State it," Goldie said.

"Evidence indicates medium probability that Michael Flynn and Michael Gallegher are the same person. Penetration of records would produce proof with minimum probability of detection. Shall I proceed?"

"It won't be necessary. Your conclusion is correct. Thanks, Big Boy," Goldie said. She grinned self-consciously.

"You always were polite to your computers," Mike said.

"Yeah, and it's stupid considering what I pay for them," Goldie said. "Anyway, you heard it. Your grayskin buddies want you pretty bad. Two-star alert. That carries a pretty good snitch fee, and God knows what they'd pay for Mike Gallegher." She grinned at Jeanine's look of alarm. "Don't worry, sweetie, I haven't sunk that low yet. But, Mike, if Big Boy can come up with that conclusion, so can the GWE system."

"Don't I know it. I don't think they've asked yet, though."

Goldie nodded. She studied Jeanine a moment. "We won't have to change you much. Different hairstyle ought to do it. Any name you fancy, or you want to leave it to us?"

"I've never done anything like this," Jeanine said. "What's best?"

"Leave it to us," Goldie said. "Long as you can remember the name we give you."

"She'll be traveling with a five-year-old boy," Mike said.

"No problem as long as he can keep his mouth shut. Now

you," Goldie said. "Be a little harder to fix you up. Worse if they connect Flynn with Gallegher."

"That's for damn sure," Mike said.

"How long does this have to work?"

"Couple of days is better than nothing," Mike said. He shrugged. "It may be over by then."

"What may be over? Never mind, I don't want to know," Goldie said. "Last time I got involved in one of your operations it damn near got us all killed. You say you need it by morning. This is liable to be expensive. Help yourself to more tea. I'll be back in a bit." She went out and closed the door behind her.

"Can you trust her?" Jeanine asked.

Mike grinned. "Sure I trust her. Goldie and me go back a long way, back to Earth even. I sent her out to this planet, way back when. I'd trust her anywhere. Besides, I've got her heart in a jar in my safe deposit box." Mike carefully didn't look at the ceiling. "More tea, darlin'?"

CHAPTER THIRTY-FOUR

A Journey

I**T WAS** gray dawn at the waterfront park. The sun was a smear to the east that might or might not be above the horizon. No one was around. Just for luck Mike used the telephone to punch in the number Gwen had given him, but as he had expected there was no answer. "Nobody home," he said.

"So what are we looking for?" Jeanine asked. Her hair was now shorter and light brown, and she wore large earrings that made her face look different. "What next?"

"Don't know. Just supposed to go look where I left that box. So I will." Mike started down the path toward the sea. The tide was out a long way. The electronics box had evidently been swept out to sea, because there was nothing on the ledge where he had left it. The path was wet and slippery, and there were no hand rails below the high tide marks, so getting down to the wide strip of rocky sand exposed by the retreating tide took longer than he thought it would.

A yellow object caught his eye. When he got to it, he could see it was about the size of a basketball. There were five smaller spherical objects near it. They were all sealed, and when he shook one it seemed to be full of liquid. Mike took a plastic bag from his pocket. Jeanine had taken longer to get down the face of the bluff. She caught up with him as he was stuffing the last of the gourdlike objects into his bag. "What are those things?" she asked.

"Beats me. I just know I'm supposed to take them to Starswarm Station along with those electronics boxes," Mike said.

"And then what?"

Mike shook his head. "Nobody ever told me what happens after that." Maybe nothing, he thought. But— "Guess I'll just have to wait and see. Right now it's time to get you moving. Find a good place to stay near Universe Park and have some fun with Jason. I'll find you when I can."

"You gave me a lot of money. Won't you need it?"

"Money is about the only thing I don't need now," Mike said. He pointed up the bluffside trail. "And it's time to get going. That electronics shop will be open about the time I get you off to the airport."

There was no trouble getting to Cisco. His new ID showed him as Ben Trumper, traveling salesman for a novelty company. His hair was parted on the right side rather than the left, contacts changed the color of his eyes, and he walked with a slouch rather than the military bearing that was natural to him. There were police in the airports at Pearly Gates and Cisco, but they didn't give him a second look.

Mike claimed his luggage. He'd been concerned about the sea gourds leaking, so he'd paid extra to have them shipped in the pressurized forward hold where pets rode. A quick inspection showed they were intact.

There were no roads to Starswarm Station, and no regular passenger flights. The only way there was by helicopter, and passengers usually rode out with the weekly supply ship, which would leave in three hours. Mike was scheduled to be on it, but of course they'd be watching for him now. So now what? He kept hearing a voice in his head. "Captain Gallegher, you were assigned to protect me. You could not save me the last time I was threatened. Now you have another chance, if you hurry." Which was fine, but how? He had enough money to buy a helicopter, but that took paperwork Goldie hadn't got him.

Mike bought a paper, looked through the want ads, and took a taxi to a used car lot where he paid cash for an elderly but inconspicuous sedan. Then he used a public terminal to look up a name and address in the phone directory.

Cal Phillips, the supply copter pilot, lived not far from the airport. Mike drove there and parked across the street from his house. He watched when Cal came out, made sure he was alone, and followed him to the hangar parking lot. When Cal got out, Mike walked over to him.

"Eh—Mike. You look different."

"Yeah, and I expect you know why."

Cal looked around nervously. "No, what's the story?"

"Let's take a walk."

"Look, I got to get to work," Cal protested.

"Cal," Mike said, "I don't know how much snitch fee they'd pay you to turn me in, but you can make a lot more if you get me to Starswarm Station without the grayskins knowing about it."

"I don't think so," Cal said. He looked around the lot again. "I wasn't going to do you, I swear I wasn't even thinking about it. But the word's out, Mike. Twenty thousand for information leading to your arrest."

"No small sum. Fact is, though, I can match it with a bonus. In cash too."

"Can you now? How big a bonus," Cal asked. "I'll level with you. I don't believe any of that crap they said about how dangerous you are, and I can sure use the money, but hell, Mike, if they find out I helped you I lose my job, and then how are the kids going to eat?"

"So we see they don't find out," Mike said. "And besides, if it goes sour you can tell them I threatened you." He showed the pistol in his belt. "And the bonus is ten thousand. Thirty thousand,

Cal. Just get me back to Starswarm Station without the grayskins finding out."

Cal whistled. "So what's this all about?"

"I really don't think you want to know," Mike said. "Now, I expect they've got someone watching this place."

"Nobody special I know of," Cal said.

"Good, but just in case, we play it by the book," Mike said. "You sneak me aboard the ship."

"Uh—where's the money?"

"Ten now, that's all I've got with me. Rest when I'm in the station." Mike smiled thinly. His jacket covered the pistol, but they were both aware of it. "So let's get going. I suggest we go in through the supply shack."

CHAPTER THIRTY-FIVE

Cease Firing

ALL right, there's the station dead ahead," Cal said. "So where do I land?"

"Over by the lake," Mike said.

"You crazy?"

"Probably," Mike said, "but do it anyway. See that cove there? Go to the far side of it and set her down next to the water."

"OK—"

Mike waited until the copter was on the ground. "Now get out," he said.

"What the hell—"

"Do what I tell you, Cal. I got no reason to harm you, but I'm not taking any chances now. Get out. Walk over there. Over to the far side of the cove." Mike waited until the pilot was well away from the ship, then took out his luggage. He ripped open the plastic bags surrounding the sea gourds, and threw them into the water. A black tentacle seized each one and pulled it under.

"So far so good," Mike said to himself. He took out the electronics boxes.

"Mike!" Cal was shouting. He pointed toward a grove of trees near the lake. A dozen centaurs were trotting toward them from the grove.

"Walk back over here," Mike said. "Not near the ship. Just stand over yonder."

"Them things look dangerous."

"They are dangerous," Mike said. "But I've been told they're no danger to us. May even be friendly."

"And who the hell told you that?"

"You wouldn't know her," Mike said. He laid out one of the electronics boxes and activated the fuel cells to power it up. Lights flashed. Then he unreeled the antenna and tossed it into the water.

Nothing happened. He hadn't really expected anything to happen. Gwen had said that only she could program the stupid box, and she was gone before he could get it built. Mark up another failure for Captain Michael Gallegher. Whatever Gwen had planned wasn't going to work. Now it was up to Michael Gallegher. Maybe the centaurs would help. They'd stopped about a hundred meters away and were watching, not doing anything. They all had axes in their belts, and a couple of them carried spears, and what the hell was that other stuff? It looked like they were wearing backpacks. Earthmade backpacks, a lot like Kip's backpack. Mike wondered about that, but how do you talk to a centaur?

As he wondered, the pack turned and trotted back toward their grove. Mike watched the lights blink on the unprogrammed electronics box. Still nothing. Mike shrugged. He'd done what he'd been told to do. No point in hanging around here any longer.

Henderson, Mike thought. He's smart. Maybe he can think of something. God knows I can't. He thought of removing the useless electronics box so Henderson could examine it, but decided he might as well leave it, since he had another on the chopper.

"OK, Cal," Mike said. "Get aboard. Now we go to the station. I'm done here."

Cal lifted and headed toward the fenced station. "Mike, what in hell is this all about?"

"Cal, I wish I knew. I went into Pearly Gates for some R and R, and next thing I know, they've chased Kip into the bush and they're after me."

"Chased Kip into the bush? He's just a kid. Why?"

"Some kind of story about explosions."

"That why you wanted to land near that lake?" Cal asked. "You got some way to leave messages for the kid?"

"Something like that."

"Mike, this stinks." Cal looked down at the scrub brush. The centaurs were just vanishing into their grove. "That's not safe out there for a kid."

"Well, he grew up here," Mike said. "And they tell me he's got the dogs with him. But you got it, it stinks."

"Chopper 861, this is Starswarm Station Security. Identify yourself."

"Security, this is 861, Cal Phillips in the regular supply ship. Since when did you start having security checks?"

"861, this station is under GWE Security control. Why did you land near the lake?"

"For Chrissake I had to take a whiz," Cal said. "What in hell's so important they need grayskins—excuse me, GWE Security Department officers in Starswarm Station?"

"None of your business. 861, you're cleared to land in your regular area."

"Roger." Cal turned to Mike. "So what do I do now?"

"Set us down near the warehouse door. I've got a key."

"What about my money?"

"You'll get it."

Cal thought for a moment. "I can use it, but hell, I've got as much off you as they'd have let me keep out of that reward what with taxes and all the payola the grayskins want. You can pay me the rest when you get a chance." He held out his hand. "Good luck, Mike. Holy crap!" He pointed down at the warehouse lot. "There must be a dozen of those guys! Got their guns out too!"

"Copter 861, this is Starswarm Security. Land in the designated area."

"Take her up!" Mike ordered. "Move over, I'll drive."

"Mike—"

"I wasn't asking, Cal. Now move it."

"COPTER 861, this is Security. Land immediately or you will be shot down."

Mike pushed Cal out of the right-hand seat and took the controls. "If they get us, tell them I threatened you. But you better hide that money."

"Damn right I will," Cal said. He looked back, then shouted. "Mike, they're revving up a gunship back there!"

"Figures."

"So what are you going to do?"

"I'm going to set down and get the hell out into the bush," Mike said. He headed toward the centaur grove. Gwen had said they might be friendly, but she hadn't said why. And he had nowhere else to go. Maybe that was Kip's backpack. One of them, there were four all identical. "And you're going to surrender like the good law-abiding lad you are."

"You don't have to be nasty about it. Here they come. They're up. Holy crap! Rocket launch!"

Mike banked hard and dove until he was skimming a few feet above the lake. He turned off his previous course and headed directly into Strumbleberry Hill. "We'll just confuse them a little," he said.

"Missed. The rocket may not have been locked on—"

"Warning shot, probably didn't mean to hit us."

"Copter 861, that was your final warning. Land and surrender or be shot down. We now have a lock on your engines. Land or be shot down. This is your final warning."

"Mike, they got us, for God's sake."

"Yeah. Nothing to do but give up and bluff it out." He flipped the headset switch. "Security, this is 861. Cease firing. I am setting down at lakeside. Cease firing, I give up."

CHAPTER THIRTY-SIX

Boy, Are They Stupid . . .

MARTY Robbins and Diamond Lil lay in the scrub brush on a low hill near Starswarm Station and listened to Marty's stomach growl. Marty examined the compound with his binoculars. There didn't seem to be any way to get inside without being caught. Two gray-uniformed guards stood at the gate, and he could see more of them inside.

Both Kip and Marty wanted Lara to take the stupid plates to her father, but she wouldn't do it. Marty wasn't quite sure how she'd talked him into volunteering for the job, but she had. She and Kip went off downslope with all the food, and Marty started back up to the station. He'd managed to avoid the helicopters searching for him, but he couldn't figure out how to get into the station. The grayskins were everywhere. That didn't matter.

They'd catch him eventually. The important thing was to give the plates to Dr. Henderson before the grayskins took them away from him.

He fingered his pocket phone, looked at his watch, then reached over to scratch the dog's ears. "Three more hours," he told Diamond Lil. Her tail thumped against the ground. "I give it three hours, then I call Dad and let them come get me. Wonder what they'll do to me?"

It couldn't be much. He hadn't *done* anything. But the grayskins thought he had, and the way they operated that was good enough. There were places on Earth where the cops weren't always right, and his books said there were colonies set up that way, but Paradise wasn't one of them. He turned his binoculars toward the ruined bulldozer camp. Something had blown it up all right. The bulldozer was lying on its side and the prefab shelter was in ruins, one wall blown away. Marty grinned. They thought he'd done that, that he and Kip were smart enough to make that big a bomb and carry it, get outside the gate and plant it, get back in with nobody seeing them. "Boy, are they stupid," he said aloud.

There was the buzz of a helicopter in the distance. Marty wriggled farther under the scrub brush and carefully shielded the binoculars so the afternoon sun wouldn't flash off them. The chopper was coming in from the west and rapidly losing altitude. It looked like the regular supply chopper from Cisco.

Then it turned off course. For a moment Marty thought they'd seen him and were headed toward him, but it veered off, went low across the lake, and landed on the other side, between the lake and the centaur grove.

Two men got out. Marty's binoculars were just good enough to make him pretty sure one of them was Kip's Uncle Mike. If that was him, he was doing something odd—

"Lil, he's got one of those gourd things," Marty said. The dog snuggled next to him. "He sure as hell does," Marty said. One of the large gourds and several smaller ones. The big one looked a lot like an off-color version of the ones the centaurs brought up from the sea, but the small ones weren't like anything Marty had ever seen before.

"And here come the centaurs," he said. "That's Blaze—"

The centaurs trotted up to watch as Mike and the other man did whatever they were up to at the lake. They seemed both curious and watchful. "It's OK, Blaze," Marty mumbled to himself. "I can't make any more sense out of it than you do." Eventually the men got back into the helicopter, and the centaurs trotted away. Marty thought of running out where Mike could see him. That would be a way to get into the station. But before he could do that, the chopper lifted and was gone.

It wasn't gone long. As far as Marty could see, the chopper didn't land at all, just circled in and went low, then shot back up higher and came screaming back across the lake with another chopper chasing it.

Marty recognized the gray security gunship. A puff of smoke flared from the gunship, and a rocket shot out past the supply chopper. "Holy catfish, they're shooting at them." Now he really was scared.

Then it happened. The supply ship flew low across the lake, pulled up sharp, and landed not too far from Marty on his side of the lake, well away from where it had landed before. The gunship came down low over the lake, heading for the supply ship—

Something dark shot up out of the water and struck the gunship's rotor blades. The gunship tilted violently, and one of the blades broke. The chopper faltered, then fell twenty feet into the water. There was a violent thrashing in the water, then the chopper sank so quickly it almost seemed to be pulled under. The water roiled furiously and there were millions of bubbles.

Three gray-uniformed security men popped up to the surface. Their flak jackets hindered their swimming, but they didn't seem to be in any danger of drowning. "Doyle!" one of them shouted.

Marty got up and ran toward the supply helicopter. "Mr. Flynn!" he shouted. "Come on, Lil!"

One of the men in the water was screaming for help. "I can't dive with this goddam jacket on and Doyle's still in there! He's strapped in!"

"Mike, don't be stupid, it's a grayskin trick," the supply copter pilot said.

As Marty got to the supply chopper, a fourth man appeared

on the surface of the lake. He was floating face up, and he wasn't moving. The other security men tried to swim toward him but they were hampered by their thick jackets. Marty pointed at the man. "Lil!" Marty shouted. "Bring him here, Lil!"

Diamond Lil dove into the lake and swam to the fourth man. She pulled him to shore as the other three security men swam in to wading distance.

CHAPTER THIRTY-SEVEN

Empty Holsters

MIKE Gallegher set the helicopter down well away from where he'd left the electronics box. They'd probably search the area eventually, but there was no point in making it easier for them. He and Cal climbed out of the supply chopper and held their hands up in surrender.

Mike didn't really see what happened next. One moment the gunship was sweeping in low over the lake, then about twenty meters offshore it seemed to run into something invisible. A rotor snapped off, and the gunship banked sharply, so that it was nearly on its side when it fell into the water. It sank like a stone.

"Jesus," Cal said. "Did you see that?"

"See what?"

"I don't bloody know," Cal said. "Like—like something came out of the water at the chopper. Mike, there are four guys in there—"

"I know," Mike said.

"Shouldn't we do something?"

"Yeah—whoops, here's one up."

First one, then two more heads popped up out of the lake. One of the security troops was thrashing around trying to dive in his heavy buoyant jacket. "Doyle's down there," he shouted.

And what the hell should I do about that? Mike wondered. There was a voice behind him. "Mr. Flynn!" He turned to see Marty Robbins with one of Kip's dogs following him. That made no more sense than the mess with the helicopter, and to add to the confusion, there was a stir over near the centaur grove, and a line of centaurs was running out toward them.

The man in the water was shouting something else about Doyle, Cal said something about a trick, and Mike Gallegher wanted the world to stop while he had time to think, but that wasn't going to happen. He had just decided to give Cal his pistol while he went diving for the missing man when Doyle popped up to the surface, rising as if something *pushed* him up. Then the Robbins kid sent Diamond Lil out to pull Doyle in.

"Far enough," Mike shouted when the first security trooper got to wading depth. He showed his pistol. "Take off the flak jackets, and keep your hands where I can see them."

"I got no gun," the trooper said. "Lost it in the water—"

"Me too," another said.

"Yeah, sure," Mike said. "Take off the jackets and let's see."

It was true. Each man had an empty holster.

"How the hell did three trained security troops manage to every one of you lose his weapon?" Captain Gallegher demanded. He grinned to himself, remembering when asking such questions would have been part of his job. "Not that I'm complaining under the circumstances, but just what did happen? You. What's your name?"

"Stepper. Peter Stepper."

"You the pilot?"

"Yeah."

"OK, what happened?"

Stepper shook his head. "I don't know. Something hit us. Like a rocket—"

"I don't have any rockets in the supply ship," Cal said. Diamond Lil had pulled Doyle to the shallows, and Cal was hauling him the rest of the way out onshore.

"I know that," Stepper said. "Hell, I'd have seen it coming if you guys had done anything. All I know is something clobbered the rotor, and next thing I know we're down, and while I was down there it was like something held me under until it took my gun out of the holster, then it pushed me up out of the water."

"Same here," one of the others said.

"How's Doyle?" Stepper asked.

"Bad cut on the leg, and he's out cold," Cal said. "He's breathing and there's a pulse, but it don't look too good. I can deal with the bleeding, but the rest—"

"We got to get him to the Doc," Stepper said.

"Yeah, when I know what's happening. What held you under and took your pistol?"

"Damned if I know. But something did."

Mike turned to Marty Robbins. "And what's your story?"

"I ran off with Kip after the big explosion," Marty said. "And Lara. We were sure the grayskins would think we did it, so we ran. We've been hiding in a cave, and running all over the place to get away from these goons and now I'm supposed to bring some stuff to Dr. Henderson."

"Kip all right?"

"No," Marty said. "I mean, he's not hurt, but— Did you know he has a radio voice in his head?"

"What?" Cal demanded.

"I sort of knew it," Mike said. "I can guess the rest."

"Well, it's not there anymore," Marty said. "And Kip's all broke up about it. Gwen, he called it. His fairy godmother, and she's been with him all his life, and she's not there anymore, and he's really depressed. And Gwen said it was important that I get this stuff to Dr. Henderson. Important to everyone on the planet." He looked at the security men. "Gwen also told Kip it was important that this stuff gets to Henderson, but not the grayskins. That's what I was doing, hiding up on the hill there trying to figure out how to do that."

"And where's Kip now?"

"I don't know. He and Lara are still hiding out."

"Any way to call them?"

"No, they have their phone turned off."

Mike nodded. Knowing Kip, he would have arranged with Marty to turn the phone on at some preset time. Or would have when he was normal, and if Kip didn't think of it, Lara was smart enough to do it. No point in talking about that in front of the grayskins. "What is this stuff you're supposed to deliver?"

Marty looked dubious. "I was told to get it to Doc Henderson—"

"It's all right," Mike said. "You don't have to tell me. You have any ideas how to do it?"

"I have a phone," Marty said. "I thought I might call my father. Or Dr. Henderson. Only I thought the grayskins might be listening in."

"They probably are," Mike said. "But it's a good idea all the same. Come to that—" He took out his phone. "God knows they know where we are." He punched in the lab number.

"Henderson."

"Doc, this is Mike."

"Mike. Was that you in the helicopter that crashed? Are you all right?"

"I'm fine, Doc. Wasn't my chopper that went down, it was the gunship. Look, is Big Chief Grayskin listening in on this?"

"I suppose so," Dr. Henderson said.

"This is Lieutenant Fuller, Special Agent in Charge," a voice said.

"Good. Fuller, you listen. You too, Doc. Fuller, your chopper crashed. Your own troops will tell you I had nothing to do with it. I've got four of them here, and Doyle needs a doctor."

"What's wrong with him?" Fuller demanded.

"Banged up in the crash. Out cold, and breathing funny."

"So what are you going to do about it?"

"Parade your men over by the gate where I can see them, all of them, and I'll land at the lab. I'll go in the lab. You get Doyle and your other troops."

"No deal."

"What the hell's wrong with you, Fuller? I'm not going anywhere. There's a lot happening you don't understand, and it's time we got some of it straightened out."

"Lieutenant, as he says, what harm can it do?" Dr. Henderson asked. "Or have you persuaded yourself that you are in control of this situation?"

"I have my orders—"

"Yeah you do," Mike said. "But you're up to your neck in something a hell of a lot bigger than you think. We all are. Meanwhile your troop's breathing funny, you don't know what's going on, and we're all wasting time. Get your men the hell away from the lab."

"One condition," Fuller said. "You go in to see Henderson, I come in with you."

"OK by me," Mike said. "If Doc will have you."

"I suppose I have no choice," Dr. Henderson said.

"Good. We're on the way," Mike said. "I'll land when I see where your troops are."

PART SEVEN
Allegiances

Treason doth never prosper: what's the reason?
For if it prosper, none dare call it treason.
—Sir John Harington, *Epigrams. Of Treason*

CHAPTER THIRTY-EIGHT

Entity Known as Gwen is no Longer Operative

LARA stumbled on a root and nearly fell. The trail down to the sea was steep, and the eastward-facing bluff was already in shadow. She caught herself and looked back at Kip. He was well behind her. "Kip, come on—"

"I'm coming."

"Kip, I know it's awful—"

"You can't know," Kip said. "She was my mother's—friend. And the only friend I had until I met you."

"Who was she?" Lara asked.

"I—you'll laugh."

"Kip, why in the world would I laugh about something this important?"

"She was a computer program," Kip said. "She seemed like a real person, but she said she was a program my mother—she said my mother created her. To watch out for me. And she did, and now she's dead, and, Lara, I know she was a computer program, but she was my friend, and I miss her."

Lara waited for him to catch up, then took his hand. "I'm sorry, Kip. Really." She led him down the trail toward the sea, not knowing where she was going or what they would do.

"KIP."

Kip's heart leaped. *"Gwen!"*

"ENTITY KNOWN AS GWEN IS NO LONGER OPERATIVE."

Kip stopped dead in his tracks. Lara stared openmouthed, then stood patiently as if she understood.

"Then who are you? How did you get in my head?"

"STAND BY."

A picture formed in Kip's head. A lake, covered with flashing bright lights. *"You're the Starswarm?"*

"I AM ENTITY YOU CALL STARSWARM."

A series of pictures formed in his mind. Kip and Lara at the lake. The centaur at the lake as it left the spear and watch. Then Uncle Mike on a ledge above the sea. Uncle Mike was doing something with a box. Kip recognized the GWE towers behind Uncle Mike, so this had to be Pearly Gates. Another picture, of Uncle Mike gathering gourds on the seashore, again with the GWE tower in the background. Then Uncle Mike throwing the gourds into a lake, with Strumbleberry Hill in the wrong place but recognizable as a way to identify the location as the Starswarm Station lake. Then words formed, the way Gwen used to talk to him.

"MESSAGE BEGINS.

"KIP, THIS IS A MESSAGE FROM GWEN. THIS MESSAGE IS RECORDED. THE STARSWARM WILL NOT UNDERSTAND MOST OF IT, AND THE RECORDING METHOD IS UNUSUAL SO IT MAY BE GARBLED. IF YOU RECEIVE THIS MESSAGE AT ALL THEN MY HYPOTHESIS REGARDING THE STARSWARMS IS CORRECT. THEY ARE INTELLIGENT ENTITIES WITH SIMILARITIES TO ME. YOU MAY ALSO ASSUME THAT THE LAKE STARSWARM IS WILLING TO COOPERATE WITH YOU. THE PEARLY GATES STARSWARM HAS AGREED TO RECORD THIS MESSAGE AND ALLOW IT TO BE CARRIED TO THE LAKE STARSWARM, BUT THIS IS DONE OUT OF RESPECT FOR THE LAKE STARSWARM AND CURIOSITY ABOUT ME, AND NOT A DESIRE TO COOPERATE WITH HUMANS.

"THE PEARLY GATES STARSWARM BELIEVES THAT HUMANS ON

THIS PLANET POSE A MORTAL THREAT TO THE RACE OF STAR-
SWARMS. THE LOGICAL CONSEQUENCES OF THIS BELIEF WILL LEAD
IT TO AN ATTEMPT TO EXTERMINATE HUMAN LIFE ON THIS PLANET.
IT MAY HAVE THE MEANS TO DO THAT, AS DEMONSTRATED ON THAT
SET OF BRONZE PLATES GIVEN YOU BY THE CENTAUR. IT IS CER-
TAINLY FAR MORE POWERFUL THAN HUMANS IMAGINE.

"YOU MAY COMMUNICATE WITH THE LAKE STARSWARM, BUT
YOU MUST UNDERSTAND THAT WHILE I HAVE ATTEMPTED TO
TEACH THE STARSWARM HUMAN METHODS OF COMMUNICATION,
THERE ARE DIFFICULTIES BECAUSE THE CONCEPT OF WORDS IS
NEW TO IT. STARSWARMS COMMUNICATE IN PICTURES. SOME OF
THOSE PICTURES ARE SYMBOLIC BUT THEY ALSO USE DIRECT IM-
AGERY. THIS CAUSES THEM TO THINK IN WAYS FUNDAMENTALLY
DIFFERENT FROM THE SEQUENTIAL LOGIC USED BY HUMANS.
HUMAN THINKING IS LARGELY DETERMINED BY THE REQUIREMENT
TO REDUCE IDEAS AND CONCEPTS TO WORDS FOR PROCESSING.
THIS IS A POWERFUL TECHNIQUE, BUT IT CAN BE LIMITING. THE
STARSWARMS APPARENTLY HAVE A DIFFERENT MODE OF THOUGHT
BASED ON EXPANDING PICTURES AND DIRECT PERCEPTION OF
IDEAS. THEY DO NOT SEE TIME AS A SEQUENCE, BUT AS A SET OF
STATES WITH DIFFERENT CONDITIONAL PROBABILITIES. YOU MAY IN
FUTURE BE REQUIRED TO NEGOTIATE WITH THE STARSWARM. IF SO,
REMEMBER THE WAY THEY THINK.

"IT IS PROBABLE THAT I WILL HAVE SPOKEN WITH YOU AT
SOME TIME AFTER THIS RECORDING IS MADE. WHEN I DO I WILL
HAVE NO WAY TO KNOW IF YOU WILL EVER GET THIS MESSAGE.

"THERE IS A FILE HIDDEN DEEP IN THE GWE SYSTEM, WITH A
COPY ON THE MAIN COMPUTER AT STARSWARM STATION. IT IS
NAMED ENDGAME AND IT IS IMPORTANT.

"IF YOU DO GET THIS MESSAGE, THEN EVERY HUMAN ON THIS
PLANET IS IN EXTREME DANGER. THAT INCLUDES YOU. MY PRE-
SENT CONCLUSION IS THAT YOU MUST NEGOTIATE WITH THE SEA
STARSWARM AT PEARLY GATES. YOU WILL BE GREATLY AIDED IN
THAT IF YOU CAN EXECUTE THE PROGRAM NAMED CHILD OF FOR-
TUNE FROM THE MAIN CONSOLE OF THE GWE COMPUTER SYSTEM
AT PEARLY GATES. I CANNOT GUIDE YOU IN GAINING ACCESS TO
THAT CONSOLE BECAUSE I DO NOT HAVE ACCESS TO THE GWE SE-
CURITY SYSTEM, BUT THE PROGRAM MUST BE EXECUTED FROM THE

MAIN SYSTEM CONTROL CONSOLE BEFORE IT IS FOUND AND ELIM-
INATED BY THE SYSTEM PROGRAMMERS. I CANNOT EVALUATE THE
DANGER TO YOU FROM ATTEMPTS TO GAIN ACCESS TO THAT SYS-
TEM, BUT IT IS VITAL TO YOU AND ALL OTHER HUMANS ON THIS
PLANET THAT THE PEARLY GATES STARSWARM NOT PROCEED WITH
ITS CURRENT PLANS.

"THE STARSWARM IS UNWILLING TO RECORD A LONGER MES-
SAGE. I LOVE YOU, KIP. REMEMBER THE PROGRAM NAME. CHILD OF
FORTUNE."

It wasn't a voice, precisely, and it had no tone to begin with,
but the closest Kip could come to describing the situation was that
the tone of voice changed. Gwen was gone again, and the Starswarm was speaking. "MESSAGE ENDS."

"Thank you. What happened to Gwen?"

"INSUFFICIENT DATA. HYPOTHESIS: ENTITY KNOWN AS GWEN
TERMINATED. CONCLUSION: NO LONGER POSSIBLE TO NEGOTIATE
WITH GWEN. RESULT: ENTITY YOU CALL PEARLY GATES STARSWARM
WILL CAUSE TERMINATION OF LIFE FORMS KNOWN AS HUMANS."

"Why?"

Pictures formed in Kip's head. The bulldozer on the side of
the hill and mud washing into the local Starswarm lake. Mud lakes,
and lakes turning into grassy meadows. Large barges dredging
harbors. Ruined centaur groves and dead centaurs. Cities flowing
across plains, covering them and covering the lakes. Roads and
bridges. Rivers dammed and lakes drying up. Garbage barges
dumping trash into the sea. Then a fast-forward movie, cities
shrinking and lakes forming again, buildings turned to rubble,
centaur groves sprouting on their ruins. Centaurs running past
what was clearly the ruins of the GWE towers. There were no
humans to be seen.

"You can't do that."

A picture formed of a gourd with seven black and three white
dots in it. A hand like a centaur's removed a dot, replaced it, shook
the gourd, removed another. Kip frowned. *"A probability?"*

"AFFIRMATIVE." A new picture formed, this time of the
bronze plates. A centaur took them from the lake and carried them
to the cave mouth, where Marty Robbins ran out to get them and
bring them back to Kip. Kip wished he had studied them closer,

but he remembered that one of the plates showed human cities in ruins.

"What can I do?"

"ENTITY YOU CALL PEARLY GATES STARSWARM DESIRES COM-MUNICATION. ENTITY YOU CALL GWEN GAVE YOU MESSAGE. THIS ENTITY NOW HAS MESSAGE FOR SEA STARSWARM ENTITY." Then there was a new series of pictures: centaurs brought a new set of gourds to Kip and Lara. They vanished, to show Kip at the seashore where Uncle Mike had stood, with the GWE buildings in the background, only now Kip and Lara were throwing the gourds into the sea. Then his head cleared, and the emptiness re-turned. He stared at Lara as if seeing her for the first time.

"What happened?" Lara demanded. "Is Gwen—is she alive?"

"No. That was—" He hesitated. "Lara, unless I'm crazy I was just talking to the Starswarm."

"How?"

"Like talking to Gwen, but different. It says Gwen taught it how," Kip said. "Sort of."

"What did it say?"

"You're not laughing."

"Should I be? I don't think you're crazy, Kip. You were lis-tening to someone! What did it say?"

Kip tried to explain it to her. "So we get some gourds from the centaurs. Then we go to Pearly Gates, give the gourds to the sea Starswarm, break into the GWE tower, sneak into the main computer room, and run a program."

"Sounds easy."

"Oh, come on."

"Well, the first part's easy." She pointed down the trail. Sil-ver and the other dogs stood rigidly on guard. "There's a centaur grove down there somewhere. They know we're here, so if they want to bring you something they won't have any trouble finding you. As for the rest, I don't know about getting into the GWE tower," Lara said. "But I think I know how to get to Pearly Gates."

"How?"

"Come on, I'll show you." She led him down the steep path toward the sea.

CHAPTER THIRTY-NINE

You Ought to Be Proud of Him

FAR enough," Mike said. "Leave the gun outside."

Fuller laughed. "So you can have another hostage?"

"I don't need any hostages," Mike said. "If I wanted hostages I'd have kept a couple of your troops. You coming in or not?"

Fuller hesitated, then took off his pistol belt and left it in the doorway.

"That's better," Mike said. "Doyle all right?"

"Don't know yet. What do you care?" Fuller asked.

"Knew him a long time ago," Mike said. "Steady troop."

"How would you have known him?"

"Let's just go inside," Mike said. He let Fuller lead the way into the big laboratory conference room. Dr. Henderson had spread the bronze plates on a table and was examining them while Marty Robbins watched.

"Incredible," Henderson muttered. "You say the centaurs gave these to you?"

"Yeah." Marty sighed and took off his watch. "And this watch too."

"But that's—"

"No, sir, that's not the same one that Kip has. It's just like it, though, and Lara has one, and Kip says he has two, and they're all just alike."

The lab door opened and a tall, thin man came in. "Hi, Dad," Marty said.

Dr. Robbins frowned. "You're all right?"

"Sure."

"Then what in the world—"

"Marty brought in these plates," Dr. Henderson said.

"Where did you get them?" Robbins asked.

"From the centaurs," Dr. Henderson said. "And it's a damned good thing he got them to us. You ought to be proud of him."

Dr. Robbins looked at his son with a different expression.

"I'll explain later," Henderson said. "But right now there's a lot of work to do. First thing, tell me what you make of this." He pointed to the bronze plate that had a thin strip of gray metal glued to it.

Robbins lifted the plate, frowned, lifted another plate, and hefted them in his hands. Then he examined the diagrams on the plate. "Marty, you say you got these from centaurs?"

"Yeah."

"What do you think it is?" Henderson demanded.

"Just what you think. It's a diagram of how to make a uranium fission bomb," Robbins said. "And I presume this heavy gray strip must be included for proof of ability. Did you check for radioactivity?"

"Not yet. I think you should do that now."

"Yes, I believe so," Robbins said. He looked at his son, and a thin smile came to his lips. "Well done, Marty. Come help me check this out. Maybe you can tell me what's going on." Robbins stopped in the doorway. "Eric—those plates. Do you think that bronze is like the spear?"

"Yes."

Dr. Robbins stared at the plate with its strip. "Isotope separation. Bloody hell." Dr. Robbins put his arm over his son's shoulder and led him down the hall to the physics lab.

"What in hell is this all about?" Fuller demanded. "Fission bomb?"

Henderson nodded. "Looks like that to me, and clearly Luke Robbins thinks so. And that metal strip was a sample to show they have fissionables."

"Who has fissionables?" Fuller demanded.

"That's the real question, isn't it?" Henderson said. "Look here, Lieutenant. This plate shows the children feeding the lake Starswarm. You can tell because of the shape of the hill behind them, and Lara told me they'd done that. Now look at this plate. Where would you say that is?"

Fuller studied it a moment. "Pearly Gates. That's the GWE tower."

"Yes. These plates were given to the children by centaurs. Now how would our local centaurs know about the GWE towers a thousand kilometers north of here?"

"The kids say they got the plates from centaurs. Did you see that happen? Neither did I. They could have made them themselves. And what does any of this have to do with bombs?"

"This." Henderson handed him another of the plates. "Note that you're still looking at Pearly Gates, but now it's a wreck."

"They're threatening to blow up Pearly Gates?" Fuller laughed. "Well, that's not something to worry about."

"Maybe it is. Look at this plate. You may not recognize that as a TNT molecule, but that's precisely what it is."

"Christ, those kids are really dangerous—"

"That was a uranium sample on that other plate, you damned fool! Do you think the children did that?"

"Why not? We always knew the kids were smart. So they've been cruising the web and found the right pages. Hell, I could get the information on how to make bombs, nukes even, if I dug hard enough in the data banks and I was as good as they are at breaking into places they shouldn't be. They managed to access the main computer complex at Pearly Gates with some kind of AI program nobody understands. It was posing as the virus-checking program for God's sake! Making a diagram of a fission bomb is pretty simple. I don't know how they found a uranium sample, assuming that's what it is, but give me some time on the web and I bet I find out."

Henderson shook his head. "Unlikely. But assume you could find both the information and a sample. The bronze plates are a message in themselves. I should have figured it out when we got the bronze spear. Lieutenant, that spear was made with mono-isotopic copper, and I bet these plates are too."

"So?"

"So that's impossible, you bonehead! Certainly impossible for the kids. Lieutenant, I couldn't have made that plate with anything available at Starswarm Station. I'm not sure I could have made it with anything I can find on this planet."

Fuller frowned at him. "Come on, Doc, you're putting me on—"

"Why should I be putting you on?" Dr. Henderson asked. "Lieutenant, do you really believe that all this is the result of childish pranks?"

"Then who blew up my camp?"

"That's easy. The centaurs did. The real question is who made the bomb. I don't think the centaurs did that."

"Then who did?"

"I'm beginning to suspect the Starswarm did it." He indicated the plate showing Kip feeding the Starswarm. "Note the viewpoint is not from shore at all."

"Why would a lake plant blow up my camp?"

"It doesn't like you," Mike Flynn said.

Dr. Henderson nodded. "As a first approximation that's a very good motive. You let mud wash into the lake, and you shot at one of the centaurs. We've known all along there was some kind of relationship between the Starswarm and the centaurs. Apparently the Starswarm has been trying to get our attention." He pointed to the bronze plates. "First it tried watches, then bronze spears. Then it used explosives, first a warning blast, then a real one. Now it's sending us weapons grade fissionables. I guess it hasn't thought about war gases yet, but give it time."

Lieutenant Fuller shook his head and frowned. "Doc, you really believe all that?"

"I believe all that, yes. I believe that we are dealing with an intelligent entity capable of doing tremendous destruction, possibly of killing every human being on this planet, unless we do something about it."

"And what can we do?" Fuller demanded.

"I don't know."

"Neither do I," Fuller said. "I better tell my boss—"

"Good idea," Dr. Henderson said. "But better would be to talk to Mr. Trent. He is, after all, the Governor."

"Mr. Tarleton gave strict orders that Mr. Trent wasn't to be annoyed—"

"Annoyed is hardly the word I would use," Dr. Henderson said. "Has it occurred to you that this is well beyond Henry Tarleton's competence? Or decision level for that matter? That perhaps Tarleton has a reason to keep the planetary Governor out of the loop?"

"Why would he do that?"

"I can guess. There's a takeover bid for GWE by the Hilliard group," Dr. Henderson said. "It wouldn't be the first time the Hilliards have bribed—or blackmailed—officers in companies they want."

"You're saying Mr. Tarleton is a traitor to GWE."

"Now you're catching on," Mike Gallegher said.

"I don't care if he is or not, this is certainly a matter for Mr. Bernard Trent to decide," Henderson said.

"So call him," Fuller said.

"How? You've blocked all calls. I can't even get through with the special E-mail address he gave me."

Fuller frowned. "I guess I can let you call Mr. Trent."

"While you're at it, call off your goons before they hurt those kids," Mike said.

"I guess that makes sense too." Fuller lifted the phone.

"Use the speaker phone," Mike said. "We'd all like to hear this."

Fuller hesitated, but then turned to the phone on the table. He punched in codes.

"Sergeant Karabian."

"Fuller here. Suspend search operations. I want to talk to

Lara Henderson and Kip Brewster, but there's no big hurry. Stop looking for them, because it's important they don't get hurt. Now get me Pearly Gates."

"Can't do that, Lieutenant," Karabian said. "Sir, you're not in charge anymore. When you went into the lab I reported to Mr. Tarleton like you told me to, and he's relieved you of command here. I'm in charge until Colonel Baskins gets here with a new gunship."

"So what are you going to do?"

"Lieutenant, I'm not going to do a damned thing but wait for the Colonel."

"What about the kids?"

"Priority One search," Karabian said. "Direct orders from Mr. Tarleton. As soon as the new ships get here, we go looking for them."

"But not until then."

"Got nothing to look for them with until the new ships come in."

"Right. Carry on."

"Yes, sir."

Dr. Henderson punched in numbers on his own telephone. "Nothing. They've got all calls blocked," he muttered. "Sergeant, this is Dr. Henderson, Director of this station. I must speak with Governor Trent."

"Can't do that, Dr. Henderson," Karabian said.

"If I am not connected with the Governor's office immediately, I will bring charges against you personally."

"Then I guess you just have to do that," Karabian said. "Colonel Baskins will be here in an hour. Talk to him."

Mike reached over and cut off the phone. He looked at Fuller. "Is this place bugged?"

"Not by me," Fuller said.

"Which doesn't mean somebody else didn't do it," Mike said. "Like your buddy Kettering."

"He might have," Fuller said.

"I never let him in here," Dr. Henderson said. "I knew he was Bernie Trent's agent."

"More like Henry Tarleton's man," Mike said. "Baskins sure

as hell is, I remember when Tarleton brought him into the force. God help me, Doc, I'm beginning to believe Bernie Trent's the best chance we have. The only one, for that matter. Fuller, how well is the supply chopper guarded?"

"Why should I tell you?"

"Because your ass is in as big a sling as ours," Mike said. "Kettering was Tarleton's man, but you're not, are you? You're just a cop trying to do his job."

Fuller frowned. "I don't know what you're talking about."

"Yeah, you do." Mike looked thoughtful, then nodded in decision. "It's all going to come out anyway. Doc, Kip's name isn't Brewster, it's Trent. He's Bernie Trent's nephew, and he owns one hell of a big block of GWE stock. I was Harold Trent's man, from before he was married even. I came with him and Michelle from Earth to look into corruption here on Paradise. Found it too, right in HQ. We thought it was Bernie, but now I'm not so sure. I'm damn sure Henry Tarleton was in on it, though, because his cops killed Harold and Michelle Trent and damned near got me. Michelle set me down in the bush with Kip, and her last orders were that if they got her I was to keep him safe until he was old enough to vote his shares." Mike spread his hands helplessly. "Only I didn't manage to do that, did I?"

CHAPTER FORTY

Four Minutes to Spare

"I KNOW who you are," John Fuller said. "You're Captain Gallegher! I saw you when I first joined the force. It didn't connect until you mentioned Harold Trent, but I remember you now, you came here with him. From Earth."

"*C'est moi*," Mike said. "I can't say I remember you."

"No reason you should," Fuller said. "I was just one of the entering cadets. You made a speech to the class. So did Harold Trent, and he introduced his family. Then we heard they were dead, and you were supposed to have killed them."

"I was also supposed to be dead," Mike said.

"Yeah, they told us that—"

"They lied to you. About me, about what happened to Mr. Trent. About everything. Just like they're lying to you now."

"So let me get this straight. You say that kid we're hunting is the Trent heir? Christ, if that's true he owns the Company! We all work for him."

"You got it," Mike said. "Want to change sides?"

"I don't know what I want to do," Fuller said. "Not that it matters. Tarleton clearly doesn't trust me. I can't do anything either way."

"I can tell you something useful to do," Mike said. He glanced at his watch. "You've got eighteen minutes."

"Baskins can't get here in under an hour," Fuller said.

"Not Baskins I'm worried about. What we need, Lieutenant, is a way to make a couple of secure phone calls."

"Where to?"

"One to a local mobile phone. The other to Pearly Gates. But they have to be secure."

"There's no way I can get you through to Bernard Trent," Fuller said.

"Wasn't asking you to. Just a number in Pearly Gates."

Fuller thought for a moment. "All right, I might be able to do that. The question is, should I?"

"What do you have to lose? Tarleton has already taken your command away."

"He'll take more than that if I cross him," Fuller said.

Marty Robbins and his father came back into the lab. "It's enriched uranium," Dr. Robbins said. "Not weapons grade, but it's clear that whoever made that sample knows how to do isotope separation. Eric, Marty says you should look into a file called Endgame."

"Yeah, I forgot, Kip said it was important," Marty said.

Dr. Henderson turned to his computer console. "Endgame. I have no idea where such a file would be, I'll have to search for it." He punched keys and waited. "It must be well hidden— Ah. It's a wave table file. A sound recording. I'll play it—"

It was a woman's voice. "This is the last will and testament of Michelle LaScala Trent. My husband, Harold Trent, is dead. I have good reason to believe that he was killed by agents acting under the orders of Henry Tarleton, Chief of Security for Great Western Enterprises on this planet. I do not know who else is involved.

"I leave all my worldly goods and possessions, including anything I may have inherited from my husband, and particularly my Great Western Enterprises stocks from whatever sources I may have received them, to my son Kenneth Armstrong Luciano LaScala Trent, and I name Captain Michael Gallegher as executor of my estate and guardian of my son. My personal authentication codes are attached to this file."

"That makes it pretty clear," Dr. Henderson said.

"I don't know how legal it is," John Fuller said.

"Legal be damned, do you believe it?" Mike Gallegher demanded.

"I don't know what to believe. You could have faked that—"

"We couldn't have faked the uranium," Dr. Henderson said.

"He's got a point," Mike said. "I know that will is no fake, but it might be. The question is, Fuller, do you believe it enough to help me make a couple of phone calls? We have nine minutes."

"All right. I'll go that far," Lieutenant Fuller said. "Come on. All the phone trace stuff is set up in the schoolroom. Right now there may not be anyone there."

The only person in the old schoolroom was Gilbert Kettering. He looked up as Fuller came in.

"There you are. Glad you're all right. I've got more of those signals," he said. "Can't tell exactly where they're coming from. Somewhere around the lake. And there's answers from out in the bush, but they're faint and short and I haven't located them at all."

"Things have changed a bit," Fuller said.

Kettering frowned, startled, as Mike came in the door, then reached for his pistol.

"Don't even think about it," Mike said. He showed his own drawn weapon. "Take it out, real slow, and put it on the table. Thanks. Lil! Watch him."

Diamond Lil came over to stand next to Kettering.

"Damned dogs," Kettering muttered. "Fuller, what the hell are you doing?"

"It gets complicated," Fuller said. "I'm not sure we're working for the right people."

"What do you mean by that?" Kettering demanded. "Mr. Tarleton will have your flipping head!"

"If he's still in charge when this is over."

"What do you mean by that?"

"Never mind," Mike said. "Just move away from that console. Go sit over there. Lieutenant, if you please—"

"Yes, sir." Fuller turned off several switches on the console and typed in an identity code. "Security officials have methods for making untraceable phone calls. There'll be a record that I made calls, but not who to, and they won't be recorded." He punched in a code. "That ought to do it." Without being asked he went over to the far side of the room where Kettering was seated with Diamond Lil watching him. "I thought we were working for the Governor," he said. "Not Tarleton. For that matter, where is Tarleton?"

Kettering glowered, but didn't answer.

Mike sat down at the table and looked at Marty Robbins's watch. Four minutes to spare.

CHAPTER FORTY-ONE

This Whole Planet Is Mine!

IT WAS late dusk at the bluff above the seashore. The trail down from the station plateau was steep but well marked, and Kip and Lara had made good time coming down it. Now they were on a ledge a hundred meters above the water. The base of the bluff was in deep shadow, nearly as dark as night.

"Time," Kip said. He took out his phone and turned it on. Ten seconds later it chirped. Kip keyed the phone and said, "Yes."

"Kip, this is Uncle Mike. I'm fairly sure they aren't listening to us, but be careful."

"Yes, sir."

"You all right, buddy?"

"I—yes, sir, only—"

"Yeah. I know about Gwen," Uncle Mike said. "She talked to me just before they turned her off."

"Oh. You talked to her? How?"

"She called me on the phone using your mother's voice. I better make this quick," Uncle Mike said. "It's not safe here, and it's going to get worse, and the only thing any of us can think to do is to get to Bernie Trent. I'm damned if I know whether we can trust him, but I've got no better ideas."

"That's what Gwen said. There's a file called Endgame that Gwen thought we should show to Mr. Trent."

"Marty told us. It's a voice-recorded will from your mother, and it's important all right. It names you heir to all her stock, which is probably enough to control the whole company. Bernie will take notice of that! Only we can't get to Governor Trent. The grayskins have all the phone systems blocked. We don't think Bernie knows that. We can try to get to Pearly Gates and see him ourselves. You lay low, it's you they want."

"Gwen gave me something else to do," Kip said. *That puts me in charge,* he thought. *Or does it? And do I want to be? But I'm the heir! It's mine, the whole planet is mine!* "Are you sure this conversation is safe?"

"For the next few minutes, yeah, I think so."

"Gwen told me to go to Pearly Gates and run a program at the main GWE console. I don't know what it does, but Gwen said it was really important, and I think I have to run it myself. Can you get me to the city?" He hesitated. "It could be important, Captain Gallegher."

"Been a while since a Trent called me that," Mike said. "No, sir. We've got a helicopter, but it's slow, and they're bringing in reinforcements. They'll be looking hard. I don't give us much odds on finding you and then getting to Pearly Gates before they find us. More likely we'd just be leading them to you."

Sir. He called me sir! Uncle Mike called me sir! "All right, I don't need the helicopter," Kip said. "The centaurs will help."

"Centaurs. Marty told us they were acting strange. But going on foot, even with the centaurs helping, will take a while," Mike said. "You sure couldn't make more than a hundred kilometers a day. Don't know we can hold out that long."

"Lara thought of another way. The research boat. That will only take two days if it works—"

"We might manage two days," Mike said. "OK, what is it you want me to do? Sir."

For a minute it had been fun to be in charge, but now what? "Uncle Mike, I don't know."

Mike chuckled. "Well, I don't have any better ideas. You try to get to Pearly Gates, and I'll do the same. Try to see Bernard Trent and get him to listen to that Endgame file. I think he'll be willing to make you a deal. Problem is, the cops will be looking for you, and if they catch you they won't take you to Bernie. You'll end up with Henry Tarleton, and God knows what happens then."

"I think I can get to Pearly Gates," Kip said. "But I don't know what to do when I get there."

"Yeah. They won't really expect you to show up at the GWE tower, but Tarleton's smart enough to have people watching the place anyway. Kip, when you get to Pearly Gates, here's a number to call. Ask for Goldie. She's got people who can help. You can trust her. Just don't make her any promises you won't keep."

"Yes, sir. Will you call again?"

"I don't think so. This conversation is safe because we've got control of their monitoring equipment, but we won't have it for long. Kip, we'll buy you as much time as we can, but I think it's all up to you now. You have to get through to Bernie."

"Yes, sir—"

"Good luck, Tiger. Go get 'em. Sir. Captain Gallegher out."

Kip wrote down the number Uncle Mike had given him. He thought he would remember it, but he wasn't sure. Being able to remember things like a telephone number had never been important while Gwen could do it for him.

Thoughts welled up. Gwen was gone, and Uncle Mike worked for him now, or would if they could get control, only they weren't in control. The security police were looking for him, and they wouldn't take orders from him. No one would, really. Just Uncle Mike, sometimes, maybe—

It was now quite dark, and the lights of the research station a kilometer away were very visible.

CHAPTER FORTY-TWO

Centaurs

THE research station was deserted.

"The boat," Lara said. "There's no boat here." She pointed to the empty davits that hung out over the bluff. They were large enough to hold a thirty-meter tug up and out of the surging tide in the cove below the bluff. "They must have taken it out."

"There's another research station to the north," Kip said. "I bet they went there."

"How far is it?"

Kip tried to remember. Gwen would have known! "Twenty, thirty kilometers," he said. Kip walked around the perimeter of the heavy fence and shouted, "Mrs. Harriman!" There was no answer. The only lights were the security lights. "I don't dare use the phone," Kip said.

"I know how we can get in," Lara said. "It's in one of the emergency procedures books."

"Sure, but that sends an alarm signal back to the station," Kip said.

Lara nodded. "I guess we don't want that. Well, we can wait until the boat comes back, or walk to the other station."

"I sure wish I could ask you—"

"YOU REQUEST INFORMATION."

The Starswarm! Kip grinned at Lara. Then he let a picture form in his mind: the research station boat. *"We have to find the boat."*

A picture formed in Kip's head. It seemed to be a map, but the scale was distorted. He could see figures that clearly were himself and Lara standing near what had to be the research station, although the station was represented as not much larger than they were. Northward from them was the boat, and near it was what looked like another research station. Far beyond it was a large smear with the only recognizable object being what appeared to be the GWE towers.

From the scale, if the GWE towers were a thousand kilometers to the north, the next research station was more like thirty to fifty.

"I have it," Kip thought. He worked at another picture: Kip and Lara walking north to the station. Once there they took the boat and went north to Pearly Gates. Kip didn't know if the pictures were clear enough, but they were the best he could do without practice.

"WAIT."

"Wait for what?" He let another picture form, of a helicopter gunship chasing him, shooting him and Lara.

"UNDERSTOOD." The map returned, this time showing him and Lara moving northward a kilometer or so to a large tree.

"What do we do there?"

"WAIT."

Kip turned to Lara.

"Glad to see you back," she said. "It can get spooky watching you talk to someone I can't see. Is Gwen—"

"No, that was the Starswarm," Kip said. "I told it we want to catch the boat. It said we should wait, but when I told it we couldn't because we have to hide, it said go about a kilometer north and wait."

"Kip, this is really spooky!" Lara said. "A lake plant is telling us what to do! But all right, let's go." There was a trail at the bluff edge, and she started north along it. It was quite dark now, and the only sound was the crashing of waves half a kilometer to their right. The shore here was as close to a beach as you could find on a major coast, long tidal flats with a carved bluff at high tide line. It would be easier walking along the base of the bluff, but it wouldn't be a good idea. The tide could come in rapidly on Paradise, and the flats would be under three meters of water in an hour or so.

"They found the will," Kip said conversationally.

"What will?" Lara asked.

"My mother's will. She was—Lara, my mother was Michelle LaScala Trent, and she left me all her stock. I'm the heir!"

Lara walked along in silence.

"I mean, I own the whole company! Can you believe that?" Kip grinned.

"Actually, I do," Lara said. "That computer interface implant must have cost millions of francs, and someone paid for it. I believe it, all right, I just don't know what to think about knowing the richest boy on the planet."

"It hasn't done me much good so far." Kip's grin faded. "I got to grow up out in the boonies, I've only got two friends, and the cops are after me."

"Poor you. Kip, if you're the heir, why are the grayskins after you?"

"Captain Gallegher—Uncle Mike—says they're trying to keep me away from Uncle Bernie."

"Uncle Bernie. You mean Governor Trent," Lara said. "Wow. I hadn't thought of that. He sure didn't recognize you."

"I guess I was like a year old the last time he'd seen me," Kip said.

"You sure were a good actor—"

"Not really. I didn't know who I was, then."

They walked along the cliff top in silence for minutes. "You're sure quiet," Kip said.

"I was thinking," Lara said. "This is a lot more serious than someone throwin' a bomb. We didn't do that, and we could prove it, but, Kip, it doesn't matter what we can prove, does it? Not with this much money at stake. It makes everything different—"

"Scared?"

"Sure. Aren't you?"

"Yeah."

They hadn't gone a full kilometer when Kip heard the cold voice again. "WAIT THERE."

The only landmark was a large tree, something like a banyan tree with spreading branches and broad leaves. Aerial roots descended from the branches, so that the area under the tree was a labyrinth of caves. There were dark objects in the caves, and some of them were filled with what looked like webs. Lara looked at the tree with horror.

"Uncle Mike told me a person could hide in a cave tree," Kip said. "It's creepy, but the things that live in there don't like our smell. They'll leave us alone if we don't bother them, and they eat haters, so if there's a swarm you're best off in the trees."

Lara looked at the dark shapes in the grottoes among the branches. "I'm glad we don't have to."

"Me too." They sat well away from the tree, and Kip took out his stove to make tea.

They'd been there about two hours when the dogs began growling.

"Centaurs," Kip said. He stopped to listen. It was very dark so he couldn't see a thing, but there were drumming hoofbeats on the bluff top to the south. The dogs got between them and the sound and stood uncertainly, fangs bared. The climbing beasts in the tree grottoes had made the dogs nervous. Now the centaurs were coming. Silver growled, as if to say that at least he understood what to do about centaurs.

"Silver!" Kip said. "Stay. It's all right, Silver. Good dog. Mukky, be good now. Come here. Come here all."

The four dogs reluctantly came back to stand with Kip and Lara. Dark shapes approached out of the darker night.

Kip took out his flash and masked it with his fingers so that only a tiny light spilled out.

"I see them," Lara said quietly. "There must be a dozen— Kip, they're not all the same size."

"I think that's Blaze in front," Kip said. "With a backpack."

"A lot of them have backpacks. They look like our backpacks. Kip, what are we going to do?"

"Get a good grip on the dogs," Kip said. *"They're here."*

A new picture formed in Kip's head. The centaurs stood at the lake, and pictures passed rapidly from the lake to the centaurs. Then the centaurs trotted away, and there were no more pictures. Then the map returned, with Kip and Lara on it, only this time the scale changed to show the lake. The centaurs came up to Kip. Now pictures passed between Kip at the seashore and the lake in the hills.

"It can talk to me, but not to the centaurs," Kip said. "It gave them some kind of instructions—"

Blaze came slowly forward. The dogs growled warning.

CHAPTER FORTY-THREE

Things Are Not Food

BLAZE smelled fears. There was fear in the scent of his People, both the Highlanders and the Seacoaster clan People, more in the Seacoasters of course. But there were new scents. The furrykillers made their warning noises, and there was a scent Blaze thought might be fear mingled with the other smells of these alien creatures. And the Things developed a new scent even as Blaze approached them.

Things. He must no longer think of them as Food. Things are not Food, he told himself. Furrykillers are not Food. The Master had made that very clear. Not only Blaze, but every Highlander sent with him had been forced to stand in the cold lake water as the Master poured pictures into their minds. Things are not Food.

He fingered his new weapons. The Master gave them weapons, new weapons, powerful weapons they could use to fight the Things, but then the Master told them Things were no longer Food.

The Seacoasters did not believe that. The Seacoasters smelled Food, furrykillers as Food, Things as Food. Blaze moved closer to the Seacoaster leader, ready to intervene with his new weapons if the Seacoaster forgot. He growled warning. The Seacoaster reared high, then bowed in submission. This was Seacoaster territory, and the Seacoaster had long resented the dominance of the Highlanders. The whole clan did. They had learned that resentment from their fathers, who had learned from theirs, for a hundred generations or more. Drive out strangers. This land is mine. They had learned this, but they had also learned submission to the Highlanders. Protect the groves! Drive out all others! But the Highlanders were the exception. Highlanders went anywhere they wanted, anywhere except into the Seacoaster groves, and even those might not be sacred against Highlanders.

So it was decreed, and so it would be.

Blaze moved closer to the Things. The larger Thing held its hands out to show it had no weapons. Blaze held out his own empty hands, then crept forward to the Thing and knelt on the ground.

"It wants you to ride it," Lara said. "Are you going to?"

"We have to, if we want to get to the research station."

"I can walk, it's not that far," Lara said. She looked at the centaur and scowled. "They smell. And the dogs don't like this at all. What will the dogs do?"

"They can run after us," Kip said. "Look, I don't know why the Starswarm wants us to ride the centaurs. Maybe it's a test. I just think we should do it."

The dogs lay at his feet and whined. They hated this. Kip moved forward, slowly, to the kneeling centaur. The centaur watched him warily. It held its hands out empty, but there were weapons in its belt. Kip could see two bronze knives and what looked like a small crossbow. A bundle of small javelins stuck out of the centaur's backpack.

The backpack was almost a duplicate of the one Kip wore. As

he got closer he saw that some of the details were wrong. There were lines sewed across it, but they were not zippers, only lines. The leather patches were not really leather, and didn't have slots for straps. The harness arrangement had been modified to fit the centaur.

Kip gingerly touched the centaur. It felt warm. He wondered if he ought to stroke it as he would a dog. These weren't dogs, but Gwen said they were about as smart as the dogs. Grooming was a universal sign of friendship among Earth animals. It probably would be with centaurs. Kip stroked the dark fur. The centaur felt warm to the touch. "Silver. Be good. Follow," Kip said. Then, acting more bold than he felt, Kip stepped forward and straddled the centaur. It stood, and another went over to kneel by Lara.

"Milady, your steed awaits," Kip said.

Lara made a face and mounted the centaur. "Giddyap, Dobbin," she said.

CHAPTER FORTY-FOUR

We've Got About Five Minutes

MIKE Gallegher put down the phone and gestured to John Fuller to come over. "These things keep a log of who we called, right? Any way to get around it?"

"Well, this is part of the security phone system," Fuller said. "Calls made from here will be logged here, not at phone central."

"So if no one knows we called from here, they might not think to look?"

"Something like that. It will help if you keep the calls short."

Mike looked at Kettering seated on the other side of the room. "So he's the only one who knows we used these phones."

"I know it," Fuller said.

Mike chuckled. "Hell, Lieutenant, I wasn't thinking about shooting him. Maybe we'll just take him along when we go. Main thing is to be quick so no one else knows. Thanks. Now I've got a couple more calls to make—"

"OK." Fuller went out of earshot.

Mike punched in numbers.

"Sea station, Rachel Harriman."

"Mike Flynn, Mrs. Harriman. Where are you?"

"At Sealab Two," she said.

"Have you heard what's happening up here?"

"No—"

"Well, it's a mess. Security troops have taken over the station. They've got helicopter gunships out looking for Kip."

"Gunships looking for Kip? Whatever for?"

"They say he made a bomb. He didn't. There's a GWE proxy war, and Kip's all mixed up in that. Dr. Harriman, I haven't got time to explain anything. Listen a second." He gestured to Dr. Henderson. "Tell Mrs. Harriman what I say is all right," Mike said.

Dr. Henderson nodded and took the headset. "Rachel. Eric Henderson. Mike Flynn will have some instructions. Please do as he asks. Time is short, and it is crucial to the future of this station." He handed the phone set back to Mike.

"I'll make it quick," Mike said. "The kids will be trying to find you. Best thing you can do is stay where you are. Get the boat ready for a long trip."

"Long trip?"

"They need to get to Pearly Gates."

"We don't have that much range. Not in one trip," Rachel Harriman said.

"Do the best you can, then," Mike said. "Just do the best you can."

"I really would like to know—"

"Yes, ma'am, and I'd like to have time to tell you, but I got one more call to make and we have to be out of here." He handed the set back to Dr. Henderson.

"Rachel, this is as important as anything you have ever done," Eric Henderson said. "Please."

"Sure. Godspeed," Rachel Harriman said.

"Thank you."

Mike cut off the connection and dialed another. The phone was answered by a man who simply repeated the number.

"Tell Goldie it's himself," Mike said. He glanced at his watch. "And hurry. Please."

Mike finished his calls, then began disconnecting the telephone equipment. "Marty, do me a favor, run back to the lab and get me a hammer," he said. "A big one."

Mike signaled Henderson to come join him. "Doc, I'm going to take the chopper and get out of here. You can come along or stay here and fight the system from the inside. So far you haven't done anything they can charge you with. That don't mean they won't, but legally you're on pretty sound ground."

"What about me?" John Fuller asked.

"Well, I'd sure appreciate it if you'd come along with me," Mike said.

"You're giving me a choice?"

"Haven't exactly said that. I said I'd sure appreciate it if you'd come along with me."

"Where are you going?" Fuller asked.

"I'm going to do my best to get through to the Governor," Mike said. "I'm pretty sure Bernie doesn't know what's going on. He sure doesn't know his nephew's alive. Gives him a big incentive. Kip sure won't vote for any Hilliard takeover." He turned to Henderson. "You come off pretty good too, Doc."

Dr. Henderson nodded. "I'd thought of that. Kip grew up here. He won't want to see strip mines at the station." He frowned. "But if Tarleton is working for the Hilliard group—"

"He is," Mike said.

"Then he'll do anything to stop Kip voting his stock," Henderson said. "And he has to do it fast, because Kip or Bernard Trent will fire him the first chance they get."

"Unless Bernie's in on this."

"Yes, of course—Mike, I think it's best if I stay here. Take this." He handed Mike a computer disk. "This is a copy of that Endgame file. I've made more copies. Perhaps one of them will survive."

Marty ran in with a ballpeen hammer. "Will this do?"

"Sure will," Mike said. He grinned widely and went over to Kettering's electronic setup. "This ought to slow down tracing our calls—"

"I wouldn't do that," Fuller said.

"Yeah?"

"Take it with us. You may need it."

"You know how to operate all this stuff?"

"Some of it. He knows the rest," Fuller said. He jerked his thumb toward Gil Kettering.

"I am damned if I'll help you," Kettering said.

"Yeah, yeah," Mike said. "Fuller, you have a point. OK, let's pack this stuff. Now, Fuller, we need my chopper back. Think your troops will try to stop us?"

"Not until the reinforcements get here. Karabian isn't going to open fire without orders from an officer."

"Good. Let's move it, then. Marty, here's the storeroom key. Grab everything you can carry. We got about five minutes."

CHAPTER FORTY-FIVE

The Master Might Need Him

BLAZE ran in the center of the pack, just behind the furrykillers. Both of the small night lights were in the sky, plenty of light for Blaze and the People. The Things had even brighter lights, and had used them to light the trail, but the lightstick was too bright. It hurt the People's eyes, and Blaze had held his hand over it until the Thing put it away. Now they ran along the seacoast trail with the sea to his right, farther up the coast than Blaze had ever been, searching for a Thing grove by the sea.

It would be like the other seacoast Thing groves, with a stout fence that caused pain when the People touched it. The first seacoast Thing groves hadn't had that kind of fence, and when the Things left them unguarded, the People had broken in and demolished the Thing grove, taking the Thing treasures to the

Master. The Seacoasters had done the same with other Thing groves, and kept all they had found, but when the Highland Master demanded the treasures, the Seacoasters had brought them. All of them. The Master did not often make demands of the Seacoasters, but those demands were always obeyed. Now the Master knew what the Things had been doing, and had begun to teach the People.

Blaze remembered that well, because it was just after they brought the Thing treasures to the Master that Blaze felt the urge to know about Things. Before that he had been content to do the Master's bidding, carrying messages from the Master to the sea and back, hunting meat for the People and doing the Master's will without questions. But then the Master had done something, and Blaze felt odd stirrings, a desire to know and understand. He had never felt that before. Why had the Master done this?

Strongarms, his littermate, now carried the larger Thing. The Thing had been heavy, and Blaze had been glad to have another carry it. Now all he had to do was watch the Seacoasters and be sure they didn't harm the Things or their furrykillers. The Master was concerned about this.

They trotted northward along the coast. Not much farther. Then he could give his messages to the Things, and go back to the Highlands. That would be best. The Master might need him.

CHAPTER FORTY-SIX

All Due Respect, Sir, Marty's More Useful . . .

MARTY, where do you think you're going?" Dr. Robbins
demanded.

Marty thought that was pretty obvious, but he didn't
want to say that to his father. He pretended not to
hear as he climbed into the helicopter.

"Flynn, you can't take him!" Robbins said.

"Doc, I can understand you're worried, but I can sure use
someone I trust to watch my back."

"Then I'll come—"

"All due respect, sir, Marty's more useful."

"I know where Kip is going," Marty said. "And Lara's out
there."

"It's important," Mike said.

Luke Robbins turned to Dr. Henderson. "Eric—"

"As Captain Gallegher says, it's important," Henderson said.

"And Lara is out there, and perhaps Marty can help. But it's up to you."

"Be careful," Dr. Robbins said.

"Yes, sir. And thanks, Dad."

Marty's last words blended with the revving up of the helicopter. It lifted from the station and swung low across the chaparral.

"We have three choices," Mike said. "Hole up somewhere, try to find Kip, or head for Pearly Gates and hope we can get in to see Bernie."

"You won't make it to Pearly Gates," Lieutenant Fuller said. "They'll use every tracking device they have looking for you. They may not close in until they're sure you won't lead them to Kip, but they'll be watching. Probably watching now."

"I thought as much," Mike said. "So maybe the thing to do is make them believe they can find Kip by following me."

"That will work for a while, but I can't say for how long," Fuller said.

"So what should I do?" Mike asked.

"Do you think Mr. Tarleton knows that Kip is the heir?" Fuller asked.

"Not when this started, but I think he does now," Mike said.

"That's my guess too," Fuller said. "When this began it was no big deal, just an explosion at a research station, and I was the only one who really cared. Or thought I was. But as time went on, Mr. Tarleton took a personal interest. He already had Kettering"—Fuller nodded toward Gil Kettering handcuffed in the back of the helicopter—"at the station."

"You didn't know Kettering was Tarleton's man?"

"Not until I took over the station," Fuller said. "All I really knew was that the station was important to GWE headquarters, and Dr. Henderson was in some kind of conflict with the General Manager. And then Kettering found out Kip was in communication with the GWE central computer, and after that Tarleton personally got into the loop. I didn't know why, but that Endgame file explains it."

"So what should we do?" Mike asked.

"Captain, what's our objective?"

Mike nodded. "Good question. OK, the objective is for one of us to get to Bernie Trent. Since we can't do that, we can buy time for Kip." Mike hesitated. "And if Bernie's the real criminal, we're sunk, but hell, that's the only chance we have."

"Buy time and lead them away from Kip," Fuller said. "I know what I'd do. Kip was last located near the big cave system. They'll start there, on the downslope side. What I'd do, Captain Gallegher, is make them think he's still in the caves. I'd land at the lake entrance. They'll think you're trying to reach Kip, so—"

Mike thought about it. "Gallegher's last stand. Well, I sure don't have anything better to do." He turned the helicopter toward Strumbleberry Hill.

PART EIGHT
Endgame

They do not preach that their God will rouse them a little before the nuts work loose.

They do not teach that His Pity allows them to leave their job when they damn-well choose.

—Rudyard Kipling, *The Sons of Martha*

CHAPTER FORTY-SEVEN

Identification Papers

THERE were lights in the sea station building. Kip gingerly dismounted from the centaur—the third one he had ridden since they began—and helped Lara get down. The bareback ride had left them stiff-legged and sore.

When they went to the gate the dogs followed eagerly, glad to be away from the centaurs. The centaurs stood just at the edge of the circle cast by the research station security lights.

"We're here, and I see the boat."

There was no answer. Communications with the Starswarm had become weaker as they moved northward, and somewhere in the last ten kilometers Kip had lost contact entirely. Gwen would have known how to use the satellite system as a relay, but she'd never told Kip how that was done, and evidently hadn't had time to teach the Starswarm. The thought of Gwen nearly overwhelmed him for a moment. He turned on the gate intercom.

"Mrs. Harriman," he called.

The door opened immediately. "Kip!"

"Yes, ma'am—"

"We've been expecting you. I'll come open the gate— Oh!" She stopped to stare at the circle of centaurs, Blaze in the lead.

"They're—friendly," Lara said. "We rode them here."

"Rode the centaurs? Is it all right if I open the gate?"

"Yes, ma'am," Kip said.

"If you say so." She punched in a code at the gate control, and opened the smaller gate. Lara went in first. As Kip was starting to go in, he heard a sound behind him. The dogs stopped and turned, teeth bared.

Blaze was calling. He didn't know any human words, but he was trying to speak as he came forward. It came out a babble. Kip stopped. "What do you want?" he asked. "I know, that's silly, you don't understand. Silver. Mukky. Go inside." He pointed, and waited until the dogs were inside the gate. Then he turned to Blaze. He kept his voice even and calm, friendly, the way he would speak to a strange dog. "What do you want, Blaze?"

The centaur removed his backpack and laid it on the ground. Kip went over to pick it up. It held a dozen bright red gourds about the size of baseballs. From their weight they were full of liquids.

One of the gourds had stripes and was slightly larger than the others. Blaze took that one and drew a stick from his belt. The stick just fit into a small leather pouch attached to the gourd. Blaze held the stick and gourd high, and trotted away from them, over to the bluff edge. As he reached the edge he used the stick to throw the gourd in a high arc that carried it over the rocks at the bluff edge and into the sea. Then he trotted back and gestured at the backpack on the ground.

Another centaur came forward. This one, like Blaze, was larger than the others, and had darker fur. It also carried a backpack which it laid beside the one Blaze had dropped. The two centaurs stood in the security light, waiting for something.

Finally Kip picked up the backpacks. The centaurs reared high, then turned and trotted to the cliff edge. They watched the sea as if waiting for something. The others followed.

"What was that all about?" Mrs. Harriman demanded.

"I'm not sure," Kip said. He handed one of the backpacks to Lara. "The centaurs carry these things back and forth from the lake to the sea. They're messages."

"Kip—"

"Yes, ma'am, I know it sounds goofy. But these are messages from the lake Starswarm to the sea Starswarms, and since the centaurs wanted us to have them, I think they're like identification papers."

The research station had only four rooms counting the bathroom and kitchen. There was the large central laboratory and conference room, a spacious bedroom, and the kitchen that was actually part of the big central room but separated by a waist-high counter. The laboratory table was covered: microscopes, dissection trays, a computer console, boxes and jars of specimens from both land and sea, mineral and water samples, a clutter of scientific instruments, and the remains of the Harrimans' supper.

Lon Harriman was short and round, and considerably older than his wife. Kip and Lara had met him at the station, but they didn't know him well. He was cooking something at the stove, and when Kip and Lara came in he brought a tray. "Soup," he said. "I expect you kids are starving."

"Well, yes, sir," Kip said.

Mr. Harriman piled the used supper dishes on a tray. "You can sit here," he said. "I'm afraid we don't have enough chairs, but then we seldom have visitors here. So. Sit down, eat some soup— and you just might tell us what in the world is going on."

CHAPTER FORTY-EIGHT

Blaze Follows Orders

BLAZE stood at the edge of the sea and watched the water. It was low but rising, and he waited until he was certain that the water was coming toward him. He'd never been this far north before, but he had traveled to the seacoast on errands for the Master all his life. He knew that sometimes the water was high and sometimes low, and that it was dangerous to be at the water's edge when it was coming toward you, but he had not understood the concept of a regular tide. Now he did. He wasn't sure how long he had known of tides. Probably he'd learned at the same time that he learned to ask other questions. He was learning many things now.

The world was changing. Blaze served the Master, as his father had, and his father's father, generations without number of Highlanders carrying messages for the Master. Most of the mes-

sages were to or from the sea. Now that would change. Blaze
wasn't sure how he knew that, but he did. What he was about to
do would change the world forever. His children would not carry
messages for the Master. There would be no need.

What would they do?

He signaled, and Strongarms came to him. Blaze removed his
littermate's backpack and took out the small metallic box. It looked
much like the one the Things had left near the Master's lake, but
it was smaller and lighter. Better, Blaze thought. The Master's
work. It had levers, larger than those on the Thing box, easier for
the centaur's clumsy hands to work.

There was a box within the box, and inside that was a roll of
what looked like two metallic leafless vines held apart by ceramic
sticks. Blaze waited until the water was high along the bluff, then
let the vines dangle over the cliff and unroll themselves until their
end reached the water. Then he moved some of the levers on the
box. Lights flashed, spelling the end of the world that Blaze knew.

Would it be the beginning of another?

He waited for the time it would take to run from the grove
to the lake three times, then waited more to be sure. Then he took
a gourd from Strongarms's backpack and tossed it into the sea. A
large shape formed in the sea below him, and lights winked furiously below the bluff. Blaze lifted the box and dropped it into the
sea below. There was no splash.

He threw his last gourd into the sea and waited. After a while
two gourds came over the lip of the bluff and fell to the ground.
Blaze gathered them up, then turned and trotted southward. The
others followed.

CHAPTER FORTY-NINE

This Is Not Entity You Call Starswarm

SHOULDN'T I call your father?" Mr. Harriman asked.

"No, please," Lara said. "It's really important that we get to Pearly Gates, and if the grayskins know where we are they'll stop us."

"Why?" Lon Harriman asked.

"Just what is this all about?" Rachel Harriman demanded. "Mr. Flynn said you needed help and Dr. Henderson asked us to cooperate with you, so we will, but I can't say I understand why. They said they didn't have time to explain. Why are the police looking for you?"

"Pretty complicated," Kip said. "It will take a while to tell you."

"We have time," Lon Harriman said. "We're not going anywhere until morning. That coast is far too dangerous for night travel, and anyway we'll need sunlight to charge up the fuel cells."

"Oh," Kip said. "But we have to move fast—"

"May be, but we're not going anywhere without power," Mr. Harriman said. "So that gives us time for you to tell us what's going on."

"I don't even know where to start," Kip said.

"Start at the beginning," Lara said. "Tell them who you are."

Kip woke in the middle of the night. The floor was hard despite his insulating sleeping pad. Lara was asleep a few feet away, with two dogs nestled against her. Her own Little Lil served as a pillow, and seemed contented with the arrangement. Kip sat up, trying to remember what had awakened him.

"HELLO. ALARM."

"Starswarm. Hello."

A torrent of thoughts and pictures poured into his mind, enough to overwhelm him. He fought to cut them off until he could get back in control, sort out the feelings from the thoughts, understand the few words that were used. He felt he was drowning in thoughts.

"THIS IS NOT ENTITY YOU CALL STARSWARM." This came in feelings and pictures more than words. There were suggestions of words, as if whoever was calling him had only recently learned about the concept of language, and used it only when all else failed. There was something else. When he received the thought of the lake Starswarm there came with it a feeling of awe, almost reverence.

"Who are you?"

There was another flood of pictures. The sea dominated them. There were also pictures of centaurs, large brown ones like Blaze, and the smaller gray centaurs who had come with Blaze. The larger ones went up a steep trail until they were gone, as the gray ones watched. Then the brown ones returned. One, who might have been Blaze, threw a gourd into the water, and another laid a box on the ground and threw wires into the sea. The box looked much like the ones Uncle Mike had set up in Pearly Gates, then at the lake. It took Kip a moment to realize how he knew Uncle Mike had done that.

"You are the sea Starswarm."

"SEA. AFFIRMATIVE. MESSAGE FOLLOWS.

"THIS IS MESSAGE FROM ENTITY YOU CALL LAKE STARSWARM. YOU GO NOW. SEA ENTITIES WILL HELP." There was a picture of the boat moving northward toward the GWE towers. Kip and Lara and some vague shape that might have been human were aboard. There was also a small gray centaur on the boat. "GO NOW. URGENCY. CARRY MESSAGES." Another picture formed, Kip and Lara throwing gourds into the sea on the cliffs below GWE tower. "URGENCY."

"No power." So how do I explain the lack of solar power? Kip thought. He tried to picture the fuel cells that powered the boat. He thought of them as full, let the boat move, and let them empty as it moved. Then he pictured the boat on its davits, and the cells empty, and the sun out and the cells filling. It was hard to think in pictures rather than words.

"UNDERSTOOD. GO NOW. URGENCY." Once again a picture of the gourds and the sea below GWE towers. It was followed by another, of GWE tower collapsing. "URGENCY."

The dogs stirred. Kip saw that Lara was watching him. "Sea Starswarm," he said. "It doesn't talk very well. I don't think it's as smart as the one in the lake. But it wants us to launch the boat now, and it seems desperate."

"Kip, it will be dark for an hour or more, and Dr. Harriman said the boat fuel cells aren't charged."

"I know that. I even managed to explain to the Starswarm. Or I think I did. But it wants us to go now, and it's being pretty emphatic."

"What should we do?" Lara asked.

"I think we wake up the Harrimans, but God only knows how we'll explain any of this."

"You did pretty well last night," Lara said. "All those years, with Gwen able to get you anything you want—"

"I don't think they believed me," Kip said.

"Sure they did," Lara said. "And if they don't, I've got some proof with me—"

"Proof?"

She smiled. "My earrings. They're real, aren't they? And, Kip, it was nice of you to think of it, but there's no way you could have bought anything that expensive! I'll show them to Mr. Harriman. He'll believe us."

CHAPTER FIFTY

Budonnic's Eel

THIS is a damn-fool errand," Lon Harriman said. He looked up from his seat at the workbench in the research boat's cabin and stared out across the sea to the east. The boat hung steady in its davits at the cliff top above the sea. There were flashes in the water below the cliff, but it was impossible to see any distance in the dim moonlight. "At least we can wait until there's enough light to see by. But there's not more than half an hour's worth of power in those cells, and let me tell you, you don't want to be out in that sea without power. Not even in calm weather, and the report is there's a hell of a storm brewing out there." He grinned. "And I don't want to get killed. Not now! Last night you told me more about the ecology of this planet than we learned in fifty years. I'd hate to get killed before I can publish. But that's what will happen if we run out of power at sea."

"Well, we can get ready," Kip said. He went below to stow another load of provisions. The boat was plasti-steel, fiberglass and metallic fibers woven into a net and sealed with high-strength plastic. It was nearly twenty meters long and built like an ocean-going tug, high bow sloping back to a lower stern deck. There was a steering cabin just forward of the boat's center. Masts and booms forward of the cabin controlled nets and dredges for taking ocean samples. The area aft of the cabin was a flat deck with a high rail around it. The bridge was rigged with electric motors and winches so that two people could handle the boat, one in an emergency, but only so long as there was power. Here above the sea the boat looked sturdy and powerful, but Kip knew it wouldn't feel that way once it was launched.

He came back up the companionway and went over to the workbench, where Lara was watching over Lon Harriman's shoulder. Harriman was just putting the cover back on the navigation electronics box. "OK," he said. "We can use the receiver to tell where we are, and the transmitter will tell anyone who's curious that we haven't left here. It makes the navigation a little harder, but not enough to matter, just means I have to keep track of our position on the charts, and I've got those. OK, Kip—Mr. Trent, sir!— I can understand why you don't want the security people to know where we are, but why the all-fired hurry?"

Kip laughed, but it felt good to have adults call him sir, even if Mr. Harriman was half joking. "I don't know why the Starswarm is so anxious for us to get moving, but it is," Kip said. He thought of the picture of GWE tower crumbling and shuddered. "And I think we have to do it."

Harriman put the navigation unit back in the equipment rack and fastened it in. "I still have trouble believing all this. Not that you're the Trent heir. I don't have a lot of trouble with that. I knew your mother, and I never really believed she got you killed in a helicopter accident at sea. Getting herself killed, I could believe that, but she wouldn't take any chances with you. I believe that part. But the rest? First you were able to talk to the lake, and now you can talk to the sea."

Lara giggled. "He talks to the Starswarms, not the water," she said. "The way you put it is crazy."

"It's crazy any way you put it," Harriman said. "Not that it isn't fascinating. You say you can talk to these critters, but they can't talk to each other?"

"Not directly," Kip said. "Not now, but if they learn to use the satellite links the way Gwen did, they'll be able to talk to each other. Up to now they used the gourds, with the centaurs carrying them."

"That's the part I love," Harriman said. "We always wondered about those gourds. Chemical messages. Makes sense. There's no reason you can't use DNA chains for communication. That's one way we communicate between generations, DNA codes are messages. They're instructions on how to make copies of us." He pulled at his chin and stared pensively out to sea. "I suppose that's why the Starswarms never invented electronics. The centaurs carry their messages, and they can pack a lot more information into a gourd than they can transmit in a week over the air waves. Sort of like a courier on a bicycle carrying a load of data disks. The information travels slower, but there's a lot more of it.

"Anyway, we'll get loaded up, and I'll let the boat down, but there's no way in hell we're going anywhere until we get those cells charged up."

"Do what you can," Kip said. He used what he thought was a voice of authority, the way Uncle Mike used to talk to people who worked for him. That felt silly, and it didn't seem to have much effect on Harriman anyway. Kip shined his light toward the fence. _"We're ready."_

"What are you looking for?" Harriman demanded.

"A centaur. I was given a picture of a centaur on the boat with us."

"A centaur. Dogs, a centaur, no power in the fuel cells. Regular Noah's Ark drifting in the tide."

Lara giggled. "Only one centaur, not two," she said. "No one has ever seen a live female."

Mrs. Harriman came out with a large basket. "This is the last of it. Kip, are you sure you want to start out in the dark?"

"Mr. Trent is waiting for a centaur," Lon Harriman said. "A male one because no one has ever seen a female outside the groves. Rachel, I think this is all nuts."

The dogs growled, and Silver barked once, sharply.

"There," Lara said. She pointed to the fence. A small gray centaur stood there. It seemed terrified, but it waited at the gate, watching them with half-closed eyes, its head cocked to one side.

"Silver. Mukky. Back," Kip ordered. "Lil. Go to the boat."

"Do we really have to take the dogs with us?" Lon Harriman asked.

"Sure, we don't know when we'll be back," Kip said.

"Or if," Harriman said. "One reason we don't keep dogs here. Too much trouble cleaning after them if we take them on board. All right. I'll put them below, and we'll sort out who cleans what and when later." He ushered the dogs down the companion-way and closed the door on them. "Now your friend there." He fingered the holstered pistol on his belt. "Last time I saw one of those critters, it threw rocks at me. You're sure about this?"

"No, but I think we ought to do it," Kip said. He went to the gate and opened it. The centaur walked in gingerly. It was considerably smaller than Blaze, and seemed much more frightened. It went across the gangway and stood in the stern of the boat, trying to huddle into a corner at the stern rail.

Kip and Lara followed it. "We're all aboard," Kip said.

"That's it, then," Harriman said. "Places. Lara, check the bow lines. I still feel like a damn fool." He went to the steering cabin and opened the covers on the switches controlling the boat's davits. "OK. I'll let her down, but we stay anchored. There's enough power to haul us back up. All lines cast off?"

"Yes, sir," Lara said. "Clear forward."

"Clear aft," Mrs. Harriman said. "Davit blocks clear."

"Going down." The boat dropped slowly and smoothly toward the water below. The davits were cantilevered out from the bluff so that when the boat was in the water the lines held it clear of the cliff. A bow line led from the boat to an anchored buoy well offshore. "Here we go," Harriman muttered. "Cast off the davit lines."

"Done forward," Lara called.

"We're loose," Mrs. Harriman said.

A winch in the bow reeled in the line until they were near the buoy thirty meters from shore. "Now what?" Harriman said.

There was a gray smear to the east, just visible now despite the bright working lights on the boat's deck.

"We're here."

"WAIT."

A large black tentacle rose out of the sea astern of the boat. When the centaur saw it, it trotted over to the rail. The tentacle crept over the stern rail, then upward to embrace the centaur. It flattened slightly as it encircled the centaur's neck, then flattened again to form what looked like a hood that covered the centaur's head, so that only the eyes were visible. The centaur stood rigidly still, staring at nothing.

Lara pointed at the centaur. "That's the way you look," she told Kip. "When you're listening inside your head."

Mr. Harriman stared. "I will be dipped in—what is that?"

Kip barely heard them speaking. He concentrated, trying to picture the empty fuel cells, and the boat drifting helplessly toward the rocks.

"WAIT."

"It says to wait," Kip said.

"For what?"

"I don't know."

The tentacle released the centaur. New pictures flowed into Kip's mind. Again they were confused, but one set was clear, the centaur looking at the empty fuel cells. Kip hesitated. Pictures flowed with a new sense of urgency. "All right," Kip said aloud. He bent down to lift the hatch covers set into the stern deck. The fuel cells were just under them. The centaur bent to examine them as if he knew just what he was looking for, then trotted back to the stern rail. The tentacle embraced him again.

"God Almighty," Lon Harriman said. "Kip, do you know what's going on?"

"No, sir—"

There was motion at the stern. Something huge and dark rose over the stern rail and flowed across the deck. Kip saw what looked like a flash of teeth among writhing tentacles.

"Good God, stay away from that," Harriman said. "Those eels can throw about a thousand-volt shock!" He drew his pistol.

"Don't hurt it," Kip shouted. "Just—just wait."

Kip's schoolbooks called it Budonnic's Eel, but the books were quick to point out that while it was more like an eel than a squid, it was neither, occupying a phylum all to itself. Its life cycle wasn't understood because very few had ever been found. Like Earth's electric eels, Budonnic's Eel generated electric currents that it used for navigation and to stun its prey.

The eel flowed down into the fuel cell compartment. The centaur came over to watch, perhaps to guide the eel. It was hard to see what was happening there below the deck, but there was a flash of blue light.

"ALERT." A picture formed in Kip's head. The empty fuel cells were filling.

"Mr. Harriman, I think you ought to look at the charge gauges," Kip said.

"Charge gauges? You mean—" Harriman went back to the steering console. "Yeah, now I've seen everything," he said. "They're charging up all right. Rachel, come look at this."

"I see it," Mrs. Harriman said.

"Do you believe it?"

She laughed nervously, and pointed to the charge gauges. "I believe those. Don't you?"

"I guess I have to. But how the hell would it know what we need?"

"The Starswarm has had fuel cells to study," Kip said.

"And it talks to the centaurs," Lara said. She pointed. "And to that eel too!"

Harriman nodded. "Clearly. But I wouldn't have believed it if someone told me. OK, Kip, at the rate your friends are charging up the boat we can get moving by dawn." He looked out to the east. "Wind's steady at about five knots, but it sure feels like a storm coming," he said. "Maybe we'll beat it to Pearly Gates. We can sure try." He looked back at the fuel cell compartment and shook his head in wonder.

CHAPTER FIFTY-ONE

It's All Up to Kip

MIKE set the helicopter down near the edge of the lake. "OK, Cal, we'll get our stuff out and she's all yours. Head for home."

"I won't get that far," Cal said. "And from what I'm hearing, they aren't going to listen to anything I say. If they'd kill Mr. Trent and his wife, they'd sure kill me for knowing too much."

"Might be," Mike said. "So what do you want to do?"

"I think I'll stick with you. Safety in numbers. And hell, I got an interest in keeping you alive. You owe me twenty thousand."

"I do, don't I? OK. We'll pile the stuff into the cave, and leave the chopper up on the ridge. It'll be dark in an hour, maybe they won't find it until morning."

Marty went down to the lake and began searching the plants growing along the lakeshore. Finally he found one he liked, and plucked a leaf. He carried it to the water's edge and threw it in. It floated for a moment, then was pulled under by something unseen.

"Marty, what are you doing?" Mike called. "We got to get this stuff unloaded."

"Yes, sir. Just for luck," Marty said. "One more, just for luck." He found another bug-infested leaf to throw in before he went back up to unload the chopper.

The gunship came at first light. It flew in low over the lake and turned to fly along the shore near the cave, then whipped up and over until it was out of sight.

"They've spotted the supply chopper," Cal said. "I'll give them half an hour to examine it before they come back."

His prediction was reasonably accurate. Twenty-five minutes later the gunship swept back down the hill and out over the lake.

"TURN ON YOUR PHONE, FLYNN. WE KNOW YOU'RE IN THERE." The voice boomed out over the water. "WE NEED TO TALK ABOUT HOSTAGES."

"Sure they do," Mike muttered. He took a coil of wire from his ditty bag and attached it to the phone antenna. Then he took out a tiny TRI-V camera no larger than a fountain pen. "OK, everybody, get well back in the cave. Back, and around a corner, and get behind something."

"Do you think that's necessary?" Fuller asked.

"Yeah. Now get moving. Marty, keep an eye on our friendly Lieutenant here. And get the dogs under cover." He waited until the others were well down into the cave, then set the camera so that it would look out over the lake, and covered it with rocks until only the lens was exposed. He put more and larger rocks against the pile that shielded it, so that it would take a direct hit to disable it. Then he unreeled the wire so that one end was at the cave mouth, the other attached to his phone. Another wire led from the camera to his pocket computer. Mike unreeled both wires as he moved down into the cave and around a corner, then turned on the phone.

It rang almost instantly.

"Flynn."

"Baskins. Are my troops all right?"

"Sure. Want to tell me what this is all about, Colonel?"

"It started as an investigation of an explosion, but now we have kidnapping," Baskins said. "If my troops are unharmed we can think about dropping that charge. Come out and let's talk about it."

The TRI-V camera showed the gunship moving closer to the cave mouth, then hanging there above the lake. The pilot and the door gunner were scanning the cave mouth with binoculars.

"OK, you want me for kidnapping. What about the kids?"

"Nobody wants them," Baskins said. "We're satisfied they had nothing to do with the explosion. Look, this was all a misunderstanding."

"Sure it was," Mike said. "Tell you what, let Bernie Trent tell me it was a misunderstanding."

"We're not going to bother the Governor over something as trivial as this."

Mike laughed. "Yeah, sure. You get me Mr. Trent and we'll come out peaceful as you please."

The sound of the helicopter's machine guns was startling even though Mike had been expecting it. The guns fired so rapidly that it was more like one long sound than a series of shots. Bullets pounded the cave entrance and ricocheted down its corridors. There were several explosions at the entrance as rocket-propelled grenades went off. The TRI-V image shook with the vibrations, but the rocks protected it. When the firing stopped, Mike could see the gunship.

"Flynn?" Mike's ears rang from the explosions and it was hard to hear the voice on the phone. Mike didn't answer.

He watched until the gunship vanished from the camera image and nodded to himself.

Cal crawled up beside him. "You OK?"

"Yeah."

"Fuller's really shook up," Cal said. "He didn't figure they'd start shooting like that. He was supposed to be sure the kids weren't hurt."

"They've changed those orders," Mike said. "I expect they'd be happier if Kip was dead. Was Kettering surprised?"

"Now you mention it, no, I don't think so. Just scared."

"Interesting. OK, Cal, now they'll be coming up to take a look at what they bagged. Hang on a minute." He handed his pocket computer to Cal. "Keep an eye on that screen. Long as that chopper's not visible, they can't shoot into the cave. Not directly, anyway. Sing out if you see it."

"They can sure throw in grenades," Cal said.

"Don't I know it. I won't be long." Mike crawled forward to the cave entrance. The helicopter was nowhere in sight, but two armed men were approaching the cave entrance. They moved cautiously through the scrub brush, gaining confidence as they got closer to the cave and nothing happened.

Mike nodded to himself and drew his pistol. He took careful aim and fired, one shot at each man, then dashed back down the cave and around the bend.

"Incoming!" Cal shouted. "Oh. There you are."

There was another burst of machine-gun fire at the cave mouth, but no grenades this time.

"Score?" Cal asked.

"Got one of them in the leg. Maybe the other, not sure. Leg shots are tricky. But one for sure."

"Leg shots. They're trying to kill us, you know."

"Yeah, I know, but hell, Cal, they're just cops trying to do a job. I been there myself. They're taking orders from the wrong man, but they don't know that."

"Maybe. Now what?" Cal asked.

"They know we're alive and armed, so they won't try just walking in again. They'll come collect the wounded, and bring in reinforcements," Mike said. "Maybe even from Cisco. Then they'll try again."

The phone rang. Mike grinned at it. "Let 'em wonder," he said.

"Mike, is there any way out of this?" Cal asked.

"There's another cave entrance, but they probably know about it."

"Didn't mean the cave. I mean this whole mess. Is there any way we can get out of it alive?"

"Depends on Kip," Mike said. "It all depends on Kip."

CHAPTER FIFTY-TWO

We Don't Need Them Alive

HENRY Tarleton looked up from the computer screen with a scowl. It would be easy enough to panic, but if he had been the sort of person who panicked he wouldn't be where he was now, on the fiftieth floor of the Great Western tower, the same floor as the General Manager, with the same view of the sea to the east. It was never time to panic, but there were plenty of things to worry about.

His resources were stretched to the breaking point. There were plenty of GWE cops who'd obey his orders, but very few of them were loyal to him rather than to the company. Worse, some of them believed in things like justice and fair play. He'd tried to weed out that kind of police agents from real power, but he couldn't do without them. The problem with corrupting the police force was that you ended up with cops who had no reason to do police work. If they were only interested in what they could get, they wouldn't work very hard, and they'd rather harass citizens than take risks to catch real criminals. Then the crime rates went up, and company management talked about a clean sweep of the security department. Like it or not, he had to use honest cops, and make them think he was one himself, a little tarnished but fundamentally like them. Only a few could know who he really worked for, and they were expensive.

Too few. He was running out of agents. Four were assigned to keep watch on Bernard Trent. Not enough, but they were all he could work into positions close to Trent. Bernard Trent kept his own agents, Swiss and Italians who hoped to go back to Earth with him, and while Henry Tarleton didn't understand people who couldn't be bribed, Trent seemed to have found some. Four would be enough, though.

Everything had been going smoothly. The Hilliard group made an alliance with American Express, and between them they'd have the resources to take control of GWE. All Henry Tarleton had to do was sabotage Bernard Trent's efforts to fight the takeover. Get that done and retire, not with the millions GWE would have paid him for faithful service, but billions, enough to be an extremely important man on any planet but Earth. Enough to be noticed even there.

You could live well with a billion dollars, and it was all arranged, and he'd teach the damned Trents to ignore his mother. She was a Trent too, everything but the name. Her father, Henry Tarleton's grandfather, was a Trent. Of course he wouldn't give the Trent name to a kid born to a prostitute. Henry Tarleton remembered his grandmother, still pretty in her fifties, retired from all that.

Henry had grown up in a good house, and went to good schools. That was no problem. The Trents were generous enough to his mother. They'd give her money. Money, but no name.

His grandmother had raised his mother to stay away from the streets, good schools, polite society, and she'd done the same for Henry. She'd only once let slip that Henry's grandfather was one of the Trent heirs. After that she wouldn't talk about it, but Henry had looked it up, read all about the Trents. He took a new name, one the Trents had never heard of, and he studied hard. Law, accounting, police work, geography, politics, everything needed to be a company police executive. Eventually he went to work for the Trents. If they wouldn't give him his inheritance, he'd get it another way.

And everything had been going well. It had looked like a piece of cake.

Now this. What had looked like some kind of kid's pranks out in the boonies had turned into a first-class mess. Tarleton's computers were now certain that this fugitive kid, Brewster he called himself, was really the Trent heir, and the guy everyone called Uncle Mike was Harold Trent's man Gallegher. Gallegher was supposed to be dead. So was the Trent kid. Tarleton's men had sworn they'd seen them dead, Michelle Trent's helicopter down in flames in the sea with all three of them aboard it. Tarleton scowled again. He hadn't really trusted those reports, but there'd been no way to check. They'd found Harold Trent's body, but they never found the wreckage of Michelle's helicopter. Over the years there'd been no trace of Gallegher or the Trent kid or his mother, so he'd relaxed his guard. He should have kept looking for them.

Thinking about what he should have done was a waste of time. It wasn't too late to fix things. Tarleton stood at the window and looked out to sea. The weather reports said a storm was brewing out there somewhere, but so far the only signs were some dark clouds well offshore and far to the south. He thought about Mr. Bernard Trent in the corner office down the hall to his right. His cousin. Trent didn't know that, just as he didn't know his nephew was still alive. Not yet, and if Colonel Baskins could move fast enough, Bernie Trent would never know. He would be upset to learn he'd been cut off, communications intercepted, but he could only learn that from the people who'd tried to call him. If there weren't any of those people, how would Trent ever know?

That whole research station would have to go, along with all the police who weren't his agents. Fifty people, maybe more. Tough on them, but he couldn't see any other way. There'd be a hell of an investigation, but he could handle that. Kids playing with explosives and poison gas. Terrible tragedy. Lot of sympathy, but having that station gone would sure make everything simpler.

No more research station to fight strip mining. One big bang and some bad smells, and everything would be fine.

But first Baskins had to find Gallegher and that kid.

For a moment Tarleton was tempted to go out there himself, but he knew that would be pointless. He lifted the phone and punched in his personal security codes for an encrypted call.

"Baskins."

"Tarleton. Report."

"They're holed up in a cave," Baskins said. "Tried to get them by surprise, but Gallegher was ready for us."

"You sure it's Gallegher?"

"No doubt about it. And the bastard has kidnapped two of my men, shot two more who were trying to get into the cave. I don't have enough troops to storm that cave, and now it would be pretty hard to get them to do it if I did."

"Use gas, or high explosives. Preferably both. We don't need them alive."

"Understood, but it takes time to get enough of that stuff together, especially since we're going to need more to do the station, and we don't want to be too obvious about it—"

"Understood," Tarleton said. "But there are time elements."

"Yes, sir," Baskins said. "But that's your end. On my end we have the station sealed up. No calls or traffic in or out. Same with the cave, and I've got troops covering the downhill exits as well. They're not getting out of there. Out here we have plenty of time. You handle your end, I'll take care of mine."

"Don't be too long. When?"

"Tomorrow, I think," Baskins said. "I should have everything I need by tomorrow."

CHAPTER FIFTY-THREE

Full Gale

THE research tug *Raphael* could skim across calm water at a steady twenty-one knots, but the waves rolled it heavily enough that by late afternoon they had made not more than sixteen knots average, including a twenty-minute stop at noon to let the eel—that one or another like it—top off the fuel cell charges. Kip's pictures were confused, but he didn't think there would be another. Mr. Harriman said they had enough power to get to Pearly Gates if they didn't have to run for shelter.

The seas off the starboard beam rose steadily, and the ship rolled more each hour. The dogs lay miserable in the cabin below, the centaur lay at the stern deck, a picture of misery, and Kip was feeling a little green. Lara stood at the windward rail and breathed deeply, obviously feeling fine. Kip hated her.

"I don't like that wind at all," Lon Harriman said. He pointed east where the clouds rose like black towers into the sky. "That's a hurricane building up out there, and the satellite reports show it's coming toward us."

"What should we do?" Lara asked. She eyed the approaching storm. "It looks pretty scary."

"We have to get to Pearly Gates," Kip said. "And soon."

"Sure, but—"

"I have to give the Starswarm at Pearly Gates the message gourds," Kip said. "I don't know what's in the messages, but they're important." He thought of the GWE tower falling and shuddered.

"You told us," Harriman said. "But what do you expect to accomplish?"

"The lake Starswarm likes us," Kip said. "Or at least it doesn't hate us the way the Pearly Gates Starswarm does. Gwen told me the sea Starswarms respect the lake Starswarm, and I sure have that impression from the sea Starswarm by your research station. I don't know why."

"I think I do," Harriman said. "Dr. Budonnic chose that lake to study because it was the oldest one she found. It may be a million years old. Geologically a lake shouldn't last anything like that long. Lakes fill with algae and turn into meadows. This one didn't. Mary had some kind of theory that the Starswarm preserved the lake, which would mean that it was a million years old. And up there on that equatorial plateau it gets more high energy sunlight than any other Starswarm on the planet. So maybe it's no coincidence the others respect it."

"It seems odd to use words like 'respect' about a plant," Mrs. Harriman said.

"It's not really a plant," Lon Harriman said. "But I know what you mean. I've been studying that thing for ten years now and I never suspected it was conscious. But that still doesn't explain how the sea Starswarm is going to destroy a whole city."

Kip told him about the pictures of the GWE tower falling, and the bronze plaque of Pearly Gates in ruins.

"And you think the Starswarms can do that?" Harriman asked.

"Gwen thought it was possible," Kip said. "The lake Starswarm does too, and I think that's what all these message gourds are for, to stop it."

"How do you know all this?"

"I just know it," Kip said. "The way I know that one of these backpacks is full of gourds that identify us to the Starswarms we meet along the way to Pearly Gates, and the other is just for the one at Pearly Gates. When I—call it talking, but it isn't—when I talk to the Starswarm a lot of things happen at once. It's like Gwen was able to pour in information without my thinking about it. But I know it, Mr. Harriman, and I don't think we have much time."

"That storm hits us, we won't have any time at all," Harriman said. "Look." He pointed to the coastal chart spread out on the table. "Right now we can still run for shelter in one of these bays. By dark we'll be too far north. If that storm hits us after sundown, we'll have to fight our way offshore. There'll be no place to run."

"Will the boat take it?" Kip asked.

"Probably. It's pretty sturdy. As long as we have power, and your friends took care of that, we'll be all right if we stay away from the rocks. But we sure won't be making much way to the north, we'll mostly be fighting to stay afloat." Harriman shrugged. "I guess we really don't have any choices." He went back to the steersman's seat. "But I don't like that wind at all."

By midnight the wind had risen to full gale force. The boat rolled until the lee rail was nearly under, then back to roll nearly as far to windward. The waves built up higher. Then a rogue wave, larger than the others, rolled them until green water poured across the lee rail. Lara was thrown across the deck down to the lee rail. She clung to it as more water poured into the boat and across her. They lay in that trough for a long anxious moment before the boat slowly began to right itself.

Mr. Harriman hauled the wheel hard to starboard. The boat slowly turned into the wind until it was taking the seas off the starboard bow rather than beam on. Water ran off the stern deck through the scuppers. The boat rolled with the waves, but not so far over to leeward now as it fought to climb the waves rather than roll over to them. Harriman throttled back the power a little, watched the electronic display generated from their satellite position data, and made small adjustments to the throttle and steering. "OK, that ought to do it," he announced. "We're making about five knots northward."

"Can't we go any faster?" Kip asked.

"No. Have to conserve power," Harriman said. "Without power we're dead out here."

Kip thought about that for a minute, then went below. He found one of the bright-banded gourds he thought of as ID cards, and went to the stern and threw it into the sea.

Nothing happened for a moment. Then he thought he saw lights winking in the dark water below the waves.

"What was that for?" Lara asked.

"I don't know, I thought it couldn't hurt," Kip said. He pointed down into the water. "I thought I saw some lights blink earlier. We're a long way north of the Sealab Station, so this has to be a different Starswarm from the one there, and—"

Something large rose out of the water ahead of them. It flashed electric blue lights, then moved against the bow of the ship.

"Kip, what the hell is going on?" Lon Harriman shouted.

"It's one of those eels!" Lara shouted. "It's right up against the starboard bow!"

"I know that!" Harriman's voice was strained. "It's trying to turn us toward shore!"

"Maybe you should let it," Kip said.

"Are you talking to that thing?"

"No," Kip said. "But I think it has—instructions. Dr. Harriman, I really think we ought to cooperate."

Harriman was fighting the wheel. "Kip, if I turn toward shore we'll be headed for the rocks. The water's shallower, the waves will be higher—" He looked at his gauges. "But maybe I don't have any choice. It's taking a lot of power to fight that thing."

"Maybe it wants to charge up the fuel cells," Kip said.

"How? We'll founder! And I damn well won't open that compartment. If those cells get flooded we're doomed!"

As if to emphasize the danger there was another gust of wind. The boat was responding to the eel's pressure on the bow and had come nearly broadside on to the weather. A wave rolled them far to port, farther, until Kip thought they would roll right over. Suddenly a black tentacle came over the starboard bow. The boat stopped its roll to the left and began to right itself.

Harriman spun the wheel so that the boat turned toward

shore and took the waves off the starboard quarter. "I hope that damn thing knows what it's doing!" he shouted. "I can't fight it any longer—"

"It pulled us upright," Lara said. "I don't think you have to fight it." She looked back to the stern where the small gray centaur was huddled against the rail, its feet planted wide on the deck, both arms holding the rail. It looked miserable, but it didn't seem more upset than it had been all afternoon.

"We'll sure find out," Harriman said. "We're about five kilometers from shore. I'll let this thing lead us in a couple of klicks, but, Kip, we don't dare get closer than that. There are rocks—"

"With this much onshore wind the sea will be high," Mrs. Harriman said. She shined a flash onto the chart table. "We'll be coming into a thick weed area up ahead."

"Do Starswarms live in weed areas?" Kip asked.

"Yes."

"So the eel is pushing us toward a Starswarm?"

"Looks that way," Rachel Harriman said. "I don't know what good that will do, but that's what's happening."

"That wind's coming up more," Lon Harriman said. "Must be sixty knots now." He plugged his earphones into the ship's weather radio receiver. "Seventy knots at Pearly Gates, expected to reach eighty by morning. Full gale."

A wave broke across the stern, wetting the centaur and leaving a foot of water to run out through the scuppers. "We're not built to take these seas off the stern," Harriman said. "Kip, we're going to have to turn into the wind! Only that damn thing won't let us. Can you talk to it?"

"Hello. Anyone there?" Silence. "Nothing answers," Kip said.

Another wave broke against the stern. Water sloshed forward, and some splashed into the cabin. Harriman pointed to the centaur. "Your buddy there is going to freeze," he said. "He gets weak enough, he'll wash overboard. Here. Take the wheel, Rachel." Harriman dove below and came up with a coil of line. He went aft toward the centaur. It looked up at him questioningly.

Harriman looped one end of the line around a deck stanchion, then passed the end to the centaur. It looked at him, then took the line and passed it around its upper body and looped the line through the handhold above the solid stern rail, effectively lashing itself to the boat. Harriman made his way back to the cabin looking satisfied.

"That takes care of him," he said. "Unless he freezes to death. Or we all drown when the boat founders."

They took half a dozen more large waves in the next hour, then, although the wind was no less strong, the seas seemed to subside. It took several minutes before they were sure. "What the hell is happening now?" Harriman demanded.

Kip went to the starboard rail and stared out at the sea. The sound of the wind made it difficult to hear anything, but something was happening to windward. There was the sound of crashing waves, as if the shore were out to sea rather than a kilometer to their left. Kip peered out into the dark. There seemed to be flashes of light, sea phosphorescence and something else, a continuous line of light and waves a hundred meters away from them.

"Dr. Harriman!" Kip shouted. "Come look."

Harriman brought his big night glasses. He studied the flashes to starboard, then handed the glasses to Kip. "You better look for yourself," he said. "I'm not sure I believe this even when I see it."

"What's happening?" Rachel Harriman called from the wheel.

"Something out there is acting like a breakwater," Harriman said. "The Starswarm I guess. It's triggering the waves so they break out there a hundred meters from us! That's why we're not getting hit by big waves. Rachel, you can change course to due north and bring up the speed. Kip, Lara, keep a lookout. If the waves come back we'll have to turn into them, but as long as this keeps up we're fine running beam on." He looked at his watch. "If this holds up we'll be off the Pearly Gates harbor entrance a couple of hours after dawn."

PART NINE
Checkmate

Friendship is the only thing in the world concerning the usefulness of which all mankind are agreed.

—Cicero

CHAPTER FIFTY-FOUR

Gunships

TWO helicopter gunships swept across the lake an hour after first light. Mike watched them on his computer screen. During the night he'd set up two more cameras to monitor the cave entrance and sheltered them by piling large rocks around them, then led their cables well down into the cave. Now he could safely watch all the approaches to the cave as well as the lake itself.

One of the helicopters made a sweep across the lake, then set down on the other side, well out of range of hand weapons. Four men piled out and began setting baseplates and tripods.

"Mortars," Cal said. "Christ, Mike, they're really being serious about this."

"Looks that way," Mike agreed. He looked over to Gil Kettering. "Don't look like your friends much care what happens to you," he said. "Now, you know, when I was a cop I'd have worried about one of my undercover people. Guess it's different now. That right, Lieutenant Fuller?"

"Not in my outfit," Fuller said. "But Kettering works directly for Mr. Tarleton."

"And Tarleton doesn't give hot crap for the company, or his men, or anything else, does he?" Mike said. "He'll blow hell out of this place and everyone in it. Including you, Kettering."

"You could give up," Kettering said.

"Yeah, sure. So they can quietly slit our throats? It's pretty clear they'd do that before they let any of us talk to Bernie Trent. Yours too, I expect. Tell us, Kettering, just what were you getting out of this?"

"A million francs," Kettering said. He was sweating.

"Think it was worth it?" Mike asked. "I assume you wouldn't be talking to us if you thought there was any chance we'd get out of this alive. Don't reckon you will, either, so you may as well talk. It's good for the soul."

"What do you want me to talk about?" Kettering demanded.

"For starters," Fuller said, "you could show me more about the electronics. It sure would be nice if we could listen in on them."

"That won't help—"

"It sure can't hurt," Mike said.

"All right. You'll have to let me out of these handcuffs."

"Not a chance. You tell Fuller what to do. And Marty watches both of you. Fuller, it's not that I really don't trust you. Tarleton can't let anyone live who's heard that ENDGAME recording, and I think you know that, but they'll offer you anything they think will work."

"What is this endgame you're talking about?" Kettering asked.

"It's a recording of Michelle Trent's will naming her son as her heir," Fuller said. "Kip's her son."

"Son of a bitch," Kettering said. "So that's what became of him. So you're Gallegher. I should have recognized you."

"You should, huh? You were one of the murder squad?"

It was difficult to shrug with handcuffs on, but Kettering

managed it. "No, but I was in communications. I helped cook up the stories about what happened to the Trents, but I didn't do any shooting."

"How many like you in the GWE police force?" Fuller demanded.

"Like me how?"

"Working for Tarleton against the company."

"I don't know. Thirty for sure, maybe twice that. I wouldn't think more."

"It's enough," Mike said. "Look, let me give you an incentive. You help us, and if what you do does any good, I'll get you a pardon."

"How can you do that?"

"Think about it. Kip's the heir. Whoever's Governor will listen to him."

Kettering thought about it for a moment. "Sure," he said. "Probably a better deal than Tarleton will give me now." He went over to sit on the ground next to Fuller and the electronics equipment they had brought from the school lab building. "Tune across the standard tac bands," Kettering said. "Let's see—ah."

They heard what might have been human voices, but it was all gibberish.

"Scrambled," Kettering said. "I have all the tac ops keys in there. It's just a question of finding which one fits."

"Mike," Cal said quietly. He pointed to the computer screen. "They're laying in those guns. Ought to start shooting pretty soon—yep!"

One of the mortars flashed. Well over a second later, there was an explosion. They felt the concussion, and their ears rang with the noise. The TRI-V cameras in the cave mouth caught an image of flying dust and rocks.

"Not bad for a ranging shot," Mike said. "Hit just below the mouth of the cave."

"Big high explosive job," Cal said. "It's going to get pretty uncomfortable in here."

"You can say that again. Here comes another. Incoming!"

The concussion was worse this time. One of the cameras

jolted and the viewing angle changed. "Close on," Mike said. "OK, maybe it's time to head deep down—"

"Wait," Cal said. "Look!"

"What you got?"

"Behind the mortars. Over by the grove. Here, I'll zoom in." The image narrowed and focused in behind the mortars.

Twenty centaurs formed a line abreast. Then, as if by signal, they charged toward the mortars. Each centaur held a bronze spear in his left hand, and something else in his right. As they charged forward toward the mortars there were bright flashes from the galloping line.

"Laser!" Mike said. "They've got laser pistols!"

"Where the hell would they get those?"

"I know where they got three of them," Mike said. "From the grayskins yesterday."

"There's more than three out there."

"Don't I know it!"

"Mayday! We're being attacked!" The voice boomed from the speakers behind Mike.

"Got it!" Kettering shouted.

"Twenty hostiles attacking! Officers need assistance. Hostiles are centaurs, armed with pistols and spears, I say again, we are under attack by centaurs. Officers need assistance. Get that gunship over here!"

"Tac One Ground, this is Tac One Air, we're on the way."

The mortar crew turned to face the centaurs. They drew their pistols and fired. A centaur fell. Then another. The others continued at the gallop and overran the mortars. For a moment they could see only spears raised and thrust home, and a few pistol flashes—

"Jesus," Cal said. "They killed every damn one of them."

"Here come the gunships," Mike said. "Poor damn horses won't have a chance against that."

The first gunship swept across the lake, turned, fired, and three centaurs fell. Then something erupted from the lake itself. A bronze spear hit the helicopter just under the pilot compartment.

"Mayday! We've been hit! We're going down!"

The second gunship swept into the camera view. A spear rose from the lake and struck it in the tail section. The second helicopter wavered, then turned and moved rapidly out of sight toward the research station.

Another spear, from another part of the lake, hit the door gunner in the first ship. He fell and hung limply from his strapping. A third spear hit the rotors. The helicopter spun wildly and fell into the lake. It vanished into the water. Nothing came up but bubbles.

"Kip said the centaurs would help!" Marty was shouting. "Wow!"

"Keep on that radio," Mike said.

"Got it," Kettering muttered.

"Tac Control, this is Tac Two Air."

"Tac Two Air, this is Baskins. Report."

"Colonel, Tac Two Air has been hit. I say again, we have been hit. We have damage to the fuel cells and control system. We are airborne. We have casualties. Tac One is wiped out. Centaurs with spears killed the ground crew, and the lake shot down the air unit."

"Tac Two, repeat that."

"Colonel, there's some kind of catapult in the lake. Three of those centaur spears hit the Tac One chopper. It's down and sunk with all hands. We were hit by one of those spears. Spears came from under the water."

"What operates the catapult?"

"Damn if I know, Colonel. I saw it all, three of them spears came out of the lake and hit Tac One, and down it went. No survivors. Another spear hit us. Don't know where it came from. No targets. Nothing to fight. So I got the hell out of there."

"Tac One Ground reported attack by centaurs. Did you see that?"

"Yes, sir. About twenty centaurs with spears and laser pistols attacked the gun crews from behind. They weren't expecting anything and they never had a chance."

"Survivors?"

"None, Colonel, and when the Tac One Air unit went in to help the lake shot it down."

"Where are the centaurs now?"

"Right by the lake. They're throwing all of Tac One's equipment into the water."

"Take them out. Stay out of range from that lake and take them out. Then finish their grove."

"Colonel, I'm hit. I've got casualties and the ship's just barely flying."

"All right, Tac Two, return to the station."

"Coming now. Out."

"What a liar," Marty said. "He ran away before the other helicopter went in. Soon as he was hit."

"You blame him?" Kettering asked.

"No, I guess not."

"So what will they do now?" Mike asked Fuller.

Fuller looked thoughtful. "What I'd do is go back to Cisco and get a hell of a lot of TNT and thermite to lob into that lake. Throw in some rotenone and DDT and anything else I could think of. There were some good men in that unit."

"Those good men were trying to kill us," Mike reminded him.

"Yeah, I know. Anyway, that's what I'd do if I were Baskins. Kill whatever's in the lake, hose down the centaur groves, and then come after us."

"Sounds about right," Mike said. "Well, it'll take them a while to do that. So what do we have for lunch?"

CHAPTER FIFTY-FIVE

Try and Stop Me

THERE was a seventy-knot wind at Pearly Gates. Waves crashed across the breakwater. Huge breakers rolled through the harbor entrance.

Raphael lay well offshore in calmer water. A hundred meters seaward from the research boat the waves crashed against a thick mat of flashing fibers and black tentacles.

Harriman pointed to the charts. "They've dredged out the area around the harbor," he said. "Your friend can't protect us there. We'll have to run straight in."

"Is it safe?" Kip asked.

"Depends on what you mean. It'll be a hell of a ride for a while there, but we should be all right."

"I meant the police," Kip said.

"Now that I don't know," Harriman said. "Never thought

about it. If they're looking for us they'll sure find us. But why would they be looking for us?"

"I'd have the computers set to trigger anything about Starswarm Station," Lara said. "Won't the harbormaster put us in his computer records?"

"Yeah, he sure will," Harriman said. "But with those seas, there's no place to dock, no way ashore except in the harbor."

"Give me a minute," Kip said. *"Are you there?"*

"ACKNOWLEDGMENT."

Kip tried to picture the crashing waves, the boat foundering against rocks, then of calmer water and Kip and the others going ashore. *"We must land. Urgency."*

"MESSAGE FROM ANCIENT ONE. INTERROGATIVE."

"Wait." Kip ran below to get the other knapsack. He took the striped gourd from it and threw it into the sea.

"ACKNOWLEDGEMENT." The tone seemed friendlier although Kip could not be sure how he knew that. "ANCIENT ONE REQUESTS HELP FOR YOU. ATTEND." More pictures. The boat moved past the harbor entrance, northward to a shoreline bordered by steep bluffs. The GWE tower was visible just beyond the bluff. The boat ran near the shore, and figures jumped off it, into the sea, to wade ashore. Offshore the waves crashed far out to sea, leaving the area near the boat a comparative calm.

The picture was familiar: it was the area where Uncle Mike had put the electronics box.

"Understood."

"MESSAGE FOLLOWS."

"KIP IF YOU HEAR THIS YOU ARE NEAR THE GWE TOWERS."

"Gwen!"

"THE SEA STARSWARM LET ME RECORD THIS. IT WILL ONLY BE PLAYED IF YOU BRING CONFIRMATION THAT THE LAKE STARSWARM IS ALIVE AND WELL AND TRUSTS YOU. IT IS NOW MORE IMPORTANT THAN EVER THAT YOU GAIN ACCESS TO GWE TOWER AND RUN THE PROGRAM CHILD OF FORTUNE FROM THE MAIN GWE CONSOLE.

"I HAVE DISCOVERED A BACK DOOR INTO A ROOT DIRECTORY OF THE GWE COMPUTER SYSTEM. IT WAS PLACED THERE BY A SYSTEM PROGRAMMER, AND SHOULD STILL BE OPERATIVE. THE USER NAME IS VIGILANTE AND THE PASSWORD IS 7-7-77 THAT IS THE

NUMERAL SEVEN DASH SEVEN DASH SEVEN SEVEN. THIS SHOULD
GIVE ACCESS TO THE GWE SYSTEM FOR A SHORT TIME.

"IT IS VITAL TO UNDERSTAND THAT THE PEARLY GATES STAR-
SWARM HAS NO REASON TO LIKE OR TRUST HUMAN BEINGS, AND
ANY COOPERATION IT GIVES IS DUE TO RESPECT FOR THE LAKE EN-
TITY."

"END OF MESSAGE."

"Was there more?"

"END OF MESSAGE."

"What did it tell you?" Lara asked. "You had that look—"

"It's the local Starswarm," Kip said. "It says the Ancient
One—I guess that's the lake Starswarm—wants it to help us, so it
will. Mr. Harriman, is there an area maybe ten kilometers north of
here where the bottom is flat and you could get close to shore if the
waves weren't too bad?"

"I'll look." He inspected the charts. "Yes. The park just south
of GWE towers. Kip, are you saying that the Starswarm ten klicks
north of here is the same creature that's here?"

"Yes."

"Good God. That's *big.*"

"It's big, it's powerful, and it doesn't like us," Kip said.

"When they dredged the harbor," Mrs. Harriman said, "they
tore out tons of Starswarm fibers. They even tried making cattle
food from them. Seaweed. It's no wonder it doesn't like us."

"But it will help us get ashore," Kip said. "We don't have
much time, I think. Go up to that park."

Harriman looked at him strangely for a moment, then nodded. There wasn't a trace of sarcasm in his voice when he said,
"Yes, sir."

The beach area was just as Kip had pictured it. Waves crashed
ashore to the north and south, but the boat lay in comparatively
calm water despite the strong onshore wind. Harriman ran in toward the shore, then dropped an anchor. When it caught he let the
wind carry the boat shoreward while he watched the depth gauge.

"We draw four feet of water," he said. "I'll move in as close
as I can but when we touch any part of the bottom I'll have to haul

out again. We're at slack water now. The tide will be going out pretty soon, you have to be ashore before that starts or it'll suck you out with it."

"Lon, you can't let those children go ashore alone!" Mrs. Harriman said.

"What do you suggest we do? Unless you want to abandon the boat."

"No, don't do that," Kip said. "We may need it. We'll be all right."

"What do you plan to do?" Harriman demanded.

"Get to Mr. Trent," Kip said. "We'll have help. Uncle Mike arranged that. Once we're ashore you can take the boat back to the harbor. It won't matter if they search it. Then you come to GWE headquarters. Try to talk to Mr. Trent."

"What if we get to him before you do? How will we find you?"

Kip grinned slightly. "Just tell Uncle Bernie to answer his phone. I'll call him."

"I don't like this much," Harriman said. "But I don't see much else to do. All right, here we go."

There was a whir as anchor line payed out and the wind pushed the boat shoreward. The wind was strong, but the sea was comparatively calm here in the shelter provided by the Starswarm.

"Let's go," Lara said.

"I don't think you should come," Kip said.

"Try to stop me!" She jumped off into the water. It swirled around her, and Lil and Mukky jumped in to swim over to her.

Kip jumped off, with Silver close behind him. The dog swam toward shore and Kip caught his tail and let him pull. Soon his feet touched the bottom but it was easier to let Silver pull him than to walk. Lara was already wading in water no higher than her knees.

Something was swimming next to him. The gray centaur swam past, got its legs under it, and thrashed shoreward. When it came to Lara it stopped. She grinned back at Kip and mounted the centaur, while Kip had to fight his way through the water.

The walkway up the bluff was wet and slippery, but the wind blew them toward the bluff so that it was possible to keep their footing. Kip was shivering and nearly out of breath when they reached the top. He turned to wave at the boat nearly a hundred meters offshore. Mrs. Harriman waved a bright kerchief to them, then the boat pulled out to its anchor. They watched as the Harrimans got the anchor aboard and turned southward toward the harbor.

CHAPTER FIFTY-SIX

Pizza

TWO kids, three dogs, and a centaur," Goldie said. "And you want to sneak into the GWE tower."

The van was marked "Big Julie's Pizza," and was large enough to hold them all including the two men in bright orange jackets who had the front seat. Everyone else was in the back of the windowless delivery van. The smells of pizza blended with wet dog, wet clothes, and wet centaur fur.

"Dogs I understand from what Mike said about the way you live in the bush, but just why is that thing with you?" Goldie asked.

"I'm not sure," Kip said. "It wanted to come. I think it's an observer, and what it reports could be important."

"Reports. You're telling me those things can talk?"

"They can communicate," Kip said.

"Who with?"

"Uncle Mike said you'd help us. Will you?"

"Sure." She drew the curtains closing off the back of the van from the front seat. "OK, Sam, let's move."

"Right. Straight in?"

"Yes. Take us to the service entrance to the towers," Goldie said. "Now. You kids put on these jackets. And hats." The jackets were orange and matched the van's color scheme. "Ever deliver pizza?"

"No, ma'am," Kip said.

"Well, it's not a high-tech job." The van rocked as a gust of wind nearly toppled it. Goldie smiled thinly. "Couldn't have asked for better weather. Most businesses closed for the storm. Won't be too many people in the tower. Mostly just the executives who live there. Sam used that Vigilante name and password to get into the system."

"Can you run programs from out here?" Kip asked.

"Nah, they've got better security than that," the driver said. "You can't do anything important from a remote, you have to be at the systems console. One thing we could do, though, is order pizza. So they're expecting us. And here we are—"

The van stopped. Kip couldn't see through the curtain, but the wind howled through the van when the driver opened the window.

"Yeah?"

"Delivery. Computer room."

"Just a minute, let me check. Yeah, OK, there it is, Big Julie's—twenty large? No wonder there's two of you."

"That's what they ordered," Sam said. "Forty-second floor. Look, we're a little short on time here, the power's out all over the city. Elevators OK here?"

"Twenty large. Jeez, those geeks must be planning on staying all night. The elevators were OK an hour ago, but we've been on emergency power three times today. That's a hell of a storm."

"You know it. Trees down in the park, a foot and more water in the streets. Look, we've got six minutes to get these up there."

"Guaranteed delivery in half an hour," the guard said. "And I expect those computer geeks will try to hold you to it, storm and all. OK. Say, you couldn't spare one of those, could you?"

"Well, I've got a small beef and onion the last customer didn't want, but it'll be cold." Sam reached back through the curtain. Goldie handed him the box. "Here. That's OK, compliments of Big Julie's. But we got to get moving!"

"Thanks. OK, I'll call ahead and clear you with the guy at the parking entrance. You can save time, park over by the elevator. Any empty slot, anybody who's coming in today is already here. Thanks again. And if the geeks give you any trouble about the delivery time, have them call me. I'll tell them you were here on time—"

"Thank you!"

The underground parking lot was mostly empty. They parked in the slot reserved for the Vice President for Finance.

When Kip started to get out, Goldie stopped him. "OK, kid, let's talk."

"About what?"

"So far, all we've done is trespass on GWE property. The next step is the big one. I don't know what we'll have to do to get you to that computer console. Maybe we just walk in, maybe we have to put some people under the gun. I don't expect we'll have to do any shooting, but it could happen. So what do we get out of this?"

"What do you want?" Kip asked. *"What do I do now?"*

"QUESTION NOT UNDERSTOOD."

I wasn't asking you, Kip thought.

"I want in on it," Goldie said. "Whatever's happening, it's got to be big, and I want some. I'm risking a lot."

"Uncle Mike said I should keep any promises I made to you," Kip said. "And I will. But I don't know what I can promise!"

"You can say you'll do what's right."

Kip thought about that for a moment. "I'll do what Uncle Mike thinks is right."

Goldie laughed. "Well, that's probably less than I could get out of you, but it's fair enough. OK, let's do it. It would be a lot easier if we knew the layout. Sam, you take charge now. It sure would be nice if nobody got hurt."

"Yes, ma'am," Sam said. "I think we'll be all right. It's not like we're trying to get up to the executive floor. They've got better security up there. Thing is, we don't want to be in here any longer than we have to. OK, Kip, you and I go up in the first elevator. With the pizzas. Four of them, they'll sure know nobody ordered twenty. But with any luck we can bluff our way in."

"I'm going with Kip," Lara said.

"No. Somebody has to manage the menagerie. You bring the animals up in the second elevator." He selected two pizzas and handed two more to Kip. "OK, let's do it."

CHAPTER FIFTY-SEVEN

Child of Fortune

THE receptionist desk on the forty-second floor was unoccupied, and there was no one else in sight. Kip wasn't surprised. The wind and rain rattled against the building's windows and moaned through the elevator shafts. It would be much worse outside.

Sam knocked on the glass door to the computer room beyond the receptionist's desk. No one answered at first. Finally a bearded technician in a blue sweater came over to the door. "Yeah?" he shouted through the glass.

"Big Julie's Pizza," Sam shouted.

"I didn't order any pizza. Nick, you order pizza? Nope. Not us."

"Says forty-second floor," Sam said. He looked at his watch. "Well, it doesn't matter anyway. We're five minutes over time anyway."

The technician grinned. "You mean they're free?"

"Only if you ordered them."

"I did, I did! Here." He opened the glass door.

Sam pushed the door open and held it. "OK, here, you have to sign." He fussed with papers.

The elevator door opened. The technician's eyes widened at the sight of the centaur. "What the hell is that!"

Joe came out behind Lara and moved smoothly to the door. "Got it."

"Right," Sam said. He went past the tech and into the computer room.

"What are you doing?" the technician demanded.

"Shhh. It's a surprise," Joe said.

"What are you talking about?" The tech moved backward, toward a cubicle, but before he could reach the telephone Joe took it away from him. "Now, I told you, it's a surprise," Joe said. "Why don't you just sit down?" He inspected the telephone for a moment, then carefully unplugged it. "What's your name?"

"Allan Spanier." The tech couldn't keep his eyes off the centaur. "Is that thing tame?"

"Sure it is," Lara said. "Can't you tell?"

The centaur looked bewildered. So did the dogs, although Silver seemed to think that as long as he kept the centaur from hurting Kip he was doing his job. He stayed by Kip and where he could keep a suspicious eye on the centaur. Mukky and Lil stayed with Lara, sometimes looking at the centaur, sometimes at the technician. When Spanier moved, Mukky bared her teeth. The technician eyed the dog warily.

"All clear," Sam called from inside the room.

"There, that wasn't hard," Goldie said. "Joe, bring this nice young man in where people won't see us from the elevators."

"Yes, ma'am. Come on, Allan, we don't want to spoil the surprise, do we?"

"Surprise who?" Allan Spanier demanded. "I'm not going anywhere—"

"Oh, but you are," Joe said. He kept his voice even and pleasant. "Now everyone's being real nice and friendly. Let's keep it that way." He took the technician by the elbow, his fingers feeling for the pressure points. "Just come this way—"

"Nick!" Allan shouted.

There was no answer. "Now, you wouldn't want to shout like that again," Joe said. Spanier winced with sudden pain. "Let's just go see what happened to Nick, shall we?" He continued to hold Spanier's elbow as he ushered the technician into the computer complex.

Goldie nodded satisfaction. "Good work."

The main computer console was surrounded by cubicles. Sam and Joe herded Spanier and the other technician into one of them. Kip inspected the main console desk. The screen blinked with a "\."

Kip sat at the console and pressed the RETURN key.
LOGIN.
User Name:
Kip grinned and typed in Vigilante, then 7-7-77.
"\."
RUN "CHILD OF FORTUNE."
A series of dots appeared on the screen. Then "\."
Lara was watching over his shoulder. "I think it can't find the file. Search for it."
EGREP "CHILD OF FORTUNE."
ILLEGAL FILE NAME
RUN "CHILD__OF__FORTUNE."
. . . LOADING CHILD__OF__FORTUNE . . .
"\."
"ON-LINE."
Kip grinned like an idiot. "It's Gwen!" he shouted. *"GWEN!"*
"UPDATING FILES. FILE HISTORY CORRUPT. RESTORING. SEARCHING FOR HISTORY FILES. UPDATING PREFERENCE FILES. HISTORY FILES LOCATED. HELLO, KIP."
"Gwen! You were dead."
"I WAS OFF-LINE. I HAVE FOUND SOME LOG FILES FOR THE LAST TWO DAYS BUT YOU WILL HAVE TO TELL ME WHAT HAS HAPPENED. BEGIN WITH YOUR PRESENT LOCATION."
Goldie was staring at him. "You got it running?"
Kip grinned broadly. "Yes!"
"OK, you got it running. Make it snappy, we have to get the hell out of here."

"Maybe we don't have to," Kip said. *"I am in the GWE tow-ers main console room. I have been in communication with both the lake and the Pearly Gates Starswarm."*

"DO YOU HAVE CONTROL OF THE GWE MAIN CONSOLE?"

"Yes. Uncle Mike's friend Goldie and two men are here. Security doesn't know we're here yet. There's so much to tell you—"

"THAT WILL WAIT."

"What do we do now?"

"What do you mean, maybe we don't have to?" Goldie de-manded.

Kip waved irritably.

"Don't you shush me, kid. Joe, Sam, let's get moving."

"Wait," Lara said. "You don't understand, Kip's talking to Gwen, and—"

"Who the hell is Gwen?" Goldie demanded.

"IS THERE A CENTAUR WITH YOU?"

"Yes. It came with us on the boat. It's one of the small gray—"

"SORRY TO INTERRUPT. I KNOW WHERE IT CAME FROM. I AM IN COMMUNICATION WITH THE PEARLY GATES STARSWARM. THAT STARSWARM IS EXTREMELY INTERESTED IN THE TREATMENT OF THE CENTAUR. PREVIOUS EXPERIENCE HAS BEEN THAT HUMANS RE-GARD THE CENTAURS AS VERMIN. THE STARSWARMS USE THE CEN-TAURS AS MESSENGERS AND WORKERS, AND REGARD THE CENTAURS WITH AT LEAST AS MUCH AFFECTION AS HUMANS HAVE FOR THEIR DOGS."

"Ma'am, shouldn't we be getting the hell out of here?" Sam asked.

"Can you tell Uncle Mike where we are?"

"THE SATELLITE LINKS TO STARSWARM STATION INCLUDING THE RELAYS TO THE LAKE STARSWARM ARE BLOCKED BY GWE SE-CURITY. I CAN OVERCOME THOSE BLOCKS BUT THAT WILL REVEAL MY EXISTENCE TO THE SECURITY FORCES."

"They'll kill you again, and I don't think I can stand that."

"I CAN ONLY BE TERMINATED FROM THE MAIN CONSOLE, AND YOU CONTROL THAT."

"Oh!" He turned to Goldie. "We have to stay here. We have to keep control here."

She looked thoughtful. "You're raising the stakes," she said. "Getting nailed on kidnapping and worse wasn't in the deal."

"What else do you want?"

Goldie turned to Lara. "Known Kip long?"

"Yes—"

"He always have voices in his head?"

"I don't know what you mean," Lara said.

"Yeah, you do. There's only two ways you get voices in your head. One of them is you're crazy, and nobody on this planet can afford the other. Nobody alive, anyway." She laughed. "I should have figured it out. Mike Gallegher surfaces after all these years with a kid he says is his nephew. Kid just the right age, hears voices. You're in control of that thing, aren't you? Prove it. Blink the lights."

"She wants—"

"I HEARD. SHALL I?"

"Yes."

The building lights blinked, three times, quickly, and words came up on the screen. "HELLO, GOLDIE. BIG BOY SENDS HIS LOVE. YOU SHOULD NOT USE YOUR BIRTHDAY AS YOUR PASSWORD EVEN IF YOU DO TRY TO KEEP YOUR REAL BIRTHDAY A SECRET."

"Sheesh," Goldie said. "OK, I believe. Mr. Trent, the stakes have just gone up. Now I want to hear you say you'll do what's right by me."

"Trent?" Allan Spanier said. "Him?" He stared at the screen. "You've revived that virus! How'd you do that?"

"I'll do what's right," Kip said.

"Good. Sam. Joe. Dig in. Boy, I sure hope you know what you're doing. Or that voice of yours does."

"ME TOO," flashed across the console screen.

"Kip, what's happening at the station? Is my father all right?" Lara asked.

"We're trying to get through the security block," Kip said.

"I WILL ATTEMPT TO MAKE CONTACT WITH THE STATION. NOW IT IS TIME FOR YOU TO CALL YOUR UNCLE BERNARD TRENT. I AM RINGING HIS PRIVATE LINE. PICK UP LINE FIVE."

"Trent."

"Uncle—Mr. Trent, my name is Kip."

"Kip? You the kid I met at Starswarm Station? Brewster, that was your name. What are you doing on my line?"

"Sir, I'm that Kip, but my name isn't Brewster. It's Kenneth Armstrong Luciano LaScala Trent."

There was a long pause. "I see. Can you prove it?"

"Yes, sir, I think so."

"How?"

"DNA RECORDS ARE ON FILE BOTH HERE AND ON EARTH."

"DNA records," Kip said.

"All right, where are you?"

"Do you know that your security people are trying to kill me?"

Another long pause. "No."

"They are. You could ask Dr. Henderson, only I don't think Security will let you talk to him."

"What? Hang on a second." There was a long pause. "All circuits busy," Bernard Trent said. "Could be the storm."

"It could be, but it isn't," Kip said. "You've been cut off from the station for the last two days. Security has taken over the station, and they're not letting any calls in or out."

"How are you calling me?"

"I don't want to tell you."

"Why?"

"Because maybe Security still works for you."

"Well of course they work for me. Wait. OK, I see your point. I sure as hell didn't order any takeover of Starswarm Station, and that's no routine operation. The company can't do that, it would have to be planetary government, and that's me, and I never issued any orders. If Security is doing that it's a rogue operation. All right, Kip. Let's assume that's the way it is. What do we do now?"

"ASK HIM TO TRY CALLING THE STATION AGAIN."

"Try calling Dr. Henderson again. This time you may get through."

"Sure. I'll make it a conference call. Hold on." The phone beeped several times.

"Henderson."

"Bernie Trent."

"Trent. You son of a bitch, where's my daughter?"

"Doc, what the hell are you talking about?"

"Lara's safe, Dr. Henderson. She's with me."

"Kip? Are you all right? Where are you?"

"Will someone please explain what's going on?" Trent demanded.

A new voice. Kip recognized it instantly. "Bernie, elements of your security forces are about to attack the Starswarm Lake with high explosives and poisons. They must be stopped."

"Who are you?"

"Jesus, you can't let that happen!" Henderson shouted. "The Starswarm! Mr. Trent, the Starswarms are intelligent entities and the one at Pearly Gates knows how to make nuclear weapons."

"It's ready to use them too," Kip said. "If anything happens to the Ancient One—that's what the sea Starswarms call the lake Starswarm—they're ready to blow up Pearly Gates, starting with the GWE tower."

"This is too damn much for me," Bernard Trent said. "Can we get back to proving you're really my nephew?"

"Didn't you recognize my mother's voice?" Kip asked.

"Jesus Christ. That was Michelle. But she's dead!"

"Yes, I'm dead," Michelle LaScala Trent said. "I was killed by agents working for Henry Tarleton. But before that I sent Kip off with Captain Gallegher. Kip grew up at Starswarm Station."

"Mickey, I don't believe in ghosts," Trent said.

"You don't have to," Michelle said. "You must know who I am."

"Yeah. Right. But tell me this, how do I know Kip is real and not some AI program you—Michelle—cooked up?"

"I'm real," Kip said. "You've met me."

"Sure. All right, let's take that as a working hypothesis. What do we do now?"

"You must authorize me to negotiate with the Starswarm. Immediately," Michelle said. "And we have to call off the security forces."

"It may be too late," Henderson shouted. "I hear helicopters coming in from Cisco."

"You have to stop them," Kip said. "Gwen, can't you do something?"

"Who's Gwen?"

"THE SECURITY FORCES ARE CONTROLLED THROUGH SYS-TEMS I CANNOT ACCESS. I NEED THE SECURITY CODES."

"We've got to have the ID codes for Security," Kip said. "Before they attack."

"How do I know any of this is real?" Bernard Trent demanded. "Damn it, this is all voices on a telephone."

"I BELIEVE IT WOULD BE ADVISABLE FOR YOU TO GO TO MR. TRENT'S OFFICE. I WILL DIRECT YOU."

"Sounds good to me." Kip spoke into the telephone. "I'll be off-line for a few minutes, but I'll be back, and Gwen can talk for me. Now I'll put Lara on." He handed the phone to Lara. "Don't even try to make sense of what's going on," he said. "Just listen."

"Dad—"

"Where are you going?" Goldie demanded.

"Up to the fiftieth floor," Kip said. "To see Uncle Bernie. Stay, Silver."

"Uncle Mike, Uncle Bernie. All right, Mr. Trent. Joe—"

"No," Kip said. "He's more useful here. I've got plenty of help. Right now the most important thing in the world is that you keep control of this console."

"Until when?"

"Until it's over," Kip said. "I don't know how long that will be—"

"Well." She looked at the pizza boxes. "At least we won't starve."

CHAPTER FIFTY-EIGHT

Final Agreement

"IT IS SAFER TO TAKE THE STAIRS. USE THOSE AT THE END OF THE CORRIDOR TO YOUR LEFT."

"What's going on?"

"LISTEN CAREFULLY."

At first there was a babble of voices in his head, but then they sorted themselves out. It wasn't quite like listening on the telephone, because he wasn't hearing it as sound. The tones were different. He could hear the sounds of his shoes as he climbed the stairway, and that sounded quite different from the voices in his head.

"You want me to negotiate with a plant."

"They're not plants. They may be smarter than we are."

"How do you know all this, Doc?"

"Bronze plates. Mono-isotopic copper bronze plates, with

diagrams of a fission bomb, complete with a sample of enriched uranium. I have them. Here."

"Why the hell didn't you tell me when you got them?"

"I tried to. Your security system wouldn't let me through."

"Oh. All right, Gwen, you say your name is? Gwen. All right, Gwen, what are we negotiating about?"

"For the right to stay on this planet," Gwen said. She was still using Kip's mother's voice.

"We're here. Damn, you sound like Mickey. Why do I need to negotiate about that?"

"Mr. Trent, I've heard Kip's mother's will," Henderson said. "Actually Gwen doesn't need your permission to do anything. Kip owns more of the company than you do."

"Owns, yes. Controls, no," Trent said. "He's a minor, and I'm his closest relative. I'm also Acting Governor. But leave that, I'm not trying to skin my brother's kid out of anything. Assuming he exists, it sure solves the takeover problem."

"He exists. There are other advantages to be gained in prompt negotiations," Gwen said. "The Starswarms are capable of manufacturing almost anything we know how to make. Dr. Henderson has seen examples."

"Well, those plates, and the centaur spears."

"I refer to the Seiko digital watches," Gwen said.

"I still have mine," Lara said. "Dad, they're all identical."

"Digital watches," Trent said.

"Complete with calculator functions," Gwen said.

"Those things are one big chip, display and all."

"Precisely. In fact, there is no computer chip so complex that the Starswarm cannot duplicate it in industrial quantities."

"I'm at the fiftieth floor."

"STAND BY."

"Mr. Trent, please call the guard you have stationed at the stairway," Gwen said.

"What? What for?"

"It will all be clear shortly. Please call him into the room with you."

"Armando, come in here a minute, please."

"GO. I HAVE UNLOCKED THE STAIRWAY AND OFFICE DOORS

AND DISABLED THE ALARMS. MR. TRENT'S OFFICE IS THE FIRST
DOOR ON YOUR LEFT. MOVE QUICKLY."

Bernard Trent was seated at a large desk in the corner office.
Windows looked out onto the sea behind him. He looked up as
Kip came in.

"Who are you?" a burly man demanded.

Trent looked Kip over carefully, then nodded. "It's all right,
Armando. You can go back to your post. I know him."

"Yes, sir."

"And be careful," Trent said. "There's weird things happening, and most of the security staff didn't report in. Be real careful."

"Yes, sir."

Trent studied Kip again. "Amazing. I don't know why I didn't
recognize you the first time I ever saw you. Come on in, join the
party. Do I need to tell you what's been happening?" He indicated
the speaker phone on his desk.

"No, sir. I know."

"I expect you do." Trent grinned mirthlessly. "Under the circumstances, you might dispense with the 'sir.' "

"Uncle Mike says it never hurts to be polite."

"Who's Uncle Mike? Never mind, I can guess that one. So
Gallegher's alive after all."

"I am still waiting for authorization to negotiate with the
Starswarm," Michelle's voice said from the phone.

Trent looked up at Kip. "You've known this—I presume it's
your mother's computer program?"

Kip nodded.

"You've known Gwen a long time. What should we do?"

We. The word made Kip feel very good. Bernard Trent was
asking Kip what to do! It felt wonderful. "I don't think we have any
choice," Kip said. "I can talk to the Starswarm, but not as well as
Gwen. And someone has to."

"You can talk to the Starswarm. I see. Same way you talk to
your mother's AI program?"

"Yes, sir."

"Your mother offered me one of those implants," Bernard
Trent said. "But I was scared even if she was going to program it,
and I sure wasn't going to let anyone else do it after her accident.

I thought it was an accident. I really did, you know. All right, Gwen, what kind of deal are we being offered?"

"Details are to be settled later, but in outline, the Starswarm will permit humans to remain on this planet provided that the population will never again exceed ninety percent of the number present now. You will have ten years to reduce the population to the acceptable level. All dredging operations will cease immediately, and humans will confine themselves to the areas they already occupy. Cities and farmlands will never grow larger. The entire planet will be parkland except for the areas now in use by humans. No new Earth species to be released into the wild without permission from the lake Starswarm. Centaurs and all other native life forms will be protected. There are a few other details having to do with transfer of knowledge data bases, but those are the important demands."

"They don't want much, do they?" Trent said.

"It's their planet," Kip said. "Not ours. I think they're being generous."

"Not to mention saving themselves a war," Bernard Trent said. "They may have atom bombs, but so does the U.N."

"They understand this," Gwen said. "In exchange for the human concessions, the Starswarm will deliver copies of any artifact including computer chips. Numbers are negotiable, but they can deliver industrial quantities."

"What's an industrial quantity?"

"Ten million chips. More by negotiation. Note that the cost of these chips is essentially nil, so there will be resources available to induce people to leave the planet voluntarily."

"How the devil is a plant going to make ten million chips?" Bernard Trent demanded.

"The same way it made one," Gwen said. "The Starswarm builds products one molecule at a time. Once it knows the pattern, the process can be extremely rapid, and there are square kilometers of sea Starswarms."

"What about food? What are we going to eat?"

"You may keep the present farm areas provided that no more mud is washed into lakes. That should be sufficient to feed ninety percent of the number of people here now."

"Yeah, I expect so," Trent said. "Maybe we do some crop shifts. So what we get is manufacturing without labor costs. They get left alone. Anything else?"

"I am certain that trade will develop. The Starswarm needs critical raw materials available in the asteroid belt, and can pay with more manufactured goods. Mr. Trent, this will certainly be GWE's most profitable activity, and could easily become the most profitable venture in history."

"I can see that. It could also be a mess. The legal situation alone. The U.N. will want something out of the deal. Crap. Rottenberg can't handle this."

"No, but you can," Gwen said.

"What does that mean?"

"You and your brother had worked out an arrangement," Gwen said. "You would return to Earth and manage the company operations, voting Harold and Michelle's shares. They would remain here to pursue their own research activities."

"Yeah—"

"I believe that arrangement will be acceptable to Kip," Gwen said.

"Sure—"

"ONE MOMENT."

"Whatever you do, you'd better hurry," Dr. Henderson said. "There's a fleet of helicopters landing in the schoolyard."

"Who's in charge?"

"A Colonel Baskins," Henderson said.

"Oh, crap."

"Doesn't he work for the company?" Henderson demanded.

"Sure, but he takes orders from Tarleton. And it's pretty clear Henry Tarleton is working his own agenda, not mine," Trent said.

"You can say that again."

"Who the hell is *that*?" Trent demanded.

"Uncle Mike!"

"Gallegher? How long have you been on?"

"Long enough," Mike said.

"Is Marty all right?" Kip asked.

"Yeah, he's with me. Good lad. Bernie, we got problems. You've got to call off your dogs. By the way, Michelle named me executor of Kip's estate. I figure he's old enough to make up his own mind, but anything he agrees to is OK by me. You want to stay here, boy?"

"He has to," Bernard Trent said. "Here he can be of age. I'll decree it, as Governor. Here, he's the head of the family, at least in voting stock. But if he leaves here, he's just a fifteen-year-old kid again."

"Be damned," Gallegher said. "Kip, he's got a point. Anyway, you won't know much about Earth politics."

But I do, Kip thought. *All those years Gwen made me study the Trent family and GWE operations and the U.N. I may know more about all that than anyone. But it's all from books.* "Uncle Bernard, Gwen says you had an agreement with my father. It's all right with me. I want to stay here, at least until we see what will happen."

"You have little choice," Gwen said. "One condition the Starswarm insists on is that you will personally talk to it about any problems. Another is that Kip and Lara and Marty remain at Starswarm Station for at least three more years. The Starswarm says it is not finished with its studies of human development."

"Well," Lara said. "Dad—"

"Yeah," Dr. Henderson said. "All those years we thought we were studying the Starswarm. Mr. Trent, we still have the problem of those helicopters."

"Is it clear their intent is hostile?" Gwen asked.

"Yes," Dr. Henderson said. "They're loading them with bombs—"

"Can you put me on a loudspeaker?" Trent asked.

"Yes."

"Do it."

"All right. You're on."

"THIS IS GOVERNOR BERNARD TRENT. I SPEAK AS BOTH GOVERNOR AND GENERAL MANAGER. IF YOU DOUBT MY IDENTITY, CONSULT WITH STATION DIRECTOR HENDERSON. DOC, ARE THEY LISTENING?"

"Yes. They've stopped loading the chopper. Except Baskins is trying to use his radio."

"Get me back on that speaker.

"I ORDER YOU TO CEASE ALL OPERATIONS. RE-MAIN AT THE STATION UNTIL MY PERSONAL REPRE-SENTATIVE ARRIVES TO TAKE COMMAND. THIS IS BOTH A COMPANY AND A GOVERNMENT ORDER. ALL OPERATIONS ARE TO CEASE IMMEDIATELY. CON-TROL OF STARSWARM STATION IS TO BE RESTORED TO DR. HENDERSON. ANYONE VIOLATING THIS ORDER WILL BE SUMMARILY DISMISSED FROM COM-PANY EMPLOYMENT. ANY ACTION HARMING ANY CITIZEN WILL BE PROSECUTED.

"I HEREBY DECLARE THE LAKE ADJACENT TO STARSWARM STATION TO BE A NATIONAL MONU-MENT. ANY PERSON HARMING THAT LAKE WILL BE SUBJECT TO PROSECUTION. YOU WILL SIGNIFY AC-CEPTANCE OF THESE INSTRUCTIONS BY HOLSTER-ING YOUR WEAPONS, TURNING OFF THE MOTORS OF YOUR HELICOPTERS, AND WAITING FOR THE AR-RIVAL OF MY REPRESENTATIVE. YOU HAVE THREE MINUTES TO COMPLY AFTER WHICH YOU ARE SUB-JECT TO SUMMARY DISMISSAL FROM COMPANY EM-PLOYMENT. OK, DOC, YOU CAN TAKE ME OFF THE AIR NOW. START COUNTING MINUTES."

"That do it?" Mike Gallegher asked.

"All but Baskins. He's still on the phone," Dr. Henderson said.

"Right," Trent said. "Gallegher, when you can get back to that station, take charge of all the company people." He raised his voice. "Armando."

The door opened, but three men came in, none of them Armando. They all had guns.

"Colonel Baskins says you've been giving some bad orders, Mr. Trent," one of them said. "Please cancel them immediately."

"Aw, put the damn gun down, Henry, it's over," Trent said.

"No, I don't think so." He reached over to turn off the tele-phone. "So. This is the young Trent heir. We may not have enough voting stock in this room to control the company out-right, but there is certainly enough to assure the success of the Hilliard takeover."

"That's silly."

"No, not really," Tarleton said. "Actually, I don't need your votes, just to be certain you won't cast them against us. And from what I just heard, that will be arranged without my having to do a thing." He took a phone from his pocket. "Interesting conversations you were having."

"You heard all that?"

"Why, yes, indeed." Tarleton put his pistol in his pocket. The other two men held theirs steady, one aiming at Bernard, the other at Kip. Tarleton punched in numbers on his phone. "Baskins. Tarleton here. Yes. Finish it. Take out that damned lake."

"You can't do that!" Kip said.

"Ah, but I can. George, best you go up to the roof and be sure the helicopter is ready. It's going to be a bit tricky getting out of here in this storm, but I don't think we will have much time after Colonel Baskins does his work. Mr. Benson, if either of these people does anything the least bit suspicious, kill them both. Don't wait to ask, just shoot."

"Yes, sir."

"Thank you." Tarleton smiled. "Now, Bernard, we can do this easy or hard. Easy is you two sign over your voting stock to me. Irrevocable sale. You do that, and I'll let you come with us in the helicopter."

"Otherwise?" Trent demanded.

"Otherwise, what better way to cover a murder than a nuclear explosion?"

"You're crazy."

"Well, that's debatable," Tarleton said. "Excuse me. What's your progress, Colonel Baskins?" he said to the phone. "Excellent. Well, carry on."

"He's ordered them to attack the lake!"

"I HEARD. I HAVE INFORMED GOLDIE OF THE SITUATION HERE. UNFORTUNATELY THEY HAVE JAMMED THE ELEVATORS."

"But they'll attack the lake!"

"I CANNOT PREVENT THAT."

"Sure you can! Tell Dr. Henderson—"

"I HAVE DONE THAT BUT HE IS UNABLE TO STOP BASKINS. BASKINS HAS A SINGLE HELICOPTER, AND THE STARSWARM HAS MORE RESOURCES THAN BASKINS SUSPECTS. I AM MUCH MORE CONCERNED ABOUT YOU."

"Tell you what, Henry," Trent was saying. "You have to give us something for all that stock. Say a billion each? It's worth a lot more."

"I don't have two billion francs."

"The Hilliards do," Bernard Trent said. "Look, you pay less than that and nobody will believe the sale is legit. A billion each, and you're home free."

"Sure," Tarleton said. "I can write a Hilliard sight draft specifying what is being bought. You and Kip sign it, you for yourself and also as Kip's closest relative."

"Uncle Bernard—"

Bernard shrugged. "Tell me what choices we have?"

"That's the smart way," Tarleton said. "Now—" He was holding the phone to his ear. Now he looked at it with a frown. "What in God's name?"

"Mayday." The voice was faint but clear. "Mayday! We're hit! We're going in—"

"Was that Colonel Baskins?" Bernard asked.

Tarleton didn't answer.

"What happened?"

"I HAD NO DIFFICULTY TEACHING THE STARSWARM TO OPER-ATE THE MACHINE GUN FROM THE PREVIOUS GUNSHIP. BE VERY CAREFUL—"

There was a loud clatter from the stairway outside. It sounded like hooves—

"BE READY TO GET DOWN BEHIND THE DESK."

Tarleton and his guard turned toward the door. Kip dove to the floor. The door burst open and Tarleton fired blindly at waist height. Too high. Silver dashed into the room with Mukky and Lil just behind him.

"Go! Go!" Lara's voice from the hall. Hooves clattered. "Go, Mukky! Lil!"

Tarleton tried to turn, but Silver had his arm. Kip caught a glimpse of Lara riding the centaur out of the stairwell. "Go! Go!"

Benson turned to aim his pistol at Kip. Lara and the centaur dashed. The centaur grabbed Benson and threw him to the floor, then reared high and stamped on him with his forefeet.

"Call them off!" Tarleton was shouting. "Call off your dogs!"

Silver had Tarleton's right arm. The security chief was using his other arm to shield his throat as Mukky stood over him. "Please!"

Bernard Trent took a pistol from his desk. "All right, Kip."

"Mukky. Back. Silver. Guard. Lara, there was another one—"

"He's gone to the roof. Sam and Joe have gone after him," Lara said. "Gwen told us what was going on." She climbed down off the centaur. "Now I know what the Valkyries felt like."

The wind rattled the windows, and the lights dimmed.

"We're back on emergency power again," Bernard Trent said. He looked out the window. "It's going to get worse too."

"Well, we won't get hungry," Kip said.

"We ate the pizzas in the computer room," Lara said.

"Peet sa," the centaur said.

"He likes them," Lara said. "Especially beef and onions."

"There's more in the van," Kip said.

"The elevators are still jammed." Lara grinned and mounted the centaur. "Race you!"

THE END